Risky

SERIES DUET

USA TODAY & WALL STREET JOURNAL BESTSELLING AUTHOR

CHARITY FERRELL

Risky

Editing by: Hot Tree Edits

Proofreading by: Jovana Shirley, Unforeseen Editing, www.unforeseenediting.com

Prologue

GABBY

I **STUMBLED** toward the dim light shining through the open doorway, unsure of what the fuck I was doing. Inhaling a deep breath, I slowly raised my sweaty hand, knocked on the door, and then made myself known.

A set of glazed-over blue eyes squinted in my direction. "Gabby?" Dalton rasped, his tone uncertain, as if he imagined I was there. He slowly surveyed our surroundings, double-checking that I was alone.

I'd never had an actual conversation with this man before.

Sure, we'd said quick hellos in passing, but that was it.

"What are you doing here?" he asked.

I didn't know how to answer his question. I'd been asking myself the same thing continuously for the past twenty minutes while contemplating if I should come into his room and attempt to seduce him. It was a random, spur-of-the-moment thought that my drunken brain had convinced me was a good idea.

When I raked my eyes down his body, I found he was no longer wearing the black tuxedo jacket he'd had on downstairs. His white dress shirt was half-unbuttoned, giving me a peek of his hard, muscular chest, and untucked from his pants. Everything about this man oozed pure sex. I stared at the carpet as I wavered closer to erase the distance between us and stopped directly in front of his towering body.

His breathing hitched as his sharp gaze leveled on me. Nervousness swept through me when I reached forward, grabbed the back of his neck to pull his face toward mine, and then smashed my lips against his.

He reacted immediately, his mouth claiming mine in a deep kiss and allowing my tongue entry. I explored his mouth, tasting the sweet combination of whiskey and peppermint candy as our tongues danced together. I wanted to savor that taste forever, memorize it, and make my own drink so I could consume it later.

A deep growl escaped his throat as he lowered his large hands to cup my ass over the silk dress I was wearing to pull me into him roughly. The movement forced his growing arousal to rub against my leg, directly beside my core, causing my body to melt into his instantly.

"Gabby," he breathed out while attempting to pull away.

Tightening my hold on him, I moved my hand to grip his hair, not allowing him to move. "Don't say anything," I whispered, pulling his bottom lip with my teeth before kissing him again.

Our lips slid against each other's hurriedly as the real world drained itself out of my thoughts. We wobbled backward until I felt my heels smack into the edge of the steel bed frame. I gasped when I was pushed back against the mattress, and the weight of him hovered above me.

Our hands were frantic as we touched each other, us racing to see who could get the other naked first.

He was better at it than I was.

More skilled.

My dress was the first to go. Dalton stroked my shoulder softly before sharply pulling the knot holding it together around my neck and then slowly dragged the expensive material down onto the floor. I suddenly became strongly aware of my pulsating heartbeat when his hand ran up my bare leg and stopped abruptly at the top of my thighs.

"This might be a bit more complicated to get off." He half-laughed, half-slurred.

What the ...

I lifted myself onto my elbows to glance down at what he was looking at and cringed when I realized what was happening.

Shit, my damn Spanx.

There was nothing unsexier than having to stop mid-hookup because the guy didn't know how to get off your goddamn Spanx.

Heat flushed from my core up to my cheeks. "Between my legs," I panted, unclasping my bra, desperate for his touch again.

His gaze jumped from my thighs and back up to me. "Huh?"

I could've died at that moment.

"The other clasps—they're in between my thighs," I explained, averting my eyes away from him.

What a way to put a damper on the mood, Spanx.

His lips drew together. "Oh ... okay."

He went back to the task, concentrating hard, and dropped a hand directly between my thighs. Inching his fingers apart, he gently pushed my legs open wider. Instead of unclasping me, his thumb glided over my clit torturously. I trembled in anticipation of what was coming next.

My head fell back, my eyes slamming shut at the same time I felt the Spanx loosen around my midriff, and he dragged it down my legs before tossing it alongside my dress. He slid off the bed and walked toward the doorway.

"W-what are you doing?" I stuttered, nervously peeking down at my naked body.

Is he about to ditch me because he doesn't like what my Spanx was hiding?

My hands shot down to cover myself as I suddenly became insecure.

"The door," he explained, gesturing to the wide-open doorway that led straight out into the main hall.

I sighed. Thank God he noticed because my brain wasn't comprehending anything but how badly my body ached for him. If anyone found out what we were doing, chaos would erupt, and my ass would be in a shit-ton of trouble. He'd be shunned by his family for even touching me.

The door slammed shut, and his fingers wrapped around the handle to lock it before he stalked back to me. I focused on his body and the way his chest heaved in and out slowly.

"You sure this is okay?" he asked, returning to me. His eyes locked with mine while awaiting my answer and the fate of our night.

My slow nod was all the confirmation he needed. His lips twitched into a wide grin before he lowered his mouth to my sensitive earlobe, nibbling gently before raining kisses down the nape of my neck. His touch was more distinctive than anyone else I'd ever been with. He wasn't rushing to squirm his fingers into my panties or frantically unzipping his pants to make sure he received his pleasure. No, he took his time—his touches slow, precise, and skilled.

"You're the sexiest woman I've ever laid eyes on," he whispered.

I whimpered when his chilly hands dipped down to my breasts, palming and massaging them while his lips continued to kiss my neck.

"When you walked in tonight, I couldn't help myself from imagining what was under that sexy-ass dress you were wearing," he continued, licking my neck before sucking down hard. "It's even better than I imagined."

I moaned, and my hips rotated underneath him when he squeezed my hard nipples.

"Why are you still dressed?" I panted, pushing my weight into him before running my hands underneath his shirt. His skin was sweaty but soft as I traced my fingers against the hard muscles lining his chest. I needed more of him.

A deep growl escaped from the back of his throat. "Give me a minute, baby."

His lips moved southward, between my breasts, and he replaced his hands with his mouth on my nipple.

I squealed, my back arching.

"Does that feel good?" he asked, moving his mouth to my other tightened nipple and doing the same thing.

"God, yes," I moaned, licking my lips and pushing him forward.

As good as what he was doing to my body felt, I craved more.

I brought myself up and unbuttoned the rest of his shirt before rubbing his growing erection through his pants. "You can't be the only one having all the fun, can you?"

My behavior—how in control I was in the moment—shocked me. This wasn't me, and I'd blame it on the bottomless glasses of champagne I'd downed earlier when this all came to blow up in my face.

He groaned, his teeth biting into his lower lip, and he rolled his hips, moving into my hand. "I guess you're right."

Leaning up, I dragged his shirt off his body, threw it across the room, and smiled in victory when he shuddered at the feel of my fingers sliding down his waistline. His muscles tensed when I brushed my fingers back and forth and flicked the button of his pants open. Sliding the zipper down, he tugged his pants to his feet.

My eyes widened at the sight of the large bulge coming from his boxer briefs. He cursed when I ran my hands over his hardness and moved into my touch. When I pulled his boxers down, my lips parted at the view of his erection. Wrapping my hand around his length, I stroked him.

"Fuck yes," he muttered, pumping his hips to the same rhythm as my hand before slowly massaging my breasts.

Tiny sparks lit up my body, and the more excited he grew, the faster I stroked him.

"Baby, not so fast." He wrapped his hand around my wrist to stop me.

I raised a brow. "It doesn't feel good?"

"I fucking love it, but I want to enjoy it longer."

He pushed me down on the bed before sliding to the edge to open his nightstand, where he pulled out a condom.

"Is this okay?" he asked, stroking himself.

I paused, relishing the view of him. "Yes," I croaked, opening my legs wider in assurance.

He brought the wrapper to his mouth, ripped it open with his teeth, and rolled the condom over his throbbing erection before positioning himself directly in front of my entrance.

Holy freaking hell.

This is actually going to happen.

My chest caved in when he moved the tip in circles around my opening, and I groaned in pleasure at the pulse-pounding moment that was approaching.

"You're so wet," he said, gently sliding into me.

I pulled in a deep breath and held it in.

"And, fuck, so tight." His face scrunched up as he entered me more.

I shut my eyes, praying he wouldn't discover the reasoning for that. I held my breath as he broke through my barrier, and then my body shot forward in pain at the throbbing sting that pulsated through me.

"Holy shit!" I yelled out in horror, my legs tensing up.

His body completely stilled, and his eyes snapped wide open. We did a stare down, neither one of us sure of what to say or do.

"Please tell me you're not a virgin," he said, finally breaking the awkward silence. He slammed his eyes shut and threw his head back in dread while I contemplated lying.

I gulped, and his head shot down to look straight at me.

"I don't think I am anymore," I nervously replied.

There was no way I was still a virgin after feeling like my vagina's walls had been ripped apart with a machete. I was slapping the next girl I heard say she got off her first time and it didn't hurt. That shit killed.

"Jesus, fuck," he groaned.

My body went rigid when he started pulling out of me, but I grabbed his ass to stop him.

"Keep going," I begged.

He'd already broken through. All I needed to do now was get through the pain.

His mouth flew open, his wide eyes studying me. "You're out of your damn mind if you think I'm taking your virginity tonight."

I shut my eyes and took a deep breath.

He was right. I was out of my damn mind.

But there was no way I was letting him say no to me.

GABBY

Six Months Later

THE ONLY SOUND I heard was the click of my favorite heels as I dreadfully walked into the swanky reception area. I cursed myself for not creating an excuse to get out of interning for a business owned by people who despised my existence.

Clueless on where to go, I strolled toward the young blonde receptionist animatedly talking on the phone. All I was given before my first day at the new job was an emailed handbook and schedule. I'd almost made it to my destination when a glimpse of something caught my eye, nearly causing me to trip.

Rather a glimpse of *someone*.

Balancing myself, I shut my eyes and prayed I was dreaming. My muscles tensed when I opened them.

Nope, definitely not dreaming.

Turning around, I made a detour, my blood boiling more with each step I took toward the man sitting in a reception chair.

"What the hell are you doing here?" I hissed.

He was supposed to be thousands of miles away. Him being there messed up everything, and I wasn't prepared to see him. I'd planned to have an entire speech and escape plan ready for our next run-in.

He peered up at me with his ocean-blue eyes, and his voice was flat as he answered, "I could ask you the same question."

Six months had passed since we'd last seen each other—since I had given him my virginity. Clearly, he was as delighted to see me as I was him. At least we were on the same page.

"I work here," I snapped, perching my hands along the curve of my hips.

The corner of his mouth twisted up, and he stroked the curve of his strong jaw. "Interesting."

I hated how attractive he looked in his crisp black suit and blue tie that matched the hue of his eyes. His chestnut-colored hair was shorter than the last time I had seen him and no longer swooped in front of one eye.

"And why is that interesting?" I asked.

There wasn't anything interesting about the situation. The better word was *horrifying*.

He cocked his head to the side. "It looks like we're here for the same reason. Hello, new coworker."

When he held out his hand for me to shake, I wanted to rip it off his body.

"We can't work together," I snapped.

He dropped his ignored hand. "Why exactly is that, Gabby?"

Oh, he's testing me.

Glancing around the lobby, I noticed the secretary staring and lowered my voice. "You know why."

"Is it because I've seen you naked?"

I glared at him, knotting my fist as I considered punching him now instead of arm-ripping.

"Is it because I know what it feels like to be inside you? What it feels like to have your pussy wrapped around my cock?"

My mouth dropped.

Did he really just say that?

"You're a jackass." I wondered how much trouble I'd get into if I took one of his baby blues out with my heel. The plus would be I'd get fired and get to leave this damn place.

12

He tapped his finger against the side of his lips. "Let me get this straight. We fucked and then you completely ignored me. No calls, no texts, nothing. Oh yeah." A harsh laugh escaped him. "You also failed to mention the fact that you were a damn virgin! But I'm the jackass?"

I nodded, folding my arms across my chest. "Exactly."

He tossed his hands up into the air. "You're fucking unbelievable."

I wasn't stupid. I had known the day would eventually come that I'd have to face him. I might've been naive enough to drunkenly give away my virginity, but I wasn't *that* naive to think we'd never see each other again.

That was because I was stupid enough to break the most important rule of a one-night stand—*make sure you'll never see the other person again.*

"I was drunk," I said, rushing out the words to my bullshit excuse.

"We were both drunk," he argued. "And correct me if I'm wrong, but you were the one who came to me. You wandered into my room and climbed into my bed. I know for a fact you weren't too damn drunk to forget that."

As much as I wanted to deny the accusation, he was right. That night, he had been the only thing on my intoxicated mind.

"Whatever," I said. "And don't worry; I won't tell anyone in your precious little family, so I didn't feel the need to answer your calls."

I knew the real reason for his calls. He didn't want them to know he'd hooked up with the daughter of the home-wrecking whore they hated. They already had one embarrassment in their family. They couldn't have another.

He winced at my insult. "I called to check on you and to make sure you were okay after everything, considering you left my bed in the middle of the fucking night."

Yeah, right, buddy.

Everyone knew the Douglas family only cared about themselves. They were born without souls.

I shook my head at his blatant lie. "It doesn't matter. It happened. Now, let's move on and forget about it. Okay?"

He nodded in agreement. "You're right, but shouldn't we—"

"Dalton, babe, your dad is ready to see you now," the eavesdropping secretary called out, cutting him off, and then strolled toward us.

Her tight red dress was undoubtedly against the dress code I'd read about last night. She smiled brightly at Dalton before sending a nasty smirk in my direction.

Dalton ran his hands through his short hair in frustration and blew out a ragged breath before lifting himself from the chair. He moved around me silently before following Blondie out of the lobby and down a hallway. As soon as they were out of eyesight, I slumped down in his abandoned chair and let out a deep sigh.

Welcome to my nightmare.

DALTON

I STROLLED into my father's office and took in the new decor. "I see you've had a change of scenery."

The expensive sailboat replicas he'd lied about building had been replaced with taxidermy animals. A giant boar's head was plastered above his desk and staring straight at me. My gaze moved to the mountain lion chilling at the top of his bookcase. A grizzly bear was nuzzled against the beige wall—his paws up to make it look like he was climbing.

He smiled, sitting behind his massive desk and wearing a black suit. "I needed something manlier, wouldn't you agree?"

With his light-brown hair, bright blue eyes, and six-foot-five frame, my father and I were striking replicas of each other—except my hairline wasn't receding and I didn't wear a permanent scowl on my face.

"Sure," I lied, sitting in one of the two black leather chairs in front of his desk.

I found it creepy, not manly, but whatever. My dad had always been into weird shit.

Clasping his hands together, he leaned forward in his chair and positioned himself into what I called his power pose. It was his attempt to send a message that he was in charge.

That he was the big man.

Have at it, Dad.

We hadn't even started yet, and I was already ready to get this shit over with.

"I'm glad you're here," he said, preparing to throw out the speech I'd been waiting for. "But I need to make it clear that you are to take this job seriously. No partying. No staying out all night long. It's time to grow up. If you want to take over this company, it must be earned. There will be no free rides just because you're my son."

I nodded in understanding, knowing he'd be harder on me than anyone here to prove his point. I loathed dealing with him, and now, we were going to be around each other daily—something that had never happened.

He had been nonexistent when I lived at home in high school, and the only time he'd visited me in college was for my graduation, which he'd only done for his image. He wanted everyone to know he was the father of another kid who had graduated from an Ivy League school.

And now, I had Gabby's sudden arrival added to my stress. When I'd noticed the curvy, petite, auburn-haired woman step out of the elevator and strut across the room, she'd immediately held my attention. My cock stirred as I watched her walk toward Summer. I scratched my temple, familiarity hitting me. I knew that ass, those legs, that hair from somewhere. That body had consumed my thoughts since I'd woken up to an empty bed after taking her virginity. Hell, I even dreamed about it, even after she ignored all my calls and texts.

"I got this," I replied. "I know the responsibilities I took on."

"Perfect," my dad said, an arrogant grin on his face. "Glad we're on the same page. Now, go find Summer, and she'll show you to your new office." He dismissively waved me away, picked up his phone, and didn't grant me another word.

I pulled myself to my feet and left his office in search of his mistress—or secretary, as he called her. For someone who'd made millions hiding people's secrets, he sucked at covering up his own.

I found Summer sitting behind the front desk, filing her bright red nails and working hard.

"New office?" I asked.

She threw down the nail file and jumped up from her chair. "You're seriously going to love it," she squealed, her lips forming a sly grin. Her long fingernails went to the top of her low-cut dress, and she pulled it down, giving me a not-so-subtle view of her ample cleavage. "I'm so glad you're working here. I needed a cute new face to look forward to seeing every morning."

Swinging her hips suggestively, she led me down a hallway before stopping at a closed door and opening it. "Here you go."

Summer was attractive. We'd gone to school together, but now, she was fucking my father. No way in hell would I ever touch her.

My new office was nice but plain—white walls with generic paintings hung along them. I asked Summer to shut the door as she left and plopped down in the leather chair behind the desk. Opening every drawer, I found basic office supplies, and a few minutes later, my phone rang.

Eva's name flashed across the screen.

Goddammit. Another girl I wasn't in the mood to deal with.

"What?" I answered. "I'm at work."

Feminine laughter came from the other end as she said, "That's certainly no way to greet your future wife."

"If you were a wife I wanted to marry, you would've received a better greeting. But you're not, so that's what you get, babe." I kicked a drawer shut with my foot and made myself comfortable in the chair.

"You're so charming. I love how you act like you're the only one getting screwed over here." She didn't want to marry my ass either.

"Then, why don't you put a stop to it?"

She had to be the one to do it. Not me. I had too much to lose.

"The same reason you won't. We both love money more than our happiness."

She was right. Our parents had threatened our inheritance if we didn't go through with our engagement.

I propped my feet up on my desk. "Then, to what do I owe the pleasure of this call?"

"I'm supposed to do my wifey duty and invite my future hubby over for dinner tonight. Our parents will be there, so we have to act in love."

Our parents knew we weren't in love but still expected us to play the part. I considered it good practice for the show I'd have to put on for the rest of my life.

I grunted. "Fine, but do I at least get laid at the end of the night?"

Sex was the only good thing I got out of our arrangement. Eva was a good fuck, and when we got stuck in situations with our parents, we tended to rid out our frustrations in the bedroom.

"At least I know I'll have a spectacular sex life in our meaningless marriage," she said.

"Feeling's mutual," I grumbled, grabbing a stack of business cards with my name on them and placing them in the empty holder at the front of my desk.

"God, why couldn't my parents have stuck me with someone who actually had a heart?"

"I do have a heart," I corrected. "Just not for you."

She snorted. "And that feeling's mutual, handsome. See you tonight, *sweetie.*"

The line went dead, and I tossed the phone down on the desk. As much as I hated my parents choosing a woman for me to marry, I could've had it much worse. The wife they chose for my brother, Leo, was a fucking terror. Eva had known what the hell we were getting into from the very beginning and wasn't expecting roses and romance from me.

Chapter Three

GABBY

"YOU'RE SERIOUSLY NOT GOING to believe what the hell happened to me today," I yelled, barging into my best friend, Cora's, bedroom. She'd given me a key a few years back because she was too lazy to come downstairs and answer the door when I came over.

"Jesus, fuck, Gabby," Lane, Cora's boyfriend, yelled from the bed, where they were cuddled up, watching TV. "There's this word, not sure if you've heard of it, but it's called fucking knocking. People with manners do it before they bolt into other people's bedrooms. We could've been naked and screwing."

I rolled my eyes. It wasn't like it would've been the first time I'd walked in on them doing the deed, and it probably would happen again. Knocking was a problem for me because I'd lived alone with my mom for the first fifteen years of my life, and when you lived with another girl, you never worried about knocking.

"That's actually two words, Einstein," I corrected. "And there's no time for knocking when you're having a crisis."

I met Cora when I moved to my new high school freshman year after my mother married Kenneth. We'd gone from a tiny two-bedroom apartment into his ten-thousand-square-foot mansion. As soon as I stepped foot into the new school, Dalton's younger sister, Piper, started a hate campaign against me. Cora was the only girl who didn't play into it and shun me for having a *whore mother*, as they called it.

My mother and Cora were the only people I trusted. I was also close with Lane since they'd dated since middle school. He hung out with us more than he did his friends and was like a big brother to me.

"That's nothing new," Lane replied.

Cora smacked his arm and dismantled herself from him. "What's the crisis?" Eagerness filled her tone, and she muted the TV.

I shut the door and paced in front of her. "Okay, so do you remember how I'm working for Douglas PR this summer?"

"How could we forget?" Lane muttered.

They had the pleasure of hearing me complain about it since I found out. After taking a year of deferral from college, my mother demanded I do something productive with my time. I'd told her that I had plenty of other pastimes I could enjoy without being around the Douglas family, but she wouldn't budge. I highly doubted I could call her up now and tell her I had to quit because I'd hooked up with her step-nephew.

"Today, I walked in, and guess who I ran into?" I asked.

"Your stepdad?" Cora guessed, raising a brow.

Kenneth owned Douglas PR with his brother, Wilson, who was Dalton's father.

Yeah, I chose the most fucked up, intermingled situation I could've possibly found to throw myself ... and my vagina into.

"Dalton!" I screamed, throwing my hands up, unable to hold back his name any longer.

All day, I'd been on edge, scared I'd run into him again. The chance of that dwindled when I was led to my tiny work cubicle and told to check my email for daily tasks.

"It was Dalton Douglas ... and he is also working at Douglas PR." I pointed a hand-formed gun to my head and pulled the imaginary trigger.

"Holy shit!" Cora gasped, her mouth dropping open. Her eyes brightened as she geared up for the juicy story she knew was coming her way.

Lane rubbed his temples. "What's wrong with Dalton? That dude is cool as shit. He used to score all the hot chicks."

Shit! I forgot I never told Lane about my drunken rendezvous with Dalton. He was going to be pissed.

"Nothing," Cora quickly answered. She wasn't only attempting to save my ass, but her own as well. "Will you pretty please go get me something to drink?"

"Fuck no, Your Highness. This sounds way too fucking good, and I'm hearing every single damn word. Spill it, Gabs." He stretched out his legs, swiped his dark locks behind his ear, and interlaced his hands behind his head, waiting for my confession.

"No, you don't have to hear this," I grumbled, glaring daggers his way.

The fewer people who knew about what happened with Dalton, the better. I couldn't risk our parents finding out, especially his. They'd kill me.

His face lit up. "Holy fuck. You two hooked up, didn't you? You hooked up with your cousin." His lips twitched into a huge grin.

I swiped a book from Cora's desk and threw it at him.

He dodged it, causing it to fall to the floor.

"You know he's my step cousin, asshole."

He shrugged, the smug grin still on his face. "I know, but it sounds scandalous when you say it like that."

I turned my attention back to Cora. Her strawberry-blonde hair was braided on the side of her head, and her pale skin was makeup free. The only people she let see her without makeup were Lane and me. It wasn't that she was insecure. She was just always put together. Cora reminded me of a sweet little Georgia peach until you messed with her friends or family. Then, she turned into a spitfire.

"Your boyfriend is seriously annoying," I said, rolling my eyes.

She laughed. "Girl, you know he loves juicy gossip just as much as we do." She paused and scrunched up her face. "Probably more than we do."

She leaned over to kiss him on the cheek, but he pulled away, blocking her with his palm. "Nuh-uh, gorgeous. How long have you been holding out on me? This is grade A gossip."

I groaned, flopping down onto a fuzzy pink chair in the corner. "It happened New Year's Eve." I rolled my neck around in circles to help ease the built-up tension from the day. "It was that stupid party my mom forced me into going to. You know how miserable those things are for me, especially when you guys aren't there."

They'd gone to Lane's cabin for the holiday, but my mom made me cancel and attend the party. If she had to endure hell, I had to be at her side.

I shook my head before going on. "They had champagne, and misery loves alcohol, so I started chugging glasses of it."

Lane chuckled. "If you can't be the most popular girl at the ball, you might as well be the drunkest."

I threw another book at him, and he wasn't quick enough to dodge it. It smacked him in the side of the face before falling.

He winced, rubbing his jaw and scowling at me while I gave him a large smile.

"Anyway, during my little drunken escapade, I found myself roaming the halls of Dalton's parents' mansion and somehow landed in his bedroom. Then his bed. Then, I was naked. Then, I let him pop my cherry. And that's it." I spun around in the chair and let out a deep sigh.

"Damn, he sure got one hell of a New Year's kiss," Lane said around a chuckle.

"I'm glad you think my suffering is funny," I muttered.

"Don't forget about how you left in the middle of the night when he was passed out and have ignored him ever since," Cora said before glancing to Lane. "He's tried to call her, like, fifty times. She hits the *fuck you* button every time."

I gave her a dirty look. She was trying to get back on her boyfriend's good side. *Traitor.*

"Shit, Gabs, what are you going to do?" Lane asked, allowing Cora to snuggle back up to his side now that she'd snitched on me.

I slumped down in the chair. "Hell if I know. I've never had to deal with the aftermath of a one-night stand before."

"Good news for you, princess. You just started working at a place specializing in dealing with shit like that. I'd consider it practice."

I flipped him off. "You two seriously suck ass at crisis-solving."

Lane laughed. "Aww, look, your middle finger likes me."

I flipped him off again, bringing myself up from the chair and walking out of the bedroom. Over my shoulder, I said, "Call me later," and then stomped down the stairs. I had some serious damage control to do because I couldn't avoid Dalton forever.

"Good luck, my deflowered friend," I heard Lane yell before I made it out the door.

* * *

"Hello there, my sexy little vixen."

I jumped at the husky voice behind me and almost smacked my head against the top shelf of the fridge.

"I told you to quit calling me that," I muttered, grabbing a bottle of water and slamming the fridge shut. "It's just too weird." I scrunched up my face as I turned around to face him.

"How the hell is that weird?" Asher, my stepbrother, asked, pulling out a stool underneath the kitchen island and plopping down onto it.

"I'm your stepsister."

I'd been terrified the day I met him and was certain he'd poison my food since Kenneth left his mother to be with mine. My mother had broken up his happy home, and to make matters worse, the first time we met was at their wedding. It was only a month after Kenneth's divorce was finalized, and they made Asher attend.

Instead of hating me, he hit on me. It was a game he started and continued with every visit he made here from Miami, where he moved with his mother to be closer to her family.

If marriage didn't relate us, I'd have totally jumped on that bandwagon. Asher was only a year older than me, attractive, and athletically built from playing football for his college in Miami.

His dirty-blond hair was shaved short as he moved around the kitchen in black Nike shorts and a cutoff T-shirt with the Miami University logo on it. Trickles of sweat dripped down his forehead. He must've been working out in the basement gym.

My gaze fell to his chest, noticing the view of his muscular six-pack through the slit in his shirt. I wanted to reach over and trace my hand along the ridges.

"Haven't you watched *Cruel Intentions*? I could picture us being like them, all scandalous and shit," he said, a wicked grin on his lips.

I screwed off my water bottle cap and pointed to him. "You do know the stepbrother dies at the end, right?"

His smile faded. "Fuck, I forgot about that part."

"Why are you even here? In case you didn't notice, your dad is gone." I motioned toward the empty house.

I probably sounded like a bitch, but Asher never visited when his dad was gone. His relationship with Kenneth was strained, and he only came up for holidays and special occasions. He'd taken his mom's side during the divorce, and I didn't blame him. I would've done the same thing.

"Exactly why I'm here, kitten. No parents, no one up my ass. You're stuck with me for the next few weeks."

I slumped against the counter. "You Douglas boys never seem to go the hell away." I snatched a banana from the fruit basket next to me and tossed it at him.

His posture perked up as he caught it with one hand, unpeeled it, and took a large bite. "What the hell is that supposed to mean? I'm a fucking blast to have around, babe."

I shook my head, waving off my words. "Nothing."

There was no way I'd be more with Asher, especially after sleeping with his cousin. Not that he'd ever find out about me sleeping with Dalton. I'd never hear the end of it.

He shrugged, taking another bite of the banana. "You'd better get used to us being around them since you'll have to endure it sometimes when we get married. Plus, you'll be sharing our last name. Gabby Douglas. It's like music to my ears."

I rolled my eyes. "In your dreams."

"Oh, baby, you've been in plenty of my dreams."

I reached across the island and smacked his arm.

"So, how was your first day at the new job?"

"Miserable. That place sucks ass." I bent forward and felt the cold marble across my forehead as I smacked it against the countertop.

He tossed the banana peel onto the counter, only a few inches away from my head. "Tomorrow will be better."

I dragged my head back up to look at him. "Why's that?"

The only way it'd get better was if I was fired or Dalton quit.

His eyes twinkled with mischief. "I'll be there."

I leaned forward to smack my head against the counter again and groaned. "Seriously?"

His hand went up to his broad chest. "Shit, babe, don't get too excited. You sure know how to hurt a man's feelings."

"You mean, ego?"

"Eh, I guess you're right. Trust me, it wasn't my first job pick, but my mom and dad insisted. Plus, I'm working in IT. That's unfortunate for you though because you won't see this handsome face as much." He cupped his chin and looked up at me with a grin. "On the plus side, it'll help hide our office affair."

Him working in the IT department wasn't a surprise. Asher was a hacking genius who could get into almost anything. I was guilty myself of having him do a few things for Cora and me. Nothing illegal. We only wanted to know if she'd made it into her first-choice college, and she did. My best friend was leaving me soon while I would be stuck here doing who knew what with my life because I was so indecisive.

"I'm shaking my invisible pom-poms," I muttered, circling the island and falling onto the stool beside him.

He tapped my thigh. "I'd much rather you be shaking something else."

I shoved him.

"Come on." He hopped off the stool and held out his hand. "Let's get something to eat. I'm fucking starved. My treat, but if you spend over five bucks, you're on your own."

When I took his hand, he attempted to pull me into his side, but I stopped him, plugging my nose.

"Nuh-uh, playboy," I said. "I'm not going anywhere with you until you shower and get that sweaty shit off your body."

He slapped my ass. "Fine, be back in five, unless you want to join me?"

My foot went into his shin. "Five minutes, or I'm getting food without you and letting you starve."

Chapter Four

DALTON

GABBY

THE FIRST THING I noticed walking into Eva's parents' living room was the nasty scowl plastered on my mother's face.

"You're late," she said.

Her voice was sweet, but I didn't miss the distaste in her tone. She'd wait until the audience was gone before she let the real Victoria Douglas come out—a raging, jealous, and controlling woman who covertly hated her life.

My gaze moved from her to Eva's parents, sitting on a couch directly across from her.

"Work ran over," I replied, giving them a polite wave.

"That's nonsense," my mother argued, and I detected the slight slur in her voice. "Your father owns the company, and he arrived on time."

Great, she'd been drinking. The chances of her not making a scene decreased. My mother was an emotional drinker, and by emotional, I mean, she liked to talk shit about our dirty laundry when too much liquor was running through her system.

"Victoria, that's enough," my dad scolded like she was a child.

She slammed her mouth shut, and I gave my father a chin raise for the save. He was sitting next to my mother and had a glass of bourbon in his hand. Bourbon had been the choice of alcohol for the men in our inner circle for years. They believed if they drank enough, it emitted power into their veins.

"I had him finish some additional paperwork before leaving. It seems it took him longer than I expected," my father explained.

"I'm sorry, Dalton. You know how strongly I feel about punctuality," my mother said, her eyes staring down at the floor.

"You finally made it," Eva called out, and I turned to look at her.

Gone was her long blonde hair—now hitting the end of her shoulder blades. Usually, I wasn't a fan of short hair on girls since I liked something to grab onto when I fucked them, but Eva worked it well. She wore a short black dress that showed off her curves and gold heels that made her legs appear longer. My dick stirred in my jeans. Not wanting to marry her didn't mean she didn't turn me on.

"Hi, future hubby," she purred, giving me a fake smile and kissing me hard on the mouth. "I was beginning to think you wouldn't make it."

I scratched my cheek while grinding my teeth. "I couldn't miss seeing you, babe."

She rolled her eyes at my response.

Eva's dad clapped his fat hands together before bringing himself up from the couch. "Now that everyone's here, let's eat. I'm starving."

He straightened his hands down his expensive suit and unbuttoned a few gold buttons on his jacket. His large belly protruded over his black slacks. He wasn't obese, but he also wasn't fit. His light hair was beginning to thin and was balding in the middle. Not that he cared. Clive Monroe wasn't big on worrying about his appearance. His focus was always on the almighty dollar.

My head tilted up, admiring the crystal chandelier hanging above us, while I followed everyone through the large foyer. Their home was the epitome of old money with winding staircases and cathedral ceilings painted with clouds and cherubs.

When we made it to the dining room, a table that could fit at least twenty was already set. A group of waiters filed into the room, their hands filled with plates and glasses of wine. I immediately grabbed a glass off a tray, not having the patience to wait for them to set it down. I pulled out Eva's chair for her before settling in the one next to her. Everyone got comfortable and started the first course.

"Is this the first time you two have seen each other since Christmas?" Mona, Eva's mom, asked.

I barely noticed her mouth move from the overabundance of Botox injections she'd had. While Eva's dad wasn't one to worry about appearance, Mona was the opposite. She was the stereotypical Stepford wife. Her long blonde hair was curled into tiny spirals, hitting the top of her exposed cleavage, and her made-up skin looked flawless, but her fake eyelashes were almost obnoxious.

My attention moved away from her to my mom, whose look was the complete opposite. She was wearing a white long-sleeved blouse that buttoned down the middle, pairing it with a gray skirt and heels. It was something you'd wear to a business meeting, not a dinner with so-called friends ... future in-laws. Her hair was twisted into a tight bun at the nape of her neck.

Eva set down her wineglass, grabbed my hand, and didn't flinch once as the lie fell from her lips. "No, I visited him last month."

She hadn't visited me once at Columbia while she was at Georgia State.

Before joining the conversation, my mom wiped her mouth and took a swig of unneeded wine. "That's nice, honey. I'm sure you're ready to move in together." She glanced at me. "Dalton just purchased that new gorgeous condo with *plenty* of space for the both of you."

I brought the wineglass to my lips and took a large gulp.

Jesus, could she have made it any more obvious she was ready to get this agreement—I mean, marriage—over with?

Eva's dad was worth millions, and my parents wanted him and his thirty-something businesses on our side. I was the perfect little worm to reel the big fish in.

"We decided to wait until marriage before moving in together," Eva answered.

The forced smiles turned into grimaces, only Eva and me loving the idea.

"I mean," Eva said before pausing and letting out an un-Eva-like giggle, "what would people think if we lived together before tying the knot?"

The bright smiles reappeared like her words had hit a light switch, changing the mood. My future wife was damn good.

"You're right, dear," my mom replied before wagging her skinny finger at me. "Dalton, honey, you'd better get on that."

"Just looking for the perfect ring," I grumbled, taking another drink of wine.

I planned to have my younger sister, Piper, pick out a ring. No way in hell was I dropping to a knee and delivering a pathetic speech about how much I loved Eva. My mother wanted a public proposal, but that shit wasn't happening.

It wasn't that I hated Eva. In fact, we were friends. We dated our sophomore year of high school but broke up after six months when we realized we were better off as friends. Unfortunately, our parents disagreed with the breakup, and we'd been *engaged* for years. They were planning our marriage before I even received my high school diploma.

"My son is quite the perfectionist." My mother glared at me in warning. "He only wants the best for the woman he loves."

I almost choked on my food at the bullshit coming out of her mouth. I grunted when an elbow slammed into my rib cage and looked up at Eva.

"It'd better be a good one," she whispered, smiling.

I rubbed my side and tapped her thigh underneath the table. "Oh, baby, you're going to hate it."

"If I have to deal with you for the rest of my life, I deserve a nice big rock."

"I'll be sure to find you the nicest ring at the local pawn shop," I threw back, not able to hold back my laugh.

"Do it, and I'll be planning your funeral instead of a wedding."

GABBY

MY ATTENTION DARTED AWAY from the stack of papers in front of me at the sound of my phone ringing. I'd been at Douglas PR for a week, and not once had that damn thing rung. *Not once.*

I was beginning to think it was only there for looks. My job comprised of organizing files, emailing invoices, and being bored into oblivion. Once the other employees caught word of me being the step-daughter of their boss, they pretty much snubbed and labeled me as undeserving for the job. *Assholes.*

My focus stayed on the phone, certain I was hallucinating the noise. By the time I realized I wasn't *that* crazy, it went silent. *Oh well.* I went back to my stapling routine, and the ringing came back.

Damn it.

I set the stapler down, contemplating whether to answer it. Everyone there hated me. Asher was the only person I talked to, and he would've called my cell, so whoever was on the other end was most likely someone I didn't want to talk to.

I swiftly picked up the phone and brought it to my ear. "Uh, hello?"

"Gabrielle," the penetrating voice on the other end barked, and I instantly regretted answering. "It's Wilson. Come to my office."

The line went dead, and I rolled my eyes as I set the phone back down in its receiver. I'd forgotten how much of a jackass Wilson, Dalton's dad, was. I took a deep breath, uncertain of why I was being called into the demon's office, and crossed my fingers in the hopes that I was getting fired.

Rising from the uncomfortable chair, I ran my hands down my skirt before venturing out of my box. I walked past the rows of cubicles before reaching Blondie at the front desk. Since I had no idea where his office was, I was forced to ask.

"The almighty Wilson has summoned me," I grumbled to her and laughed at the sight of her painting her nails.

Where can I sign up for that job?

She set the brush back in the bottle and blew on her nails. "Follow me," she ordered, getting up from the chair, careful not to mess up her freshly painted pink nails.

We stopped at a wide set of French doors, and she knocked. The same voice that'd barked through the phone yelled for us to come in.

I clutched my hands together as she allowed me entry into the pet cemetery. The room of doom was packed with taxidermy animals— on the walls, bookshelves, in the corner. I was confident they were looking down at me, warning that I was his next victim.

"Thank you, Summer," Wilson said, choosing not to acknowledge me while studying her ass as she left the room.

I shuffled my feet back and forth. The guy was married but ogling his secretary right in front of me.

"Hello, Gabrielle," he finally greeted once his ass distraction disappeared. He stared at me like a lion does its prey before ripping them to shreds and having them for dinner.

I forced my lips to create a small smile. "Call me Gabby."

He always called me by my full name, and I always corrected him. No doubt he did it to disrespect me.

He shot me a smug smile and pointed to an empty chair in front of his desk. "Have a seat."

My legs felt like Jell-O as I made my way across the room and sat down.

He folded his hands in front of him on his desk. "I'm glad you're here with us."

I covered my mouth and held back the eye roll at his blatant lie. The man despised me.

"How do you like it so far?"

The next lie belonged to me. "It's great," I answered, crossing my legs and straightening my posture.

"Terrific." It amazed me at how much sarcasm dripped from one small word. "I understand Kenneth said you wanted more responsibility around here."

A tingle swept from the back of my neck to my face. I was going to kill my mom. I'd casually mentioned I was going insane from boredom at work, and she must've told Kenneth. Then, he went to Wilson.

Great.

Had I known it'd result in a chat with this jerk, I would've kept my mouth shut.

It took me a moment to decide if I wanted to deny his accusation or roll with it. The door swung open before I got the chance to reply, and Summer reappeared ... with Dalton behind her. Dalton shoved his hands into his pockets while staring at his father.

Luckily, I'd succeeded in avoiding any other awkward run-ins with him. It took some work but was worth it. I made Asher drive us to work twenty minutes early and took the stairs instead of the elevator.

"You wanted to see me?" Dalton asked, walking around Summer before halting in step at the sight of me.

I was certain I wasn't the only one working to avoid each other.

"I did." Wilson settled back into his chair and gestured to the seat next to me. "Have a seat." He shooed Summer out of the room.

My pulse raced when Dalton settled in the chair, and panic surged through my veins as to why we were here at the same time.

Does Wilson know about us having sex?

Will he fire me because of it?

"Dalton, this is Gabrielle. She's your uncle Kenneth's stepdaughter," Wilson said, introducing us.

There was nothing more awkward than being introduced to the guy who'd popped your cherry. A giant *fuck you* was at the tip of my tongue and begging to be released. My mom and Kenneth married four years ago, and I'd had the displeasure of spending holidays with his dreadful family since my mother's was nonexistent.

He knew who I was.

He knew Dalton knew who I was.

Dalton's eyes cut his dad's way. "I know who Gabby is."

Wilson gave him a smug smile and clapped his hands. "Great! I'm glad we got that out of the way." He signaled between Dalton and me. "You two will be partnering up with a new client—a *very important* client. Everything must be kept completely confidential."

My jaw dropped, my attention darting to Dalton to gauge his reaction, but his face was blank.

"Partners?" I asked, indicating between the two of us with a single finger. "As in us working together?"

I knew the answer to my question was obvious, and I probably looked like a complete idiot, but I needed some clarification.

Wilson sneered at me. "Yes, Gabrielle, I do believe that's what partnering up means."

Yeah, he totally thinks I'm a complete airhead.

Wilson raised a brow. "Unless you don't feel you are qualified enough for the job?"

Not to toot my own horn and all, but I was smart. I'd graduated with a three-point-eight GPA. It'd be a waste of breath to defend myself and tell him that though.

"I'm just the file girl. I know nothing about PR," I told him.

His face turned hard but amused at the same time. He enjoyed my pathetic attempt at getting out of this. "You're an intern. Interns do whatever the hell I tell them to do. Whether that be filing folders, getting my dry cleaning, or scrubbing my goddamn toilet. Interns have no damn say in what they do or don't do around here. Understood?"

"Dad," Dalton warned, his jaw working in circles.

I wasn't sure if he was pissed because he had to work with me or if he was sticking up for me.

"Understood," I said with a weak smile. "Is there anything you'd like me to do to prepare for tomorrow?"

Other than learn to suck it up and deal with his verbal abuse.

Wilson grunted before his eyes scanned my body. "Wear something more professional."

I peered down at my knee-length Burberry dress that I'd paired with my favorite Mary Jane peep-toe pumps. Wilson couldn't be serious. Not only was my dress ten times more professional than his secretary's, but it was also designer. Just because I wasn't born into Douglas wealth didn't mean I didn't get the benefits. My mom had given me her credit card to go out and buy new clothes for the job.

"Dalton will meet you in the morning and take you into the boardroom with him at eight o'clock sharp," Wilson said. "Don't be late." He waved me out of the room dismissively.

I hopped out of my chair, careful not to trip on my heels, and hurried out of the room.

Things were about to get interesting.

Chapter Six

DALTON

I **WAITED** until Gabby left before ripping into my father. "What the hell?"

Before today, I hadn't seen Gabby since our last confrontation. I realized she was avoiding me when I caught her sneaking out of the staircase entrance. Her head had looked both ways before she dashed down the hall to her cubicle.

"What?" he asked before dragging both hands over his face and letting out a disgruntled groan. "That girl's whore of a mother complained to my goddamn brother about giving her more responsibilities because she's bored. Of course, my brother takes that slut's side and calls me. We both know that brat is useless, so I figured I could stick her with you. You do all the work and give the twit something minuscule to appease him until we can find a way to get rid of her."

Tension flared up into my neck. He hardly knew Gabby and had no right to bash her. His disdain for her was caused by my uncle leaving his wealthy heiress wife to be with Gabby's mom, who was far from an heiress. Before marrying Kenneth, she'd worked nine-to-five, lived paycheck to paycheck, and lived in a small apartment.

"Don't take your hate for her mother out on her. She seems decent," I said.

I averted my eyes to the wall behind him to appear as casual as possible. He couldn't know I'd taken the insults somewhat personal. The man could read people like a damn book. That was why he was so good at his job. It was a trait I admired, growing up, until I realized who he truly was.

He worked his jaw from side to side. "Not taking anything out on the girl. She's working here, is she not? I'd say that's rather generous of me, considering she has no experience."

"You just called her useless."

He flashed me a cold smile. "So, I did, but you can't argue that. She's not even attending college, for God's sake. According to my dipshit brother, she's taking a year off. I can't believe he'd even allow that to happen in his household. I would've kicked that damn girl out on the streets if she tried pulling a stunt like that."

It was the truth. Had any of his children decided against the college they'd chosen for us, we would've been cut off—plain and simple, no exceptions. My parents expected us to excel in academics and everything else in life.

"Mom didn't go to college," I fired back, treading into dangerous territory.

"Your mother and that girl are on two different scales of the social spectrum," he snarled, his eyes beginning to blaze fury. "Your mother comes from a well-bred family. That girl comes from nothing, from filth, from being the daughter of a whore. She'd be smart to accept the education my brother is offering to pay for and get a decent career, so that she can support herself. He doesn't need another mooch leeching off him."

"Is that what Summer is then?" I asked, noticing the instant the true meaning of my question dawned on him.

His glare focused on me, vicious and hard, like he was daring me to keep talking.

"What the hell are you talking about?" he asked, attempting to look confused and going directly into his power pose.

I leaned forward, resting my elbows on my knees, and relayed my words slowly. "Does that make Summer a whore?"

Fuck it. Someone needed to set his ass straight for once. He was constantly belittling my uncle and his wife because she was his mistress, but he was doing the same damn thing. The only difference was that my uncle had enough balls to own up to his mistakes. My dad would never do that.

"Be careful, throwing out false accusations," he warned, spit flying out of his mouth.

I snorted. "False accusations? You're married to Mom but banging Summer on the side. Summer is your damn mistress. She's the same thing that Gabby's mom was to Uncle Kenneth."

I'd be damned if I was going to allow him to treat Gabby like shit the entire time she worked here.

He opened his mouth, ready to voice his argument, but I continued talking. "Don't waste our time denying it. Everyone knows, including Mom. Given that Summer is your mistress, that'd make her a whore as well, correct?"

"You leave Summer out of this. You hear me? Whatever ridiculous notion you have brewing in that head of yours is wrong. Be ready tomorrow." He picked up the glass on his desk and walked over to the minibar in the corner of the room, filling it with cognac before gulping it down.

When I got up to leave, he shouted at my back, "And if you ever refer to Summer as a whore again, your employment here will be terminated. I don't give a shit if you're my son. You will not disrespect my employees like that. Do I make myself clear?"

Fucking hypocrite.

"Shouldn't that go both ways?" I asked, my back still facing him. "I'd consider calling your brother's wife a whore is not only disrespectful toward your brother, but also to Gabby. Both of whom are not only employees here, but your family as well."

He cleared his throat. "I'll take that into careful consideration."

I rolled my eyes and pulled open the door.

He'd never change.

* * *

Music played when I walked through the dim-lit bar and strolled past rows of occupied tables. I'd tried to get my older brother, Leo, to meet me at the strip club, but he wouldn't budge. If his wife caught him there, she'd most likely go into one of her crazy rampages, which sucked because I figured some eye candy might take my mind off Gabby. The more I saw her, the more I wanted her, and that was a huge fucking problem.

I headed straight toward the bar and pulled out a stool next to Leo before slumping down on top of it.

"Rough day?" Leo asked, an entertained smile on his face. He had a beer in his hand and looked like shit. My brother, the typical businessman who was always clean-cut and put together, appeared as if he hadn't shaved in days and was due for a haircut.

"You have no idea," I answered, signaling toward the bartender. "Jack and Coke, please."

He nodded.

"And keep 'em coming."

"Going for the hard shit tonight, huh? I see working for Dad is still fun," Leo said, taking a long swig of his beer. "That's something I don't miss."

Leo had worked for my dad until he got married and became the VP of his wife's dad's oil empire. He happily left Douglas PR, practically skipping out the door.

As soon as the bartender delivered my drink, I chugged it, relishing the burn as it seeped down my throat. "Uncle Kenneth's stepdaughter is now employed at Douglas PR as well." I wiped my mouth with the back of my arm.

He chuckled. "I bet Dad is fucking loving that."

"Even better, he decided to partner us up for my first client."

I'm fucked.

How am I supposed to focus on my client when I can't stop thinking about sleeping with Gabby again?

Leo's face turned serious. "Don't do anything stupid."

The bartender sat drink number two in front of me.

"What the hell is that supposed to mean?" I felt a slight buzz slowly creep up inside me.

"She's an attractive girl, and everyone knows how much you love attractive women."

I tilted my head to the side, a slow smile building across my lips. "You think she's hot?"

I wasn't surprised Leo didn't have an issue with her. My brother was like me and didn't care about labels or reputations like our parents.

His fingers splayed out across his glass. "For a younger woman, yes, she's attractive."

I brought my drink back up to my mouth. "Huh."

He let out a sharp breath. "Fuck, Dalton, tell me you didn't?"

"Didn't what?" I asked into my glass, fully aware my ass was busted.

"You had sex with her, didn't you? You know Dad is going to kick your ass."

I held my free hand to my heart, feigning innocence at his accusation. "What? No! Of course, I didn't have sex with her."

"You do realize I know when you're lying, right? You squint your right eye every single time. You've done it since we were kids."

"Really?" I squinted my right eye.

Why is this the first time I'm hearing about my little lie detector?

"I'd better work on that, and thanks for just now telling me, asshole."

Alcohol splashed onto my pants when he smacked me in the back of the head.

"I always knew you were fucking stupid, but I didn't think you were that stupid," he said.

I shot him a glare as I grabbed a napkin. "Stupid? I just graduated from an Ivy League college."

"For someone who just graduated from college, you're a dumbass. You had sex with our uncle's daughter."

Every single pair of eyes in the bar shot our way with looks of disgust plastered onto their faces. It was my turn to smack my brother upside the head.

"Stepdaughter," I clarified loudly to our audience, correcting my idiot brother's choice of words. "She's his stepdaughter. We are in no way blood-related."

"Blood or not, you'd better hope Dad or Uncle Kenneth don't find out." He snapped his fingers. "Oh yeah, did you also forget about Eva, the girl you're marrying?" he hissed, lowering his voice.

The asshole wanted to shout to the world that I was in an incestuous relationship but lower his voice when he talked about my engagement.

I shrugged, downing my glass. "What about Eva?"

Eva had never come to mind when I hooked up with other women because we weren't technically together. We'd made a pact. We were both free to do whatever we wanted until we got married. After our wedding, we'd be monogamous.

I wasn't happy about the whole arrangement, but I figured I could live with screwing Eva for the rest of my life. Until fucking Gabby wandered into my bedroom. I needed to fuck her out of my system because time was ticking down before my monogamous deal was going through.

"Does she know about your little affair?" he asked.

"Affair?" I held up my hand. "Whoa, whoa. We aren't having an affair. It was only once. Plus, Eva doesn't give a shit what I do. I'm allowed to do whatever the fuck I want until we tie the depressing knot that's going to strangle the shit out of me."

"Great. Now, quit sticking your dick into Dad's employees before you get your ass fired and have no one to marry."

"I'm not fucking any of his employees. It was a while back, and I'll repeat, it was only once. No need to get your panties in a bunch, brother."

He stayed silent.

"New Year's party," I elaborated.

That night had been hell for me. My dad and I argued because I'd chosen against going to the Hamptons with Eva and her family. We'd screamed, he'd thrown some shit, and I'd slammed the door in his face before leaving. I emptied an entire flask of whiskey and then some before trudging my ass to my bedroom and away from their party.

The parties got old. All my parents cared about was making themselves look good and showing us off to be the perfect family. *Perfect, my ass.* The only family member I even talked to on a normal basis was Leo.

I was undressing, ready to pass out, when I heard the knock on my bedroom door. The next thing I knew, Gabby was standing in front of me, and her mouth was on mine.

At first, I was sure I was hallucinating. There was no way she'd come to my room. Anytime I'd tried to talk to her, she'd always shy away from me. The moment her lips hit mine, I'd forgotten all about my bullshit argument with my dad, the Hamptons, parties, all of it.

When I'd woken up the next morning, desperate for another round, she was gone. I thought I'd been dreaming until I found the empty condom wrapper on my floor. I wasn't drunk enough that I'd fucked myself. She ditched my ass, and it pissed me off. But not pissed off enough to not overplay how she begged me to take her in my mind. I couldn't forget how sweet her whimpers sounded underneath me as I pounded into her tight core.

"And it just keeps getting better," he fired back. "Please tell me she was eighteen, or you're going to be hiring Dad to clear your name."

Fuck, he was right. I never asked Gabby how old she was. In my defense, I never had the chance to ask her anything.

"She was eighteen, and don't worry. She made it clear she won't say a word about it."

He cupped his hand on my shoulder. "Baby brother, chicks always say that shit until they want money or attention. You know that. Then, when you don't give it to them, they turn on you."

"She doesn't need money, considering Uncle Kenneth provides anything she needs. Plus, she hates me ... and I'm positive she's embarrassed about sleeping with me."

He chuckled. "I think I actually like the girl. But stay the fuck away from her."

I pointed at him, my body beginning to sway in my stool. "I'm sorry, did you forget the part where I told you Dad partnered us up?"

"Easy fix. Tell Dad you want to work with someone else ... or by yourself."

I snorted. "Like that doesn't make it obvious something happened between us."

"Fine, smart-ass, just keep it professional and leave your goddamn dick in your pants."

I held up my glass in a cheers motion. "I got it. I got it." I took another gulp even though I didn't need it. "How are Kelly and the kids?"

My brother smiled at the mention of his family. Well, at the mention of his children. "Claire and Oliver are doing great, but Kelly ran off on one of her me-time trips. I guess spending days shopping and drinking mimosas at the country club while other people watch our children is stressful for her. I'm caring for the kids, working sixty hours a week, and trying to find a new nanny."

That explained why he looked so damn drained and why arranged marriages were nothing but a giant pain in the ass.

"A new nanny?" I asked. "What happened to the last one?"

Kelly usually hired old, frumpy ladies to nanny, but the last was a hot petite blonde. Unfortunately for me, Kelly had warned her that if she talked to me, she'd be fired. Every time I'd walked into the same room as her, she'd run out of it.

"Kelly caught us laughing and fired her."

Typical fucking Kelly. That chick was born with jealousy in her veins. If my parents wanted to despise any wife in our family, it needed to be her, not Gabby's mother.

I cocked my head to the side. "Did you?" Being on the other side of the questioning block was much better.

"Fuck no. The poor girl was only telling me something Claire did at the park that was funny. I laughed, and Kelly went all fucking Kelly."

I believed my brother. He was unhappy but wasn't the type to cheat and ruin his family. He knew what he was getting into when he got married, and he respected his vows.

"You need to get a divorce, bro," I said, repeating the words I'd been telling him for years.

I felt terrible for my brother. He was a good guy, and he deserved happiness more than anyone in our family.

"You must really be drunk." He dragged the glass from my hand. "Just be happy Mom and Dad set you up with someone who can't be mistaken for Satan."

"Yeah," I mumbled, snatching my glass back out of his hand and chugging the rest of its contents.

I needed to be preparing for my meeting tomorrow, but instead, I was drinking away thoughts of Gabby.

Chapter Seven

GABBY

I PACED the room while nervously waiting for Dalton the next morning. As much as I'd love to be back in my cubicle, I was at least happy I wouldn't be working with Wilson.

"You ready for this?" Dalton asked, strolling into the room with a notebook in his hand.

I gulped, my eyes blazing into him. He was wearing another fitted black suit, complete with a silver tie. A diamond watch was wrapped around his wrist that matched his cuff links. His face was clean-shaven, showing off the perfect definition of his high cheekbones. He looked delicious, and it instantly reminded me of why I couldn't stay away from him that night at the party.

Some girls were attracted to guys in tight jeans and cowboy hats. Others were into bad boys, covered with tattoos, or ones with guitars always swung around their shoulders. Those guys were hot and all, but there was nothing sexier than a well-dressed man in a suit, screaming they were in charge. Power hungry. That was one of the worst traits I inherited from my mom—poor taste in men. We were attracted to men we weren't supposed to be attracted to. We craved what we couldn't have.

"Not really," I answered.

I slept terribly last night, unsure if my nerves were from being around Wilson or working with Dalton. Most likely both.

"It won't be bad. I promise." Dalton winked at me before turning and walking down the hall.

I followed him, hot on his trail, and he led us into a large boardroom like the ones in the movies. A projection screen was centered in the middle of the room and positioned in front of a long table. Black chairs surrounded the table, and my eyes immediately landed on Wilson. He was planted at the head of the table, having what appeared to be a serious conversation with a man sitting to his right. I stayed behind Dalton, using him as a barrier, and peeked at the two men.

Dalton cleared his throat, and their attention came our way.

"These are two of our interns," Wilson said, motioning toward us. "Dalton and Gabrielle."

The man grimaced. "Interns?" A worried glance swept to Wilson. "I made it clear this needed to be as discreet as possible. I can't have inexperienced interns working on this issue and run the risk of them leaking information."

I squinted in the man's direction. There was something familiar about him, but I couldn't figure it out. His dark hair was cut short and peppered with shades of gray. A few wrinkles surrounded his eyes and lips as he scowled over at Wilson.

His eyes shot to us. "No offense to you two. I'm sure you're extremely hard workers, but I need something more than what an intern can give me."

"I can assure you, you'll be in good hands," Wilson attested.

The man raised his brow. "How so?"

Wilson pointed at Dalton. "This is my son and the future owner of this company." His finger slid over to me. "This is Kenneth's stepdaughter. I chose them specifically for those reasons. Nothing will be leaked. You have my word."

The man scratched his pale cheek and moved his eyes, focusing only on me. "Stepdaughter, huh? She looks a bit young. How old are you?"

I shifted, suddenly feeling uncomfortable, and my reply surprisingly came out more confident than I felt. "Eighteen." I wrapped my arms around my chest at the same time Dalton clapped his hands.

"Let's get started, shall we?" Dalton said, pressing his hand to my side and squeezing it gently. Stepping forward, he pulled my chair out for me and then took the one at my side. Tossing the notebook onto the table, he grabbed a pen from his pocket. "What can I help you with, Governor Gentry?"

My mouth flew open in recognition. That was why he looked so familiar. I'd seen him on TV plenty of times because he was the governor of Georgia, and word was, he was gearing up for the future presidential bid.

"Call me John," the man insisted before popping his knuckles. "Now, on to business. There's a woman blackmailing me for ten million dollars. If I don't pay, she's threatening to expose me."

Expose him? I looked around at the other people in the room, none of them looking near as confused as me.

Dalton nodded. "Expose you for what?"

"We had an affair." His answer was so low that I barely caught his words. "She has plenty of evidence to prove it—texts, emails, and I'm not sure what else."

My gaze moved from John to Dalton, but he didn't even flinch at John's confession.

"When did the affair take place?" Dalton asked, scratching down notes.

John fiddled with his watch, failing to look at anyone and losing all the arrogance that had surrounded him when we walked in.

"Governor, I need you to be up front with me about everything if you want our help," Dalton said.

John inhaled a deep breath before nodding in confirmation.

"Thank you," Dalton said. "Now, have you attempted to negotiate with this woman?"

"Yes, but she won't budge." John's shoulders slumped. "She's angry I won't leave my wife and doesn't understand what a divorce would cost me. It'd ruin everything—my goals, career, reputation, all of it."

I bit my tongue, fighting back the urge to tell him if he didn't want to ruin everything, he should've kept his dick in his pants.

"And how do you know this woman?" Dalton asked.

"She was an intern on my campaign." He paused for a second and held his finger up like he'd just come up with a brilliant plan. "Maybe we can blame the messages on that?"

Yeah, I'm sure those messages were real campaign related.

Dalton shut his notebook. "Doubt that'll work. I need everything you have on this woman—dirt, blackmail, her personal information, anything you have. We'll get tech on the case immediately. For now, stay away from her. Avoid all communication. No calling. No meetups, do you hear me?"

Revulsion brewed into my stomach as I took in what was happening in front of me. He was paying us to hide his affair like a coward.

"Thank you," John said, stroking the back of his neck. "Ruin the girl if you have to. I don't care. Do whatever. Don't let her talk, *please.*"

I swallowed the lump in my throat, unable to hold back the words fighting to be released from the tip of my tongue. "To confirm, you want us to cover up your affair with an intern?"

I needed some clarification on what exactly my job was.

Is this the kind of PR they do here? Protect assholes from dealing with the consequences of sticking their cocks into women who weren't their wives?

Wilson tensed, waiting for me to say something stupid, and John's mouth fell open. He probably wasn't used to people calling him out on his bullshit.

"Gabrielle," Wilson warned.

"What?" I asked, raising a brow. "I'm curious." My eyes deadpanned on a nervous John. "If you cheated on your wife, don't you think you should man up and take responsibility for your actions?"

John stared at me, speechless. Wilson smacked a stunned Dalton's arm and motioned toward the doors.

Dalton jumped up and pulled my arm to get me out of my chair. "I forgot we have some briefs to go over," he rushed out.

His hand latched on to mine, and he dragged me out of the room and down a hallway into an unfamiliar office. I pulled out of his grip at the same time he slammed the door shut.

"Are you fucking crazy?" he hissed, his pupils dilating. "Do you want to get fired?"

I bit back a laugh and threw my hands up in the air. "Is this the kind of *publicity* you guys do around here? Cover up for philandering assholes?" I took a few steps backward and held my palms up his way. "I want absolutely no part in it."

Obviously, I wasn't cut out for the job. I had morals—not a lot, but some.

"We're a crisis PR company, Gabby. We make sure our clients' reputations stay intact and polished. Whether they're having an affair, breaking the law, or doing whatever else could possibly damage their public image, we fix it."

I crossed my arms across my chest. "Okay, that's just sad."

"We don't only work for bad guys. We do PR for charities and plenty of reputable companies as well."

I scoffed.

"I'm serious. This is our first case. We can't mess this up."

"How about you stick me somewhere they do charities then? I want no part in covering up for that sleazeball."

"Just great," he muttered, flopping down into a leather chair behind the desk. "Just fucking great."

Our eyes went to the door when it swung open. Wilson charged into the room, his face crimson with fury, and stalked my way. Dalton jumped up from his chair.

Well, shit.

"I knew it was a bad idea, allowing you to work here," Wilson said.

I dodged the spit flying out of his mouth while he got closer to my face.

"Dad," Dalton said, edging himself in between the two of us before pushing Wilson away from me.

I always knew Wilson was a raging dickhead, but this was seriously out of line.

Wilson came to his senses and took a step back before thrusting a finger out at me. "Listen here, girl. If you want to continue your employment here—and trust me, I'm only doing this because of my brother—you'd better shape the fuck up! This company exists because we please our clients! Not insult them! Do I make myself clear?"

I threw him a hateful smile. "Crystal." I wouldn't cower in his presence.

"Get her ass straight," he snarled, his finger swinging over to Dalton. "Here's his file. I want you to get this shit fixed." He tossed a manila folder onto the desk and stormed out of the room.

I slumped down into the nearest chair. "How do I put in my two weeks' notice?"

Dalton fell down into the chair beside me. "You're not putting in your two weeks."

I shook my head. "This is a temporary job for me. You think I want to fix other people's problems for the rest of my life? Definitely not. I have a hard enough time handling my own."

"Are you going to school?"

"What?" I asked, unsure how that pertained to me working in this damn hellhole.

"Are you going to school?"

"I'm taking a year off."

I didn't even want to go to college, but my mom insisted it was something I needed to do. I knew the real reason was because she never had the chance to do it herself. She'd gotten pregnant with me right before graduating high school and had to work two jobs to support us since my dad apparently fell off the face of the planet. College was never in the cards for her, but it was for me. The problem was, I had no idea what I wanted to do with my life, and going to school before then seemed pointless and a waste of money to me.

"And who's paying for your school when you go? Better yet, who supports you now?"

"My mom." I still wasn't sure where he was going with the conversation, but I had a feeling I wasn't going to like it.

"If your mom is, then my uncle is most likely the one paying for it."

I drew in a sharp breath and clenched my fists. "My mom works," I snapped defensively. I was so sick of them thinking my mom just sat around, eating bonbons, while Kenneth paid for everything. My mom didn't make millions, but she worked her ass off for what little we had.

His face dropped at my tone. "I didn't mean it like that. I was just saying, my uncle helps support you, which is a normal thing for stepparents to do. I want to warn you that if you do quit, my uncle will most likely cut you off because my dad will pressure him to do so. That will then create a problem for your mom and him. Not to mention, I plan on this being my career, and I want to take over eventually. This is my first assignment, and for some reason, we got stuck together. You don't have to do anything. I'll do it all. Just keep your comments to yourself, is all I ask."

Dammit, he has a point.

My mom was finally happy. She loved Kenneth, and he treated her right. We also didn't have to worry about our electricity being cut off or an eviction notice on the door when we came home from the food pantry.

"This is wrong," I whispered. I had to throw that out there before I gave in. I didn't agree with it, but I was doing it for my mom.

"Maybe, but we do help people, whether you want to look at it that way or not. How do you think your mom and Kenneth's affair didn't end up blowing up into some huge media circus? A millionaire VP cheats on an heiress with the woman his wife hired to design his new office. That would've made one hell of a story. You want to know why? This company. Otherwise, your mom would've been made out to be an evil home-wrecker, and her face would've been plastered on every news outlet in the country."

And the jackass has another point.

I crossed my arms. "Weird, your family seems to make up for the ridicule you saved her from by treating her like shit every time you're around her."

He frowned. "I've never said anything bad about your mom."

"Whatever," I grumbled, getting up from my chair. "Let's get this whole life-ruining thing over with."

He breathed out a rush of relief. "Thank you."

My gaze flicked to him, and my eyebrows pinched together. "I'm not doing this for you."

"I know."

"So, what now? We find some juicy dirt and launder it out to the highest bidder?" I needed a *How to Blackmail People for Dummies* book, pronto.

"First, we try to negotiate with her. We show her what we can leak if she goes forward. If she doesn't budge, we offer her money, but nowhere near ten million." He snagged the folder off the desk, opened it, and looked through the papers. "Looks like he won't pay anything over two."

"Two? As in two million dollars?" I choked out.

He nodded. "Reputations are an expensive thing."

"Some people have more money than sense." I shook my head. "What if she won't take the two million?"

"Then, we go into fight mode. We can make her out to look like some obsessed stalker and ruin her reputation. The girl will become the butt of jokes on all of the late-night talk shows."

"Let's hope it doesn't come to that."

I didn't know the girl, and it was wrong to sleep with a married man, but ruining her life seemed a bit drastic. My mother was a mistress, but she wasn't a bad person. Some women were just confused and looking for love in all the wrong places. Love made people do some stupid shit. I would blame it on daddy issues, like a lot of people did, but I had plenty of daddy issues, and you didn't see me sleeping with married men.

"Rule number two of this job: be prepared for anything," he added.

I looked over at him. "What's rule number one?"

"Don't insult the person who's paying us. Haven't you ever heard the phrase, *Don't cut off the hand that feeds you?*"

"Have you ever heard the phrase, *Don't piss off a girl with heels she can ram into your balls?*"

He laughed and pulled himself up from the chair. "Nope, never heard that one. Let's go see what we've got."

I followed him out of his office and into a room full of people sitting in front of computers.

"This is where our tech people do all their work."

I scanned the room, looking for the familiar face as fingers tapped on keys. I grinned when I spotted him.

"Hey, guys," Asher called out, waving us over.

"Got this for you," Dalton said. He handed him the folder Wilson had given him.

Asher flipped through the pages. "Your dad emailed me a few minutes ago about this. I've already found a few things." He shut the folder and snagged a sheet of paper from the printer. "Here are text messages and emails they sent back and forth, including naked pictures."

"Naked pictures of her?" I asked. *Are they really going to use naked pictures to blackmail her?*

"Of both of them," Asher answered.

A sour taste filled my mouth, and I swallowed back the impending vomit wanting to force its way up. Images of John naked were the last thing my eyes wanted to be scorned with.

"But don't worry; I didn't print any of John," Asher added.

I breathed out a breath of relief.

"I just want to throw this out there." Asher grinned. "Our governor has some grade A taste." He shot me a grin as I rolled my eyes. "Nowhere near your beauty, babe. You know you're my favorite."

Dalton snatched the papers from Asher's hand and wedged himself between Asher and me. "What else you got?"

"She's in debt and needs money. The girl has a serious shopping problem with the majority of it coming from sex shops and Victoria's Secret." His lips formed a sly grin. "Although I think that's a pretty good investment."

Dalton snapped his fingers. "Jackpot. She'll take the money."

Thank God. I'm ready for this to be over.

"Unless someone offers her more," Asher said. "She has some pretty decent proof, including pictures of them together. Oh, and look at this shiny new Mercedes."

The three of us leaned in when he clicked on the computer screen.

"Brand-new C-Class, purchased by our good ol' governor."

"What an idiot," I muttered. "Aren't these guys supposed to be good at hiding this kind of stuff?"

"Some guys think they're untouchable," Asher replied before smiling at me. "Dinner at seven though, by the way. We need to try that new burger joint that just opened up around the corner."

As much as I acted like Asher annoyed me, I enjoyed spending time with him. Every night since he'd arrived, we'd gone to dinner together, then hung out afterward.

"Be sure to wear something sexy for me, preferably see-through." Asher winked.

I slapped his shoulder, shaking my head with a grin. "I'll see you tonight, Casanova."

Dalton darted out of the room, clearly angry, and headed back to his office. He waited until I shut the door before deciding to open his big, obnoxious mouth.

GABBY

"SIT," Dalton demanded, reminding me of his jackass dad.

Ignoring his rude command, I turned around and wandered around his office, saying nothing. I was already taking orders from one douchebag Douglas. That was enough for the day.

"Nice office," I said, picking up a magazine from a rack, studying it, and then dropping it back down.

He shrugged, his eyes following my every step. "It's boring."

I laughed. "You should see mine." The only personalization I had in my beautiful cubicle was two picture frames, shoved into the tiny corner—one of Cora and me and the other with me and my mom.

"You work in here from now on."

"Huh?"

"You work in here from now on. We're partners. I don't want to go on a search mission every time I need you for something."

He was still pissed about our meeting with John. Jesus, I'd agreed to go through with the damn job and keep my mouth shut. What more did he want from me? I wasn't apologizing to him or his dad for my outburst.

"Do you and Asher have something going on?" he asked suddenly, his face turning cold.

I winced. "What? Asher's my stepbrother."

He clicked his tongue against the roof of his mouth. "That doesn't answer my question."

"I would think me pointing out the fact that he's my stepbrother is answer enough."

"No, it's not, and your attitude has already given me the answer I need."

"Oh my God! No, nothing is going on between us." Even if there was, I didn't need to explain myself to him.

"Sure looks like it."

"Then, you need to get your eyes checked because you're clearly seeing things."

He pressed his lips together in a tight line. "I'm just looking out for you, but do whatever the hell you want. Do you want to fuck my cousin, Gabby? Have at it," he snarled, his skin bunching up around his eyes. "Go screw everyone in my damn family for all I care." He snatched the notebook from his desk, threw it into a drawer, and slammed it shut.

I narrowed my eyes at him. "What the hell is your problem?"

"I just don't think it's cool, you and Asher."

"I just told you nothing is going on between us."

"Just like nothing is going on between us?"

My pulse sped up as I charged toward him. "Oh, there is absolutely nothing going on between you and me."

He stood from his chair, his chest only a few inches from mine. "I beg to differ. If nothing is going on between us

and nothing is going on between you and Asher, does that mean he's been in your panties too?"

"You're an asshole." I pushed his chest, but he didn't budge.

"Then, don't fucking lie to me."

I stiffened, my defenses rising with every passing second. "Not that it's any of your goddamn business," I spat, poking a finger into his chest, "but no, Asher has been nowhere near my panties."

His gaze leveled down on me. "Has anyone?"

"Has anyone what?"

"Has anyone else had their fingers in your panties? Inside you?"

My insides trembled, and my cheeks warmed.

"Again, that's none of your business," I breathed out, feeling my heart kick.

He stepped an inch closer, nearly stepping on my toes. "Be honest with me," he whispered, capturing a strand of my hair and sweeping it behind my earlobe.

I wanted to push him away, but I couldn't find the energy to do it.

"Have you let anyone else in there besides me? Have you let anyone else have what you gave to me? What's mine?"

I gulped, begging my brain to come to its senses. "I'm not yours," I rasped out.

He moved in closer. If I moved just an inch, our heads, our lips, would be connected. "You sure gave it to me like it was."

"I was drunk," I choked out, reusing the same excuse as last time we had this discussion. *Always blame it on the alcohol*, was my new motto.

"You still gave it to me, baby. You handed it over, no fucking questions asked. You spread your beautiful legs wide open for me and let me have it. You let me own you." His words made me light-headed.

"It wasn't yours, and you don't own me," I hissed.

"Then, why'd you do it?" he asked, grabbing my face, lifting my chin so I'd have to look at him.

I pushed away from him. "I was lonely, okay? You happy now?"

His eyebrows scrunched together. "Lonely. How in the hell could a girl like you possibly be lonely?"

A girl like me?

I felt my blood temperature rise. "Just because my mom was a mistress doesn't make me a slut, you arrogant asshole. I was a virgin before we had sex, in case you forgot."

His hands raked through his hair. "That's not how I meant it. You're gorgeous, so I don't know how guys aren't knocking down your door to take you out. It had nothing to do with thinking you're a slut because, baby, you're far from being a slut."

My mind drifted back to the only guy I dated after hooking up with Dalton. His name was Ross, and he was a joke for a boyfriend.

We broke up a few weeks ago because he was visiting his cousin's summer house and wanted to fuck other girls freely without feeling guilty about it.

"I was miserable at that party," I said, my voice lowering. "Not one person in your family talked to me. You did. I mean, it wasn't much, but you did. You said hi and asked if I was ready to graduate. I was sad and upset. I thought maybe, just maybe, you could make me feel better. But you know what?" I didn't give him the chance to answer before I continued, "I regret it. I should've never gone looking for you. I should've never gone into your room. It was a stupid mistake." I attempted to maneuver around him, but he stopped me and pushed me back against the wall.

"Don't say that," he demanded, his arm reaching out to level us against the wall as he leaned into me.

"It's the truth," I rasped out.

His weight pushed into me at the same time his lips hit mine, not giving me the chance to elaborate why then and now was a terrible idea. My brain had completely shut down.

"That was one of the best nights of my life. I've never had someone trust me as you did. I've never had someone give me something so fucking special to them."

He broke away from our kiss and ran his thumb along my jawbone. I inhaled a deep breath as he kissed me again. The taste of peppermint seeped into my mouth, reminding me of our first night together, and numbed any rational thoughts of stopping him.

My brain was screaming at me, telling me this was a terrible idea, but I couldn't pull myself away. The magnetic pull that had forced me into his bedroom was back, and I didn't have the strength to fight back.

He brushed my hair away from my shoulder and ran his soft lips along my neck. I gasped as his cold hand slid up my dress and ran across the inside of my thigh. He slipped a finger underneath the lace of my panties. I gripped his shoulder, and my knees went weak when he slid a finger down my center. I whimpered, parting my legs to give him better access at the same time someone knocked on the door.

"You've got to be fucking kidding me," Dalton said, groaning against my neck.

Summer barged in before we had the chance to break away from each other. She stilled at the sight of our tangled bodies against the wall. Dalton dragged his hand from my panties and turned around, covering my body while I embarrassingly adjusted myself behind him.

Well, this is humiliating.

"Future reference, Summer," Dalton growled. "Wait for a damn response before you barge into my fucking office."

"I'm sorry ... I didn't know you'd be so ... busy," she answered, a grin tugging at her lips. "Don't worry. I won't tell your father."

If Summer told anyone about this, I was quitting. I didn't care if it pissed my mom off.

"That would be smart on your part," he said as I stayed crouched behind him. "What do you want that is so damn important that you forgot your fucking manners?"

"Your dad wants to know if you'll be joining him and the governor for lunch, but it seems you're busy getting your fill of something else," she said. "I'll let him know you won't be able to make it. Oh, and by the way, you have some lipstick smeared on your face." She pointed to her cheek, threw him a smile, and left the room.

"Holy shit," I shrieked as soon as the door clicked shut before pushing Dalton away from me. "What if she tells your dad? What if she tells Kenneth and he tells my mom?"

My mind was running through a thousand different scenarios, and I couldn't keep up. My mom would kick my ass, and Wilson would probably have me murdered.

"She won't say anything," he said, grabbing a tissue from his desk and wiping away the evidence of our make-out session. "Trust me."

I took a calming breath and leaned against a chair. "Okay, what just happened?" I asked, coming to my senses and feeling like an idiot.

Our hookup was a one-time thing. Nothing more.

Dalton scrubbed his cheek. "Just don't say anything, okay?" he answered, tossing the Kleenex in the trash before walking out of the room.

Chapter Nine

DALTON

I'D FORGOTTEN how soft Gabby's skin felt against my fingers and how sexy she looked when turned on. Just when my fingertips reached the wet warmth between her thighs, Summer's annoying ass barged in and ruined everything. Talk about a fucking mood killer.

"This is a nice place," Gabby said, looking out the window at the high-rise apartment.

We stayed quiet for the short ride over, and I was oddly okay with that. I knew if what happened in my office was brought up, she'd tell me we needed to stop. I sure as fuck wasn't letting that happen. I wasn't going to allow her to overthink our situation. Instead, I would play it cool and wait for her to realize her feelings for me.

I tapped my fingers against my steering wheel to the beat of the music playing and muttered, "Too damn nice."

No way could a young intern in debt afford to live there. John's dumbass was no doubt footing the bill. That gave me one more thing to worry about covering up.

I cut my Tesla's engine off and swung the door open, and Gabby slid out of the passenger seat. I joined her side as we headed toward the entrance doors.

"We're here to see Ivy Hart," I told the doorman.

His thin lips formed a generic smile. "No problem, sir. Let me ring her quickly to allow clearance."

His chubby arm extended to grab the phone, but I reached out and stopped him. His eyes looked down at my hand over his before moving back to my face.

"How about you just tell us the apartment number?" I dipped my hand into my pocket and pulled out a hundred-dollar bill before sliding it into his hand.

His eyes widened before shooting to each side of the room to double-check no one was paying attention to us to witness the exchange. He crumbled the hundred in his hand before tucking it away in his pocket. Money always talked.

"Seventh floor, apartment five," he said quickly.

I grinned and tapped my hand against the counter. "Thanks, dude." I saluted him before turning around in search of the elevators.

"Of course, you bribe him with money," Gabby hissed, joining me in the elevator.

As soon as the doors shut, I wrapped my arms around her stiff body and pushed her against the mirrored wall behind us. A sharp breath kicked out of her throat, and she looked up at me nervously.

"I would shut that pretty mouth of yours, or I might have to put it to much better use," I whispered, sliding my thumb across her lips.

Her mouth fell open, and I was unable to hold myself back any longer. I leaned in to press my lips against hers, but she bent down to stop me. I darted my arm out, smacking it against the wall, and blocked her from moving.

"What happened in your office ... it can't happen again," she said, breathing heavily, almost panting, as I stared down at her.

I trailed a hand down her side and rested it on the curve of her hip. "It will happen again, baby."

She opened her mouth, ready to give me her reasoning, but the elevator dinged, stopping her.

Saved by the bell.

I leaned forward, smashed my lips against hers, and pulled away quickly.

I caught a muttered, "Jackass," come out from behind me as I stepped out of the elevator.

I laughed, snagging her hand, and walked us down the hallway. Her fingers interlaced with mine.

"You should probably let me do the talking," I said. I could see her hyping the girl up and convincing her to tell John to go fuck himself.

My knuckles slammed against the door at the same time I felt a sudden pain in my shin.

"I told you I wouldn't say anything stupid," she said, unlatching her hand from mine.

The door swung open, and a tall, skinny blonde appeared in the doorway. She matched the description of the pictures Asher had shown us. She was pretty much on display for us, only wearing a sheer nightie and a skimpy pair of boy shorts.

"Who the hell are you?" she asked, leaning against the doorframe, causing her top to rise higher, which gave a better view of her sparkly belly-button ring reflecting against the hallway light.

Gabby's heel connected with my shin again, and I diverted my eyes away from the half-naked woman to her. I wasn't trying to check her out. I was only attempting to assess what I should do with the situation in front of me.

"That doesn't matter," I answered, now focusing on the wall. "Can we come in?"

"Sorry, I don't allow strangers into my home," she answered with a snarl.

Gabby nudged my side with her hips and moved into my space. "Ivy, is it?" she asked.

The woman nodded.

"We're here on behalf of Governor Gentry. I hear you two know each other pretty well."

Ivy gasped at the same time Gabby shot her a friendly grin.

"We understand you two are attempting to come up with some type of agreement."

Damn, my girl means business.

"Oh," Ivy replied, popping the word off the tip of her tongue.

She veered to the side, allowing us to slide between her and the doorway to enter her apartment. I held my arms in the air during my pass to be sure I didn't accidentally graze any part of her. The last thing I needed was Gabby thinking I was trying to get a grope in.

"Are you going to tell me who you are now?" she asked, shutting the door and whipping around to face us.

My eyes moved around the apartment, taking it all in. Oh, yeah, Gentry was for sure paying for her crib. The apartment was almost as big as mine. Cathedral ceilings. White columns separating rooms in the open floor plan. Expensive furniture. State-of-the-art electronics. John created the perfect bachelor pad to stick his mistress in.

"We're from Douglas PR," I said, taking a seat on the couch.

Ivy blew out a noisy breath. "Of course, you are." Her hand shot out to the table, snagging a pack of cigarettes before sliding one into her mouth. "He always said you guys were the best." She lit the cigarette and took a large puff.

I scratched my jaw, still refusing to entirely focus on her. "Would you mind putting some clothes on?"

Her mouth opened, and a cloud of smoke fell out. "Wow, I think that's the first time I've ever been asked that question. He might be a keeper, honey." She pointed her lit cigarette toward Gabby, causing her to freeze up. Ivy's eyes pinned on me, and her lips slipped into an annoyed smile around her cigarette. "But whatever. I guess I can do that."

She strolled out of the room, and Gabby sat beside me.

"I can't believe you just asked her to put on clothes. You feeling okay?" She reached up and felt my forehead with the back of her hand.

I gripped her wrist, dragging her hand down my face, and pressed my lips into her palm. "I just had my hands in your panties, babe. I don't think it'd be cool if I were standing there, checking her out in front of you. The only naked body I want to see is yours." I kissed her hand again before releasing it.

I wasn't lying. I couldn't wait to get my hands back on that silky skin of hers. I'd never thought about Gabby and me before that night.

But after everything, she was all I thought about. She was constantly embedded into my brain. Now that I'd had another hit, I needed more. I was like a damn addict, constantly thinking about when I could get more of her.

Her cheeks grew pink. "Dalton, we had some silly make-out session. That doesn't mean we're going to fall hopelessly in love and live happily ever after in our golden castle."

I gripped her knee and rubbed the exposed skin. "Trust me. I'm fully aware of that." Even more than she was. "I like being around you, and I really like kissing you." I moved my hand up higher underneath the hem of her skirt. "And touching you."

She whimpered as I slid my hand up more.

"So, how about you let me keep doing those things, and I'm certain that will make both of us very happy?"

"You don't know what makes me happy," she argued, refusing to look at me.

"Then, tell me what makes you happy."

"Is this better?" Ivy's voice boomed through the room, interrupting us.

Gabby swatted my hand off her. Ivy's outfit change made little difference. She was now wearing a white cotton robe that grazed the top of her thighs. I was grateful that at least her nipples weren't saying hi to everyone anymore, and the cigarette was gone.

"Sure," I grumbled. I wanted her to get the fuck away, so I could keep talking to Gabby. "He's willing to give you five hundred thousand."

I needed to get straight to the point and lowballed the price. One of the first things I learned from my dad was always to start low. It was easier to go up than down when making business deals.

"Take it or leave it, but if I were you, I'd take the money and get the hell out of town," I went on.

"I want ten million," she replied, clearly insulted by John's offer. "I won't take a penny less."

"You talk, and you'll never get a job in this city again. Your expensive apartment here." I gestured to the space around us. "Say bye-bye."

I'd witnessed it happen so many times. Women got sick of men's broken promises and insisted they finally leave their wives. When the men refused, they'd tell anyone who'd listen about their sordid affair as an act of revenge. But in the end, it only fucked the women. They'd lose the guy who was paying for all their shit. On top of that, they'd forever be known as the other woman. When their kids would Google their name, those would be the first stories to pop up.

"You don't know that," Ivy replied.

"He's a very powerful man. Take the five hundred thousand and keep your mouth shut."

"I want ten million dollars. Now, go back and report that to that limp-dick asshole. It's all or nothing."

The couch shifted as Gabby started to get up, taking that as our cue to leave, but I grabbed her arm and pulled her back down. I never caved that easily.

I pushed to my feet and geared up for my reasoning. "What happened with you and your Economics professor your freshman year?" I asked, and her head jerked up. "Do you honestly want to be labeled as the whore who chases after married men? A ring chaser? We have these."

I pulled out the stack of pictures from my pocket that Asher had given me. I scattered the photos onto the glass table one by one. Her eyes got wide, and she picked up one of the several nude pictures.

"These photos can be easily distributed all over the internet," I went on. "Perverts will be jacking off to you."

Her body went rigid.

"What will your parents think about you then?" I pointed to a random photo. "This will haunt you forever if you go forward. You do know that, don't you? You work in politics. You're smart enough to know that. If you don't talk, we'll burn these, and you'll never hear from us again."

She dropped the photo in her hand, and it fell onto the floor. "I'm not a whore."

"I'm not judging you, but the public will."

If the chick wanted to fuck every man in this city, I personally didn't give a shit. But everyone loved a juicy scandal, especially one involving a popular politician who had his eye on being the future president.

"Four million," she countered.

"Three. Final offer."

She huffed, her overly large lips forming a scowl. "Fine, but I want the money transferred into my account by tomorrow morning."

Thank you, Jesus.

I grabbed a folded paper from my pocket. "I'll make sure it's there. Here's the nondisclosure agreement. I just need your signature here." I pointed to the line and handed over a pen.

She snatched the paper out of my hands, and her eyes scanned over it quickly. "I need to read over this, and you can come to pick it up later."

Fuck, I didn't want to get it later. I needed to get this shit done, pronto.

Her attention moved to Gabby, who was bringing herself up from the couch again. "Girl to girl, be careful. Men in this business are snakes."

"Trust me. I'm fully aware," Gabby replied, walking past us and out of her apartment.

Taking that as my cue to leave, I nodded at Ivy. "I'll be here to pick that up later," I told her.

It wasn't a good idea to leave without the signed form in my hands, but I could tell Gabby was pissed. When I'd dropped the naked pictures on the table and threatened Ivy, I caught a glance of her face, and it wasn't pretty. She'd lost respect for me for that action, and I didn't blame her.

"Well, that was fun," I said, catching up with her and sliding between the closing elevator doors as she stood there with her arms crossed.

"Fun, my ass," she replied, hitting the main floor button. "That was rude as hell. We shouldn't go around, blackmailing people, especially with nude pictures they sent to someone in confidence. That goes against my girl code. Girls aren't supposed to do that shit to other girls. It's just cruel." She shook her head, wrapping a strand of hair around her fingers and shoving it behind her ear. "Plus, I thought you said John didn't want to pay anything over two million dollars?"

"He'll pay it." There was too much on the line. I knew he'd pay more.

She eyed me skeptically. "An extra million dollars is a lot of money."

"Not to him."

She blew out a breath. "You people have serious problems. That money could go toward feeding starving kids, and they're paying it to save themselves from dealing with their grown-up actions."

I leaned back against the wall. "Welcome to the real world, baby."

Chapter Ten

GABBY

ASHER TOOK an oversize bite of his cheeseburger that was almost as big as my head and swallowed it down. "Did you get the hot chick to take the money and run?" he asked.

I nodded. "Yep."

Thank God. Her accepting the offer meant our partner work would be done, and I wouldn't have to spend any more time with Dalton. The more I was around him, the more he was tearing my defensive walls down, and that couldn't happen.

"And?" he asked, waiting for me to elaborate.

"And the case is confidential." I dragged my teeth over my straw and took a drink of water. I still felt terrible, blackmailing that girl. Even though I wasn't the one doing the actual threatening, it was still a shitty thing to do.

He held out his arm with the burger gripped in his hand. "What the hell, Gabs? I worked the damn case with you." He snatched a fry from my plate and popped it into his mouth. "I already know all the juicy gossip and lady bits of the case." His eyebrows waggled, and I tossed a fry his way. "Is she as hot clothed as she is naked?"

"I wouldn't know. She was practically naked when she answered the front door."

I'd kept my gaze on Dalton the entire time we were at Ivy's. I was waiting for him to hit on her, steal a touch, or do something asshole-ish to give me a reason to fight the feelings I had for him. But he had to go and act like the perfect gentleman ... until he pulled out the pictures. The way his face fell when he threatened Ivy let me know he didn't enjoy it. He just had to get it done. Now, I was left with nothing but thoughts of how I wanted him to touch me again.

After I'd lost my virginity to Dalton, I ended up having sex with my ex a few months later. But it was nothing like what it was with Dalton.

I'd never gotten excited like that before. I'd never panted and begged for someone's touch. When I had sex with Ross, I did it to get it over with. I knew that was what he wanted, and I was afraid he'd break up with me if I didn't give in. I never craved his embrace while his tongue slid in my mouth like I did Dalton's. I never missed his touch after he left me like I did Dalton's.

"You've got to be kidding me?" Asher asked, his dimples popping out. "Man, I knew I picked the wrong job."

"Nope, Dalton actually had to ask her to put on clothes," I answered, wiping my hands.

He dropped his burger down and held up his hand. "Hold up. You're talking about my cousin, right? Dalton?"

I nodded in response.

"Holy shit, what the fuck is wrong with him?"

I shrugged. "It was probably because I was there." And we had just almost gotten it on against his office wall just minutes before we had to leave to go see her.

"Idiot," he mumbled, shaking his head. "But I probably would've done the same thing. She's not shit compared to you."

I smiled at his compliment, and he shot me a devious grin.

He grabbed his phone when it rang. "Speak of the devil," he said, looking down at the screen before bringing it up to his ear. "Yo, dude, what's up?" He paused and listened to the person on the other line I assumed was Dalton. "Yeah, she's right here." Asher's arm stretched across the table, and he handed the phone over to me. "He wants to talk to you."

I raised a brow, and he shrugged.

"Hello?" I said into the speaker.

"I know you enjoy torturing me by ignoring my phone calls, but we're working together, so you're going to have to suck it up and hit the Answer button," he said from the other end.

I looked down at our table, noticing my phone wasn't out. "Shit, my phone's in my bag," I told him. "I guess I didn't hear it ring." I snagged my purse from the chair beside me and pulled my phone out. Fifteen missed calls from him.

"I've tried calling you a hundred times," he replied, clearly pissed off and exaggerating.

Fifteen was far from a hundred, buddy.

"Okay," I drew out. "What's up?"

"Turn on your TV," he demanded, tempting me to hang up on his rude ass. I wasn't too keen on taking orders from people.

"I'm not near a TV," I fired back.

"Where the fuck are you?"

"Dinner."

The line went silent, and I pulled the phone away, double-checking he was still on the other line.

"With Asher?" he finally asked.

"Considering *he* just answered *his* phone, I would think that's pretty obvious."

"Why the fuck are you doing that?"

"Why am I eating? The same reason everyone eats. I'm hungry, and I don't want to die."

A groan came from the other end. "I thought after today, you'd stop having your nightly dates with him."

Holy shit! Was he jealous?

"We aren't having that conversation right now," I grumbled, annoyed, and ignored the curious looks coming from Asher. "What do you need that's so important?"

"Ivy went public."

70

I almost dropped the phone down onto my plate. "What?"

"Yeah, she fucking went public and blabbed to anyone who would listen to her about her sleazy affair with our beloved governor. The office is in a fucking uproar. You need to get your ass here now."

Great, I was sure Wilson was killing puppies at the moment and hanging them up as new accents in his office.

"Fine," I muttered. "I'll be there soon." I hung up and handed Asher's phone back to him. "Ivy talked." I grabbed the strap of my bag and hoisted it over my shoulder.

Asher cursed under his breath and motioned to the server for our check. "The hottest ones are always the dumbest. Dalton should've banged her, made a sex tape, and used it as blackmail or something. I thought he was supposed to be good at this shit."

I looked at him, baffled, as he dragged out his wallet from his cargo shorts and threw some cash down onto the table. "You can't be serious?"

"That's what they do around that joint," he said, getting up from his chair. "If you fuck with them or their clients, they'll ruin your life."

"Would you do that?" I asked, opening the door to the BMW he drove whenever he visited. Kenneth had bought it for me, but I felt more comfortable in the Honda coupe I purchased from working at a department store in the mall last summer.

"Fuck no. That's why I work in the IT department. I knew my dad wouldn't let me off the hook, so I took the easy way out."

"You dig up the blackmail for them," I fired back.

He pushed the ignition button, and the engine roared to life. "True, but I don't threaten anyone or do the actual blackmailing. I just hand over the goods."

I bit back a laugh. "Oh, I get it. You're like the people who manufacture or cook the meth but don't feel bad when people overdose because you weren't the actual dealer who handed it over to them," I said, resulting in a glare from him.

"Okay, when you say it like that, it sounds pretty shitty. So, let's just say it my way," he muttered, turning into the street. "Look, I want to play football for a living, not play detective. I'm just doing this for a few weeks, and then I'm outta here."

* * *

We found Dalton in his office, slumped in his chair with his head resting on the desk. The TV in the corner of the room was playing but on mute. I read the words *Governor Gentry's Mistress Speaks Out* scrolling across the bottom of the screen with a picture of John on one side and Ivy on the other.

He brought his head up and looked at us. "Nice for you to finally show up," he grumbled, grabbing the remote and clicking off the TV.

It had only been a few hours since I left the office, but he looked like hell. His hair was disheveled, most likely from dragging his hands through it in frustration. I was sure Wilson had come in before us and ripped him a new one.

"Dude, that's so fucked up," Asher said, plopping down into a chair.

"She played us like a fucking fool. I want you to find me everything you have on her, and I mean, everything. I want to know every single time she went to the doctor. I want to know if she ever got in trouble at school. Contact her damn preschool boyfriend if you have to. Just get me something to fix this fucking disaster."

Asher snapped up from his chair. "On it," he said, squeezing my shoulder in passing before walking out of the room.

Dalton let out a loud breath and grabbed a stack of papers in front of him. "Time for damage control."

"Damage control?" I repeated. "What exactly does that entail?" Were they going to release all of her naked pictures and expect that to fix everything? "The doubt is already there, and she's shattering her image in the process. Maybe John needs to come clean, apologize to his family, the people, blah, blah, how all of those politicians do it." I'd watched the news enough to know how things like this went down.

"You're right. That would be easier."

I perked up.

"But he refuses to come clean."

My shoulders slouched down.

Well, shit, there went that bright idea.

"He'd probably have the girl offed before he'd let anyone know the affair took place."

My throat burned. "Okay, that's seriously disturbing."

If Ivy ended up dead, I knew who was to blame.

* * *

"I hate this place," I grumbled, standing in front of the familiar door as Dalton knocked for the second time that day.

The door swung open.

"You two again," Ivy snarled, apparently in the same mindset as I was. She stood in the doorway, her legs planted wide and her fingers spread out along her hips. Her blonde hair was pulled back behind her ears, and her eyes were glossy, like she'd been crying. Thankfully, she had on clothes this time.

I laughed and pointed at myself. "Oh, you remember little old us? The people you made a deal with, then completely screwed over?" I snarled, not giving Dalton the chance to even say anything. I let him take the lead last time, and it didn't work.

A smile formed on her lips, like I amused her. "I see the quiet girl actually has some sass," she threw back.

If it were another time, I probably would've appreciated her half-assed compliment, but I was too pissed off at the moment.

"Not sass, honey, an intolerance for untrustworthy, lying traitors. FYI, I despise my job, and your actions have made me come in after hours. Therefore, I'm pissed the hell off." I shoved the door open with my hand and bumped Ivy on the side on my way into her apartment with Dalton on my heels. I might've been little, but I wasn't one to back down to anyone. "Now, tell me why you did it."

"Don't push me again," Ivy warned, slamming her door shut.

Dalton stepped in front of me, blocking Ivy from seeing me roll my eyes at her.

"I told you I wanted ten million," she said, flipping her long, bottle-dyed hair over her shoulder.

"You did, but then you agreed on three. Or did you forget about our conversation because of your alcohol problem?" Dalton asked.

Her face scrunched up. "Alcohol problem? I don't have a damn drinking problem."

Dalton bit back a laugh and opened up the folder in his hand, scattering pictures back down on the table the same way he had last time we were there. "That's not what we heard."

Ivy stomped our way and looked down at the pictures, these different from the nudes.

"Look at all of these lovely pictures we have of you drinking it up and partying. I don't think too many people would want a girl like this going into their political campaign." He motioned toward a picture of Ivy dancing on a bar with her skirt pulled up her waist. "This one sure is nice."

Ivy pushed him out of the way and snatched the picture up. "This was college spring break!" she yelled, scooping up another picture. "And this one is five years old! I was a freaking teenager! You can't sit there and tell me you didn't do anything stupid on spring break."

I shrugged, looking away from her. I'd done plenty of stupid shit on spring break. I just wasn't dumb enough to put myself in the public eye, so that everyone would know.

"Do you honestly think anyone is going to care how old they are?" Dalton asked. "They only care that they exist."

She threw the pictures down onto the floor. "Release them. I don't care. I have nothing else to lose."

I caught a growl come out of Dalton's throat.

"Who paid you?" he accused out of nowhere, and my mouth shot open as I gasped.

Ivy shuffled backward. "What are you talking about now, asshole?"

Dalton stalked her way. "Who was the highest bidder you sold yourself to?"

Ivy reached around him, grabbed a handful of photos on the

table, and shoved them into his chest. "I don't know what the hell you're talking about, but I think it's time for you two to get the hell out of my house."

Dalton opened his arms, and the pictures scattered onto the hardwood floor. "Don't worry. We've got plenty of copies. I'd consider yourself fucked. And enjoy *your house* tonight because your time is limited in it."

"Fuck you," Ivy seethed, stomping behind us. She threw open the front door and pointed to the hallway.

I looked at Dalton, waiting for a signal of what to do next. He grabbed my hand and walked us toward the angered woman settled to the side of the doorway.

"Good luck," he said, engulfing me in his arms and blocking me from her body as we walked out the door. It slammed shut behind us.

"Thank you for protecting me," I said, keeping my hand in his as we headed back to the elevator. "But I so could've taken her."

He squeezed my hand. "I don't doubt that. But I put you in that situation of us having to go back over there. It's my responsibility to take care of you. I didn't want her fucking with you, or we'd have a whole other set of problems on our hands."

My cheekbones rose at my bright smile. I never had anyone protect me like that before. I grew up without a dad, so I was always on my own. "You think someone really paid her to turn on him?"

We stepped into the elevator.

"I don't think it," he replied. "I know it. Ivy is a smart girl. She knew exactly what she was doing."

"Who do you think it was?"

"That's the hard part. The governor has a long list of people who'd love to see him fall from his high horse. Welcome to our next project."

"Project that starts tomorrow?" I asked, hopeful.

He smiled, unlocking his car and opening the passenger door for me. "Nice try, cuteness, but no."

"Ah, man, this job is completely ruining my summer," I groaned, buckling my seat belt.

He got in on the driver's side and slammed the door shut before smiling over at me. "Come on, don't you enjoy hanging out with me?"

I scrunched up my nose. "Eh, not so much." I leaned forward and turned up the music as he laughed in the background.

Chapter Eleven

GABBY

I **TURNED** into Detective Gabby when I got back to Dalton's office. He'd gone to talk to his dad and told me to wait in there for him. I was a nosy person. I couldn't help it. I opened up the largest desk drawer first and frowned at my findings. The only items were a few envelopes, some business cards, and a pack of gum. Fail. I bent down and opened the one under it, hoping to find something incriminating. Nothing.

Damn it. I needed something to turn me off from him.

"Find anything interesting?"

I jumped at his voice and cried out in pain as I slammed my hand shut in the drawer. My hand screamed in agony, but I had to make myself look innocent. I shoved it back into the drawer and picked up the first thing my achy fingers could grab.

"Nope, just looking for ..." I glanced down at the object in my hand. "Gum." I snagged a piece, unwrapped it, and shoved it into my mouth to further prove my innocence. "Mmm ... this is my favorite flavor."

Okay, just because I was nosy didn't necessarily mean I was good at it.

Dalton shook his head at me, laughing, and shut his office door. I stilled as he headed my way. He grabbed the back of my chair and rolled it back. He took my hand to pull me up from the chair and replaced my ass with his before dragging me down on his lap. I squirmed, my ass rubbing against his crotch in an attempt to break free. I froze up when I felt his sudden excitement.

"Relax," he whispered, running a hand along my thigh and brushing my hair off my shoulder with the other. He rotated his hips underneath me. He wanted to make sure I knew how much I turned him on.

He didn't know it, but the feeling was mutual. His hand slid up my skirt, and I knew he was ready to finish what we'd started earlier, but I couldn't let that happen. I stopped him before he reached my core and dragged his hand away.

"Dalton, we can't do this," I whispered. I didn't want to stop, but it was the right thing to do. "Anyone can come in here."

"No one is going to come in here," he said.

I shook my head. "This isn't a good idea, period. We're coworkers. That's it. Now, stop trying to seduce me."

"You really want me to stop?" A hint of sadness was in his voice.

"I do." My voice broke at my lie, and he groaned.

This had to stop. He released his hold on me, and I got up to sit down in another chair.

"So, what did your dad say?"

He moved around in the chair, grabbing his crotch and repositioning himself. I was sure talking about his dad would fix his arousal problem.

"The usual," he answered, not looking at me.

"Ah, so he said you'd better fix it or die?"

He chuckled. "Pretty much."

"So, what do we do until we find out who the culprit is?"

He stood up, and I noticed the bulge in his pants going down. "I talked to Asher. Six million dollars was deposited into Ivy's account from an offshore one. The account number belonged to one under the name of Celine Dion."

I snorted. "You really think Celine Dion, the singer, wants to ruin the governor's life? I'm sure that woman has better things to do with her time."

I knew I was talking like I knew Ms. Dion personally, but I didn't see her as the culprit. She seemed much too smart to have anything to do with John.

He laughed at my response. "No, I don't think the real Celine Dion has anything to do with our case. People usually use fake names on offshore accounts to protect themselves."

"Oh," I replied, suddenly feeling dumb. Why didn't I know that? I felt like I had watched enough crime movies to know that.

"We're going to brainstorm here." He picked up a large corkboard and set it against the wall on a table at the other end of the room. He opened a few folders sitting on his desk and began pinning pictures onto the board.

I stood up and examined the photos. "Who's this?" I asked, pointing to a headshot of a guy who looked to be in his late twenties.

"That's John's brother, Malcolm," he answered, proceeding to put up more pictures.

"You think his brother did it?"

He shrugged. "You never know, babe. We have to look at everyone. Malcolm wanted to run for governor, but his family wouldn't allow it since John's the oldest brother. Sources say he's bitter and would love nothing more than to see his brother get screwed."

"He got screwed all right," I muttered. I pointed to another picture. "And this guy?"

"He ran against John in the last election."

I examined the board and grabbed the stack of pictures that he hadn't posted yet. "Why aren't there any women on here? Maybe he had other mistresses or something."

He grabbed a photo from the stack in my hand. "Mistresses normally don't have millions of dollars to give to other mistresses."

I huffed. "Sexist much?"

"Not sexist, babe, just observant. Normally, when a woman is a mistress, she has something to gain by sleeping with a wealthy, married man."

"Like my mom?"

He frowned. "You know I didn't mean it like that."

I rolled my eyes. "Right."

"I'm serious. I have no problem with your mom. I was just saying, in general. Your mom and this case are completely different, okay?"

"Sure," I grumbled sarcastically and headed back to my seat before twisting back around and snapping my fingers as a thought came to mind. "Maybe John was the mistress, or mister, or whatever you call guys in that situation. He could've been having an affair with a married woman. She found out he had another lover and paid Ivy to expose him in spite."

"I have no doubt the man has an extensive list of mistresses, but I don't think it was one of them who went to Ivy. They usually want money in the end, not give it away to their competition."

"Or that's why she did it. She didn't want the competition. If she paid off Ivy, John's wife would find out and probably leave him. John would cut off Ivy for telling on him and selling him out. Then, the woman gets to keep John for herself and probably needs to be admitted into a psychiatric ward as well."

He looked at me skeptically, and I gave him a playful grin.

"What? I'm a girl."

The skeptical look morphed into a grin, and his eyes ran down my body. "Oh, babe, I'm fully aware of that. I definitely haven't forgotten."

I stepped closer to him and slapped his arm. "Seriously! No one knows how the female brain works better than an actual female."

"So, if you want to ruin a guy, you just pay another girl to do it?"

"I wouldn't say that exactly, but there are different levels of craziness in girls. We're all a little bit crazy. There's your low-key, doormat kind and the kind who take no shit but do it nicely." I pointed my thumb at myself. "That's me."

He grinned.

"Then, there are your total crazies. Those are the ones who will pay other girls to get revenge, kill their husbands, stuff like that."

He looked at me, dazed. "Wow, remind me never to piss a woman off." He pinned a few more pictures on the board. "But I'll look into it."

"Will you really, or are you just saying that to appease me?"

"I'll look into it for you," he answered, tapping me on the tip of my nose.

He thought I was wrong. Hell, I was probably wrong, but it was something more than he had to go on. All he had was a board filled with balding men who didn't know how to smile and hated John. I was certain there was an entire club with a waiting list of people who wanted to see his demise.

"Watch me be right," I said smugly and skipped back to my chair. "Let's make a wager. If it's a girl, you give me a hundred dollars. If it's a guy, I'll give you fifty."

His baby blues flashed over to me, and he chuckled. "What? How is that even fair?"

"It's plenty fair. You're a trust-fund baby, and I only get a small allowance that usually goes toward my shoe addiction."

"How about if you win, I'll take you out to dinner?"

"Eh, I think I'd rather have the cash."

He laughed. "What if, if you win, I'll take you out to dinner? If I win, I'll still take you out to dinner."

"That doesn't seem like a very fair bet."

"Neither was yours," he pointed out.

I blew a bubble with my gum, and it popped as I sucked it back in. "Fine, you've got a deal."

* * *

Six hours.

We'd been brainstorming for six hours and still had nothing. Asher had reported in, informing us he was having trouble breaking into the bank's system to the offshore account but was getting closer. He was also checking out the security cameras to Ivy's place to see everyone who'd visited her.

"My brain is tired," I groaned. "This place is sucking my will to live," I added, yawning and looking over at him from my makeshift couch.

I'd shoved two chairs together and settled down across them hours ago to make myself more comfortable while Dalton continued to pin pictures and documents onto the board. He'd pin one and then pace in front of it as he mumbled questions to himself.

He glanced down at his watch. "Shit, it's after two. Does the princess need her beauty sleep?"

My eyes roamed over him. He'd taken off his suit jacket and tie, and the top buttons of his shirt were undone. His shoes were thrown across the room, and his black socks hung loosely on his feet.

"Yes, she does," I answered. "If I get anything less than eight hours of sleep, I get delusional." My lips twitched into a smile. "Oh, I'm also letting you know in advance that I'll be late in the morning." I'd stayed *way* after hours, so it shouldn't be a problem if I came in around lunchtime.

He tossed the rest of the documents onto his desk and took a few long strides my way. "Nice try, babe, but you can't come in late."

I eyed him standing above me. "Did you not just hear what I said about me and lack of sleep? I start hallucinating and might say something I probably shouldn't. You told me I needed to keep my comments to myself, and I'm definitely positive I can do that while snoozing in my bed."

He held his hand out. "Come on, sleepyhead. I'll take you home, *and* you'd better be on time tomorrow."

My leg darted out, kicking one chair away from me, and I grabbed his hand to hoist myself up. "I rode with Asher, so I'll just go get him."

He fished a set of keys from his pocket. "I'm not going to make him quit working. I'll take you home. I don't know how late he's going to be here."

"Aye, aye, captain." I gave him a salute with my hand before grabbing the heels that I'd kicked off earlier. I looked down at my bare feet. "Great. I look like I'm doing the walk of shame out of your office," I commented, strolling into the dark, empty lobby.

I yelped as Dalton's hands grabbed my waist, and he lifted me into his arms to carry me into the elevator. "We can't let that happen, can we, beautiful?"

I gripped his lean arm and peered up at him. "I highly doubt this looks any better."

"True, but at least you're not getting all that gross shit all over these little piglet feet," he muttered.

I smacked his shoulder. "Hey, asshole, I have adorable feet."

"You mean, Flintstone feet? I might let you kick your way home in the car." He wrapped his arm around my ankle and looked at the bottom of my foot. "What's this?"

"A birthmark." My mom and I had these hideous brown birthmarks on the bottom of our right feet.

"Weird place for a birthmark," he said, running his finger over it.

"I don't think there's a normal place for a birthmark," I remarked, and the elevator doors opened.

We walked through the dark lobby and out into the parking garage. He dropped me into the passenger seat when we reached his car and leaned across my body to buckle me in. Running around the front, he got into the driver's side and started the engine. My eyes shuttered as he took off, and I watched the reflection of streetlights go in and out of my view.

"Hey, sleepyhead," a soft voice whispered into my ear, and my eyes flashed open to find Dalton perched down on the ground beside me, the passenger-side door swung open.

"Did I fall asleep?" I asked, stretching my arms out and yawning. I hadn't realized I was that tired.

He smiled, unbuckling my seat belt. "Sure did." He grabbed me in his arms again and lifted me out of the seat. "Where's your house key?"

I opened my bag hanging limply off my arm and pulled the large keychain from the side pocket. His hold stayed on me as he opened my front door and trudged up the stairs.

"Which one is yours?" he asked, and I pointed to my bedroom door. He switched on the light before depositing me in my bed. He tucked me in and kissed the top of my forehead before whispering in my ear, "Good night, gorgeous."

"Good night," I murmured, my eyes unable to stay open any longer.

* * *

Cold air smacked into my body as my warm comforter was ripped away from me. "Good morning, sunshine!"

Someone was about to die.

"What the hell are you doing in my room?" I screeched, leaning forward and snatching my blanket from his grip before tugging it back over my shivering body.

"Why is Asher under the assumption I gave you permission to come in late today?" Dalton asked, raising a brow.

I snuggled back into the comfort of my bed and rested my head on my pillow. "Because I told him that. I figured being sick of being there was a valid reason for a sick day ... or at least a late one."

"I see."

I peeked up from my pillow to find a devious grin on his face. My mouth flew open when I noticed the glass of water grasped firmly in one hand.

"You do it. You die," I threatened. "I know where Kenneth hides the guns." I didn't, but he didn't know that.

He crept closer. "Get up, Gabby."

I kicked my feet against my mattress. "Fine. I'm getting up. Get out."

"Nuh-uh, your tricky ass will lock me out or something." He tipped the glass forward, and I watched the water hit the rim. "Damn, is this what it would've been like in the morning if you didn't sneak out of my bed in the middle of the night? You sure are cranky in the morning."

My eyes glared daggers his way. "I have one nerve left, and you're seriously dry-humping it. Go away, and I'll be there in a few hours." I nestled back into my pillow when a splash of water smacked me straight in the forehead, causing my entire body to shoot forward.

"That's only a preview of what's coming if you don't get your ass up." He moved the glass around in circles over my face, taunting me.

I threw the blanket back off my body and lunged out of bed. Standing up, I let out a long, tortured sigh. "I'm up. You happy? I'm getting in the shower."

I swung around to go to my bathroom but was stopped when he grabbed my arm to stop me. His tongue darted out, and he licked his lips as his eyes traveled down my body.

"On second thought, you can stay in bed," he said, noticing the tiny boy shorts and tank top I'd changed into this morning.

I broke free of his hold. "It's not like you've never seen a half-naked girl before," I snapped, crossing my arms across my braless chest.

He smirked at my reaction. "True, but damn, baby, you're seriously sexy as hell. I think we both could use a sick day."

My body loosened as his fingertips brushed down my side. A whimper left my throat, and he grinned at my response to him before leaning in closer. I immediately came to my senses, snapping out of my trance and pushing him away.

"Not happening, homeboy," I said, holding my arms out, and he stumbled back. "I'll be out in a minute."

I swerved around on one foot, walked into my bathroom, and slammed the door shut. Turning the hot lever over on my shower, I stripped down and stepped into the steaming water at the same time I heard the door creak open.

"Get out of here!" I screeched, realizing I'd stupidly forgotten to lock the door.

"Don't take too long!" he yelled. Shit, he knew my plan. "You've got fifteen minutes, or I'm coming in there and joining you."

"Don't you have any poor girls to blackmail?"

He laughed. "Fifteen minutes, baby."

Forty-five minutes later, I walked back into my bedroom to find Dalton lounging on my bed with my laptop open on his lap.

"Intrusive much?" I asked, reminding myself to put a password lock on that thing.

"Just looking at your pictures," he answered, studying the screen. "These ones from spring break are pretty hot. Who knew you were such a wild thing, Ms. Body Shots?"

I stalked across the room and slammed my computer shut. "I'm a freaking saint compared to you."

A wicked grin spread over his lips. "Oh, really?"

"Yes, really."

He jumped off the bed and grabbed a cardboard cup sitting on my nightstand. "Babe, you definitely were far from a saint in my bedroom that night. Your moaning, your reaction to my cock inside you, and the way you kissed me—that was far from a damn saint."

My face flushed, warmth covering my cheeks.

"But don't worry. I fucking loved it. I loved how bad you wanted me. I almost got off only by your begging." He held the cup out to me, and I wanted to throw it in his face.

"I never begged," I bit back, embarrassed because I was lying.

He inched the cup further my way, and I grabbed it.

"I went and got you some breakfast while you were primping," he said, choosing not to argue with me. "I knew it would take you longer than fifteen minutes." A bagel then came my way.

"How did you know these are my favorite?" I asked, noticing my bagel was covered with peanut butter and banana slices. I got it every morning before work at one of my favorite coffeehouses.

He shrugged his shoulders. "I'm a mind reader."

I took a bite and eyed him suspiciously. "You stalking me now, Douglas?"

"Fine, Asher told me."

Chapter Twelve

DALTON

I'D JUST MADE it back into my office with Gabby when Asher came rushing through the doorway, paperwork in his hand and a shit-eating grin on his face.

"It's the wife," he told us.

"What?" Gabby and I both asked at the same time.

"John's wife is the one who paid Ivy to go public," he answered.

My stomach dropped. If he was right, I was going to have a lot more work on my hands, and things were going to get really damn complicated.

Gabby jumped up from her chair and pointed a finger at me. "I told you it was a woman!" she said, doing an annoying victory dance before hugging Asher.

Yeah, I definitely shouldn't have given that girl coffee.

"You know this for sure?" I asked. I had to be positive before I could accuse my client's wife of betraying her husband. Typically, in these situations, the wives wanted to cover that shit, not expose it.

Asher nodded. "I'm positive. I finally got into the security cameras and did a facial recognition on everyone who visited her," he confirmed. "It's absolutely the wife." His eyes moved from me to Gabby while his lips formed a thin line.

"She was probably there to tell Ivy to stay away from her

husband," I said, skeptical. "There's a lot on the line for them right now. If there's word of an affair, it could ruin their entire careers. She probably had her mind on being in the White House, and Ivy was fucking that up for her."

Asher slid his hands into his pants pockets. "I thought that might be the case, but I had a hunch there was something more. I always do my research. I did some digging, and the clues are pointing straight to her for whose account the money was transferred from."

Gabby laughed, holding her hand in front of her mouth. "His wife is Celine Dion. I guess she's kicking that asshole to the curb and telling him her heart will go on."

I shot her a look, and she shut her mouth but still managed to get an eye roll in. "How could she have that kind of money to give out without John's knowledge?" I asked.

"Her family founded La Viva Vodka. She's like the vodka heiress of the world or some shit," he answered.

"Hell hath no fury than that of a woman scorned," Gabby added, not being able to keep her comments to herself. "She's pissed she's married to a cheating asshole and now wants payback." She loved this newfound information a bit too much.

"Gentry's fucked," Asher added. And so was I if I didn't get this situation taken care of immediately. "I'll let you know if I get anything else." He turned around to leave, kissing Gabby on the cheek without saying another word to me.

"He's in a bad mood today," I grumbled.

Asher was usually always one of those people who saw the best in everything. The only other time I'd seen him in a bad mood was when his dad told his mom he wanted a divorce. I remembered he came over afterward with bloody knuckles from punching my uncle in the nose and breaking it.

Gabby ignored what I said and grinned brightly. "I told you it was a woman."

I chuckled. I'd just found out terrible, mindfucking news, but she still somehow managed to make me smile. "Calm down there, Sherlock Holmes. Just because we *maybe* solved who the person was that paid her doesn't mean our work here is done."

Her feet halted, and she frowned. "Seriously? Everyone he was trying to hide it from already knows. The media, check. His wife, check. His kids, most likely check. Why does he even need us anymore? His cover is blown, and the affair is public. He probably needs to save all the money he can for when his wife takes everything in the divorce."

I rose from my chair. "We have to make everyone believe her accusations are untrue."

She stuck her palm out. "I'm sorry, but you can just look at that creep and know it's true. He looks like a snake who will stick his penis into any woman who breathes."

"Babe, our job isn't to judge them. It's to fix their problems."

She laughed. "It seems John has a problem keeping it in his pants. Maybe we should recommend fixing that by castration."

I shook my head, trying to fight my grin. "Come on, killer, and remind me to hide all the knives when we're around him next time."

"Are you going to tell him his wife is the one who has it out for him? If you do, can I please be there to witness that because I would love to see his face? Or better yet, maybe we shouldn't tell him anything and let him figure it out himself when she burns his ass." She was rambling. "That would make a great movie! Kinda like *Sleeping with the Enemy*."

"We aren't telling him anything yet," I said, pulling her into the elevator by her hand.

"You suck. Just when I think this job is getting fun, you have to go and ruin it, fun-sucker. So, what do we do now?"

"We talk to his wife."

She shrugged her shoulders. "Fine with me. I already like this lady."

* * *

I pulled in front of a massive security gate and leaned halfway out of my car window to press the speaker button. "Hello, we're here from Douglas PR. We'd like to talk to Mrs. Gentry," I shouted into the box and noticed the tiny camera at the top. I wasn't sure if she'd allow us access, but I was hoping I wouldn't have to resort to climbing over the gate and sneaking into her house. Yeah, I was that desperate.

The gate slowly opened, and a rush of air escaped from my chest.

Gabby rolled up her window and pushed her hair away from her face. "This place is seriously creepy," she said.

We drove down a long drive lined with large trees to each side of us. I circled the wide driveway, stopping in front of a massive stone house that resembled a castle from a fairy-tale book. A large fountain was placed in the middle of the driveway with the water dripping from a massive concrete lion's head. A group of gardeners were hard at work, and the stench of mulch wafted through the air as they dragged flowers out of their vans.

"Yeah, definitely a creepy murder movie," she added.

We both stepped out of the car and trudged up the steep concrete steps that led to the ten-foot wooden door.

"I've been expecting you," an older woman greeted, standing in the doorway, waiting for us. Her black hair with hints of gray stopped at the end of her earlobes as she stood up straight in her blue skirt suit. Rows of pearls were draped around her neck and hanging from her earlobes.

The vodka heiress dripped in pearls.

I huffed as I reached the top step. "You didn't do a very good job at hiding it."

Her lips formed a tight smile. "Neither did my husband," she replied coldly.

She veered to the left, moving out of our way and allowing us entry into her home. Asher was right. She was loaded. John was a wealthy man, but there was no way he could've afforded a place like this. His wife was paying the bill while he was out, playing with girls half her age, and I sensed she wasn't very happy with that.

"Why did you do it?" I asked. If my dad found out I let this happen under my watch, he'd have my ass.

She threw her arms out, motioning for us to sit down on a plush white sofa that looked like it had never been touched before. The room was filled with pictures of John and her with their children.

I knew from doing my research he had three kids who were in their twenties and one still in her teens. It sucked he was risking his entire family for part-time flings with women who only used him.

"Would you like some tea?" she asked, and I noticed a hint of an English accent. We both declined, and she nodded her head, realizing we weren't there for small talk. "My husband needed to be exposed for what he is—a no-good, cheating bastard. I couldn't be the one to do it, so I convinced one of his brainless mistresses to do my dirty work." She seemed proud of herself for pulling it off.

"You do realize we can tell him you're the one who paid her?" I asked, raising a brow.

She gave me an obnoxious laugh. "Oh, please, my dear, be my guest. I'd love for that cowardly bastard to know it was me. That is, if he ever decides to come home and face his wife and family."

"If you don't care about him knowing, why did you pay someone else to do it?" Gabby asked.

Edith looked entirely too eager to explain herself. "I wasn't trying to hide it from John. I couldn't care less if the spineless bastard knows it was me. I needed to hide my participation from the public. I will not be made out to be some scorned woman who goes and cries to the public about her unfaithful husband."

"Yet that's exactly what you did," I fired back.

Her face scrunched up, and wrinkles formed around her eyes. "I'm not going to let them know I have it out for him. That's not good for my family's name, and I'm prepared to fight anyone who makes such accusations. And by the way, Mr. Douglas ..."

I arched an eyebrow at her knowledge. She'd done her research. She knew exactly who I was.

"Your family may be wealthy, but their wealth is nothing compared to the money and power mine has."

I nodded my head at her threat, choosing to keep my mouth shut. She was the last person I needed to be going up against. She held my fate in her hands.

"My lawyers have begun drawing up divorce papers. Now that his affair is public knowledge, our infidelity clause is void. That son of a bitch won't get a dime of my money. Not even a penny."

I leaned forward, closer into her space, and rested my elbows on my knees. "So, there's no way you'd stay by his side and support him through these false claims?" I asked, hopeful. "Don't you want that White House bid? You'd make a stunning first lady." I hoped I didn't sound as desperate as I felt.

"Absolutely not," she snarled, her face serious. There was no convincing her otherwise.

I was fucked. My career had made it a few good weeks before blowing up because people couldn't keep their dicks in their pants.

* * *

Gabby fell into my passenger seat and dabbed some gloss onto her lips. "I think I like her, *Edith Gentry*," she said, imitating her proper, English accent.

"I'm sure you do because she reminds you of yourself," I replied, debating whether to tell my dad about Edith or attempt to fix it on my own.

She fixed her eyes on me and sucked in her cheeks. "What's that supposed to mean? I'm far from being a scorned woman."

I started my car and rested my hand on her thigh. "Babe, her strength and stubbornness are all you."

Gabby would've fired back the same way as Edith did if she found out a guy was playing games with her heart. I hoped to God she wouldn't see me as doing the same thing as John. I'd convinced myself plenty of times that my situation was different from theirs. She was the only girl I wanted in my bed. I wasn't touching anyone other than her, not even Eva.

"That better be a compliment, mister," she said, her eyes pointed at me.

I smiled and drove down the drive as the gate opened. "That's definitely a compliment, babe. Now, what time do you want me to pick you up tonight?"

She slumped down into her seat, her curly hair blowing in the wind from my window being half-down. "For what? Please tell me we don't have to work again."

"You won our bet. I owe you dinner." I couldn't believe I was celebrating her being right and me being fucked. "What time do you want me to pick you up?"

She sighed and leaned her head back against the headrest. "Not tonight. I'm exhausted. I didn't get my full amount of sleep, considering this rude person came into my room and threatened me with water."

I braked at a red light and peered over at her. "Come on, we won't be out late. I'll pick you up at seven. We'll go to dinner, and I promise I'll have you back before your bedtime."

After our shitty day, I needed to have a better night with her.

Chapter Thirteen

DALTON

THE DOOR SWUNG OPEN, and an unhappy shirtless Asher brooded in the doorway. "You stole my dinner date, asshole," he grumbled. "You'd better bring me something back."

I chuckled. "Like a doggie bag?"

"Ha-ha, screw you." He let me in and glanced up the staircase before glaring at me. "What the hell are you trying to do with her, man?"

His question surprised me. I liked my cousin, but we weren't that close.

"Nothing," I lied. I had no idea what was going on with Gabby, but I knew it sure as hell wasn't nothing. Something about her kept making me want to be near her all the time, even when I knew it was a bad idea.

His voice was strained when he fired back, "She's been through a lot, and she's a good girl. She's not one of your sluts who doesn't give a shit they're having a fling with a guy who's getting married. I didn't have the heart to tell her about your fiancée, but you need to. There are plenty of other chicks out there. Go find one of them to be your side ho, not her."

I held up my hand to stop him. I didn't need reminding that Gabby could hate me after she found out. "We're just going to dinner.

That's it. Nothing more." I was making it a date, but he didn't need to know that.

"Remember what I said," he warned, looking directly in my eyes.

He liked her. I fucking knew it. Asher was a good guy, a guy who deserved to have Gabby. I wasn't. I knew I was getting married, but I was a selfish bastard. I didn't want the nice, deserving guy to have her. I wanted to have her. And like all greedy bastards did, I was going to do everything in my fucking power to get just what I wanted.

Our stare down ended as heels hitting the stairs echoed through the room, and our eyes moved up to find Gabby strutting down the steps.

My heartbeat quickened as my eyes feasted on the tight, crimson-colored dress that hugged every curve of her hourglass body. Strappy high heels covered her manicured feet. I licked my lips. My gazed moved to her auburn hair falling against her cleavage in loose curls and was held back from her flawless face with a sparkly headband.

I winced at an elbow ramming into my side.

"Change your fucking thoughts," Asher muttered.

"Fuck you."

He was checking her out just as much as I was.

She hit the bottom stair, and I held out my hand to her. "You ready to go?" I asked.

"I'm starving," she answered, grabbing my hand to help her down the stairs and giving me a shy smile. She grabbed her bag from the couch, and her attention went to Asher. "You sure you don't want to come with us?"

What the hell? Did she invite him to chaperone our date? Technically, she didn't know it was a date, but I sure as hell wasn't planning on sharing her tonight.

"I'm good, babe," he answered, wrapping his arm around her shoulders and kissing the top of her head. Thank God. I was prepared to break his legs if he tried to third-wheel it. "But don't stay out too late. We've got those *True Blood* episodes we need to catch up on."

Her face lit up. "Don't worry. I'll be home shortly to see my future hubby, Eric."

Who the fuck is Eric? And why the fuck was I becoming so damn jealous?

He looked down at her and shook his head. "I don't get what you see in him."

Gabby smacked his arm, and I shifted from one foot to the other, watching their banter. "Oh, really? I don't get what you see in Sookie. She's like the ultimate slut fang-banger."

"She's a fairy. Who the hell doesn't like fairies?"

"Fang-banger?" I asked, breaking into their conversation.

"It's a *True Blood* thing," Gabby answered, like they were in some secret club. She pulled out of Asher's hold and kissed him on the cheek before joining me at the door.

I wanted to keep it low-key with her for dinner. Usually, when I went out, it would end up turning into a damn social event. Everyone either knew my dad or me and wanted to stop and talk. I didn't want anyone taking my time away from Gabby, so I brought her to my favorite Mexican restaurant. It was a hole in the wall, but I loved everything about the place.

"You look gorgeous," I said, sliding into the old, worn-out booth across from her.

"Thanks," she replied. "And thank you for dinner. I've never been here before."

She glanced around the room, taking in the decor. The stucco walls were lined with sombreros along with black-and-white photos. The bar in the front corner of the room was packed with people drinking margaritas and chatting among each other.

"Best Mexican food in Atlanta," I told her, grabbing a chip and scooping up some salsa before plopping it into my mouth. "And you're welcome even though you earned it."

She leaned in to snatch a chip. "I'm surprised. I pretty much suck at this job."

I shook my head. "You don't suck at it."

"Be honest." Her words hit me like a ton of bricks. There was a fuck of a lot more shit I needed to be honest with her about.

"You don't suck, but you're not the best. Sound better?"

"Eh, that works. I can't be perfect at everything," she joked, popping another chip into her mouth.

Our waiter brought us our food, and I inhaled the spicy scent of the fajitas sitting in front of me. My mouth watered as I dug in.

"So, why don't you have a boyfriend?" I asked, taking a huge bite.

"I'm cursed," she answered matter-of-factly, no bullshit.

I stared at her, waiting for the punch line but got nothing. She was serious. "You're joking, right?"

"Nope, I'm cursed. Anytime I've ever attempted to have an actual relationship, it's gone to complete hell. I mean, not even lasting longer than a few weeks before something goes wrong."

I reached over and snagged a bite of her enchilada with my fork. "You just got out of high school. I'm pretty sure that's not out of the ordinary."

She set her fork down. "You know how they say karma always comes back to bite you in the ass, or what goes around comes around?"

I nodded. "Did you kill someone or something?"

"No, my mom had an affair and broke up a perfectly happy marriage. Now, you'd think good old lady karma would lash out on the person who did it, but she didn't. It's done nothing but give her complete happiness, and I'm happy for her. It just sucks that she decided to torture me instead."

"Where in the hell did you get this theory?"

"I read about it. Plus, it's well known. When you mess with karma, it can mess with you or other people around you."

"Karma is an old myth that people like to use when someone pisses them off."

"I'd be careful talking that way about karma. That bitch is ruthless."

"Baby, I'll repeat, you're only eighteen. People don't find love that young. They fall in lust."

"You're right, but a lot of people *think* they find love. They have their happy, sappy puppy love, but not me. My life was fine before my mom decided to marry Kenneth. I had a boyfriend at my old school, and we were happy."

"So, what happened?"

"We moved here, and he broke up with me. He said he couldn't do the whole long-distance relationship thing."

I nodded. "That's pretty understandable."

She reached for her drink and flipped the straw with her tongue. "It's only forty minutes away." She tapped her finger against her temple. "Karma got into his head."

"Or he became a horny teenage boy," I fired back, attempting to talk some sense into her.

She frowned. "Freshman year, I dated a kid for, like, a month, and he cheated on me with a girl he met at summer camp. A guy asked me to prom sophomore year. I went, but it turns out it was just some stupid ploy to get me to sleep with him, so he could win a bet. He even slipped me some date-rape drug or something. But luckily, Cora and Lane were there for me. Also, during sophomore year—"

My fork slammed down against the plate, and my eyes saw red. "Who the fuck was that?" I demanded angrily, cutting her off.

She flicked her hand up in the air. "That's not important."

My lips curled. "The fuck it isn't. Who the hell was it?"

"Jimmy King," she breathed out. "So, anyway, sophomore year, I also went to a homecoming dance with Dirk but wouldn't put out. So, he decided to tell everyone in the locker room, and Keegan Montgomery, my friend Daisy's boyfriend, punched his face in for it. Then, guys didn't want to date me because they all thought I didn't put out. Which I normally don't ..."

I didn't catch on to everything she said because I was still trying to wrap my mind around what she had just revealed.

"Jimmy King date-raped you for a bet?" I asked. I didn't give a shit about her failed relationships anymore. All I cared about was that someone tried to hurt her.

Jimmy King was a few years younger than I was, but he was also my friend. Well, he used to be, but I doubted we would be any longer when I beat the shit out of him after hearing this.

"He *wanted* to date-rape me," she replied. "Big difference. Nothing happened."

"That is not a big difference. Why the fuck didn't you tell anyone?" I suddenly lost my appetite.

"We did. He got suspended and put on probation."

"That's it?" Why hadn't I heard about that? I was sure his parents probably paid someone to bury that shit. Shit, I wouldn't doubt if they'd hired my dad.

"Nothing happened. There are too many girls out there who actually get raped. It was ridiculous to get all bent out of shape about it. Plus, Jimmy felt bad about it. He was a dumb teenage boy who was getting peer-pressured. He made it so obvious. I think he wanted to get caught."

"He could've done it to other girls." I moved my neck around to get rid of the sudden stiffness.

"No, I overheard him talking to his friends. It was just one stupid bet."

I needed to get my mind on something else before I jumped out of the booth and hunted Jimmy down. "Why did you leave in the middle of the night?"

She flinched at my question, and I knew I'd caught her off guard.

"You sure know how to keep a conversation light." She laughed. "I'm not sure. I guess I just kind of freaked out. I wanted to get away from the impending morning awkwardness I've heard horror stories about. Plus, could you have imagined what would've happened if we got caught? You seriously would've been shunned from your family."

"That's not true."

"Your family hates me."

"They don't hate you."

She gave me a look.

"Okay, a few people in my family dislike your *mother*, not you. It may seem like they take it out on you at times. I don't think it's right, and I've never felt that way about you." Talking about my family wasn't the direction I was going for. "You know, you shocked the hell out of me that night when you came into my room."

A soft pink lit up her cheeks. "I shocked the hell out of myself. That was so not planned."

I smiled. "I'm glad you did."

She snorted. "Of course, you are. You got laid."

"True, but you gave me something special. You let me be the first person to have you."

"Okay, Romeo, I was being reckless and wanted to get it over with," she replied, suddenly looking embarrassed.

I reached over and grabbed her hand in mine. "You shouldn't have just wanted to get that over with." I was glad she did it with me, but I still wasn't too happy about her response. Was I just some random guy she picked out from a lineup?

"What was going through your mind that night?"

"First, I was confused as hell. I thought my drunk ass was imagining you. Then, you attacked me—"

Her hand left mine, and she pointed at me. "Hold it right there, buddy. I didn't attack you."

I grinned. "You attacked me."

"I kissed you!"

"More like ravished me. You had my clothes off before I even realized what the fuck was going on."

She covered her face. "Sorry, I get stupid when I drink. I was having a bad night. All of my friends had gone on vacation for the holiday, but my mom forced me to go to that damn party. I was unhappy, lonely, and drinking. Not a good combination."

"You don't have to apologize to me. You gave me something special, something you'd been holding on to for years. I should be thanking you, so thank you." I bowed my head down to her.

She gave me a small smile. "And thank you for taking care of me afterward. I honestly don't think there are too many guys who would do that."

My mind went back to that night. When we'd finished, I went to the bathroom and got her a warm washcloth. I could tell she was uncomfortable and sore. She needed something to help with the pain, so I grabbed her a few aspirin and used the washcloth to help clean up the blood before changing the sheets.

She was right though. I typically wouldn't have gone out of my way to make a girl so comfortable before. But I felt like I needed to with her. I was uncertain that night as to why, but the meaning was getting clearer every minute I spent with her. I cared about Gabby. Shit, I was certain I cared about her before we'd even had sex.

Gabby was everything I admired. She made me want to be a better person. Sure, she didn't come from the best family, but she had more fucking class than half of the girls I knew with bank accounts larger than mine. She wasn't around me because of my family's status or their money. She didn't want all that shit. She was carefree and thoughtful. She was such a good person, and I envied her for that. I could never be as sincere as her.

* * *

"Thank you for dinner," she whispered, opening the passenger door. We'd barely finished our dessert before the yawns started.

I jumped out of my car and raced around to her side to meet her. Grabbing her arm, I helped her up and wrapped my arm around her shivering shoulders as I walked us to the front door.

"I had fun with you tonight. It was much better than working," she told me.

"I'm not sure if that's a compliment, considering you hate your job," I said with a chuckle.

Her face lit up beneath the light shining down on us, and her wet, just-licked lips glistened, begging me to kiss her.

And I did.

My tongue inched out, tracing the lines of her lips before kissing her lightly and slowly pulling away.

"Get your beauty sleep, baby," I said, kissing the top of her head. I waited until she went inside before getting back in my car.

Tonight wasn't about getting my dick excited or having sex. Tonight was about making her my girl.

Chapter Fourteen

GABBY

I PLOPPED down in Asher's passenger seat and wiped my tired eyes.

"You were out pretty late last night," he said, sighing heavily in the driver's seat.

I was struck with guilt when I got home last night and walked into the living room to find him snoring lightly on the couch with the TV on. My favorite candy, Milk Duds, and an untouched bowl of popcorn were sitting in the middle of the coffee table.

"Good morning to you too," I grumbled, grabbing my makeup bag from my purse. "I didn't have time to do my makeup before leaving because I'd overslept. And not really. I got home before midnight. I'm sorry you fell asleep. I didn't realize it was that late."

He backed out of the garage and kept his eyes on the road. "Is there something going on between the two of you?" he asked.

I stopped my mascara search. "No. We made some ridiculous bet. I won, and he owed me dinner." I went back to my hunt and snagged my mascara. I unscrewed the wand and brought down the visor mirror.

Why did it seem like someone was always asking me that damn question? Dalton thought I had something going on with Asher, and Asher thought I had something going on with Dalton.

"Be careful. I know he's my cousin, but I don't want to see you get hurt," he warned, braking at a red light.

"Okay," I drew out. "We went to dinner as *friends*, not on a date. We go out to dinner all the time. It's the same thing." Granted, I'd never had sex with Asher, but he didn't need to know that.

He pressed on the accelerator suddenly, causing my body to jerk forward, and a sticky glob of black liquid landed on the side of my cheek. Before I had the chance to bitch at him for messing up my face, he continued with his lecture.

"I'm pretty sure we've never gotten it on in an elevator. So, no, it's not the same," he argued.

I grabbed a napkin from his glove box and began scrubbing my face. "What are you talking about?"

His knuckles gripped the steering wheel. "When I was checking the camera at Ivy's place, I saw you two practically dry-humping each other in the elevator. That sure didn't look like *just friends*. You were against the wall, and his hands were practically molesting you." He shook his head and pinched his lips together.

I let out a deep breath and dropped my bag back into my purse. "That wasn't what it looked like."

He pulled into the parking lot, and he shifted in his seat to face me. "Look, you don't have to explain anything to me. I just want you to promise me that you'll be careful. There's a reason why I stay the hell away from my dad's family, and I'd suggest you do the same. They're all fucked up, Gabs, even Dalton. They'll hurt anyone who gets in their way, family or not. I don't want to see that happen to you." He grabbed my hand in his and squeezed it gently. "So, promise me you'll be careful with him."

I nodded, my eyes blazing into his aqua irises. "I promise."

I appreciated Asher's protectiveness. He was reminding me of what I already knew about the Douglas family. They weren't good people, and I couldn't get myself caught up in their wrath. They'd destroy me in a blink of an eye.

* * *

Dalton was perched up at his desk when I walked in, and the news was on in the background. His suit jacket was off, hanging off the edge of his chair, and the top buttons of his shirt were undone as he focused on a paper in front of him. A grin tugged at his lips when his head tilted up to find me.

He's bad news.

I had to remember those important words of warning and manage to keep everything professional between the two of us. But I had a feeling that would be easier said than done. The guy knew how to get what he wanted, and I was the prime target on his radar.

"So, what's on the agenda today?" I asked, tossing my bag onto the floor and falling down into a chair.

"We have to go talk to Ivy again," he answered, throwing his feet up on his desk.

"Haven't you had enough of that girl?" I knew I sure had.

"I would say she's probably had enough of us as well."

It was like her name had pulled a trigger because the minute it came out of his mouth, the broadcaster on the TV began reporting about her and John's scandal. Every day, there was something more being thrown into the mix. Some of the news was about John, but most was information on Ivy. The reporters dug into her past, finding anything they could, and would stand outside her apartment building, waiting for her to leave.

Every news station in town wanted a glimpse or a statement from the governor's mistress, but she hadn't shown her face since the day she exposed John. We both looked up at the screen, and I recognized one of the photos as one Dalton had threatened her with.

That was probably our doing.

I felt bad. Ivy had pissed me off, but I didn't like blackmailing people.

"What are we going to do?" I snarled. "Threaten her some more? I doubt she gives a shit anymore, considering she's now a freaking millionaire. She's probably laughing her way to buy a new pair of Jimmy Choos."

He grabbed the remote beside him to turn it off. "You think that shoe shopping is at the top of her priority list? She's probably too embarrassed to even step out in public."

"Oh, she's over it. If I was having a shitty day and my reputation had just been canned for the rest of my life, you bet your ass I'd be shoe shopping. And purse shopping. Oh, and probably house shopping in some other state. If you can't make your day better, buying yourself something pretty will help with the problem."

He rose up from his chair and grabbed his jacket. "Then, come on, Nostradamus. Let's see if your prediction is correct."

I grabbed my bag and got up as he walked past me. "I can tell you one thing I know is true," I said, following him out into the hallway and shutting his office door.

"What's that?" he asked, turning around to look at me as he walked backward.

"One of us is right, and the other one is you," I answered, my lips opening up and laughing.

He reached out, grabbed my arm, and snuggled me into his side. "Oh, babe, you have jokes," he said, dragging me into the elevator.

* * *

"You got any advice on the stocks tomorrow?" Dalton asked.

We just left Ivy's place, and I was right. She was gone, and so was everything she owned.

With the help of another hundred from Dalton, the guy at the front desk divulged that she'd moved all her things out yesterday in the middle of the night without saying a word to anyone. He didn't know where she was going or any way to get into contact with her.

"I told you before," I said, leaning back in the seat of his car, "I'm a girl, and no one knows girls better than girls."

His eyes twinkled in amusement. "That sounds kinky, babe."

I rolled my eyes at him and smacked his hand resting on the center console. "So, does this mean we're finished with everything Ivy-related now that she's split town?"

"I'm not sure." He grabbed his phone from his pocket and looked down at the screen with a frown. "It's a text from my dad."

"Oh, yay," I muttered.

"It looks like we have to meet him and John for lunch."

I twisted my body around to face him, the seat belt nudging into my chest. "We? There's no *we* when it's regarding your dad."

I despised being around that man. Dalton signaled a turn before turning in the opposite direction of the office, and I knew there was no changing his mind. I needed to prepare myself for surviving through a lunch from hell.

"It won't be long, and I'm sure they won't say anything to you," he said.

I clapped my hands together sarcastically. "Yay! You're right. I bet they'll act like I'm not even there."

* * *

We pulled into a parking lot packed with luxury cars, and valet workers crowded the front of the large brick building. Dalton whipped the steering wheel and headed toward the valet lane while I let out a dramatic sigh. He looked over at me, his eyebrows arching.

"You see that parking spot right there?" I asked, pointing to an open spot directly across from us that was only a few steps from the front door. "We'd only have to walk a few steps." There were still a few things I was still getting used to with being around wealthy people all the time. One of them was their need to feel like they had to get valet for everything. Even if they had to walk three steps, they still got valet. It was ridiculous and annoying. "Plus, if we need to run away, it will be easier to run to the car versus waiting for the valet to bring it."

He put the car in reverse and pulled into the parking spot I'd pointed out. "Fine, have it your way, princess," he said. "I didn't want you to have to walk a few extra steps in those heels. But if my dad asks why I parked in the normal people parking lot, don't tell him it was your idea."

I reached for the door handle but stopped to look back at him. "Please tell me your dad doesn't really call it that?"

He nodded.

"That's just sad."

Wilson was such a presumptuous jerk.

The hostess greeted us when we walked into the chaotic restaurant. I'd never eaten there before, but I'd heard great things about it. I would've been excited to finally get the chance if my company were better. Instead, my first experience was going to be with two dickheads and a guy I was developing feelings for that I shouldn't.

She rushed to the back of the room, and I picked up my pace to keep up with her. We continued to follow her into a smaller room and stopped at a small table hidden from the rest of the patrons. John and Wilson were already seated, sitting next to one another and having a conversation that looked heated. When we approached, their voices quieted, and their eyes focused on us.

Wilson's eyes turned cold when they noticed me. "Dalton, you brought Gabby," he said, annoyed.

Great, I was for sure killing Dalton for bringing me along when I wasn't even wanted.

Dalton pulled out a chair for me across from John, and he took the one across from Wilson. "She's my partner in this case. Of course, I brought her," he said. His hand moved under the table, and I felt a subtle pat hit my thigh.

"Dalton, Gabby," John said, nodding his head toward us. At least he didn't act like I was completely invisible.

"Tell me you've got something," Wilson growled, and my eyes scanned the menu in front of me. "We need to know who paid the little whore off."

I peeked over at Dalton, curious if he was going to tell them the truth or not. We bided some time by the waiter interrupting us to take our orders, and Dalton took a long drink of water before saying anything.

"It's your wife," Dalton answered, his voice tense.

I breathed in a deep breath as John choked on his drink, his head jerking up. He pounded on his chest with his fist before regaining his composure.

"I'm sorry," John rasped out. "But you're wrong if you think my wife paid that tramp."

Wilson shifted around in his chair, and I could tell he was doing everything in his power to hold back the anger surging through his blood. He didn't believe us either. "I thought you'd do a better job at this, son," he scrutinized, his voice cracking in anger.

"He's telling the truth," I said, joining Dalton's defense. "We talked to your wife, and she confirmed it. She knows about your affairs, Ivy, everything."

"I don't believe you," John said, and his face began to crumble in defeat. He knew we were telling the truth. He was just choosing to reject the thought.

"Why not?" I asked, playing with the straw in my drink and narrowing my eyes at him while avoiding Wilson's death stare. "You were having multiple affairs. Did you think she'd sit around and let that happen forever?"

Our glasses shook from Wilson's fist slamming down onto the table. "Control the damn girl," he seethed.

John held his hand up, stopping anyone from "controlling" me. "Wilson, don't reprimand the girl for being honest," he told him. "Someone needed to do it. If my wife is the one who did this, the only solution to the problem is me talking to her."

My jaw fell open, shocked at John's words. I'd been expecting an entirely different reaction when we revealed the truth.

"She has your lawyers drawing up divorce papers," Dalton added.

Everyone shut their mouths and gave forced smiles to the waiter interrupting us to drop off our food.

"Do you want us to do something about this?" Wilson asked as soon as the waiter scurried away.

"No, she's my wife," John replied. "I'm not going to threaten or blackmail my own wife."

I wanted to get up and give him a pat on the back. Even if he was a douchebag, he actually cared about his wife.

Wilson worked his jaw. "She did it to you."

I wanted to punch Wilson in the back.

John scrubbed his hands over his face roughly. "You're right, but I'm the one who created this entire debacle."

I picked at my Caesar salad while they continued to go back and forth on what to do with his wife before setting my fork down. I couldn't stomach listening to them for much longer, and it certainly didn't give me an appetite.

"So, what's the conclusion?" Dalton asked, and I noticed he hadn't touched his food either.

"Just lay off for a minute, okay? I'm going to go home and talk to Edith," John spat, throwing his napkin down onto the table. His chair screeched as it slid out from under the table, and he got up. "I'll call you when I need you." He whipped around and left.

"Goddamn it, Dalton, I trusted you with this," Wilson seethed when John was out of earshot.

"His wife paying her was out of our control," Dalton said.

"You should know this before it happens. That's what a real employee of mine would've done."

He looked at us with suspicion, and I scoffed.

"You got something to say?" he challenged, his cold eyes flashing to me.

Dalton's hand cupped my thigh, squeezing it, but I ignored the gesture.

"I'm just curious as to why, if it was so damn easy, you didn't find it?" I asked.

I was probably going to get fired for back-talking him, but there was no way we could be blamed for this.

"You've got some damn nerve," Wilson snapped, picking up his knife and pointing it at me.

"Dad," Dalton groaned. "Let it go. We're all stressed, and this is the last thing we saw coming."

I was waiting, expecting fireballs to come blaring out of Wilson's nostrils as his face reddened and he pointed my way.

"I should've never partnered you up with her. I knew you were nothing but trouble, just like your damn mother, and you're holding him back."

"Don't take this shit out on her," Dalton argued before I got the chance to tell Wilson to go fuck himself. "She's the one who told me to check the wife when you had me looking at his brother."

"How cute, you're sticking up for the tramp's daughter," he said bitterly.

Heat began to rush through my head as his words seared through me.

I narrowed my eyes at him. "Look, asshole, your remarks about my mom need to stop. You know nothing about her, and she's far from being a tramp," I said.

He busted out in laughter. "I'm the wrong person to disrespect, Gabrielle. I can promise you that."

"Do you think I'm scared of you? I'm not," I croaked, leaning forward and staring him down. Okay, I was terrified of the man, but I had to hold my own. "You're nothing but a coward. You sit behind your big, bad desk and huff and puff, forcing others to threaten people for you." I jumped up from my chair, my hands beginning to shake, and bolted from the table before Wilson had the chance to tear me down with more insults.

"Gabby! Babe, slow down!" Dalton's voice yelled out from behind me as I dodged bodies before pushing open the heavy restaurant door.

Warm air smacked me in the face as I stomped across the parking lot to his car.

"I can't stand that man," I screamed, trying my hardest not to stumble in my heels at the same time I was forcing back tears.

A cold hand wrapped around my wrist when I reached the car. "I know," he said, swinging me around to face him. I leaned back against the car, and he swiped windblown hair out of my face. "I'm sorry he talked to you like that."

"Why did you make me come?"

He massaged my shoulders. "I didn't know he was going to act like that. I wanted to spend the day with you, and we hadn't eaten, so I figured it would be okay. I was wrong. I'm so sorry, baby."

I blew out a breath. "I'm not going back in there," I said, crossing my arms across my chest. My heart was racing as I silently prayed he wouldn't ask me to either.

His arms slid down to my waist, and he tucked me into his chest, resting his chin on the top of my head. "I don't blame you. I'm not either. We're in this together."

I pulled away slightly and looked up at him. "Really?"

"Really. I guess you were right when you said where we needed to park so we'd have an easier escape," he said, trying to make light of the situation and giving my hips a squeeze.

I gave him a weak smile. "I told you, I know these things."

DALTON

I SHIFTED my car into drive before swerving out of the parking lot into the busy intersection.

"That sucked as much as I figured it would," Gabby grumbled, rolling down her window, and I felt the warm sun smack me on the side of the face.

"I'm sorry—again. I feel like I just threw you into the damn shark tank," I replied, turning in the opposite direction of the office. I wasn't in the mood to go back there, and I felt bad, dragging Gabby back into the place she dreaded.

My dad had tried to stop me from going after Gabby in the restaurant. I ignored him and his rude-ass remarks, choosing to go after her over him. I knew he'd rip me a new asshole the next time I saw him, but I didn't give a shit.

"Where are we going?" she asked, her attention moving away from the road as her eyes whipped over to look at me.

I stayed quiet and chose not to answer her. Instead, I turned up the radio and continued to drive until I pulled into my complex's garage and parked into my spot.

"Hang out with me tonight?" I asked, looking at her.

She looked up at me through thick lashes and hesitated a minute before opening up her mouth. "I don't think that's a good idea," she replied.

She was right. It probably wasn't, but I didn't give a shit. All of my brain cells completely shut down when it came to Gabby. Just being around her was always a good fucking idea.

"Please," I said, practically begging. I couldn't believe I was begging a chick to hang out with me. "I need a fucking breather from all this bullshit. I'm sorry for dragging you to lunch. Let me make it up to you," I added desperately, searching for any way to change her mind.

She shifted around in my passenger's seat. "I need to get home."

I knew she was lying. The girl sucked at lying and making excuses. Her mom and my uncle were out of town, so they most likely didn't give two shits about what she did or where she stayed.

"What's the difference between us hanging out in my office or us hanging out at my house? If you're at my house, at least you won't have the chance of seeing my dad," I added, giving her a weak smile.

Her sharp eyes lifted up to meet mine. "Um, there are other people around, so we don't do anything stupid, and my clothes stay on."

"What's wrong with you not having your clothes on?" I asked, tapping my fingers against my steering wheel.

She groaned, her head falling back into the seat's headrest. "Take me home."

Fuck, wrong thing to say.

"We both need a break. We can hang out here for a while, and I'll feed you since you hardly touched your food."

"Okay, fine," she groaned.

I had to resist the urge to throw my hands up and scream out in my victory.

She pointed a finger my way and narrowed her eyes. "One hour—that's it. And that's only because you're feeding me."

I chuckled. "You sure know how to make a guy feel special," I said, leaning over and kissing the tip of her nose.

She swatted me away with her hands. "And no more kissing," she warned, palming my face and shoving me back. "Whether it be on my lips, nose, or cheek. No more kissing, period."

"What about other regions that aren't on your face? Are those off-limits for my mouth as well?" I asked, raising a brow and waiting for her answer while hoping it wasn't a smack across the face.

She crossed her arms across her chest. "I'm serious. What happened with us was a one-time thing. No more."

I held out my hands in defeat. "Okay, okay. No more."

I turned off my car and went to open up her door. She hoisted her purse over her shoulder and followed me through the parking garage to take the elevator up to my place.

"Wow, this is nice," she said when we walked through the front door.

I loved my new place. I recently bought it after I graduated and received a quarter of my inheritance. It still needed a few more touches, but I was relieved to be out of my parents' house for good. That place was the home of misery. It bred nothing but bad moods. No one was happy in that damn place.

My place had a modern look with an open floor plan. The walls were painted a light gray, and every room was filled with black furniture. I wanted everything simple and clean. A kick-ass giant TV was mounted on my living room wall, adjacent from the couch and surrounded by every gaming system they made. I wasn't big on video games, but I liked to play them when I had friends over. My mind raced, wondering if Gabby liked the place enough to stay there with me.

I shook my head. Shit, what was wrong with me? I couldn't be thinking about that shit.

I shut the door behind us, and she walked into my living room. Damn, she looked like she belonged in here.

"Really?" she asked, stopping at the glass coffee table to pick up something. She held it in the air.

"What?" I asked, looking at the *True Blood* DVD in her hand. "You guys were talking about it like it was some secret society that I was missing out on. I wanted to see what all the fuss was about." The truth was, when I'd watched her and Asher get all hyped over some damn TV show, I got jealous. I'd never been a jealous guy. So, when I dropped her off after dinner, I ran to the electronics store and bought every season. "I haven't started watching it yet. You up for some reruns?"

She flopped down on the couch and glanced up at me. "I'm, like, the rerun queen. I've seriously watched every season, like, three times."

I laughed. "Damn, babe, you really need to find something better to do with your time."

I headed into the living room and snatched the DVD from her hand. I grabbed a blanket from the edge of the couch and blew it over her body. She made herself comfortable while I loaded the DVD player. I looked over my shoulder and admired the view. The sight of her snug on my couch, wrapped up in a blanket, waiting for me to join her, was breathtaking.

"My girlfriends and I are obsessed with hot vampire boys. Every girls' night, we veg out on the couch, drink, and have hot-guy TV show marathons."

I snagged the remote from the table and positioned myself next to her. "You still close with Brenner's girl?"

My dad always invited the Brenners to all our parties. They were some big-shots in the Atlanta music scene since his dad owned one of the top record companies. Whenever they showed, Gabby always hung out with their son, Lane, and his crazy redheaded girlfriend.

"Cora, yeah, she's my best friend," she answered, smiling. "I seriously don't know what I'd do without that girl."

I stretched my legs out in front of me. "She's a little firecracker."

She and my younger sister, Piper, didn't get along.

"That's because you're related to Satan," Gabby fired back. "No offense, but I can't stand your sister."

"Not too many people can."

I loved my sister, but Gabby was right. She had a long list of people who disliked her. She was vindictive, manipulative, and spoiled. What people didn't understand though was that Piper acted out because she wanted to get attention from our parents.

"How about we order a pizza and begin our little marathon?" I asked, turning on the TV.

She shook her head, moving a strand of hair behind her ear. "Nuh-uh, I said one hour."

The menu screen popped up, and I hit the play button. "The first episode is an hour long," I said, watching the show start. "We'll watch that one and then pick up episode two next time you come over."

Her attention went from the TV screen and back to me. "There will be no next time, buddy."

She was fighting me, but I also knew she was fighting herself in the process. She wanted to hang out with me just as much as I wanted to be around her. She was just too terrified to show it.

"We'll see," I said under my breath and moved in closer to her body.

* * *

Six episodes and one large pizza later, I was still up, watching the vampire porn, while Gabby snored lightly in front of me, her back to my chest and my arm draped around her waist. Her head rested on a pillow that was positioned on top of my other arm.

When we'd finished our pizza, she yawned and snuggled closer to me, which I had no problem with. I carefully bent forward to turn down the volume on the TV and glanced down at her sleeping body. She looked so peaceful, just lying there. Her mouth was opened slightly, and her hair was sprawled out across the pillow and away from her face. Her eyelashes fluttered as her breathing settled. I knew I should've woken her up, but I didn't want to. If I did, she'd want to go home.

Instead, I turned off the TV, delicately wrapped her in my arms, and carried her over to my bedroom. It was Friday night, so neither one of us had to work in the morning. I gently laid her down on the bed, pulling down the blankets before scooting her over and tucking her in. Her mouth released a light whimper, and my body tensed up, scared I'd waken her, but she didn't stir.

Walking back into the living room, I flipped off all the lights and grabbed our trash when her phone started to ring on the table. I picked it up and saw Asher's name lighting across the screen above a picture of the two of them smiling together.

I clicked the Accept button and brought the phone to my ear. "What's up, dude? She's sleeping," I asked.

If there was ever a time when Asher wanted to beat my ass, this was it. "What the fuck? I told you not to fuck with her, and you pull this shit," he seethed.

"Chill out," I said, dumping our dirty dishes into the dishwasher and holding the phone up with my shoulder. "We were watching TV, and she fell asleep. I didn't want to wake her up. We've all had a long week."

"I'm sure you didn't want to wake her," he huffed. "I'm on my way to get her."

I kicked the dishwasher shut with my foot. "She's sleeping in my guest bed," I lied. "I'll have her call you in the morning when she wakes up."

"Fine, but one more thing."

"What's that?"

"You tell her tomorrow that you're getting married, or I'll do it myself. I don't give a shit if we're blood or not. I won't allow her to get hurt on my watch."

"Got it," I snarled, hanging up the call.

Asher was going to fuck up everything for me before I had the chance to fix it. Telling Gabby about Eva was the last thing I wanted to do. I knew she wouldn't want anything to do with my lying ass, and I'd lose her. I'd lose her because the one girl I had feelings for wasn't up to my parents' standards, and they didn't give a shit about their own children's happiness. They only cared about their own selfish needs. I kicked my shoes across the room before taking off my clothes and getting into bed with Gabby.

Chapter Sixteen

DALTON

THERE WERE a number of different ways I'd been woken up in the morning. Sometimes, it was my annoying-as-hell alarm clock blaring in my right ear. Other times, it was the girl from the night before telling me good-bye or wanting a go at round two. Being woken up by a slap in the face had never been on that list ... until now.

Good fucking morning to me.

"What the hell?!" I shouted, my eyes flying open. I raised my hand and rubbed the sudden sting on the side of my cheek. My eyes flicked over to find Gabby beside me, sitting Indian-style with a giant smirk spread across her face. "I can't believe you just bitch-slapped me while I was sleeping. Who pissed in your Wheaties this morning?"

Her auburn hair was tangled, and her eyes still looked sleepy. I could tell she just woke up and most likely was ready to flip her shit when she'd noticed whose bed she was in.

"A slap in the face is better than someone waking you up and threatening you with water. Payback's a bitch," she answered.

I blinked a few times, fighting my eyes against the sunlight coming through my blinds. "I'm pretty sure threatening someone and doing physical harm are two entirely different things. The latter being the worst."

She shrugged, tossing her messy hair over a shoulder. "Oh, well, you deserved it. I can't believe you let me fall asleep last night."

I rose up. "I let you fall asleep? I'm sorry, did you want me to wake your ass up and kick you out of my house? I figured the precious princess would need her beauty sleep. Excuse me for trying to be a gentleman, damn." I balled my hands up and rubbed my eyes. It was way too early for this shit.

She slapped my arm. "You should've called Asher. He would've come and gotten me."

"I wasn't fucking calling Asher to come get you from *my* house." Was she fucking crazy? Why would I hand her over to my competition?

She groaned, falling back against the bed. "Get over your bullshit with him. I don't know why you two seem to have such hard-ons for each other, but you seriously need to get the hell over it."

I peeked down at her. "I don't have any beef with Asher. He's my cousin. I only want him to stay the hell away from what's mine."

Her eyes narrowed into slits. "You'd better be talking about your dad's company or some stray puppy you two found on the street."

"I think you know better."

She pushed up until she was practically in my face. "This is the last time I'm going to say these words. We are—"

I inched forward, smashing my mouth into hers. The last thing I needed to hear first thing in the morning was her telling me we were nothing. She knew better. Something was going on between us, and we needed to explore it.

I was shoved back roughly, causing my back to smack against the headboard. She began to pull away from my hold, but I tightened it up. Her green eyes glared into mine, but she didn't move away to break eye contact. We stared at each other, daring the other to cave, to give in to what we both so desperately wanted. As much as I wanted to feel her luscious lips against mine again, I wanted her to be the one to initiate it.

I needed to know she wanted me as much as I craved her.

We continued our staring game, our breathing growing ragged

from fighting our desires versus our brains. I grinned, internally giving myself a huge-ass high five when she inched forward and ran her tongue across my bottom lip.

"Kissing is okay," she whispered, sliding her lips against mine and kissing me full on the mouth.

I reached my arm around her back, pulling her into me closer. "Fuck yes, kissing is definitely okay," I replied, kissing her harder.

She pushed up my body, and I straightened up, allowing her to straddle my hips. She'd taken off her shorts, now only wearing her shirt from last night and a tiny pair of panties. I raised the shirt up as her hips began to rock across mine.

Goddamn, what was this girl doing to me? I groaned out in pleasure at the feeling of her softness grinding against my aching hardness. We fit together perfectly.

I dug my fingers into her waist, and my heart thumped against my chest as her pace picked up. My lips parted, and I inched up to kiss her again as we both moved against each other.

"Take these off," I grunted, pulling her shirt and bra off her silky body feverishly.

I was rushing it, but I couldn't help it. I'd been dying for this to happen again.

She rose, her beautiful breasts bouncing in front of my face, begging my mouth to suck on her hard nipples. Leaning forward, I wrapped my lips around one, and she arched her chest forward, telling me to give her more. I sucked on her nipple, giving her what she wanted, and reached my arm back to cup her ass firmly.

Her head fell down, her hair covering both of our heads. "That feels so good," she panted.

I released her nipple before flipping us over, so I was on top. Fuck, I couldn't wait to pleasure this girl again. I racked my brain, trying to remember every touch I'd made that excited her last time.

I held myself up with one arm and admired her beautiful body, memorizing every curve. Her breasts were moving up and down along with her heaving chest as she gazed up at me. Her puffy lips were slightly parted as she waited for me to make a move.

The only barrier now between what I wanted was a pair of lacy black panties. I hooked my index finger into the strings and quickly dragged them down her toned legs to the floor.

I trailed my lips down her stomach, stopping just above her soft clit. "I've thought about touching you again every single day," I said, rubbing my hands up and down her thighs, satisfied when I noticed the goose bumps form in their wake. My cock stirred as I slid in between her legs and ran a single finger through her wet juices. Goddamn, she was so wet and ready for me. "Have you thought about me touching you again?" I rasped, rubbing my aching finger back and forth around her clit.

She nodded. "I have," she choked out, her eyes fluttering shut. She knew what was coming, and she was ready for it.

"I know you have because you're so fucking wet for me right now."

I hoisted both legs over each side of my shoulders and bowed my head down to take the first lick. The first lick was always the best. I wasn't a selfish bastard in bed. I loved pleasing the woman, and I loved eating pussy. Her head shot back as a high-pitched moan echoed through my bedroom. Fuck yeah, she was going to love this. I moved my head down lower, devouring her as the taste of her grew stronger against my tongue with each lick.

"And you taste so fucking sweet," I muttered against her.

Her fingers tugged on my hair, and my eyes dashed up to look at her. I almost got off at the image in front of me. Her back was arched, her head back, her breasts and nipples pointing to the ceiling as she gripped mercilessly onto my hair.

Seeing her like that, all her inhibitions gone and enjoying the pleasure I was giving her, was enough to set me off.

I raised an arm up to her breast, massaging it while my mouth went back to work, my tongue moving faster.

"You have to stop," she breathed out.

My head throbbed as she attempted to pull my head up. I ignored her and kept at the task on hand of pleasuring her.

"Please," she begged. "I can't take it anymore."

"Just let go," I said against her clit. I dragged my free hand up to massage her swollen clit that was begging for my attention.

"Holy shit!" she yelped, her fingers leaving my hair to grip the sheets.

I continued my torture on her pussy until she let out a loud moan as an orgasm shattered through her body. I licked her a few more times as she came down from her high, and her body went still. As bad as I wanted to watch her face while she came, I had to save that for later because I couldn't quit tasting her.

I rose up and gently brought down her legs from my shoulders.

She looked down at me nervously. "I'm not sure if I should have sex with you or not," she drew out, swallowing hard.

I moved up her body. "We don't have to have sex. I only wanted to make you feel good." And that was my cue to get my ass up and take a cold shower.

She smiled. "Thank you. That was incredible."

I bent down to kiss her on the lips, letting her taste herself, and ignored my own throb between my legs. "My pleasure."

Her eyes went from my face to my rock-hard cock, and she licked her lips. "You need help with that?" she asked, biting the edge of her mouth before her tongue swept over it again.

Fuck, I didn't want her to feel pressured, but her fixing me up sounded much more satisfying than using my own hand. I couldn't stop myself from leaning down and stroking my straining cock once.

"You don't have to if you don't feel comfortable," I reassured, my muscles jumping under my skin.

She grinned. "Oh, I want to."

Damn, my girl was naughtier than I thought.

She lifted herself up before falling back down onto her knees in front of me, her mouth landing directly in front of my standing erection. I tensed up, and I lost my airflow at the first swipe of her tongue gliding down my aching cock. I hissed as she immediately took me in her warm, hot mouth and sucked on me gently. My eyes shuttered as I tangled my fingers into her soft, silky hair. Her eyes peered up at me as she sucked me in and out, never breaking our eye contact.

Her mouth continued to work my cock as she dropped her hand down to cup my balls and massage them gently. My nerve endings stirred every time I felt those perfect lips glide against my cock.

"Don't stop. Fuck, don't stop," I gasped, moving my hips in sync with her head.

Her pace heightened, like she sensed I was getting close, and I tightened my hold on her hair.

"I'm going to come." I had to give her a warning in case she didn't want me to come in her mouth.

She didn't stop, and I took that as permission to release inside her. I growled in the back of my throat, and my head fell back as I felt my entire body jerk. She stroked me, milking every drop out of me before swallowing my cum and releasing my cock. Her arm shot out to wipe her mouth with her hand before giving me a victorious smile.

"Was that okay?" she asked, looking up at me innocently.

My entire body shook, and it took me a few minutes to come back down from the high I was riding. "That was fucking amazing," I finally answered, bending down and kissing the top of her forehead.

She grinned, clearly proud of herself.

This girl was going to ruin me. I knew it. There was no damn way I'd be able to commit to anyone else now that I'd had a taste of her again.

Chapter Seventeen

GABBY

I STRETCHED my legs against the cold leather of Dalton's couch. "I need to get home," I muttered sleepily.

We'd been lying on his couch for hours, watching TV. We were too exhausted to do anything else. Asher had called and wasn't too happy about my sleeping arrangements. I didn't blame him. He was just looking out for me because I obviously did a pretty sucky job at doing it myself.

Dalton pressed his lips to my shoulder. "I'll run you home to shower and change, but we've got somewhere to be later," he replied, wrapping his arms around me.

I leaned against him, my back getting closer to his chest while I rested between his legs. His arm darted out and ran across my bare stomach, causing goose bumps to scatter across my skin. Instead of putting my clothes on from last night, I was only wearing a bra and a pair of Dalton's gym shorts I snagged from a drawer.

As much as I wanted to deny my attraction to Dalton, I knew us being together was bound to happen again. What I was surprised about was the reaction he always seemed to get out of me.

Dalton unleashed feelings in me I'd never experienced before. Whenever my girlfriends would talk about how much they enjoyed sex, I was never able to share my own experiences. Sure, I liked messing around with guys, but I never had anything feel as satisfying as it did with Dalton. I'd never melted at someone's touch and lost control. He was giving me that, what I'd been craving all along. It wasn't only about sex either. He made me feel special. He made me feel wanted, and he liked me for *me*. Not too many people saw the girl behind the nasty gossip with the mom from the wrong side of the tracks.

"We have somewhere to be?" I questioned, lifting my chin and looking up at him. Morning stubble scattered across his cheeks, and his hair was messy from being tortured by my hands in my moment of pleasure. "Please tell me it's not work. It's Saturday, and you bet your ass I'm not going in on the weekend."

I felt his chest move as he chuckled.

"It's a surprise," he answered, squeezing my side and trailing his fingers down my arm. "I promise it's not work."

"The only surprises I like are the ones that come in a gift-wrapped box."

I despised surprises. Every single time someone said they had a surprise for me, it ended up being a surprise from hell. My mom said it was a surprise when she told me she was marrying Kenneth. She'd also told me the same thing when she informed me we were moving in with him and I had to switch schools. Since then, the word *surprise* came with nothing but pure dread.

"You've got to trust me, babe."

I shook my head. "I don't trust very many people."

Everyone always broke their promises at some point, so I learned never to get my hopes up. In the end, people never failed to disappoint you even if they swore up and down they wouldn't.

"That's a problem," he growled, kissing my neck.

I giggled as his stubble tickled along my skin but not enough to stop me from tilting my head to the side to allow him more access. "If you don't trust anyone, you don't get hurt. Simple as that."

His mouth moved to my earlobe, and I felt my clit pulsate.

"True, but if you don't trust anyone, you're pretty much setting yourself up for a lonely fucking life," he argued, his voice raspy against my ear.

I twisted my body around to face him and threw my legs under me, so we were eye-level. "I'm going to end up lonely, period. I'm cursed, remember?"

He laughed, brushing a strand of hair behind my ear. "You're not cursed, baby."

"I am too," I screeched, tossing my hands up. "We've already had this discussion, and there's no changing my mind. Eventually, you'll see for yourself." My stomach tightened at my revelation. I was afraid of Lady Karma ripping him away from me.

His hand moved to my cheek, and he slowly began to stroke it softly. "Then, call me a fucking prince, a guy witch, or whoever fixes that shit because I'm going to break that curse."

I laughed, averting my eyes and focusing on the rough feel of the couch. His hands slid down to my chin, bringing my eyes back up to his.

"I'm going to kick that curse's ass so hard, it won't come near you again," he added. "You hear me?" His fingers trailed over to my mouth, tracing the outline of my top lip back and forth.

"It's a warlock," I replied, and his hand froze.

He blinked twice before saying anything. "I'm sorry, what?"

"It's a warlock," I began to explain. "Guy witches are warlocks."

His eyes went wide, and he pressed his palms to my cheeks. "Are you fucking kidding me, babe? Out of all of that shit, you picked up that I got the male witch reference wrong. Jesus, maybe you are cursed."

"I told you."

His lips touched mine, then pulled away. He snapped his fingers in front of my face. "There, now, the curse is gone. It's been broken."

I shook my head. "A kiss that breaks the curse? This isn't a Disney movie, buddy."

A sly smile appeared on his face. "We can try some other methods then." He ran his hand across my stomach and brushed the bottom of my breasts.

My head tilted to the side. "Hmm, I guess we could do some

research." I squealed when he reached behind me and unsnapped my bra.

* * *

I looked back into my mirror to see Asher throwing himself onto my bed, bouncing up from the force before positioning himself comfortably.

"I'm thinking sushi tonight," he called out.

I whipped around and noticed the large smile on his face falter.

"Or we can go somewhere nicer ..." His eyes narrowed in on my outfit. His Adam's apple bobbed as he swallowed.

Dalton told me to dress nice but nothing too formal. I'd decided on a black pair of shorts, a bright yellow halter top with fringe at the ends, and tall black wedges with gold details along the top. My outfit wasn't necessarily too nice for sushi, but I didn't normally dress up when we went to dinner. My eyes focused on the wall behind him.

"I actually have plans tonight," I replied hesitantly, biting the corner of my lip. I felt bad, ditching him. I was half-tempted to cancel with Dalton and hang out with Asher out of guilt, but as much as I hated surprises, I was curious to know what Dalton had planned.

"No big deal," he answered, shrugging. "You hanging out with your girls tonight?"

I shook my head, swallowing the hot lump in my throat before telling him the truth. "Dalton."

He let out a deep sigh, rubbing the back of his neck. "I thought we agreed you were going to be careful around him, Gabs?"

"I am. We're just hanging out—that's it."

"You spent the night with him last night, and now, you're going on another damn date with him tonight. That sure as hell seems like more than just hanging out." I opened my mouth to argue, but his hand went up, cutting me off. "I'm not trying to play the overprotective big-stepbrother role or whatever, but when I told you to be careful, I meant it. I care about you, and you deserve someone a hell of a lot better than my cousin."

"Like you?" I snapped back, noticing the words sounded bitchier coming out of my mouth than they did in my head.

He winced at my words. Yep, they definitely sounded bitchier. I swore I had a speech impediment that made everything I said sound bitchy.

I took a step his way. "Shit, Asher, I didn't mean it like that."

He slammed his eyes shut before lunging up from the bed and walking backward, away from me. "You know what?" he said, his voice wavering. "We both know I have feelings for you."

I gaped at him, my eyes wide.

"Yes, Gabby, I have fucking feelings for you. When I first met you, I already had my mind set on hating this chick whose mom ruined my entire life. The chick whose mom caused my own to cry herself to sleep at night and move away from everyone she loved. I was expecting to gain some evil, bitchy stepsister who was using my dad for his money. But you weren't. No, the girl I met was far from that. She was compassionate and caring. She was a complete smart-ass who wasn't afraid to tell you to fuck off. I could tell you wanted nothing to do with any of us, but you stuck by your mom's side because you have such a strong love for her—for everyone you care about. You are one of the most loyal and fascinating people I've ever met."

"Asher," I breathed out, scrambling for the right words while still processing his.

"These past few weeks I've been here, I've wanted to spend all my time with you. You're constantly on my mind. I want to know what you're doing and if you're thinking about me too. You're the first thought on my mind in the morning and the last thought before I go to sleep." His face tightened. "Last night when you were with *him*, I didn't sleep a fucking wink."

"Asher," I repeated, still at a loss for words.

He was my stepbrother; we couldn't be in a relationship. Then, there was Dalton, the ruiner of everything. I had feelings for Dalton I couldn't get rid of, and I knew that would only hurt Asher in the end. I couldn't be with him if I couldn't give myself to him one hundred percent.

He took two long strides before he reached me. His arm reached out, and I inhaled a breath as he dragged his fingers along my cheek. His breathing was heavy as we focused our eyes on each other. "If the feeling isn't mutual, I understand," he said, his voice strained. "But please, don't give yourself to someone who won't appreciate what he has. Don't fucking give them to somebody who's going to use it to his selfish advantage and hurt you because that's exactly what will happen if you give in to him."

My shallow breathing matched his as we both stared into each other's eyes. His azure eyes stayed on mine, searching for my answer.

Could I do it? Could I forget everything I'd told myself and take that leap with Asher? Every excuse of how we could go wrong ran through my mind. No, he lived in Miami. It would never work. And Dalton, there was no way I'd be able to stay away from him. Whatever option I chose, I knew I'd end up losing Asher in the end. I just wasn't sure which one would be the easiest for me. For us.

I opened my mouth, attempting to speak while he waited, but no words came out of my lips. I wanted to explain everything to him. I wanted him to know *why* we couldn't go beyond friendship. Lady Karma would've started sharpening her nails at our first kiss, plotting to ruin us.

"You know I can't," I squeaked out. My answer was lame, but I didn't know how else to explain my reasoning to him.

His jaw muscles ticced. "I get it," he snarled, turning around on his heel and storming out of my bedroom.

I let out a gasp of air I'd been holding in and collapsed onto my bed at the same time the front door slammed shut. I gulped, wrapping my arms around my body as I felt the first teardrop smack into my bare knee. Sniffling, I swiped a few tears away, noticing black mascara smeared on the side of my hand. Just perfect. Rubbing my thumb over the black smudge, I grabbed my stuffed bear, Mr. Piggles, and snuggled him into my side. Mr. Piggles always made everything better for me.

My head shot up at the sound of the front door creaking open. Thank God. Asher was coming back to work things out. The footsteps grew louder, coming up the stairs, as I prepared my apology in my head.

"What's wrong, baby?"

I squinted through blurry eyes, finding Dalton standing in the doorway, his body stiff.

I hiccupped, swiping a few more tears off my face. "Asher and I got into a fight," I stuttered.

He strode across the room and fell down beside me. His hand palmed my knee and began rubbing it gently. "He'll get over it," he said, his voice gentle.

My head drooped down. "No, I was pretty shitty toward him."

I sucked at expressing my feelings to people. I'd always been that way. I bottled everything up inside. My mom was always working when I was growing up, and I had no other family, so I was responsible for taking care of myself while she was working two jobs. I didn't have a babysitter because we couldn't afford to pay one. I learned how to deal with my problems by myself. By the age of seven, I was cooking my own meals, bathing myself, and getting ready for bed by the time my mom got home.

"If there's one thing I remember about my baby cousin, it's that he forgives easily. I used to do the most fucked up shit to him when we were younger, and he would always forget about it five minutes later," he said, squeezing my leg in reassurance.

I slumped down. "This is different," I replied, picking at the fabric on my comforter. "I didn't give him a swirly or shove his head in the dirt. I hurt him."

His hand moved up my leg and interlaced our fingers. "You broke his heart."

I cocked my head to the side, gaping at him.

"Oh, come on, I'm not stupid. I know he likes you."

"You don't know anything," I argued, rubbing my free knuckle against my temple.

"I'll let you deny it, babe. That's cool. I just want to thank you."

My eyes narrowed into slits. "For what? Ripping his heart out?"

"For choosing me."

I flicked his hand out of mine. "I didn't choose you. I didn't choose anyone. We're just friends." I was lying, but I was irritated. I had just broken Asher's heart, and Dalton was acting all smug about it.

"I think this morning proved we're far from just being friends," he fired back.

He grunted when I pushed into his side. "Seriously? Get out of my house."

He groaned and slouched down next to me. "Sorry, I'm acting like an asshole." At least he admitted it. He grabbed my hand in his and kissed it. "I just wish you would quit fighting me on this."

"Fighting you on what?"

"This. You and me."

"I don't go sleeping around. I don't do casual hookups." Or I didn't used to.

His eyes locked with mine. "Babe, we wouldn't be sleeping around. I'd be with you, and you'd be with me. No one else, the two of us together. Why are you so convinced I'm this horrible person when you've never even given me a chance?"

I bit the edge of my lip. "Oh, come on, Dalton. What do you think is going to happen? We're going to be one happy couple and have your family's support?" Hell no.

"Why can't you just let it work itself out? Let us be us and go with whatever comes our way. We don't have to plan anything. What happens, happens. We both enjoy being around each other. That doesn't mean we have to skip hand in hand together to the courthouse and declare our love for each other. You said you've never had a serious relationship before—"

"What's that got to do with anything?" I asked, unhappy he was pointing out my lack of experience.

"Not every relationship has to have a planned final destination. I think that's where you're overthinking it. You've got to throw all your inhibitions out the window, let yourself have some fun, and we'll see what happens. Let's just hang out like we've been. If a moment comes and we want to kiss each other, then we'll kiss. Sound good?"

"Fine. But don't hurt me, Dalton," I said, pointing my finger his way. "I don't put myself out there for people. I'm trusting you."

He grabbed my face and rubbed my cheeks with his thumbs. "There will be no hurting, okay, pretty girl?"

My lips twitched into a smile as Mr. Piggles was pulled out of my grasp.

"And who's this ugly little thing?" he asked, his eyes studying him.

I snatched my teddy back. "Don't talk that way about Mr. Piggles," I grumbled, looking at my bright pink stuffed critter. His hair was nappy from being washed too many times, and the stitching was beginning to come loose. He was missing his right eye, and the left one was close to matching it. He was a hot mess, like me, but I'd never get rid of him.

"He's a bear," Dalton pointed out.

"Duh. What's that got to do with anything?"

I'd asked my mom for a stuffed pig one year for Christmas, but she couldn't find one. Instead, she brought me home the only thing she could find that resembled one. I made do and decided to call him Mr. Piggles to make up for his lack of piglet features.

Dalton grabbed Mr. Piggles out of my hand and gave him a handshake before tossing him back onto the bed.

He took my hand and dragged me to my feet. "I promise to take good care of her, Mr. Piggles," he said, pulling me out of my bedroom. "We'll be out late, so don't wait up!"

Chapter Eighteen

GABBY

THE NOISY CROWD blurred past us, and I watched people talk and laugh among each other, standing in concession lines. Guys were drinking beers, and girls were dressed in skimpy dresses, taking selfies and dancing.

"What are we doing here?" I asked, keeping up with Dalton's fast pace, my hand in his as we dodged the crowd of bodies.

When we'd pulled into the parking lot of the giant convention building, I whipped out my phone to see what event was going on, but Dalton plucked it out of my hand and stuck it into his pocket.

Surprises sucked. I hated being in the dark.

"You ever heard of Slayer Town?" he asked, leading us into an abandoned hallway.

I nodded. Slayer Town was one of the hottest bands out. Their songs were blowing up the Billboard charts. Their lead singer, Tristan Eisles, had just been crowned the Sexiest Man Alive.

"They've got a show here tonight," he revealed, opening a door at the end of the hall before we walked into another.

A hulking man with fat arms covered in tattoos and long hair wrapped into a ponytail stood in the isolated hallway, blocking entry to a door labeled PRIVATE.

"What's going on, Bones?" Dalton asked, and they fist-bumped.

Bones grinned, showing off a row of gold teeth. "Dalton, my man," he replied. His dark eyes flashed over to me, and he gave me an appreciative smile. "Just the two of you tonight?"

Dalton nodded, and the guy's hand around the door handle twisted before he moved out of the way to allow us entry. Loud music hit my ears as I trailed behind Dalton, my hand still clutched in his. There were probably a few dozen people sitting around on multiple setups of couches, standing, or dancing in the middle of the room. I noticed a crowded bar at the side of the room with a man behind it, slinging drinks in his hands before handing them over to people. I'd been in VIP rooms before. Lane's dad always knew the band, so we were invited to plenty of concerts, where we had our own rooms.

"Dalton fucking Douglas! Where the fuck have you been, man?" a tall guy slumped down onto a white corner couch yelled.

A skinny blonde was parked on his lap, her tanned legs hanging over the side of his. He placed both hands on each side of her hips, lifted her up, and set her back down before stalking our way.

Dalton dropped my hand and wrapped his strong arm around my shoulders, pulling me firmly into his side and resting his hand on my hip. His hold on me screamed ownership, causing my throat to grow thick.

"Working. I had to grow up sometime," he answered, shaking hands with the guy when he reached us.

"Damn, that sucks, man. That's why I chose to go to graduate school. The longer my ass is in school, the longer my parents support me while I don't do shit," he said, laughing.

His hair was blond, almost white, and gelled to the side, reminding me of a Ken doll. His bright blue shirt had the first few buttons undone, showing off his tanned chest, and a silver chain around his neck. My eyes skimmed down, noticing his jeans and sandals. I'd been to enough college parties with Lane and Cora to know a typical frat guy when I saw one, and this guy was your typical frat guy.

"And who's this beauty?" he asked, his hazel eyes darting over to me as he gave me a beaming smile.

"I'm Gabby," I said, holding out my hand.

He grabbed my hand in his and shook it. "Sheldon. It's nice to meet you, Gabby," he said, winking. He dropped my hand, and his finger moved back and forth between Dalton and me. "And how do you two kids know each other?"

"We're friends," Dalton answered, tightening his hold on me.

My stomach dropped. Friends? I hated that we couldn't be ourselves in public because we were afraid of his parents finding out.

Sheldon ran a wide hand over his thick jaw. "Friends, eh? Well, any friend of Dalton's is a friend of mine, gorgeous," Sheldon said. "Now, get your asses over here and have a drink with me." He waved his arm out, signaling to the blonde on the couch, and rejoined her side. Grabbing a bottle of alcohol, he poured a drink for the both of us.

Dalton's heavy hand rested on the small of my back as I trudged over to Sheldon and his friends.

The blonde giggled and snuggled back up to Sheldon's side as we sat across from him, and he handed over our drinks.

"Long time no see, Dalton," she purred, draping a skinny tan leg over Sheldon's thigh. Her cleavage was busting out of her tight black dress, and I crossed my arms, suddenly feeling underdressed.

Dalton gave her a chin nod before her eyes jumped to me.

"I'm Megan," she said, giving me a cheerful smile and a wave.

A sense of relief left me that she wasn't going to be rude to me.

I introduced myself and shot her a wave back before bringing the glass of strong liquid to my mouth. I puckered up my lips. "Holy shit," I gasped, swallowing hard to keep it down.

Sheldon laughed and smacked his leg. "Shit's potent, doll. I'm the best damn drink master around this joint," he said.

Dalton grabbed the glass from my hand and took a drink. "Potent enough to kill a horse." He coughed. "I see you haven't eased up on your drinking, but let's try not to kill my girl."

Sheldon raised a brow at Dalton calling me *his girl* at the same time I rubbed my hands together nervously.

"So, you two never exactly told me how you know each other?" he questioned, circling his fingers around Megan's bare thigh.

"We work together," I answered, not giving away anything else.

He drained the remainder of his drink and set it down on the table in front of us before pointing a finger at Dalton. "Already breaking the *conflict of interest* rule, my friend. I fucking like it."

My lips formed a lackluster smile. Little did he know, Dalton was breaking more than one rule by being with me. I was terrified of the reaction his parents would have if they found out about us. I was positive my little outburst at lunch wasn't going to help my case either.

"Well, well, look who we've got here," a piercing voice said from behind me. I whipped around in my seat at the same time a strong pair of hands wrapped around my shoulders and lifted me off the couch and into the air. "Why the fuck didn't you tell me you were coming, babe?" Tristan Eisles called out, wrapping me in his arms and squeezing me tight. "I've been trying to call you."

"I just found out," I said into his chest before pulling away and feeling terrible.

I'd been so busy with my new job and Dalton; I was slacking at keeping up with my other friends. He kept me at arm's length, taking me in and smiling. It had been a few months since I last saw Tristan, right before he left to start his world tour. He'd changed his hair, and I wasn't sure if I liked it. The sides were shaved, but he'd grown it out longer in the middle. A light scruff filled his cheeks and the bottom of his chin. A black V-neck T-shirt showed off his vibrant-colored tattoo sleeves, and my eyes focused on a few I didn't recognize. Black jeans hung around his waist, and he was wearing scuffed black boots. Tristan Eisles gave no effort but still didn't fail to live up to his Sexiest Man Alive title.

I glanced over my shoulder to see a grim-faced Dalton, and his eyes were piercing as he watched our exchange.

"You two know each other?" he asked.

Tristan grabbed my waist, dragged me to his side, and pressed his lips to the top of my head. "Fuck yeah! Gabby's my number one girl." He beamed, and everyone's attention was now on us. Just what I didn't need.

"Bro, why do you always hide the hot girls from me?" Sheldon yelled our way and winced when Megan smacked his side. "Baby, you know I love you." He kissed her on the lips.

Tristan chuckled, shaking his head. "I see you've met my cousin, Sheldon."

I nodded.

His gaze turned to Sheldon. "You need to stay away from her," he warned, his eyes burning.

Sheldon held up his hands. "Dude, I got my girl," he said, slapping Megan on the ass, and she giggled. "But now, I'm curious on how you two know each other." An eyebrow arched as he filled up his glass with straight vodka.

"Gabby and I, we go way back," Tristan replied, grinning like I was his own personal secret. I felt his pocket vibrate, and he fished his phone out. He glanced at the screen before looking down at me with a frown. "Shit, I got to go, but we need to catch up soon, okay?"

I nodded, and he kissed me on the cheek before disappearing from the room.

I sat back down, ignoring the curious looks and a tight-lipped Dalton.

"Why didn't you tell me you knew Tristan?" he asked, rubbing the nape of his neck.

I shrugged, blowing out my cheeks. "I'm not a bragger."

I'd met a few celebrities through Lane, but I wasn't one of those people who went around, airing it to the world. I was never a fangirl about any celebrities. They were just regular people to me. I didn't know Dalton was bringing me to Tristan's show, or I'd have told him before we got there.

He huffed. "Well, a heads-up would've been nice."

I shifted around to face him. "Can we please turn the jealousy down a few notches? First, you're jealous of Asher, and now, you're jealous of a damn rock star." I would've been flattered by his jealousy if it wasn't toward two people I truly cared about.

"I'm not jealous. I was just curious on how you two knew each other. Not too many girls can say they know the most popular rock star out right now."

I sighed. I hated having to explain myself. "We met at one of Lane's dad's parties a while back. When he comes into town, he hangs out with us sometimes." I shrugged my shoulders. "It's not a big deal. He's pretty cool."

When I'd first met Tristan, I thought he was an arrogant asshole. But he and Lane were close, so he ended up ditching the main party and hanging out with us in Lane's basement. The more I got to know him, the more his true colors came out. He just wanted to be a regular guy sometimes. It was hard for him to be able to just relax and hang out with people because he wasn't sure whether they'd sell a story to the tabloids the next day for a couple of extra dollars.

"You surprise me more every day," Dalton said, grabbing his glass and taking a drink. "But it sucks."

"What sucks?"

"I just wanted to impress you, but it seems you're a hard one to impress, babe."

I moved closer to him, our legs touching, and leaned into his side. "Buying me things or taking me to the hottest party or concert to impress me isn't what a girl like me wants. Anyone can buy flowers, candy, or concert tickets. There's more to romance than that."

His ocean-colored eyes widened in interest. "Then, what does a girl like you want?"

"It's the little things we want. We want attention, and when we're not together, we like to know we're still on your mind, whether that be random texts or phone calls. We want kisses just because the guy wants to kiss us, not because he wants to get laid. We want him to stick up for us, no matter what's on the line. We want someone who will fight for us."

I thought back to my mom and Kenneth's relationship. I hated that he didn't stick up for her like he should. I knew he loved her, but he allowed his family to treat her horribly. I wanted a guy who would tell anyone who treated me terribly to go fuck themselves, and I'd do the same for him.

His face lit up, and he leaned down to press his lips against mine.

"I'll try my absolute hardest to give you what you want, baby. I promise."

I believed him too. As much as I was terrified of karma, I was beginning to think Dalton had the power to break me away from her grip.

Chapter Nineteen

DALTON

SHE KEPT SURPRISING ME. The fact she knew Tristan but didn't brag about it shocked me. Other girls I knew would've been bursting to divulge that information until they were blue in the face to impress me.

Not Gabby. No, she didn't give a damn about any of that shit. She liked people for their character, not their status or what she could get out of them. She was nothing like my family, and I admired that.

I blanketed my arms around her sensual body, swaying to the sound of Tristan's voice blaring through the auditorium. I smiled, moving to the beat with her body as she sang along with the words and danced to the gyrating beat of the music.

We were in the front row, but there was still plenty of space from the stage to our seats. A few people from the VIP room were close to us, but I allowed the music to drown them out and focused my attention on Gabby as soon as the show started. In my mind, we were alone.

"You've ruined me, baby," I breathed into her hair, dragging the silky locks away from her shoulder and running my lips down her sweaty neck. I couldn't seem to keep my hands off her.

She glanced back at me, the color of her face changing as the disco lights swirled above us. "What do you mean?" she asked, her bright red lips curving up on one side. She knew exactly what I meant, but she wanted to hear me say it.

Before Gabby, I never knew what it felt like to look at someone and smile for no damn reason. And that smile grew each passing minute I was around her. "You've fucking ruined me. I'll never be able to settle for someone who's not you. You've taken over every thought that runs through my mind."

And that was going to be a huge fucking problem because I was set to marry someone who wasn't her. Gabby had climbed her way into my heart, thrown her bags down, and decided she was moving in.

Her tight, petite body twisted around, so she was facing me. She leaned up on her tiptoes and wrapped her arms around my neck. Her five-foot frame was nowhere near my height, and I bent my neck to look down on the most beautiful face I'd ever laid eyes on. I wrapped my arms around her back, feeling like her protector, her shield.

"You've ruined everything for me too, you know," she replied, biting the side of her lower lip. "I've always thought I'd never find anyone who makes me feel the way you do—so wanted. I've never had anyone make me feel like I mattered." Her green eyes glimmered against the bright, multicolored lights on the stage behind her. The small smile morphed into a giant one. "Not to mention, you've pretty much ruined orgasms for me. Now that I know how good they can be, I'll never be able to settle for someone else doing a half-assed job."

I couldn't hold back my laugh. "You have such a way with words, babe."

She grinned, tucking a strand of hair behind her ear and looking up at me. "I know."

My hand inched up and traced the lining of her plump, juicy lips, my finger moving back and forth between them as they parted. She was begging me to kiss her. When I couldn't hold back any longer, I leaned down, grabbed her chin, and kissed her hard.

Our kiss was aggressive but passionate. Her mouth immediately opened, and our tongues danced against each other's to the rhythm of the music. My hand grazed her bare skin under the thin fabric of her top. She pulled away, her eyelashes fluttering as she blinked up at me and licked her lips.

"Is it weird that I want you so bad right now?" she asked.

Touching her skin had excited my cock, but her words made me fully alert. "If it is, then I'm just as fucking weird, baby," I answered. I swore to God, the girl breathed by me, and my dick would immediately get hard. "Turn around," I rasped out.

She tilted her head to the side. "What?"

I placed a knuckle on each shoulder, turning her body around swiftly so she was facing the stage again. I wrapped my arms around her lower waist, pushing my erection against her ass. I grinned as a ragged gasp escaped from her throat, and she pushed back against me. This was about to be the best concert in fucking history.

I inched my hand back underneath her shirt, dipping it lower than before with anticipation. My middle finger moved back and forth between the seam of her shorts and her soft skin. My chest sank in, and my breath caught when she rotated her hips against me to the beat.

She wasn't going to play fair tonight.

And neither was I.

I dipped my hand lower, moving my fingers under her waistband and over the fabric of her lace panties. She danced against me faster, and my dick stirred as I began raining kisses down her jaw. I moved my hand in circles over her clit. Her arm looped around my neck, bringing my mouth to hers as she kissed me. Moving the thin fabric out of my way, I dragged my hand through her wetness. She was fucking soaked. I heard the faint whimper from her hit my mouth as I began to massage her clit gently.

I broke away from the kiss and licked her earlobe. "You've got to be quiet, baby. You don't want them to know I'm playing with your pretty pussy, do you?" I whispered, swiping my finger through her wetness again before returning back to her swollen clit, rubbing it rougher as our arousal heightened.

The hand not worshiping the best pussy I'd ever tasted moved down and separated her legs wider, giving me more room to pleasure her. It was a pain in the ass, trying to work her with those tight-ass shorts on, but that wasn't going to hold me back.

Her back jerked, her ass hitting my cock, as I went lower and slowly caressed her soft opening. I briefly wondered how much trouble I'd get in if I pulled down her panties and started pounding my hard cock into her tight pussy. I wasn't sure if my dad would be able to fix that one for me.

The tempo of the music changed at the same time I plunged my finger into her. The music slowed down as I added a second finger. Her head fell back against my shoulder as I pumped my fingers in and out of her wetness. Grabbing her head, I turned it around and kissed her again. It was sloppier this time, and I was sure we looked like a fucking hot mess if anyone looked our way. Her legs wide open, my hand down her pants, and her rubbing her ass against my hard cock as we kissed made for a hell of a scene.

"You want it?" I asked, my hand moving faster.

She broke away from my kiss, her head moving back against my chest, and I knew she was close. My mind rushed through the million ways I wanted to fuck her as she began to let go. Her entire body locked up against me, and she shuddered a few times before going completely limp against me.

"That was unbelievable," she puffed, out of breath.

Watching her come was one of the sexiest things I'd ever seen, and each time, it got better because I knew I was the one giving her that pleasure. I was the only guy who instantly made her panties wet when I touched her. I fucking loved being that person.

She shifted back around, kissing me again before moving her hand and cupping my aching bulge. "Your turn," she said, grinning.

Fuck, if my cock wasn't excited enough, it was now ready to burst out of my fucking jeans. The only problem was, there wasn't a way to fix it. She couldn't just pull out my cock, get down on her knees, and suck me off in front of an arena full of people. That sounded fucking awesome, but it wasn't going to be happening.

I laughed, my dick instantly hating me. "I don't think now is the best time, beautiful."

She looked around and laughed. "Wow, I'm messed up," she muttered, her gaze going to the dirty floor beneath us.

I wrapped my arms around her and sucked on her neck. "You're not messed up for wanting me," I said against her skin. "I don't want you to be embarrassed for wanting me, and don't worry. We'll have plenty of fun when we get home."

Chapter Twenty

GABBY

WHAT IN THE utter hell was wrong with me?

I was morphing into some Dalton fiend where his hands had to be on my body at all times, or I was going to flip my shit. Dalton withdrawals—what a damn thing for a girl to suffer from. No matter how many times I heard his voice whisper in my ear or felt his hands on my body, I always craved more of him. When he'd slipped his hand down my panties during the concert, it was the most erotic feeling I ever had.

"I've missed you, love."

My eyes flashed over to see Tristan standing above me. I was slouched back on a couch in the VIP room we were in earlier. He squatted down and took Dalton's abandoned seat next to me.

He looked drained. His charcoal-colored eyes looked tired, and his dark hair was tousled, dripping wet with water from his after-show shower. He'd changed out of his stage clothes into an old T-shirt and a pair of cargo shorts.

The room wasn't as busy as it had been before the show, and I knew that was the only reason he was hanging out in here. Tristan wasn't a fan of large crowds because people liked to sell stories about him.

I leaned my weight into him, hugging his side and resting my head on his shoulder. "I've missed you too. You've just been so busy with your *world tour*," I replied, grinning. "Is it everything you wanted and more?"

This was Slayer Town's first tour, and I was so proud of him. They'd just made it big when we first met, and he'd talked about how his dream was to headline on his own world tour.

He stretched his long legs out in front of him. "It's more. It's so fucking amazing, Gabs," he answered, a little grin lifting on the side of his mouth. "The new cities, the fans, everything. It's crazy to have fans that aren't just locals from the old, run-down bars we used to play at. Every night is like a fucking adrenaline rush."

I grinned against his shoulder and squeezed his arm. "I'm so proud of you."

"It would be better if you were there with me."

He'd asked me out plenty of times to come along, but I always declined. He was a rock star, and that would really set me up for a miserable time with karma. I also wasn't big on being in the public eye and being constantly scrutinized by the entire world. I couldn't even get coffee with him in public. If we were photographed together, I'd instantly be labeled his current fling who was pregnant with his twin babies.

"Although I am a tad mad at you," he went on.

"About what?" I asked.

"You give Dalton fucking Douglas a chance but not me?"

I shook my head, moving a strand of hair behind my ear. "It's not like that."

"Right," he drew out. "And how many times have you told that lie, babe? Don't think I missed the show you two put on during my show."

I looked up at him, horrified. "W-what?" I stuttered. If he saw us, I wondered how many other people knew what we were up to.

"You think I'd know you're at my show and not watch you the entire time?"

I swallowed hard and fidgeted with my bracelet.

"But I did have to look the fuck away when I saw the jackass playing with your pussy right in front of my fucking stage."

My chest caved in, and I covered my face with both hands. "This is horrifying," I groaned, keeping my face covered and shaking my head in embarrassment.

He pulled my hands away one by one. "Don't be embarrassed, love. It's sexy as fuck when a woman is open sexually. I just wish I were the one who was making you feel that good."

He smiled down at me as I bit down on my bottom lip.

"It's complicated."

I felt his hand tap my thigh before resting on it. "You, my dear, are always complex. I just want you to be happy, and you looked happy with him. Just promise me one thing."

"What?"

"If he fucks up, you'll give me a chance."

"Tristan," I groaned, tossing my head back against the couch.

"No arguing. Just promise me."

His hand stayed on my thigh as he moved forward, his face only inches from mine. I knew I should've pushed him away, but my brain was still not functioning right from the mind-blowing orgasm Dalton had given me earlier. I also hated being put on the spot, and that was exactly what Tristan was doing to me.

I knew deep down that Dalton and I weren't going to work out in the end. We were just biding time. We'd never be anything long-term. His parents would never allow it. Then, Tristan would be waiting for me to fulfill my promise.

"You mind taking your fucking hands off her?"

My head snapped up to see a red-faced Dalton. His knuckles were clenched together in tight balls, and a large vein was bulging in his neck.

Tristan peeled his hand away from me, laughing. "He seems pretty jealous for someone who's just a friend," he commented, eyeing me carefully and ignoring Dalton. "We're leaving tomorrow morning, so I probably won't see your beautiful face before then. But next time I'm in town, we're catching up. Hopefully, your relationship status will have changed in my favor."

"Don't fucking hold your breath on that, Eisles," Dalton snarled, giving Tristan a murderous glare.

Tristan laughed again, ignoring Dalton's threatening gaze, and grabbed my hand to kiss it. He raised himself up from the couch slowly, moved around Dalton's stiff body, and joined a crowd of groupies in the corner.

Reason number nine hundred and sixty-three that I would never date a rock star: groupies.

Dalton immediately threw himself down into the open seat. "You let him fuck you?" he asked, his voice harsh.

I cringed at his blunt, rude words. "Not cool."

"Answer my question, Gabby."

Damn, the whole caveman thing he was trying to pull needed to stop.

"No, I haven't, not that it's any of your damn business."

He worked his jaw. "It is my business."

I snorted. "Sorry, but it's not."

"Anyone you're with that's not me is my damn business *and* my problem."

I shifted on the couch to directly face him. "Did you want me to join a convent or something, awaiting the day when we possibly would have sex again?" I raised an eyebrow. "Let's be real." He was starting to piss me off, and I noticed the wandering eyes and curious looks turning our way.

He massaged his temples with the palms of his hands. "I don't know. Fuck, I was hoping it would only be me who's been inside of you."

"And I'm the only girl you've been with since New Year's?" His eyes flashed down to the couch, and I took his silence as the answer I'd already known. "Exactly," I snapped.

I didn't like the fact that he'd been with other girls either, but that wasn't anything I could change or be pissed at him for.

"Who was it?" he asked, his eyes back on me.

My eyes grew wide. "Seriously? You don't see me questioning you about your past flings." Nor did I want to know.

"Or they?"

I threw my hands down on the couch. "It was one guy, my ex-boyfriend. Any more questions, mood killer? I think it's a good idea if we don't talk about past relationships."

"We need to talk about this shit. That's what people in relationships do."

My head whipped up, and my breathing hitched. "What did you just say?"

"I'm not repeating all of that."

"You said we were in a relationship," I said, suddenly finding myself trying to fight a smile.

Damn it, I was supposed to be pissed at him.

His head jerked back. "What the hell do you think we are?" he asked.

"Are we boyfriend and girlfriend?"

"I'm not one for labels, baby. We can be whatever you want to be. I can be your boyfriend, your lover, your idolizer, your friend." His hand slowly stroked my cheek.

"What would you prefer we be?" I was suddenly feeling dizzy.

"I'll be whatever you want to be," he answered.

"Idolizer? I think I like that," I replied, letting out a giggle.

"All right, girlfriend-slash-lover-slash-idol, are you ready to go?" he asked, taking my hand and lacing our fingers together.

"I think I like that one better."

Our hands didn't separate the entire time we walked out of the building and to his car.

* * *

We barely made it through the door before our mouths connected and our hands reached for the other's body. The ride back to his place had been pure torture. We'd played a sick, sadistic game of battle of the touches. I'd slowly run my hand down his arm as he steered through traffic. When we'd hit a stoplight, he'd fire back by trailing his fingertips across my bare thigh, stopping just at the hem of my shorts. Tingles between my legs had roared to life, ready for more of his touch, but the moment he sensed it, he'd move his hand away and give his attention back to the road. Then, the game would start back over. That car ride was the most excruciating thirty minutes of my life.

"I've been craving you all night," he breathed against my lips.

He flipped the light switch as he pushed me against the wall and ground his erection against my core. I squealed, feeling his strong hands lift me up in his arms. He slipped his hands underneath me, holding me under my ass as I began to grind into him, begging for a stronger connection. I needed to be closer. I wanted our bodies to become one.

Our bodies slid against each other's perfectly. His hands fell away from my ass, and my legs fell limp against the floor. Grasping my hips with one hand, he quickly unbuttoned my shorts with the other.

"God, yes," I moaned.

His hand dipped under the waistband of my panties and went directly to my clit, massaging it with the tip of his finger. My head rolled back, smacking against the hard wall as I melted into his touch.

"Let's go to bed, baby," he whispered.

"No," I panted, barely finding the strength to get that one syllable word out of my mouth. "This is perfect."

I slid my hands between the buttons of his shirt, sliced through the opening, and ignored the sound of them scattering along the hard floor. I was a woman on a mission to get him naked. His hooded gaze looked down on me as a mischievous grin spread over his thick lips. He shivered as my fingertips ran down his hard chest. My touch lingered near his nipples before I leaned down and licked one.

He growled, pushing my legs together to rid me of my shorts and dragging my panties along with them. He threw them across the room, and his hands moved to my thigh, rubbing up and down slowly before shoving them apart roughly. His moist lips smashed into mine again, kissing me full on the mouth at the same time he slipped a finger inside me. My body jerked against the wall, and I held my breath when he slid another finger inside, curling them upward.

"Ride my fingers, baby," he whispered into my ear.

I happily obliged. A wave of tingles flowed from the center of my body down to my core as he slammed his fingers into my rotating hips over and over again. It was coming. God, it was coming, and it felt so damn good. I lost complete control of my body, handing it over to him as waves of pleasure rushed through my veins.

His fingers slid out of me, and he wrapped my limp legs back around his waist to hold me up. "When I'm inside of you for our second first time, it isn't going to be against my damn wall," he grunted, walking toward the bedroom.

I giggled, still riding the high of my orgasm. "Our second first time?" I asked. "I don't think that counts."

"Every time counts with us. Every touch. Every kiss. Every time I slide my dick into that hot pussy of yours. Every fucking time counts," he breathed into my ear.

I giggled again. Apparently, I turned into an annoying schoolgirl when I was turned on, which was disturbing.

The bedroom lit up, and he tossed me down gently onto his unmade bed. I could still sense the smell of sex from our morning fun on the sheets. I inhaled it deeply as my sluggish eyes focused on his lean body slithering up mine, lust filling his face. He took my mouth in his, grinding his jeans-covered erection between my bare legs. The fabric was rough against my skin, but I didn't let that stop me from pressing back into him.

My heart pounded against my chest when he pulled away, shedding the rest of our clothes until we were both bare for each other. He reached down and cupped my breast before his mouth attached to my hard nipple, his teeth raking against it before sucking hard. My entire body lit up, and I shut my eyes as he slid inside of me slowly with his mouth still working my nipple. I opened up my legs wider, adjusting to his large size, and he began to rock in and out of me. My head fell back against the cold pillow as I cried out in pleasure.

"Look at me," he grunted, slowing down his pace while I urged him to do the opposite. "I want to see your face as I keep sinking deeper inside you."

My head flew up, my eyes fastening on to his fiery ones as he began to thrust harder inside me. I lost control of my body, of my mind, as I ground against him, rotating my hips as our sweaty skin slid against each other's. The room quickly became filled with nothing but the sound of our slapping bodies and deep moans.

"Oh my God," I whimpered, knowing what was coming.

My inner muscles clenched, and I begged it to stop, to let us keep going, but I felt every muscle in my body loosen, and I went limp against the bed. Dalton continued to pound into me, his hand moving to my clit to massage it in circles.

"One more time," he insisted. "Give it to me one more time, baby."

"Nuh-uh," I said, moving my head back and forth against the bed. "That's not happening."

There was no way he was doing that. I was done. My body was drained of all energy. I gasped as his hands went down to my ass, moving me into a sitting position with my torso tilted up as he continued to thrust into me faster. My eyes feasted on our connection. His wet cock was covered in my juices as he slid in and out of me.

I licked my lips. That image alone was enough to send me over the edge again.

And it did.

My shaking fingers ached as I dragged them through his hair and down his neck to his chest. I reached for a nipple, twisting it with my hand, and he groaned, his head falling back.

A loud growl came from the back of his throat as his entire body stilled and his muscles tensed. "Holy fucking shit, you feel so damn good," he rasped.

I whimpered, and my limp body fell against the bed, no longer able to hold myself up. He pounded into me a few more times before doing the same thing.

"Oh fuck," he said suddenly.

My head shot up and looked over at him. "What?"

"I forgot a condom," he said, crushing his eyelids together. "I never forget a fucking condom."

"Okay, the last part of that sentence was unnecessary," I said. The last thing I wanted to hear while his cock was still inside me was him talking about other times with girls who weren't me. "I'm on the pill," I assured quickly, "and I'm clean."

He exhaled a breath of relief. "Thank God. I'm so sorry. You felt so good, wrapped around my fingers. I couldn't wait to feel that with my cock."

I patted his arm and leaned up on my elbows to kiss him. "It's all right. We both forgot." I couldn't blame him when I hadn't thought about it either. It was just as much my fault as it was his.

He pumped into me a few more times, grinding our hips together before sliding out of me and falling to my side. I stayed on my back as he turned to his side next to me and wrapped his hand around my torso.

"Every time gets better with you, babe," he said, kissing my hair. "You always send me over the fucking edge."

I smiled, feeling the same way. Even with my ex-boyfriend, I'd never felt that strong sexual connection like I had with Dalton, and my feelings with him weren't just about sex. The little things he did—kissing my hair, moving me away from Ivy, and chasing after me against his dad's wishes—made me feel so protected.

I snuggled into his side. "What's your biggest fear?" I asked, and he looked down at me curiously. "Come on," I groaned. I wanted us to get deeper ... to share something more. "I'll tell you mine if you tell me yours."

His head fell back. "Ending up like my dad," he answered. "I don't want to be that man who puts business and power before everything, especially his family. I don't want to be manipulative and sour. When I get the company, I'm going to change some shit, but I've got to ride it out until he's done." He bent down and swept my sweaty hair away from my forehead.

"You're nothing like him," I said, squeezing his hand.

He crushed his eyelids together, and a pained expression crossed his features. "Your turn."

I sighed. "Ending up like my mom." It was strange. Our parents were so different but not what we wanted our future to look like. He drew up an eyebrow. "In regard to relationships, my mom's track record is terrible. I have no idea who my dad is, and she's slept with I don't know how many married men, wanting them to save her, to be that knight in shining armor."

"Have you ever tried looking for your dad?"

I shook my head. "No. I'm not going to go looking for someone who doesn't want to be found. He knows I exist. He knows he has a daughter out there and is choosing to do nothing about it."

"That's his loss," he whispered, trailing his hand down my arm.

"Growing up, my mom always had nice boyfriends, but they were never enough for her, you know? She always had to have the power-hungry, ambitious men who had money. The only problem was, men like that are always married. Kenneth wasn't the only married man she's been with," I confided in him something I'd never told anyone else. Not even Cora. "My mom would insist over and over again that they were going to leave their wives for her and start a family with us, but it would never happen. False hopes and broken promises are all she got. I know I'll never put myself in that situation. I don't care who it is."

His shoulders dropped, and his face fell. "Sometimes, it's complicated for men like that. They get stuck in situations they can't get themselves out of, and they coward up. My uncle is one of the most stand-up guys I know. Sure, it wasn't cool that he had an affair, but he did the right thing in leaving my aunt. I know for a fact he wouldn't go through all of that to hurt her in the end. Plus, he brought you to me, so I owe him a lot." I grinned, and he bent down to kiss me before going on. "No one would ever be stupid enough to choose someone over you."

He gave me a forced smile, and I knew something wasn't right. I shut my eyes, praying he'd live up to his words when it came time to pick his family or me.

Chapter Twenty-One

GABBY

"I HAVE something to tell you, but no judging," I said, looking back and forth between the two girls sitting to each side of me.

It was Sunday afternoon, and I'd just left Dalton's house before heading over to Cora's. We were having our weekly girl time and lying out by the pool, soaking up the hot sun.

"Girl, you know we'd never judge you," my friend Daisy said, brushing her dark hair away from her face and stretching her olive-toned legs against her lounge chair.

Daisy had moved from Indiana during our senior year when her boyfriend got murdered during a school shooting. She'd been having a hard time dealing with it, so her parents shipped her to live with her aunt, who was also my mom's boss at the interior design company she worked for. We instantly clicked, and I considered her one of my best friends.

There were times I wished I could move away and start over fresh like she did. No one knew all the shit she'd been through, except our inner circle. If I got out of Atlanta, no one would know about my mom's scandal or how I'd moved to upper class because my mom spread her legs to a married man and then talked him into leaving his wife.

The only problem was, I had no family to run away to. My mom was the only family I had. Like me, she never knew her dad, and my grandmother was a drunk who left her to take care of herself when she found out she was pregnant with me.

Cora clicked her tongue across the roof of her mouth and took a sip of lemonade. "I don't know," she replied, pushing her Chanel sunglasses farther up her nose. "The last time you said something along those lines, you admitted to losing your V-card to a Douglas. Now that you're working with said card-swiper Douglas, I'm afraid this has something to do with him."

I pursed my lips, slouching back against the lounge chair. "I hate how you know me so well," I grumbled.

She grinned, leaning over and kissing my cheek. "We're besties. That's how it's supposed to be. We're supposed to be able to read each other's minds. I know when you're upset, pissed, mad, turned on—"

My hand flew up to stop her words. "Uh, you have no idea when I'm turned on, freak."

Cora shot me a playful grin. "Girl, I've watched you during some of our shows. I so know when you get turned on."

"She's right," Daisy agreed. "Your breathing gets heavy and—"

I tucked my knees into my chest. "Okay, okay. I get it," I shouted, cutting her off and waving my hands in the air.

This discussion was charting into unnecessary territories. We always discussed my friends' sex lives, but mine was hardly ever brought up. It was mainly based on the fact that the majority of the times I'd ever had an orgasm was when I'd given it to myself.

"Fine," Cora said. "Someone isn't in a fun mood today, so give us the scoop, or we're going to continue talking about all the weird shit you do when you're turned on."

I wiped my hands down my sweaty legs nervously and sat up straight as I mentally prepared my confession in my head. "Okay," I drew out. "Dalton and I pretty much hung out all weekend."

"Hung out or hooked up again?" Cora threw back.

I shrank in my chair and chewed on my lower lip. "Kind of both."

Cora bent over and smacked my arm. "You dirty hooker! I knew there was a reason you weren't texting me our normal standard texts a day. How the hell did you let that happen?"

My eyes focused on the deep blue water of the pool ahead of us. "We had some work lunch with his dad, and it was mortifying. His dad seriously went on some wild tangent about how slutty my mom is. I got pissed off, said some choice words, and stormed out. Dalton ran after me."

Daisy's hands clapped together. "He ran after you? Now, that's romantic," she said, her voice bubbly.

Cora grabbed a grape from the table beside her and tossed it over my body at Daisy. "No! Not romantic. Dalton's not a Prince Charming," she yelled.

Daisy caught the grape and popped it into her mouth. The girl had recently found love with her boyfriend, Keegan, so she'd been all butterflies and candy hearts lately. I was happy for them. They'd both been through terrible shit in their lives and were perfect for each other. Plus, Keegan was a hot piece of ass, and Daisy got him to leave Dalton's crazy-bitch sister, Piper, and settle down with her. That was my girl.

"Anyway ..." I continued. I wasn't going to listen to them go back and forth on how unromantic my sexing it up with Dalton was. "We left. Dalton suggested we go back to his place instead of the office."

Cora snorted, rolling her eyes. "Of course, he did. He wanted to get his slimy hands in your pretty little panties. Damn, Gabs, I thought you were smarter than that."

I knew Cora wasn't trying to give me a hard time. She was just looking out for me. Like Asher, she didn't want to see me get hurt. She knew Dalton's reputation wasn't a pretty one when it came to relationships or lack thereof. Plus, she knew how vicious the Douglas family could be when you got in their way. She had her fair share of dealing with Piper, who was our age and dated Lane for a week when they were on a break. That was three years ago, and we still heard Piper gloat about it even though Lane didn't touch her evil ass.

I fiddled with the string of my bikini bottoms. "I think we've established that I make stupid decisions." You could call me the queen of bad decision-making. I blamed it on genetics from my mother.

"Okay, I thought you were smarter than that *now*, after you'd given him your almighty V-card drunkenly."

"I just want to point out that he obviously liked what you gave him since he's coming back for more," Daisy said, bringing up a hand and holding it up. "That's my girl."

I slapped my hand against hers to give her a high five. "Thanks, girl."

Cora groaned, stretching her legs out. "Did you two have sex again?" she asked. "We need to get to the point so I can have my lecture ready." Her question lingered in the air, and her eyes bulged out at my reserve. "Gabrielle Nicole Taylor! You freaking gave him your goodies! You weren't supposed to hand over the goodies again! You were supposed to find a nice, good boyfriend who got along with Lane to give your goodies to!"

I pulled my hair up into a ponytail and snagged the ponytail holder around my wrist to wrap it around my thick hair. "I know! The goodies are supposed to be protected and all, but I'm telling you, he was pulling out all the give-me-your-goodies cards," I replied.

There was no way I would've been able to resist Dalton. There was no way any girl would've been able to resist him when he had his soft hands on her body and was whispering naughty words in her ear with his raspy, sex-filled voice.

"I'm sure she got his goodies as well," Daisy said, laughing. "And from what I've heard, they're pretty damn good."

"Daisy, don't encourage it," Cora said, frustrated.

"What's so bad about her being with him?" Daisy fired back.

She didn't know much about Dalton, except for the fact that he popped my cherry, so she was clueless about his endless amount of hookups and playing the field. She also didn't know about the inner Atlanta circle. Even though my stepdad was in the inner circle, I was still considered an outcast to everyone else, especially Dalton's parents.

They'd do everything in their power to tear me down if they found out about the two of us.

Cora's face turned serious. "Gabby's already under the crazy misconception that she's cursed. She and Dalton being together," she said, pausing to shake her head, "terrible idea. They won't work out." She gave me a sympathetic look. "Sorry, babe, but I'm just being honest."

"Thanks," I grumbled, forcing a smile. Why did the truth always suck?

She turned her attention back to Daisy. "When they don't work out, Gabby will be even more convinced about this stupid curse shit she's obsessed with. That will result in her not wanting to give another guy a chance, ruining the odds of us having a double wedding together. I want her to be happy, and Dalton Douglas will destroy her."

"Maybe they'll work out," Daisy said, looking at me and smiling.

"Look, you two, I'm telling you right now, there will be no wedding bells ringing in the near future for us," I said. "But I think we're kind of dating-slash-friends-with-benefits. Dalton pretty much told me he wouldn't be messing with other girls while we're together. I believe him. Plus, we work together, so it would be pretty hard for him to hide a relationship from me."

"What about his psychopath family?" Cora grumbled. "Sorry to break it to you, but Piper will not be allowed entry to my wedding."

"Dalton and I aren't going to be getting married," I choked out. As much as I cared for Dalton, I knew we'd never be able to be more than what we had now. "Let me just do the friends-with-benefits thing, okay? I've never done this before."

"Babe, *friends with benefits* is a bullshit term. People can never be friends with benefits because one person eventually establishes feelings for the other. I can't see you giving your body up like that to someone just for a good time. You have feelings for him," Cora said. My mouth parted, ready to argue, but her words ran over my chance. "You don't need to deny it. I get it. It's hard not to fall for guys with that much charm. I just want you to know I'll be here for you, no matter what happens. If he breaks your heart, I'll be there with my best-friend glue gun, fixing you up."

I leaned over and gave her a sideways hug. "That's why I love you."

"Then, I'll be driving to his house to kick his door in to use my best-friend scissors to cut off his weasel cock."

"And that's also why I love you," I said, laughing.

Chapter Twenty-Two

DALTON

MY KNUCKLES GRIPPED the weight bar as Leo stood behind and spotted me. "You going to tell me why you were MIA all weekend?" he asked, glaring down at me and looking for answers.

I grunted, pushing the bar up one last time before leveling it down onto the stand. "You my babysitter now?" I growled, angling around on the weight bench. I wasn't in the mood for Detective Leo's interrogation.

His lips tightened. "I ran into Sheldon this morning, getting coffee."

I raised a brow. "Oh, did you?"

I already knew what was coming. Sheldon had the biggest fucking mouth. That was why he could never keep a girlfriend and none of us told him shit at the frat house. He didn't do it intentionally. The poor guy just had no filter and couldn't control what came out of his mouth.

"Sure did, and he mentioned something very interesting," he said.

"And what was that?"

"You were at a concert with some hot chick you worked with." He squatted down next to me. "I'm curious on who this hot chick is because the last time I checked, Eva didn't work with you." He lifted the bottom of his old T-shirt and wiped the dripping sweat off his face.

I held my arms out and stretched. "I went to a concert, yeah. Is that okay with you, Dad?" I swiped the towel covering my water bottle from the floor and wiped my drenched face. This was the last damn conversation I wanted to be having.

"Was it Gabby?" he questioned, his face grim.

"You're wasting your breath, even asking that." I brought myself up from the hard leather bench. "And quite frankly, it's none of yours or anyone else's damn business who the hell I'm spending my time with." I navigated around his perspiring body, snatched up my water bottle, and dashed up the stairs to the cardio center, hoping he wasn't going to follow me. My brother didn't always finish his workout with cardio like I did, and I was hoping today was one of those days.

His footsteps were loud behind me, but I ignored him. I wasn't in the mood to hear one of his lectures. I had an awesome fucking weekend with Gabby, and I wasn't about to let his bullshit ruin my high.

"Here's my next question," he called out as my foot hit the top stair, and we headed toward the treadmills. "Why are you such a dumbass?"

I turned around swiftly and walked backward. "Don't patronize me because I'm not acting like Mommy and Daddy's little puppet like you do, brother." I halted at the last treadmill at the end of the row and hopped on. Pushing a few buttons, I began jogging while Leo jumped on the one beside me.

"Not cool," he scolded. "I'm just trying to help you. Dad came over last night for dinner and was bitching up a storm about you."

"He's always bitching," I huffed, picking up my pace.

Talking about my dad pissed me off, which meant I needed to push myself harder to get rid of all the pent-up frustration that he brought out. I wasn't going to let my dad dictate whom I spent my time with like he did my brother. If I wanted to hang out with Gabby, I was going to hang out with the girl who made me fucking happy.

My brother's speed slowed down. "He knows something is going on between the two of you. I tried to detour his thoughts away from the idea, but our dad's not stupid. You know he isn't going to allow whatever the two of you have going on to continue."

I didn't need Leo to confirm what I already knew. I knew the moment I decided to run after Gabby what the consequences would be. I just wasn't sure how severe yet.

My feet slammed against the rubber, and I smacked a few buttons to increase my slope. Running always helped me clear my head. "Dad doesn't control who's in my bed," I replied.

"Yet he does control your livelihood. Remember that."

My hands firmly gripped the safety grips, my knuckles turning white. "Fuck me, you're beginning to sound just like him, Wilson Jr."

That was my parents' trick. If you didn't go to the college they selected for you, they'd cut you off. If you didn't marry the person they wanted, they'd cut you off. They always hung money and our inheritance over our heads like a fucking game. Them cutting us off was worse than any spanking or grounding they could've threatened. We were identical reflections of them, wrapped up in different skin. We wouldn't know what the hell to do without our money.

"I'm just being a realist and thinking with the right head. Obviously, the only one working on you is the one between your legs," he argued.

I grinned. "I can reassure you that both of my heads function extremely well."

"Your head below better find someone else to sink himself into because Uncle Kenneth will kill you. Find another chick, or better yet, screw your fiancée."

"I don't want to find another chick or fuck Eva."

He shook his head, looking down at the ground. "Damn, Dalton. There are plenty of other girls out there."

I grabbed my water bottle, taking a long chug. "Believe me, I've fucking tried."

Leo stopped dead on his treadmill, holding himself upright by the safety handles and breathing hard. His gaze fixed on me. "You have feelings for her, don't you?" he asked, unease lining his features.

My eyes averted away from him and focused on the TV ahead of us.

"Holy fuck me," he cried out, eyes wide. "You do." He slapped his side. "You had to pick the one person you're not supposed to have feelings for."

I threw my hands out in front of me and shook my head. "It's not like I planned it. If I knew this shit was going to happen, I would've kicked her out of my room that night."

"That's a lie."

I let out an exasperated sigh. "Fine, you're right. But I would've done something differently."

No, I wouldn't have. There was no damn way I would've ever been able to turn Gabby to go away. He raised a questioning brow, and I stopped my machine.

"This girl, she's getting to me. I feel the constant need to be around her, and when I'm not, all I do is think about her. Or what she's doing. Or how I can get her to come hang out with me. It's like she's taken over my damn mind."

"You're falling in love with her."

My head whipped up, fully alert. "What? No."

"Don't try to bullshit me. I know a lovesick fool when I see one, and you, my friend, are a lovesick chump." He jumped off his treadmill and slapped me hard on the back. "And you're also fucked because you can't love her. You need to fix that shit."

"And how do you suppose I do that, genius?"

"You've got to do it the hard way—cut her off. No communication, nothing. Tell Dad you can no longer work with her. Shit, tell him you don't like her anymore. He'd be thrilled to hear that." We began walking back toward the locker room. "And make sure you fix the squinting-the-eye shit before you do. He'll see right through your twitching ass," he added, laughing.

"Screw you, asshole," I said, scanning my card to open my locker and dragging my bag out.

Even though we worked out at a five-star gym, I still showered at home. Public showers weren't my thing. I snatched my bag out of the locker, unzipped it, and fished out my phone. Leo started to complain about his wife as I slid my finger across the screen and tapped on Gabby's name before I began typing.

ME: What are you doing?

I was already sucking at the whole cutting-her-off thing. A few seconds passed before my phone beeped.

GABBY: Lying out by the pool at Cora's.

I grinned.

ME: In a bikini?

GABBY: Nope. Nude.

I blinked and reread the message before replying.

ME: Send me a pic.

GABBY: No, perv. If I learned one thing from my ridiculous job, it's never to send naked photos. Can't have you black-mailing my ass.

ME: You suck.

My phone vibrated again, but instead of another text, there was a photo. I opened it up, enlarging it, and felt my cock instantly twitch. I licked my lips as I studied the picture.

It was a shot of her wearing only a barely there black bikini. Her head was chopped off, but I'd still recognize the tanned skin and hourglass curves from anywhere. I coughed, readjusted myself in my thin shorts, and silently prayed I didn't get a hard-on where other men were showering.

ME: Tease. Come over.

GABBY: Can't. But you can come over here. The boys just arrived.

ME: Boys?

My fingers grew sweatier as I typed that last message. Was she hanging out with other guys?

GABBY: Keegan and Lane.

I breathed out a rush of relief that it was just two guys but was still worried about Keegan. I knew Keegan through my sister, and he wasn't the guy you wanted around the girl you liked. I swore that guy could snap his fingers, and girls would fall at his feet, ready to do whatever he wanted.

ME: Be there in thirty.

"You're texting her, aren't you?" Leo asked, peeking over my shoulder at my phone screen.

He grunted as I elbowed him in the stomach and tossed my phone back into my bag before he had the chance to catch a glimpse of Gabby's picture.

"How do you know I'm not texting Eva?" I ask, dragging my car keys out of the side pocket and sliding my sunglasses on.

He smirked. "I've seen you talk to Eva for years. You don't smile like a giant cheese fuck when you talk to her. Your face doesn't melt or light up when you look at her pictures."

I stopped, and my head swung back to look at him. "Did you just say my face doesn't melt? Where the hell did you hear that was a sign of love?"

He laughed, grabbing his bag and hoisting it over his shoulder. "Kelly's been leaving her romance novels in the bathroom. A man's got to have some entertainment, doing his business, so I just grab one of those bad boys. They're actually pretty good."

I followed him out and headed toward our cars parked side by side. "Dear God, I need to get you away from her," I commented, banging on the hood of his Bentley before getting into my car.

* * *

"Hey there, cherry-popper," Cora yelled when I walked through the iron gate of her massive backyard.

Her family had money, although I wasn't sure how. I knew of her because she was Lane's girlfriend, but her parents never hung out in our social circle. That didn't surprise me though because Cora was a snarky little shit, and I was sure that would've been frowned upon by parents in our clique.

A small group of people were spread out over lounge chairs that surrounded the large pool area. I spotted Lane in the corner, manning the stainless-steel grill with his head bouncing up and down to the music in the background.

"Cora!" Gabby shrieked, jumping up from her chair and smacking her on the arm.

My eyes burned on Gabby, still wearing the black bikini she'd sent me a photo of. The strings to her top were tied tight around her neck, pumping up her cleavage, and my mouth watered as I licked my lips.

Fuck, I wanted to swipe over those bottoms and sink myself into her warm pussy.

"What?" Cora asked, laughing hard as Gabby fell back onto her lounge chair. "Everyone knows he's the one who swiped your sweet little V-card."

I couldn't hold back my laugh as Gabby stuck her fingers into a glass and flicked Cora with water. "I told you to be nice to him," she warned.

Cora threw her hands out my way. "I am being nice. I'm letting a Douglas step into my yard without shooting him or setting him on fire." Her eyes shot my way. "No offense, Douglas, but you got to let me get a few jabs in."

"You're good," I replied, walking closer to them. I knew Cora had beef with my sister, so it wasn't personally against me.

Gabby grinned and gave me a tiny wave. "Please excuse my friends," she commented, her cheeks blushing.

Damn, she was adorable.

Cora snorted. "Excuse us?" Her green eyes angled back at me. "No, be very afraid of us because I will personally stick your ass in my torture cheating device if you hurt her," she warned.

I blinked, tilting my head to the side. "Torture cheating device?" I questioned, instantly regretting it. Anything with the words *torture* and *cheating* in it couldn't be good.

"Don't do it," Gabby said.

"You'd better do it, girl," a dark-haired girl to the other side of Gabby yelled out.

I didn't recognize her, but I did recognize the guy whose lap she was sitting on. Keegan Montgomery. I knew my sister had a thing with him in the past, and I'd busted her a few times, sneaking out to meet up with him. I was just thankful he wasn't there to visit with Gabby.

Lane appeared at Cora's side, sat down at the edge of her chair, and rested his hand on her thigh. "I'm with Daisy on this one, babe," he said. "I've got to let another man hear this, so he feels me." His attention turned my way. "Plus, you won't be too afraid to narc on Cora when my ass goes missing someday."

Cora took that as a go because she leaned forward and grinned. "I've kind of, sort of invented this pretty little device in my head."

"And on paper," Lane added.

Cora smacked his shoulder. "You see, if Lane ever cheats on me, I'm going to tie him to a chair in his garage and set up this entrapment device that can only be removed if he cuts his penis off. I haven't completely configured the logistics of it, but it's in the process."

I felt my cock instantly ache, and my arm reached down to cover it. "Damn, girl, you're fucking brutal," I said, wincing.

"Why don't you tell him the best part?" Keegan laughed, pointing to Cora.

"Oh." She grinned, flipping her hair back behind her shoulder. "Then, I set the garage on fire, leaving him with two choices: either he burns to death or he cuts off his own penis."

"I told you, man. You've got to feel for me," Lane said, falling back against his girlfriend's legs and looking up at me.

I scratched my temple and set my attention on Cora. "Has anyone ever told you that you might need professional help?" I asked, my eyebrows scrunching up.

She grinned. "Nope, my parents just tell me I'm creative."

"Creative enough to write the next *Saw* movie," Lane retorted.

She slapped him hard on the shoulder. "Anyway, the conclusion of this discussion is that if you make Gabby cry, I'll basically kill you," she added, shrugging.

"Noted. If I want to live and keep my penis intact, I'll be sure to not piss her off," I replied.

God, I was definitely hiding from Cora if Gabby found out about

Eva before I figured out a way to break it off. I planned on talking to my dad when I got back to the office and telling him I wasn't going through with the wedding.

Lane clapped his hands together. "Now that we've gotten the threats out of the way, it's time for some grub." He shot up from the chair and slapped me on the back before heading back to the grill.

I strolled over to Gabby's side before bending down and kissing her straight on the lips. "Hi, baby," I whispered, allowing my mouth to linger on her lips for a few seconds before breaking away.

"Hi," she breathed out, and I noticed her body tense up. Scooting over, she made room for me on her chair, and I noticed why she'd clammed up. Everyone's full attention was on us, and they were all sporting huge-ass grins on their faces.

"You two are seriously so adorable," the girl they'd called Daisy squealed, clapping her hands together.

My hand rested on Gabby's thigh, and she stretched her legs out, resting her feet on my lap while everyone else got up to eat.

"Is everything okay?" I asked, massaging her feet.

She nodded, rubbing the back of her neck. "Yeah, it's just strange."

"What is?"

"Having you here with my friends, hanging out. I hope you're not completely terrified of them. I don't usually bring guys around. They can tend to be overprotective at times."

I gripped her hip with my free hand and kissed her forehead. I was glad she had friends that stuck up for her and had her best interests at heart. "The dark-haired chick named after the flower, not so much. Cora though, I think she might be out for blood," I said, laughing.

She moved up and rested her head on my shoulder. "She'll get used to you. You're going to need to suck up to her though."

"I'm glad she's backup for my girl. I'll go buy her some shoes or shit. That'll get me on her good side."

She grinned, slapping my side. "Don't get too cheesy on me." Her hands went to the edge of my shirt, and she looked up at me mischievously. "Did you like my picture?"

"Oh, I loved that picture," I replied, raising my hands up so she could slip my shirt over my head. She tossed the shirt down on a pile of clothes beside us and ran her fingernails across my chest. A smile built across my face, and I bit my lip. "Babe, you'd better quit before I take you right here in front of your friends, and I'm sure that's not going to keep me on their good side."

"They'd love a good show," she said, her tone serious.

I froze up, blinking as I gazed down at her.

She slapped my stomach. "I'm kidding!"

I blew out a breath.

"You sure? Because I'm good with ripping off your clothes right now."

"They'd probably be happy I'm getting laid," she joked, grabbing my hand and dragging me to her friends to fill our stomachs.

* * *

"Are you having fun?" Gabby asked.

I was treading water between her parted legs while she sat at the edge of the pool. I rested my hands on her palms and brought myself up to eye-level with her. "Anytime I'm with you, I'm having fun."

Her smile grew wider. "I like to hear that."

"Who wants to see me do a cannonball?" Lane yelled, and I turned around to see him running straight for the pool.

"I'd rather see you get hit by one," Cora shrieked, throwing her hands up to block her face when he smacked into the water, sending a giant splash her way. Her mouth fell open, and she pulled wet hair away from her face, giving her boyfriend a murderous look.

I nibbled on Gabby's cheek before kissing her. I loved being able to touch and kiss her freely without worrying about someone going and tattling to my parents. She moaned, grabbing my hand and moving it higher onto her thigh, just inches away from her core.

"Mmmm, you want to play?" I asked, rubbing my thumbs across the inside of her thighs, moving it closer to where she wanted.

She nodded, and I leaned in closer.

"Answer me, baby. You want to play in the water? You want to get wetter?"

She nodded again.

"You have to tell me what you want."

"Damn it, Dalton, I want ..."

My free hand grabbed her around the ankle, and I pulled her into the water quickly as she screamed, kicking her feet.

"I'm going to kill you!" she screamed, gasping for air when she shot up from the water, ready for revenge.

I laughed as her hand shot out to splash me, but I whipped around and dunked her head back under the water. When I released her, I dashed across to the other side of the pool. She came back up, gaining control of herself before swimming my way. She gripped my shoulders when she reached me, pressing down onto them roughly, attempting to dunk me but failing miserably. I was stronger and over a foot taller. There was no way she was taking me down.

"Nice try, babe, but it's not happening," I said, wiping water out of my eyes and taking in her plump breasts in my face as she continued to try and take me down.

"Oh, watch this," she yelped, her fingernails going into my shoulders as she jumped up again.

I froze when a second pair of cold hands landed at the top of my head. Oh shit. All of a sudden, before I had the chance to fight back, I was pushed under the water and held my breath. I spat out a mouthful of water when I resurfaced.

"Cheater!" I shouted at the two cackling girls high-fiving each other across from me. I pointed a finger at Daisy. "You're not allowed to help. That's against the rules."

Daisy splashed me. "We make the rules around here, Douglas."

They relished in their victory until Keegan grabbed Daisy around the waist from behind while she shouted expletives and threats before he dunked her under. She attempted to push him away, but he kept his hold on her and kissed her when she got back up for air. I swam Gabby's way, and she dashed to the other side of the pool, afraid I was out for vengeance at the same time Lane threw Cora in. I held my hands up in surrender and grabbed Gabby, so she couldn't get away.

All of us stayed in the pool for the next hour, laughing and playing games until Gabby looked down at her wrinkly fingers and proclaimed it was time to get her ass out.

"You staying at my house tonight?" I asked, wrapping a towel around her shivering body and kissing her bare shoulder. She tasted like vanilla and chlorine.

She shook her head, wrapping her arms around my dripping wet chest. "No, I have to stay home tonight."

"I'll stay there with you." I rubbed my hands down her soaked hair, and her bright emeralds gazed up at me.

"That's probably not a good idea. I told Asher I'd hang out with him and talk about everything that happened. I feel bad, ditching him all the time to hang out with you."

She was right. I didn't need to piss off Asher, so he'd go and tattle before I had the chance to break things off with Eva.

I frowned. My bed was going to be lonely as fuck without her. "Fine, you go hang out with the other guy who's obsessed with you," I said, running my hands down her cold, quivering arms.

She pushed my side, laughing. "Asher isn't obsessed with me."

"Baby, he is. But I trust you." I'd never dealt with the feeling of jealousy before, but it was boiling inside of me every time I thought about her with someone who wasn't me.

"How very sweet of you." She giggled. "I promise you are the only guy on my mind."

I raised an eyebrow. "No one else?"

She shook her head. "No one else but you, Dalton Douglas." Her hand went up to her mouth. "I can't believe I'm falling for a damn Douglas."

"Believe it, baby, because there's no taking it back."

Chapter Twenty-Three

DALTON

"YOU WANTED TO SEE ME?" I asked, my arms wide as I entered my dad's office and fell into a chair.

I hadn't talked to him since I left his sorry ass at the restaurant, so I could chase after Gabby. He'd warned me before I did it, threatened me not to go after her, but his words went in one ear and out the other. Just because he wanted to live up to being the world's biggest asshole alive didn't mean I wanted to follow in his brooding footsteps.

"We need to talk about that little stunt you pulled. I expect you to never disrespect me like that again. I'm your father," he retorted, falling into his power pose and giving me a smug look.

I scoffed at the mention of disrespect. If you ever went against anything my dad said, you were immediately pegged as being disrespectful, no matter what the circumstances were. I pulled at the tight collar around my neck. "Then, maybe you should stop being such a disrespectful prick yourself," I replied.

I wasn't in the mood for his shit that morning. I was sleep-deprived and groggy. I'd been on the phone with Gabby all night and ended up having to jack off afterward. Even on the phone, her sweet and tantalizing voice made me hard as a rock.

His lips formed a sour grin, and I tensed up, nervous about what I was about to get smacked in the face with. My dad didn't smile for no reason. No, Wilson Douglas only smiled when he was about to mutilate someone. My stomach twisted in knots. Curiosity on whether the victim would be Gabby or me. Or both.

He snatched a file folder sitting on the side of his desk and tossed it my way. I stretched forward to grab it. His eyes fixed on me as I opened it and scanned the contents inside. My heart pitched to my throat as I reread the words a few times written on the papers inside. His grin was a *fuck you, I always get my way* grin. That grin was going to hurt both of us.

"Your mother worked on this all weekend," he said, blindsiding me. "Eva's already approved everything. The invitations will be sent out this week. The ceremony has been booked, but they're still deciding between a few locations for the rehearsal dinner. I'm guessing you're not filled with any great ideas?" he asked.

My hands balled into fists, crinkling the ends of the folder. Fuck no. I didn't have any ideas for the wedding of doom I was supposed to be a part of. The only idea I had in that moment was how satisfying it would feel punching him in his face.

I slammed the folder shut. "I would appreciate it if you'd consult with me before you make plans for my wedding," I snarled, working my jaw.

He lifted a glass to his mouth and took a giant swig. I internally cringed with disgust. It was barely past eight in the morning, and he was already drinking. Someone get this asshole to an AA meeting, pronto.

"I'm not ready to get married yet, and you have no damn right to push it. I agreed to marry Eva, but give me time, damn," I went on. I tossed the folder back onto his desk and ran my hands through my hair roughly.

I'd intended on coming into his office to inform him I wanted to cancel the wedding. Now, everything had been shot to hell since they went behind my back. He knew it was coming, and he figured out a way to prevent it. There was no way I could stop it if the invitations were already being sent out.

He reclined back into his chair, crossed his legs, and held his hands behind his head. "Whatever you've got going on with that girl, end it now. I won't tell you again."

I didn't need to ask which girl he was referring to. He knew about Gabby. He wasn't an idiot. I was sure anyone could've watched me around Gabby and seen how much of a lovesick puppy I was becoming.

I bit back a laugh. "So, wait," I said, my voice grim as I raised one finger. "You're allowed to have a mistress, but I'm not?"

His eyes narrowed, and he shifted in his chair. "Oh, son, you can have as many mistresses as you'd like *after* your wedding. Have yourself a whole damn harem for all I care. But until you tie the knot, you need to keep your dick in your pants and straighten your ass up. I won't have you ruining this for me. You need to think about your family and the business, not about sticking your cock into some whore."

My face burned at his attempt to toy with me. That bastard was pushing my buttons. He wanted me to snap, so he could teach me another lesson. "What if I choose not to marry her?" I asked, not playing into his games. Every muscle in my body locked up as I waited for his response.

He choked on the drink he was taking and slammed the glass back down onto his desk. I watched cognac liquid splatter all over a large stack of papers. "What if you don't marry Eva?" he sneered, mocking me. "He wants to know what if he doesn't marry Eva." He looked up at the ceiling as though he was talking to God. His gaze shot back down to me, and fury lined his features. "If your dumbass chooses not to marry Eva, your life will be over as you know it. You'll be unemployed and broke. I will take everything you have. Say good-bye to your inheritance, your car, and your new, shiny condo you just bought. With my connections, I'll be sure you never get another job in this city again. I know you're not willing to give all of that up for some silly fuck fling. Keep her on the side, I don't give a shit, but you will be marrying Eva if it's the last thing you do."

I swallowed the giant lump forming in my throat, and a twisted smile crossed his face. He knew he was winning.

"In my opinion, you can find a much better side piece than that girl anyway. Don't take after your uncle and screw trash," he added.

I sprang out of my chair before I did something stupid, but I turned around to look at him before leaving. "You're a fucking asshole," I snapped bitterly.

"I'm sorry, what was that?" he yelled from behind me.

He heard my words. He was just waiting to see if I'd challenge him. I stomped the few steps I was away from his desk. My fist slammed onto it as I leaned my body across it to look him dead in the eyes.

"I said, you're a fucking asshole."

His mouth dropped open at my bravery.

"You sit behind this big fucking desk and judge people when you're ten times worse than they are. You're a fucking hypocrite."

I knew my ass was about to get fired, but he'd end up rehiring me later. If he fired his own kid, it would look bad on him.

He threw back his head in laughter. "It's about time you grew some big-boy balls. But you're still marrying Eva. Now, sit your ass down. We have more matters that are far more important than your love life."

My lips pressed together in a thin line, and I took a step back. "What could be more important than my love life to you? You seem to want to control it like I'm your own personal puppet you can pimp out for business deals."

"We need to talk about John," he said, ignoring my insult.

I sat back down and rested my elbows on the armrests. I was trying my hardest to cool off. "Have you heard from him?" I asked.

I hadn't heard anything from John since we told him about his wife. I was hoping they figured it out personally and wouldn't need our help anymore.

"He called me last night. His wife admitted to being the one who paid off Ivy. You were right. She wants a divorce. We're in the works of attempting to convince her to change her mind, but it's failing. Right now, our main goal is to get Ivy to go back on her word to the media. We also need to make sure news of her wanting a divorce doesn't leak. That will do nothing but tarnish his image more."

"Wow, what a shocker. You didn't hire me because you thought I'd be wrong," I fired back.

"You can't go off leads. I wasn't sure, and I had to have the hard facts before I could justify accusing someone of that." My dad was a meticulous thinker. He never opened his mouth unless he replayed it through his mind a few times.

"So, what does Gentry want us to do?"

"You need to get to that little whore he was sleeping with and talk her into going back on her word."

"She's gone," I replied. "She moved out all her shit from the place Gentry was paying for. We don't know where she went." I didn't want to admit I'd been slacking on my job of looking for her.

"Find her," he demanded.

I adjusted the cuffs on my shirt. "His wife paid her six million dollars. I'm guessing she was smart enough to make her sign an agreement that she wouldn't go back on her word. Even if we find her, trying to talk to her is pointless."

He pursed his lips. "Nothing I tell you to do is pointless. Find the damn girl. Get her to change her mind. Fuck her. Kill her. I don't give a shit, just fucking fix it!"

I didn't even bother asking him whether he was serious about killing her. I wasn't sure if my dad was capable of being a homicidal maniac, but there were rumors that he had people killed before.

"There's a price for everything," he'd say.

"On it," I growled, getting up from my chair for the second time with a headache emerging.

"Great. Now, get the hell out of my office," he said, letting me know our great father-son bonding time was finished.

I turned on my heels and left his office. Heading in the direction of the person I knew could help me out, I stormed into the room and headed his way.

"What's up?" I asked, patting Asher on the shoulder.

He was sitting in front of his computer, concentrating hard and punching buttons on the keyboard. I was probably the last person he wanted to talk to, but he was one of the few IT guys who knew about John's case. My dad would've flipped his shit if I had anyone else work on it.

He glanced over his shoulder, eyeing me suspiciously. "What the hell do you want?" he snarled, clearly still pissed off at me.

It wasn't my fault Gabby had chosen me over him. He needed to get over that shit.

"You going to act like this every time you see me now?" I questioned. "Because it's starting to get old, baby cousin."

"You trying to play Gabby is beginning to get old too," he fired back.

One of the biggest things I admired about Asher was his loyalty. When he gave you that, he was on your side all the way. He'd done the same thing with his mom through his parents' divorce. He stood by her side the entire time, not letting the family waver his options to stay and live with his dad. I knew he'd do the same for Gabby. He didn't live to impress the Douglas name, so he had nothing to lose with siding with her. His mom had money and would never cut him off.

I patted him on the back. "I'm going to do it, man. I'm just figuring out the best way to not fuck it up."

He shrugged my hand off of him. "You're lying," he accused. "There is no best way to tell her you're playing her."

"I'm not lying, and I'm not playing her. I just don't think it's a good idea to do it at work." I was lying. I was planning on telling her. I just didn't know when. I was waiting to see if I could figure out a way to get out of my marriage with Eva.

He twisted around in his chair, his gaze leveling up at me. "Do it by the weekend, or I'm doing it for you," he threatened, his eyebrows scrunching together.

I held out my hands in defeat, letting him think he'd won. "Fine. She'll know by this weekend, all right?"

"Come hell or high water, she'll know from one of us. Now, what the hell do you want?" he snapped, his jaw set.

Damn, he needed to get laid.

"We need to find Ivy," I answered, pointing to the computer.

"Why? We know who paid her."

"I guess we need to get her to go back on her statement."

He snorted. "Good luck with that."

I ruffled my hands over my face. "Tell me about it. I'm fucked."

"I'll get it," he said, waving me off.

Damn, maybe he wasn't the most forgiving person in our family.

I walked to my office to find Gabby sitting behind my desk in my chair. Her high-heel-covered feet were propped up on my desk, and she was talking animatedly to someone on her phone.

I leaned against the doorframe, my arm above my head, and watched her laugh at the person on the other line. I swallowed, terrified she was slipping out of my grasp, that our time was going to be over too soon. I didn't want to, but I knew deep down, it was going to happen if I didn't stop being so chickenshit and stand up to my parents. I was a grown man who was scared of Mommy and Daddy not being happy with his choices.

God, I was so fucking pathetic.

A grin spread over her red lips when she glanced up and saw me watching her. She bit the side of her lip. "Girl, I have to go. I'll call you when I get off," she said, sending me a tiny wave, and I threw my chin up at her. She hung up the call and tossed her phone down onto my desk. "How long have you been standing there and eavesdropping?"

I smirked, crossing my arms across my chest. "Why do you ask that?"

She shrugged, fiddling with a small necklace around her neck. "Just wondering."

I smirked. "Were you talking about me?"

She rolled her eyes and snorted. "A little full of yourself, Douglas."

I pulled my arm around my back to grab the door handle, taking a step forward, and the office door clicked shut behind me. "I think you were."

Her skinny hand reached forward, grabbing a pen, and she flung it my way. I laughed, not even bothering to move away because the pen smacked into the wall inches away from my stationary body.

"Baby, you've got terrible aim," I said, chuckling and pointing to the fallen pen.

She flipped her middle finger up.

"I hope it was good things you were saying about me."

She leaned back in the chair. "Eh, not really."

I raised a brow.

"My friends think I'm totally crazy," she added.

"They're not too far from the truth, babe."

She hopped out of my chair and moved around to the front of my desk. She was wearing a knee-length red skirt with a denim shirt tucked into it. A few of the top buttons were unbuttoned, giving me a mesmerizing view of her cleavage. I darted my tongue out, licking my lips while savoring the sexy image of her pulling herself up with her arms to sit on the edge of my desk.

"Not about me, idiot," she said, and my eyes darted down to her bare legs. "They think this"—she motioned between the two of us, breaking away my stare—"is going to end up in a massacre." She paused, the tip of her finger moving to the side of her mouth. "Well, Cora does. Daisy thinks you're hot." Her head tilted to the side. "I think she's right too."

I grabbed my tie with my knuckles, loosening the hold around my neck. "I think you should keep listening to Daisy," I suggested.

"No, I think Cora's right."

I took a few long strides, closing the small distance separating us. I halted at the corner of my desk she was parked on, dividing her legs and putting them to each side of my waist.

"Gabby," I muttered, grabbing her chin and bringing her lips to mine, "I'd never intentionally hurt you."

She pulled away from me, her eyebrows drawing together. "Intentionally? That sure gives me a lot of hope." She paused and rubbed the back of her neck. "Are we going to tell our parents about us or continue to keep hiding it?"

I closed my eyes, my head falling back in torture. I'd been avoiding that conversation with her as much as I'd been avoiding the one about me being engaged to another girl. "I'm pretty sure my dad already knows about us after our episode at lunch."

Her head flew up, almost whacking me in the chin. "Did he say something to you?"

I shook my head, rubbing the bottom of her chin. "No," I lied. "I'm going to talk to him about us soon. I don't want to lose you. I don't want to lose us over them."

She blew out a long breath, her eyes fluttering shut. She almost looked pained, like she knew our future was destined to end in heartbreak. She knew how my father was. We were both going one day at a time, dreading the impending day when we'd have to give each other up.

"You know they hate me. They're not going to let you be with me," she whispered.

I pressed my lips to her cheek before moving them above hers and kissing them lightly. "Look at me," I said, stroking her cheek as her eyes flashed down on me. "They're not the one dating you. I am. I don't care what anyone thinks about us being together. We're the only ones in this relationship. All that matters is that I want you, only you, and I think you're fucking amazing."

She leaned back, setting her palms down against my desk, and held herself up by leaning back on her elbows. "Why is that? Why do you like me?"

I moved closer into her. "You're unlike anyone I've ever met. You're beautiful, kind, and a complete pain in my ass." She gave me a look, and I chuckled. "Which I completely adore," I quickly added. "You make me laugh at times when I thought I'd never laugh. You make me feel better about myself, even when I do bad things. You've made this shitty job I have here actually enjoyable with your presence. You've made me defy my parents, which is something that no one has ever brought out in me. You bring me to my damn knees, baby, and I'm not letting that go. You're mine and only mine for the keeping."

She rose up, and her soft lips met mine. "I'm all yours if you're all mine," she whispered against them, sliding her tongue against the opening between my lips.

I opened my mouth, allowing our tongues to move slowly against each other.

"I think we can make that happen," I said, breaking away from her.

She gave me a bright smile before I leaned back in to explore her mouth, this one more heated. She tasted like coffee beans and vanilla as I swirled my tongue with hers and pulled her forward. Half her ass was off the desk while I gripped it in my hold, cupping it firmly. I ground my cock against her thighs and rubbed it directly on her core.

Her head dipped back, and she groaned out in pleasure. My hand went to her mouth to block out the noise. God, I loved how just feeling my arousal got her so worked up. My free hand reached down to the hem of her skirt, pulling it up her waist swiftly before pulling her ass up higher. I squeezed a supple ass cheek in my hand before slapping it gently.

"Holy shit," she yelped, biting her lower lip to keep from being loud and raking her nails down my chest.

I spread my fingers out, inching my hands up higher onto her thighs, and traced the edge of her panties as she shuddered underneath me. I breathed in harshly at the feel of her using both hands to squeeze my nipples. Our bodies were a tangled mess.

"Would you like it if I slid your panties over like this?" I asked, staring up at her and kicking my leg out to open her wider for me.

I pulled the tiny fabric over, so her clit was exposed. I could tell just by looking at her that she was soaked. She licked her lips as my thumb went to her clit, rubbing her tender spot in circles over and over. She moved into my touch, her hips rotating as I increased my speed.

"Would you like it if I fucked you against the edge of this desk? My dick pounding into you as I gripped your ass and masked your screams with my mouth?"

"God, yes," she moaned, freeing her hands from under my shirt to unbuckle my pants and pull them down.

My throbbing cock fell out with need, and I fought back the desire to immediately bury myself inside her. I sank a finger into her entrance, and her body bucked against my hand as I finger-fucked her hard. She bit the side of her lip, her face scrunching up as she tried to control her whimpers from growing too loud. She ground against my hand, her breathing growing more ragged with each thrust of my finger until her body grew limp and fell back against the desk.

"How are you so damn good at that?" she moaned, her chest moving in and out as her breathing heightened.

"I love making you feel good," I answered, and her hand reached down to stroke my cock a few times before rubbing it around her wet entrance.

I groaned, and she brought a finger to my mouth.

"We have to be quiet, remember? Or else we'll be fired," she said, giving me a sly grin.

My eyes shot down, watching her play with herself with my cock. I breathed hard, my fingers clenching the hard wood of the desk before quivering as she pulled me inside her. My strokes were slow and deep as I took my time, giving it to her.

"We'll figure everything out, baby. I promise," I whispered before thrusting into her one last time.

Chapter Twenty-Four

GABBY

SOFT MUSIC from the orchestra played at the front of the room as Atlanta's elite congregated throughout the large ballroom. I strolled down the wide stairway, arm in arm with Asher until we reached the bottom floor. Every woman was covered in an expensive ballgown and glittered in diamonds. Men were clad in their tuxedos, showing off their expensive watches and trophy wives.

Welcome to another typical Douglas party.

Douglas parties weren't fun parties. I liked to refer to them as one-up parties. Every person in the room wanted to one-up the other. It was all about who was the richest, the strongest, and the most powerful. Dalton's parents always went all out for these parties for that exact reason, making them formal affairs, which I absolutely despised. As much as I loved shopping, I hated wasting my money on expensive ballgowns I'd only wear once for two reasons. First being that I didn't frequent them that often. Second being that the only ones I did attend were theirs, and I'd be spit on if I wore the same dress twice. Lord forbid I re-wear clothes.

Caterers were scurrying around, their hands full with trays covered with food and glasses of champagne. I was definitely staying far away from anything that contained alcohol.

I'd always hated attending these damn parties, but I wasn't

dreading this one as much as usual. I had Asher on my side, and Dalton would be there too. I'd talked to him earlier on the phone. He had to go to dinner with his parents before the party, so we planned to just meet each other here. Plus, Cora had called me earlier and revealed she and Lane were coming with his parents. So, I was now going to be surrounded by my favorite people with me tonight.

Cora and I had gone dress shopping. I fell in love with the long red gown I was wearing the moment my eyes landed on it. The strapless bodice was form-fitting around my chest, contouring my body to my knees, then flaring out. It reminded me of a Jessica Rabbit look. I'd used my wide-barrel curling iron to curl the ends of my hair in thick spirals, applied minimal makeup with winged eyeliner, and finished my look with a bright red lip. I wasn't a big fan of overdoing my makeup, but I always had to have something on my lips. I felt naked without a good lipstick or gloss.

My mom and Kenneth had gotten home this morning, so they insisted Asher and I ride with them, which sucked. I wouldn't be able to ditch out early without them finding out. They usually allowed me to drive by myself, so I didn't have to hang with them the entire time.

"There's my baby brother," Wilson called out, approaching us with a drink in his hand. The man always had a drink in his hand.

That was my cue to get the hell out of Dodge. I tugged on Asher's arm and pulled him away from our parents before Wilson reached us. I hadn't seen him since the whole lunch from hell, and talking to him wasn't at the top of my priority list. I'd be one happy camper if I never had to talk to the jackass again.

"I hope you weren't wanting to talk to your uncle," I said, stopping us at the corner of the room.

Asher and I had made up after our fight. It took me a few days to convince him to forgive me, but when he did, I explained everything to him. He wasn't happy with my decision to not give him a chance, but he understood where I was coming from. I couldn't bear to lose our friendship.

"Hell no. He's been trying to get me to stay here the rest of the summer and keep working for him. Apparently, I'm a natural at finding blackmail on people," he answered, grabbing a tart from a tray and popping it into his mouth. He glanced around the room and shook his head. "God, I forgot how fucking excruciating these parties are, and I've only been here five minutes."

"You should stay all summer," I told him.

He was going back to Miami tomorrow, and I didn't want him to leave me. I was going to miss him. We'd grown closer the few weeks he'd been here, and I hated seeing him leave. He was Team Gabby, and I loved having someone on my side.

"I would if I could, babe, but I can't miss team conditioning." Asher played football for the Miami University Hurricanes, and summer practices were getting ready to start.

"I think I'm going to sneak into your suitcase and come with you," I said, leaning into his side.

He tucked me under his arm. "I have no problem with that. You know you're welcome to come visit me anytime."

"I plan on it," I said, smiling and grabbing a bottle of water. "I'm definitely going to come watch you kick some gridiron ass."

He grinned, looking down at me. "You'd better."

"What's happening, hot stuff?" Cora yelled, bouncing on her heels and coming our way.

We'd just watched *Sixteen Candles* the other day, and she'd greeted me like that every day since.

"I knew you'd look like a hot sex kitten in that dress. God, I wish I had your curves, you lucky thing." She smiled, giving me a giant hug.

"You're perfect, baby," Lane said, coming up from behind her and wrapping his arms around her torso.

Cora was wearing a green dress with a slit up her thigh that only a size zero could pull off. Which I definitely wasn't.

"I seriously love that color on you," I said, admiring her dress.

"Why, thank you, Gabby," Lane replied. "I always knew I looked fierce in black." He modeled a pose in his black tux, and Cora smacked his stomach.

"Quit stealing my compliments," she huffed, giving him a bright smile.

"You guys remember Asher?" I asked, pointing to my stepbrother, watching our interaction beside me.

He'd lived in Atlanta until the divorce his freshman year, so he still knew people around there.

"Hell yeah. I used to kick your ass in football on the playground," Lane said, chuckling.

"Yeah, right, man. You know I got past your sucky-ass defense every time. Plus, who's the only guy who made varsity his freshman year?" Asher argued back.

"Dude, that's only because you had fucking frog legs. This dude would jump over kids like that damn leapfrog game."

"Seriously?" Cora broke in their argument. "Both of you were deformed pubescent boys in middle school."

"Eh, I guess you got a point there," Asher said, pulling Lane in for one of those side-hug things guys did.

Lane grabbed a glass of champagne for him and Cora before looking over at me. "I would've grabbed you one, but we all know you don't make the wisest decisions when you have alcohol flowing through your system," he said, doing a cheers motion before chugging the entire contents. "Wouldn't want history to repeat itself, would we?"

I rammed my heel into his foot, and he jumped.

"Funny, asshole. Do you want to be wearing your next glass?" I asked.

He gave me a side hug. "You know I love you, Gabs." He stopped and pointed at me. "Actually, I have to love you, or Cora will dump my ass. But you're like the little sister I enjoy tormenting."

I slapped his side, and he moved away from me to wrap his arms around Cora's shoulders.

"There's my grandparents, babe. We'd better go say hi. You kids stay out of trouble." He pointed back and forth between Asher and me before saluting and walking away with Cora.

"Do you ever miss it here?" I asked Asher, curious.

"Not really. My mom won't admit it, but I know she was miserable with my dad. Plus, she's a hell of a lot cooler in Miami. She doesn't have the constant anxiety of having the Douglas approval over everything she does. These people will exhaust the fuck out of you. They judge you on your hair, your clothes, fucking everything," he answered.

"Oh, I know," I muttered.

They'd done the same thing to me since the first time I met them. I eventually learned to deal with it, but my mom was still dying for their acceptance. Deep down, I knew she was scared that if they didn't accept her, Kenneth would end up leaving her.

"So, no, I really don't miss it. I enjoy visiting you, my dad, and my old friends, but that's really it," he added before grinning. "Plus, girls wear a lot less clothes in Miami. They go grocery shopping in their bikinis."

I rolled my eyes. "Of course that would be your favorite part."

"I didn't say it was my favorite, but it's definitely high on my list."

I was glad Asher got away from here before he ended up like them. He was such a better person.

An older woman I recognized as Kenneth's sister came up and began talking to Asher, taking his attention away from me. I glanced around the room and spotted my mom standing alone in the corner. I hated when Kenneth left her at these parties. I knew he didn't do it purposely. He didn't realize my mom didn't have any friends here.

I headed toward her, dodging the group of bodies conversing.

"Have you shanked a bitch yet?" I joked, coming up from behind her, and she jumped.

"Gabby," she whispered, holding up her hand to her chest. "If they hear you, they'll hate us."

She looked great for her age. Her auburn hair was the same color as mine but cut to her shoulders. Even for being in her late thirties, her face was wrinkle-free and not because of plastic surgery. She had pure, natural beauty, and I hoped to God I inherited that from her.

I smiled warmly at her and shrugged. "Eh, I think we're pretty used to that."

Her voice dropped, and she pursed her pink-colored lips. "Just because I'm used to it doesn't mean it makes it any better. I wish they'd actually give me a chance."

She was getting agitated, and I immediately knew someone must've already said something to her. I hated when they made her feel this way. She deserved so much better.

I grabbed her hand. "Mom, half of these people are losers. If they're going to sit around and judge someone before they even know them, they're losers. They're the ones missing out on getting to know what a wonderful, caring person you are."

It pissed me off that they treated my mom like that. She'd spent her entire life trying to take care of the two of us with what little she had.

"At least Wilson kept his mouth shut around me, which is surprising. It's that damn wife of his. Oh, and his son. What's his name?"

"Dalton?" I questioned.

"Dalton," she repeated. "Yeah, that one. He came over and said hello. He told me you two were working together, and you were doing a great job. See, I told you you'd do great there."

My heart fluttered at Dalton talking to my mom. I knew his family wouldn't be too happy about it, but he was doing it for me. He was showing me that he'd never said anything bad about my mom and he had nothing against her.

"Hey, honey, I want you to meet someone."

We both twisted around to find Kenneth with John standing next to him.

Oh, great, one more asshole to add to the party list.

John's face paled when his eyes hit my mom, like he'd just seen a ghost. I looked away from him and back over to my mom, who pretty much had the same expression on her face. What the hell? My stomach churned. I was certain my mom was added to John's list of mistresses.

"Hi, John," my mom said finally after taking a moment to find her words and avoiding looking at him. "I mean, Governor Gentry," she quickly corrected.

John let out an awkward laugh. "Nonsense. Call me John. We don't need formalities, Shelia."

"Do you two know each other?" Kenneth asked, pulling my mom into his side and kissing her on the lips.

"We went to high school together," my mom answered, playing with her hands.

Kenneth smiled. "Wow, what a small world. You never told me that, honey." He was either clueless to the obvious tension or was choosing to ignore it.

"Small world indeed," John agreed. "I'm sure she didn't find it necessary to say she knew little ol' me." He looked around her, straight at me. "Is Gabrielle your daughter?" He looked back and forth between us a few times, like he was taking in the similarities between my mom and me.

My mom nodded slowly. "She is."

John's eyes narrowed. "Huh. I had no idea. She's a beautiful girl. I guess she gets that from her mother."

Okay, it is now getting weirder. I couldn't believe the scumbag was hitting on my mom in front of her husband.

My mom grabbed Kenneth's hand. "Thank you," she said uncomfortably, still avoiding eye contact.

"I'm going to go find Cora or the bathroom or something," I said, my voice trailing off as I eyed the awkward scene in front of me. I moved around my mom's body, resisting the urge to ram my knee in John's balls when I made my way around his penetrating stare.

I jumped as I felt warm hands wrap around my body before I made it to the restroom to check my makeup.

"You look so damn sexy right now," the husky voice breathed into my ear. "Did you save me a dance?"

I whipped around, still in his arms, and his hand moved down to cup my ass as he leaned me into the wall.

I looked up at him. He was dressed like all the other men in the room, wearing a black tuxedo with a bow tie around his neck, but none of those other men stood out like he did to me. None of them made butterflies swoop around my stomach at the sight of them, fluttering their wings and making me feel good. None of them made me want to rip their clothes off and have them take me against the wall either.

"You don't look so bad yourself, handsome," I said, pointing my finger into his chest before running my hands down. "Are you sure you're allowed to dance with the daughter of the home-wrecker?"

"Do you think I really give a shit?"

I grinned, loving his response. He was becoming my protector, the one thing I'd been longing for my entire life.

"If any of them say shit to you, I'll set them straight. No one is going to talk bad about my girl and get away with it."

"Then, you'll probably have to set the entire room straight," I joked.

No one talked to me at these functions. They all knew who my mom and I were from the gossip mill.

"Always my smart-ass princess."

He grabbed my hand resting on his chest and kissed it before engulfing it in his to drag me away from the corner. I groaned in nervousness. Staying in that corner with him sounded like a much better time than going out there with everyone else. I stayed by his side as we walked back into the ballroom that was now growing busier. Things were about to get interesting.

We were only inches away from the dance floor when Wilson's voice called out Dalton's name. I froze in my tracks. I was for sure he noticed our connected hands. Dalton whipped around, and his parents were directly behind us, like they'd been on our trail the entire time.

"I've been looking around for you, son. Why didn't you greet me when you arrived?" he asked.

"I had things to take care of," Dalton answered.

He glanced down at our connected hands. "I see. Dancing with my intern was one of them?"

I winced at the low blow, but I had a feeling that was just the warm-up. The full fight show was coming soon. I just knew it.

"Cut that shit, Dad. Don't disrespect her like that."

"Gabby, honey, that dress is just darling," Victoria, Dalton's mom, said, giving me a mocking smile.

I wanted to rip that smile off her face and shove it up her ass for whatever snide comment she'd said to my mom.

"Thank you. Yours is very lovely as well," I complimented.

She was wearing a long-sleeved black gown, and her neck was dripping in so many diamonds that I was close to going blind. She was just asking for someone to rob her.

"And there's my other son!" she shrieked, clapping her hands together as Leo came strolling our way.

Thank God. Saved by the sibling.

I didn't know Leo that well, but I knew he and Dalton were like polar opposites. Dalton was the fun party guy, and Leo was the serious family guy. The only features they shared were physical. Oh, and Leo wasn't a total asshole to me either, so I guessed the Gabby-hating gene didn't reproduce in everyone. Leo gave his mother a kiss before saying hello to everyone.

Dalton had tucked me into his side, his hand resting on the small of my back as his family began to banter back and forth about mergers. I stood there silently, begging for the conversation to be over so I could scurry away.

"And there's my future daughter-in-law," Wilson shouted, waving to a short, blonde-haired woman.

She smiled, coming our way, and I took in the bright blue dress she was wearing, paired with a gold pair of chained heels I desperately wanted to snatch off her feet and stick in my closet.

Huh? Leo must've gotten a divorce.

"Your new wife is gorgeous," I said, not completely catching on to anything happening around me.

Leo looked over at me, then immediately turned to Dalton, giving him a tight glare. The woman stopped to give Dalton's parents a hug before kissing him directly on the lips. His entire body went still, and the glass of water in my hand fell, shattering across the floor without me even realizing what was happening. It was like all the butterflies swarming in my stomach lost all their air and died.

I jumped. "I'm so sorry," I rushed out, leaning down to pick up the broken shards, but Dalton stopped me. As much as I wanted to shove him away and tell him to never put his hands on me again, I couldn't make a scene.

"Gabby, dear, it's all right," Wilson said, grinning. "We're all a bit clumsy at times."

I gave him a weak smile and wiped my wet hands down my dress.

"I don't believe you two have been introduced," he added smugly. "This is Eva. She's Dalton's fiancée."

I forced a smile on my lips, begging myself to hold back the tears. I wouldn't cry in front of them. I wouldn't allow them to see they'd hurt me. Karma had finished sharpening her nails and her drink, and she was now ready to ruin me.

"Hi," I choked out. "His uncle is my stepdad."

She gave me a heartfelt smile. "It's nice to meet you." She was nice, and I felt bad for hating her, but I couldn't help it. It was like she was an added pawn in the game to break my heart. "You two have been working together too, right?"

I nodded.

Had he told her about me? Did he call her late at night, complaining about his day while they planned their future together? Or was she in on the scam? Did they want Dalton to date me, so I'd get heartbroken and quit working at Douglas PR?

A million thoughts were running through my packed mind, causing me to panic. Without saying another word, I dashed away from them, holding my dress up while I searched for somewhere to hide.

Chapter Twenty-Five

DALTON

MY JAW CLENCHED as I held my anger back. I wanted to fucking kill him and wring his neck in front of his entire audience he was trying to impress. I knew the only reason he'd invited Eva behind my damn back was so he could catch me off guard. I fell into his mousetrap just like he'd wanted to. He didn't give a shit if he embarrassed Gabby, who was innocent in everything. That was most likely his strongest intention. He knew if she found out about Eva, she'd probably dump my ass. Her mom might sleep with married men, but my dad knew how to read people, and I knew he didn't think Gabby was the same way.

I rushed after Gabby's fleeing body, following her into an empty room and slamming the door shut behind us.

"Baby," I choked out, hesitantly taking steps closer to her as my heart raced inside my chest.

I had no idea how I was going to fix it. I reached for her arm, but she whipped around to face me. I winced at the sudden sting on the side of my cheek.

Yeah, she was fucking pissed.

"I deserved that," I said, rubbing my jaw with my fingers and moving it around.

"Damn straight you did," she hissed, her voice breaking in the end. She was trying to hold back her tears. I could tell. Gabby was too strong to let me see her cry over my deception. "You're getting married!" she screamed, shoving her palms against my chest to push me away from her. "Did you really think I wasn't going to find out? Really?"

I stumbled back as she pushed against my chest again before grabbing her arms to stop her. "It's not like that," I croaked out. "I don't want to marry her."

She bit back a laugh. "Then, why in the hell are you doing it, huh?"

"My parents set it up years ago. I have no choice."

She pulled her arm out of my grasp. "You're a grown man, Dalton. I'm pretty sure you have the same rights as anyone else to tell your parents you don't want to do something!" She shook her head at me. "Jesus, grow some damn balls and stand up to your dad!"

I held out my arms, ignoring her insult even though it was true. I knew I should tell my dad to go to hell, but I feared losing everything.

"Can we please just figure this out? I don't want to lose you," I begged, running my hands over my face roughly, wanting to pull the skin off to mask the anger.

She sliced her hands through the air and shook her head. "I won't be the other woman. I can't believe you'd even ask me that after everything I've told you."

I clenched my fist, fighting back the urge to shove it through the fucking wall. "Goddammit, Gabby! I'm not asking you to do that!" I couldn't lose her. I'd be damned if I lost her because of my parents' games.

"Then, what do you want from me?" she challenged, swiping fallen hair away from her puffy face.

"Fuck!" I dragged my hands through my hair and pulled at the roots. "I don't know. I don't want to lose you."

Her eyes went dead cold. "You get married, you lose me."

My knees buckled. *"You lose me."*

"Can't we find a way to work this out?"

She pursed her lips, her face laced with disgust. "Absolutely not."

I knew she wasn't going to budge. Gabby had a will of fucking steel.

"Do you love me?" I asked desperately.

I already knew the answer. She did. Maybe if she heard herself say those three words, it would change her mind. She'd realize she wanted to be with me, and we'd figure it out together.

"Do you love me?" she fired back, her eyes fighting to blink away the impending tears.

"You know I fucking do! You know I love you!"

I'd never actually said those three words to her or any other girl, but I knew I did. You figured out how strong your feelings were for someone real quick when they were walking out the door to leave your ass. I'd never felt anything like this. I loved her, and now that I finally experienced what that word truly meant, it was for a girl I couldn't have. She was getting ripped away from me, and there was nothing I could do to stop it without losing everything I'd worked my ass off for.

"Then, prove it," she said, her tiny body walking around mine to leave, but my arm dashed out, my hand grabbing her arm to stop her.

Proving how much I loved her would mean risking my entire future. Could I really give up everything for the girl I was falling in love with? I knew if I broke off my engagement with Eva, my dad would never let me go back on it. If I chose Gabby over her, everything would change.

"Anything, baby," I said, my head spinning. I grabbed her hand and clutched it in mine, never wanting to let it go. "I can do anything but that."

The tears finally broke through as I spotted one sliding down her cheek. I swiped it away with my thumb, and she flinched at my touch.

She leveled her gaze on me, and her voice turned hard. "I'm only going to say this one more time. I will never—and I mean, never—be the other woman," she said, snatching her hand out of mine and taking a step back. It was like she'd taken away my entire world with that one action. "Go marry Eva and have yourself a happy little life because I won't be in it."

"I'll never be happy if you're not in my life," I rasped out, reaching for her, but she was too far away.

"You also won't be happy without power, money, and whatever the hell else makes your guys' world go round."

I decided the best attempt would be to grab her again, but she recoiled at my touch. Turning around, she walked toward the door. Her hand hit the doorknob, and she looked over her shoulder at me.

"Go be with your fiancée. I'll be sure to send you a nice wedding gift."

The door creaked open, and she disappeared.

I picked up a chair beside me and threw it against the wall while my heart kept telling me I needed to go after her. I needed to make this right. But my brain was telling me to stay put.

What if Gabby left me and I was left with nothing? No money, no family, nothing because I'd been a fool who risked it all for love. I picked up the chair again and kicked it this time. I should've never fucking lied to her. The chair got thrown again. I should've just told her everything in the beginning, but I was too afraid. I was a pussy. That one lie cost me everything.

"Okay, killer, let's calm down," a recognizable voice said behind me, and I turned around. Eva grinned. "I like her. She's a little fire-cracker. No wonder your parents hate her."

Fuck, I'd forgotten there were two entrances into that room. I hoped no one else had heard our fight.

"You like her enough to convince her to be my mistress?" I asked, hopeful, even though I knew neither of them would go for that.

Eva snorted. "Hell no. We made a pact that when we got married, we'd be married. No other people. Plus, even if I did, I doubt she'd even go along with it. That girl is headstrong as hell. I'm almost jealous."

I grabbed the chair I'd been assaulting, flipped it upright, and sat down. "You can be that way too, you know."

She grabbed another chair and positioned it across from me before plopping down on it. "So can you. But you know what the sad thing is?"

"What?" I asked.

"I have nothing to lose with this circus they're calling a marriage. I don't have someone who loves me like she does you. You actually have that. You have someone who makes you happy, but you turned your back on her to make your parents happy. I promise you'll regret that decision for the rest of your life." She shook her head. "And now, I'm going to have to deal with it," she grumbled, clearly unhappy.

I huffed and collapsed my head between my legs. "I'd lose a lot more than just their happiness, and you fucking know it."

She leaned forward and grabbed my jaw with her manicured hands, bringing my head back up to look at her. "And look what you're losing if you go through with it. If you forgot already, she just ran out the door a few minutes ago in tears."

"I didn't fucking forget."

Eva was right. I would never forget this night. Gabby's broken face would haunt me forever. Letting her go would be my biggest regret.

"Then, go get her," she said, slapping my side and gesturing to the door Gabby had run out of. "Before it's too late."

"You think if that was an option, I wouldn't fucking do it? You think if I had the opportunity to snatch that damn ring off your finger and put it on hers, I wouldn't?"

Eva dragged the ring off her bony finger and handed it over. "Then, go do it."

I looked at her, baffled.

"If you don't go find her and we go through with this marriage, how are you going to feel when you see her with someone else? Someone who took your chance because you couldn't man up? How are you going to feel when she's giving some other guy the attention she gave you? She's smiling at his jokes and laughing. She won't even notice you because you ruined her. That will burn your heart when you realize you're not the person making her happy anymore. You won't be that guy for her again if you don't go. So, here, take this damn thing and go before it's too late."

I scoffed. "You'd love that, wouldn't you?"

Our engagement would be broken, but she wouldn't be the one to blame. She'd still get everything she wanted.

She shrugged. "To be honest, I wouldn't mind marrying you. Trust me, my parents could have stuck me with someone much worse than you. I'm risking something by giving you this back. They may stick me with some weirdo creep. I'm doing this because we're friends, and I care about you."

Chapter Twenty-Six

GABBY

MY HEART THUMPED against my chest as I charged out of the room and away from him. Trying my best to control my breathing, I searched through my clutch for my phone as I headed toward the exit, dodging bodies left and right.

Screw this party.

Screw these people.

I scrolled down to Cora's name and smacked my finger against it until I heard ringing come from the other end of the line. It continued to ring until I got her voice mail.

I scrolled down a few more names and dialed Lane's number. Voice mail again. I'd just begun dialing the number for a cab when Lane's smiling mug popped up on my screen with an incoming call.

Thank God.

"Hello," I answered, trying to control my shaky voice as I held the phone up to my ear.

"Hey. I saw you called. Where you at?" he asked. I could hear the commotion of the party around him.

"Outside. Can you please take me home?" That moment is when my voice broke. I wasn't sure if it was because I was talking to Lane or I'd reached my limit. The tears came trickling down, and I sniffled. I'd let my guard down and gotten betrayed. I was such a fool for thinking it could've been different, for thinking *he* could've been different.

"Meet me at the front door," he said quickly.

The line went dead. I wobbled over to the corner in my heels, rubbing my hands over my face in an attempt to stop the tears, and fell down onto a bench. I bent down and ripped my shoes off my feet. I was sure if anyone saw me wandering around barefoot with my heels in my hands, they'd be horrified, but I didn't give a shit. I was beyond the point where I cared any longer. The moment they began messing with my heart was the moment I realized all of them were dead to me.

"Gabby!" I heard Cora's screechy voice yell, and I pulled myself up from the bench while gathering my clutch and shoes in my hands. "What the hell happened?" she shrieked when I turned the corner and ran into them.

Her almond-shaped eyes narrowed when she took in my crying face, unruly hair, and bare feet. She grabbed my elbow, pulling me in for a hug, and I shook my head in response. I wrapped my arms around her tighter, feeling defeated as I bawled into my best friend's arms. I wasn't ready to talk about it yet. She rubbed my back in understanding. I was an idiot. I'd pissed off Lady Karma, and now, the bitch was coming back with full vengeance.

"I gave the ticket to the valet, and they're getting the car for us. Whose ass do I need to kick?" I overheard Lane's loud voice say behind Cora.

I let out a light giggle at Lane's protectiveness. "No one. I just want to leave," I said, pulling away from Cora and swiping a few more tears off my cheeks.

Cora wrapped her elbow around mine. "I don't blame you, babe," she said. "This party blows."

The valet brought up Lane's car to the front door, and my two friends settled my weeping body into the back of his Escalade.

The car ride was silent. I couldn't help myself from checking my phone every thirty seconds. Maybe, just maybe, if he called, it would change things. If he called and apologized, telling me he wanted to be with me, I could forgive him. But as the minutes trickled by, my patience began to fade. By the time we reached Cora's house, it was gone.

I couldn't go home. I didn't want to face any of the questions about leaving early from my mom or Asher. I'd texted them, letting them know I was staying the night with Cora before shutting my phone off. The only people I cared to hear from were with me. Cora had called Daisy and told her she needed to get her ass to her house because we were having an emergency girls' night.

I stripped out of my dress, and another round of tears erupted. I wished I couldn't feel a damn thing. I wasn't normally a crier. I was always the girl who held my emotions in, never letting anyone know I could be hurt. My body felt cold as I threw on a pair of pajama shorts and a tank, shivering as I ran my hands down my arms and studied the dress I threw down. As much as I'd loved that dress, it was never going to get worn again. It was tainted and had entirely too many bad memories.

I scrubbed the makeup off my swollen face, having to spend extra time to get off the mascara streaks running down my sore cheeks. My eyes were red, and I knew they'd have dark circles around them by the time I woke up in the morning. I ran trembling fingers down the curls I'd spent too much time on getting ready. I'd wanted everything to be perfect for me, but it ended up being hell.

I flicked the light switch to Cora's bathroom off and walked into her bedroom, avoiding everyone's stares. I didn't want their pity. I collapsed onto her king-size bed and drew my limbs in close to my body to create my own Gabby wall.

"Whose ass do I need to kick?" Keegan asked, his lips pressed flat.

I gave him a weak smile. "No one who matters," I grumbled.

I hated saying that Dalton didn't matter, but it was the truth. I didn't matter enough for him to be honest with me. I didn't matter enough for him to stick up for me when his dad tried to humiliate me in front of a room full of people. I didn't matter enough for him to choose me over some stupid business deal. Therefore, he no longer mattered to me.

Good-bye, Dalton. Catch ya on the flip side, motherfucker.

He laughed. "If you change your mind, let me know."

I squinted my wet eyes over to him. He was sitting on the edge of the bed next to Daisy. I could tell they'd been lying around his house because they were both wearing their pajamas. Keegan's dark hair was disheveled, and Daisy's was pulled back at the top of her head. She was wearing an overly large sweatshirt that I knew Keegan was the owner of; it practically swallowed her tiny frame.

He leaned down and kissed Daisy on the forehead. "Make your friend feel better, baby," he said, rubbing her shoulders.

She smiled, tilting her head up to kiss him.

"If you two kiss and start acting all lovey, I swear on everything I own, I will kill you all," I threatened, stopping their public display of affection. Shoot me now. I was the love-hater, surrounded by lovesick idiots.

Keegan pulled away from Daisy and held his hands up in surrender. "My bad, girl." He leaned over the bed and ruffled his hands through my hair before standing up. "I just want to throw this out there. Guys do stupid shit sometimes. Ask Daisy. I fuck up all the time."

Daisy nodded in agreement. "He does."

"I'm an idiot," Keegan continued. "Sometimes, you have to understand that's what we are—fucking idiots. We're dumb as fuck, and you have to forgive us sometimes."

Forgiveness wasn't a word that existed in my book. I'd given Dalton an hour to call me before shutting my phone off. My forgiveness had a timeline, or it was cut out for good. I picked up one of Cora's fuzzy pink pillows and threw it at him, his head bobbing to the side as it smacked him in the face.

He grinned. "Shit, okay, never mind. Hate the prick. We will all hate his sorry ass. Just be nice to me because you get seriously scary when you're pissed off. It's like you get taken over by demons."

I flipped him off and sagged against the headboard.

Daisy pointed toward her boyfriend. "See, I tamed my bad boy," she told me.

My head whipped up to look at all of them. "My bad boy forgot to mention the fact that he was engaged," I fired back, finally clueing them in.

"Oh fuck," came out of Lane's mouth at the same time, "Dumbass," came from Keegan.

It was nice to know they were on my side. I assumed it was mainly because they wanted to keep getting laid by their girlfriends, but I'd take it. The more people on my side, the better.

Keegan tossed the pillow I threw back on the bed. "I think this one is out of my league. I'll let you ladies handle this," he said. "Let us know if you need any manly advice; otherwise, we'll be in the basement, playing video games."

Lane followed him out of the bedroom and shut the door.

"How the hell did you not know he was getting married?" Daisy questioned as soon as the room cleared. "Don't you have to attend all of their holiday dinners and parties? How could you have not known about her?"

I slouched back against the headboard. "He never mentioned it, and she's never been around that I know of. Plus, it's arranged or something," I answered. I believed Dalton when he said that because I'd overheard Wilson talking about how he'd arranged Leo's marriage for a business agreement.

Daisy scrunched up her face. "What, are we in the fifteenth century? People actually still arrange marriages?"

"They do it as business agreements sometimes. Your kid marries mine, and I'll merge our companies, or we'll always do our business with you. Stupid shit like that," Cora explained for me. "It's fucked up."

"You rich people are seriously weird," Daisy replied.

She came from a small town. Her mom was a homemaker, and her dad was a cop. It took her a while, just like me, to get used to the extravagant lifestyles the people around us had.

I held out my hand in protest. "I'm not rich. I'm only guilty by association."

I knew Kenneth wasn't going to support me forever, and I'd eventually be out on my own. I was almost certain I wouldn't have millions lying around to spend when that time came either. Unlike the majority of the kids I knew, I wasn't receiving some large inheritance.

We both looked over at Cora, and she shook her head.

"Nuh-uh, I'm not rich either. My parents are." She pointed to herself. "This girl lives on a limited allowance, so let's not put me into that category, please and thank you. Plus, we're not douchebag rich. We're cool rich, as in my parents would never pimp me out for a business deal. Big difference," she added, her face serious.

"So, what are you going to do?" Daisy asked.

I sighed. "I really have no idea."

"I'll tell you what she's going to do. She's going to march into that asshole's office, kick him in the balls, and then quit the ridiculous job," Cora proclaimed.

"I can't quit my job," I replied.

There were two reasons I wasn't going to quit even though my brain pleaded with me to. The first one was that I wasn't a quitter. The second was that I knew that was what they wanted. They wanted to see me weak. That wasn't happening. I'd look Wilson in his ugly face every day at that office before I'd let him know he broke me down.

"Boo, you suck," Cora groaned. "We need more time together. But whatever you do, don't cave to that jackass."

"He was so charming though," Daisy said.

"Exactly. You don't trust guys who are charming. A boy who's charming and knows the right things to say means he's had practice, and you don't want someone who's had a lot of practice with other girls. You want to be a new experience."

"What if he leaves her?" Daisy asked. "What if he decides not to get married?" She was still in what I liked to refer to as the honeymoon stage.

"Either way, he lied to me and then let me find out in front of a crowded room of people I can't stand." I had a small feeling in the back of my head that made me wonder if the entire thing was planned to get me out of there. I couldn't see Dalton doing that, but then again, I didn't see him smashing my heart into a million pieces three hours ago either. "He should've been up front with me. Then, when I confronted him, he basically asked me to be his mistress." I pursed my lips and clinched a pillow into my hand. "I am no one's mistress."

Cora scooted closer and wrapped her arms around me. She knew how sensitive that topic was for me. "He's a jackass," she said, rubbing my back. "You deserve someone better, girl. You deserve someone who will be open and honest with you. I want you to find happiness so bad —you have no idea."

The tears started, and I shook my head. "That will never happen." I sniffled.

"Get rid of that curse bullshit, seriously. You've had a couple fails at love, but so has everyone else," Cora responded. "I mean, look at Daisy. She was in love, and her boyfriend got murdered."

Daisy smacked her arm. "Uh, hello! Sensitive topic."

Cora tapped her thigh. "Sorry, girl, but I had to make a point. If you can get past the death of a boyfriend, Gabby can get past this asshole."

She gave her a smile but groaned at the same time. "Fine, I guess I'll be made into an example."

"Promise me you won't give up, Gabs. I will find you the perfect guy if it's the last damn thing I do," Cora added.

"I probably need to hand over my rights to pick a boyfriend. I obviously don't know what the fuck I'm doing," I told them.

Daisy grabbed my hand in hers and squeezed it. "What doesn't kill you makes you stronger, babe."

I scoffed. "What doesn't kill you fucks you up mentally." I leaned back against the headboard and moaned. I was done talking about my disastrous love life. "I need to get my mind on something else."

Cora jumped up from her bed and smiled brightly. "Guess what I've got recorded?"

"Tell me it's not *True Blood*," I muttered.

"You let him ruin it for you, didn't you?" Cora accused, raising a brow. "You know better than that! You do not share shows unless it's turned serious."

"It's his fault!" I said, throwing my hands down on the bed. Every time I watched *True Blood* now, I'd be reminded of the philandering jackass who played me.

"I'll give you time, but I know you'll cave eventually," Cora said, flipping through the DVR menu. "Good thing for you, we've got plenty of other options. I'm thinking we need some *John Tucker Must Die*."

"Oh yeah, I think that's exactly what we need," I replied, grabbing a pillow and getting comfortable.

I knew the day would come when my heart would get broken. I just wasn't expecting it to hurt so damn bad.

DALTON

"I **TOLD** you this shit would blow back in your face, dumbass."

I winced at the loud voice. Sunlight beamed through my bedroom window when my curtains were pulled open. I groaned, covering my eyes with my arm. My head felt like it was full of scotch and anger, which couldn't be any more correct for what I'd been going through last night—glasses of scotch and lashes of anger.

"Go fuck yourself," I growled, grabbing the pillow underneath my head and shoving it over my face. I needed more time to soak in my self-pity before discussing my fuckup with him. "And while you're at it, get the hell out of my house."

Leo chuckled. God, was his laugh always that damn annoying? I instantly regretted giving him a key.

"It's hard for me to fuck myself and walk at the same time, asshole. I was never that great at multitasking," he fired back.

"Practice makes perfect," I moaned against the pillow. My head felt like an overused kickball.

"Don't get pissed at me because you got your ass busted. I warned you. You were too fucking delusional, trying to play two girls, to know you were about to get burned."

"I don't need to hear *I told you so.*"

I'd slept with Gabby's name on my lips, hoping I'd wake up in the morning and everything would have all been one big nightmare. Gabby hadn't left my lying ass, and my dad didn't deliberately fuck me over. But it wasn't. The nightmare was my real fucking life.

"You should've warned me Eva was coming."

If Eva never showed, none of that shit would've happened. Instead of Leo being the first goddamn face I saw in the morning, it would've been Gabby's.

"I didn't know your fiancée was coming, or I would've given you a heads-up while you were hanging out with your girlfriend."

"Shut the curtains and get the fuck out!"

My stomach grumbled. Fuck, I shouldn't have drunk that much. When I realized Gabby was done with my lying ass, I drank myself into oblivion. I wasn't sure how I landed in my own bed, but the only person I knew who would drag my sloppy ass to bed was my brother. He was always there to save my ass. He was also always there to be the one to say *I told you so.*

He slapped his palm down on my bed. "No can do, brother. You have to get your ass up. It's Claire's birthday, and you promised her you'd be there."

Fuck. The last thing my head needed was little runts running around, screaming, and being surrounded by my family.

"Tell Claire I'll take her wherever she wants to go for her birthday next weekend." I paused. "Tell her I'll take her shopping."

My baby niece was only turning seven, but the girl already had a handbag collection to make a grown woman jealous. She'd take me up on that offer and clean out my wallet while doing it.

"She doesn't want to do something next weekend. She wants you at her party. So, you'll be there."

"Today's obviously not a good day."

"Look, drunk ass, you knew this shit was bound to happen. I told you so, but you never seem to listen to anyone. Now, you made a commitment to my daughter, and she's expecting you. Get your ass in the shower, or I'm going to start my own rock concert in here with your pots and pans."

That was the one thing about Leo—his kids were his everything. You disappointed his kids, and he'd kick your ass.

I threw the pillow off my face and squinted his way. "Fine, but you need to tell Dad not to say shit to me."

"I'll talk to him," he assured, blinking.

It was nine in the morning, and my brother looked like he'd been up for hours, which didn't surprise me. He was wearing a pair of jeans and a black button-down dress shirt. He'd never go all casual. The jeans were the best you'd get. I was certain he was also the one who'd done all the planning for Claire's party while Kelly didn't do shit.

"Be there at one," he reminded, slapping my leg before walking toward the doorway and then turning around. "And you got her something, right?"

"Purse." I had Gabby pick out a birthday present for Claire.

He snapped his fingers. "Good job, baby brother."

When I heard the front door shut, I stumbled out of bed and fell down on the floor. Jesus, was I still drunk? I practically crawled to my bathroom, lifted up to turn the shower on, and hopped in when the water was still cold. I deserved the torture.

I shivered as the cold water began to warm up and hit my body in splatters. I lifted my head up, letting the water pour straight down onto my face as I let my regrets sink in.

I slapped my hands against the crisp tiled wall, my head falling limp, and internally screamed at myself. I was questioning everything I thought I wanted in life. The perfect job, money, and to make my dad proud of me. None of that shit mattered without Gabby. What I'd thought I wanted turned out to be the thing that ruined me.

After showering, I dried off my body and grabbed my phone, scrolling through the Outgoing Calls list. I'd called Gabby twenty-one times. I thought I'd officially become a stalker when I hit the double digits. I tapped my finger against the screen, calling her again.

I was a dumbass. What made me think she was going to answer my calls when I couldn't even go after her? My call went straight to voice mail. She probably blocked me for my excessive calling.

* * *

Claire's birthday party was being thrown in the backyard at my brother's house. I walked into a swarm of balloons, screaming children, and castle jump houses. I dodged a few kids' aim with water guns and spotted four grown women dressed up as princesses. I headed over to the patio tables, where the people over seven were sitting, and grabbed a bottle of water.

"Look who sobered up."

I twisted around to find my dad's eyes fastened on me. He was sitting at a table alone with a pink cup covered with flowers in his hand. Even though the cup was juvenile, I was sure there was most likely alcohol in it. The man would be the one to patronize me for drinking at an adult party when he was getting wasted at his own granddaughter's damn princess party.

"Not here, Dad," I said, pushing my Ray-Bans farther up my nose. Those things were staying on all day, or my eyes would burn out of their sockets.

He scoffed, shaking his head at me in disgust. "Now is not the time to rehash how you drunkenly called me a heartless bastard in front of a crowd of people."

Fuck. I'd forgotten about my outburst last night. Instead of chasing after Gabby, I'd decided to take my frustrations out on my dad. I'd taken a couple shots and confronted him in a not-so-subtle way.

I pulled out a chair with balloons attached to the backrest and sat down across from him. "How about we rehash how you set me up to ruin what I had with Gabby?" I asked.

"You shouldn't have had anything with that girl. You should feel lucky I didn't cut your ass off after that debacle, but I understand people make mistakes, especially when they're in *lust*."

I rolled my eyes at his sideways insult.

"As a Douglas, you shouldn't make amateur mistakes like that. Don't let it happen again."

"How very noble of you," I sneered. I was well aware he was going to throw that party in my face for the rest of my life.

He took a swig of his drink. "How's everything going with the governor's case? I've noticed you've been slacking."

My eyes deadpanned on him. "I haven't been slacking. Ivy's been staying with her parents, so it's been complicated, getting in touch with her."

Gabby and I had attempted to visit her for days, but her dad would come out, threatening us with a shotgun to get off his property.

His fingertips tapped against the table. "How's that so hard? Do a stakeout and wait until her parents leave."

"Tried it. They don't leave her home alone."

"Then, you need to sneak into her bedroom and be certain she listens to what you have to say. Those petty little threats you made about her naked pictures and alcoholic problems are minimal compared to what will come if she doesn't start working with us."

"He threatened us with a gun," I explained, rubbing my brow in an attempt to ward off the excruciating headache still pounding against my brain.

"Did he shoot you?"

I pointed to my unwounded chest. "Obviously not."

"Exactly. You played right into his games like a pussy. He was never going to shoot you."

I leaned into his space. "You know him well enough personally to be sure he wouldn't put a bullet in my head?"

He picked a peanut out of a bowl in the center of the table and tossed it into his mouth. "He knows who you are. Any man would be stupid to fuck with me."

I snorted loudly. "News flash, Dad: not everyone is terrified of you."

He growled deep in this throat. "They should be if they know what I'm capable of."

I looked back as I felt a heavy slap on my back.

"Let's not talk about that shit at my daughter's birthday party.

People are going to think we're in the mob or some shit," Leo said, jumping into the conversation and taking the seat next to me.

"We practically are," I muttered.

"You look like dog shit," he said, grinning.

"I feel like dog shit."

The stagnant smell of cheeseburgers on the grill next to us began to waft through the air, causing my stomach to tremble. I hadn't eaten anything all day in fear I'd vomit it up, and that smell wasn't helping my cause.

"You need to tell your brother to stay away from that whore's daughter," my dad snarled to my brother.

"Dad," Leo warned.

My dad had more patience with my brother than he did me.

"You told me to talk about something else," he threw back, knotting his hands together.

"Let me clarify myself since you children don't understand. Any talk about guns, threats, and whores is off-limits, okay?"

"Fine," my dad grumbled. "Just talk some sense into your brother." His face pinched together, and he pointed a thumb my brother's way while looking at me. "Why couldn't you be more like him? He's always done what he's told, never rebelled against me like you and your sister have."

"Because I have a set of balls," I replied, cursing as Leo's finger came out and flipped me in the ear.

"Funny, asshole," he muttered.

"Having the balls to act out like an imbecile doesn't make you intelligent, son. Stay away from the girl, and I'm not going to tell you again."

My fists clenched into tight balls as I counted to ten in my head, hoping that would calm me down. "That shouldn't be a problem now that she hates my ass, thanks to you."

"Then, my work paid off," he said, clearly proud of himself for fucking up my life.

I rolled my eyes, exhausted, and no longer wanted to waste my energy arguing with him. I'd let him think he'd won, but I wasn't going to let him determine my happiness. I was planning on explaining everything to Gabby Monday morning.

"Look who finally decided to show up," a squawking voice shrilled, causing me to wince. She sounded like a squirrel getting strangled while sucking on helium.

My eyes narrowed on Leo's wife, Kelly, as she walked up to my brother's side with my mom behind her. The two wicked witches were there to cause havoc on the princess party. I was just waiting to see which one would cast the spell first.

I lifted my water bottle up her way. "I've been here for a while, Kelly. You've just been too busy, complaining about lifting a finger, to notice your guests."

We'd never gotten along since day one. The moment I met her, I knew what kind of woman she was, and I despised those types of women.

She scrunched her makeup-packed face up. "Whatever, Dalton. Just don't get wasted and embarrass my daughter like you did your parents last night."

"The only person embarrassing your daughter is you," I snapped back, gesturing to her outfit of choice.

It was a children's party outside, and she was dressed in a tight black cocktail dress and six-inch heels. Claire had confided in me, asking me why her mommy wasn't like her friends' moms—caring, nice, and present at her ballet recitals. I'd told her that her mom was too busy and my brother liked to have her all to himself. I'd grown up with invisible parents my entire life. It sucked ass. I was glad that Claire had my brother. He was doing the job of the mom and the dad.

She rolled her eyes. "Screw you, Dalton. Go disappoint your parents some more."

"Go disappoint your husband some more," I fired back.

We could go back and forth for days. She thought I was a raging asshole, and I thought she was a raging bitch.

Leo slapped my arm. "Cut it out," he said, his eyes pleading with me to quit provoking her.

My mouth slammed shut for the sake of my brother. Kelly

stomped away when she realized I was done with our game, and my mom sat down next to me.

"We need to talk about your wedding," she commented, and I slammed my head down onto the table.

This day was going to be worse than I thought.

Chapter Twenty-Eight

GABBY

"DID YOU KNOW?" I snarled, standing at the edge of our pool when Asher emerged from the water. He was leaving tonight, and we'd planned to spend the day together before he left.

He shook his head, water flying toward me, and rubbed his eyes with his knuckles. "Fuck," he groaned, grabbing on to the edge of the pool and holding himself up while looking at me.

"You knew." His reaction told me the answer I was dreading. "How could you not tell me?" I yelled, stomping my foot onto the concrete and clasping my hands against my hips.

"I tried warning you! You wouldn't listen to me, damn it."

His muscles flexed as he pulled himself out of the pool and grabbed a towel from the edge. My eyes widened, watching the water droplets trickle down the hard ripples on his chest. My mouth watered as my eyes traveled down until the drops smacked into the concrete below him. I might've been pissed off at him, but I couldn't stop myself from eye-fucking him.

"You said he was bad news," I replied when I regained control of myself. If he noticed I was staring, he didn't mention it. "You failed to mention the fact that he was getting married!"

He snapped his fingers before throwing the towel over his shoulder. "Next time, I'll know to be more descriptive in my warnings." He bunched the towel in his hands and ruffled it through his hair. "It's not like it would've mattered anyway, babe. You were so fucking obsessed with him; it was ridiculous."

I wiped the sweat forming around my hairline. "I wasn't obsessed with him."

He rolled his eyes and rubbed a hand over the dark stubble against his cheeks. "Whatever, Gabby. You were too damn blind to see the signs. You ignored my warnings. Why couldn't you trust me?" He drew his hands out, and his face fell.

He'd wanted me to trust him enough to take his word, but my idiot ass didn't. Now, I was stuck with a broken heart and a broken friendship.

I kicked at the ground. "I did trust you, but you can bet your ass I don't anymore."

"What the fuck?" he shouted. "You don't trust me now?" A harsh laugh escaped his throat. "I didn't do shit, except try to help your ungrateful ass."

A lump wedged itself into the center of my throat. In less than twenty-four hours, I'd lost two people I thought truly cared about me but didn't. "You were trying to help me by not telling me he was engaged?"

"I wanted to—believe me, I did—but I didn't know how. You were so damn set on him being this good person, and every single time I tried to convince you otherwise, you'd get all defensive and shitty."

"I would've listened pretty damn well if you'd told me he was putting a damn ring on someone else's finger."

He grunted. "Yeah, right. You say that now, but you would've told me I was lying."

I was getting more pissed by the second. "You know what? You're an asshole, just like them. You're just like every other Douglas out there!"

"That's where you're wrong, sunshine. You're the one turning into them, not me."

Heat flushed through my body as his words seared through me.

"Go fuck yourself," I yelled, charging toward him.

He let out a loud yelp when my palms pressed against his chest and pushed him back into the water. I twisted around on my heels, grabbed my car keys, stormed to my car, and sped out of the driveway.

* * *

My hair blew with the wind as Adele blared from my car's speakers. I steered my car while wiping the trickles of tears falling down my face. I continued to drive for hours until I reached the old park my mom used to take me to play when I was younger—before she married Kenneth and my life did a one-eighty. I slouched down onto an old, rickety bench and stared at the warm colors of the sunset, watching the ducks glide across the water and children running around, playing.

I knew it was too late when I got home. I'd waited until I knew Asher would be gone for his flight before I came back. It was a shitty thing to do, but I was still pissed at him. He could've stopped me from putting myself in that situation with Dalton. He could've stopped my heart from getting smashed into a thousand pieces. He could've stopped the painful feeling in my chest that felt like my insides were swelling up inside me.

I parked my car into my spot in the garage, noticing most of the lights in the house were out before heading up to my bedroom. I dragged each foot up stair by stair restlessly before reaching my bedroom and flipping on the light. I headed straight to my closet to grab a pair of pajamas before deciding to take a hot bath.

"You missed Asher leave," my mom's voice called out.

I halted, turning around and looking at her.

"He waited until the last minute, and you never showed, Gabby. You also turned off your cell phone. What is going on with you?"

I tossed my pajamas back onto the top of my dresser and slumped down onto my bed. "Nothing. We just got into an argument, and I needed time to cool down." I shrugged my shoulders and avoided looking up at her. "I guess I just lost track of time."

"He's on his flight now, but you need to call him tonight and apologize."

I nodded. I'd eventually apologize to Asher, but there was no way that was happening tonight. I'd planned on keeping my phone off and taking a hot bath, where I could plot my escape from everyone.

"Now, get some sleep. You look exhausted," she added.

I whipped my head up and opened my mouth before she left. "Do you ever feel bad about what you did?" I asked suddenly.

Her eyebrows drew together. "Bad about what?"

"You know, having an affair with Kenneth and being the other woman." I couldn't believe I was actually going to have this conversation with her.

She walked forward, erasing the distance between us before sitting down on my bed. Her skinny hand gently patted my leg. "I'm not proud of the situation we got ourselves into, but I would never take it back."

"But he had a wife," I pointed out, my voice wavering.

I didn't understand how she didn't feel guilty. I hadn't even known Dalton's fiancée, and I felt bad for her. My mom had attended dinners and planned Kenneth's office design with his wife.

Her eyes averted down, and she played with a button on her leopard-print pajama top. "You're right, but he also was unhappy with her."

I cringed, my lower lip curling. I hated when people used that bullshit excuse. If they weren't happy, they needed to get a divorce. It was that simple. "So, not being happy justifies you being able to cheat? You're not with the one who makes your heart skip a beat anymore, so you have an affair? How could you inflict that pain on another woman?" I hated that she was trying to condone the fact that she'd stolen another woman's husband, but not as much as I hated myself in that moment. I was the other woman to Dalton's fiancée. I was my mother. "Don't you hate people calling you a home-wrecker? Didn't you think about all the damage it would cause?"

She nodded, and I noticed her eyes grow glossy. "It hurts, but their insults aren't worth me being unhappy. Their vindictiveness doesn't change my feelings for Kenneth or his feelings for me. That's all that matters." Her posture picked up, and she paused to examine me. "Why all of a sudden are you asking me about this?"

I pressed my hair back with both hands and shrugged. "No reason. Just curious."

"Okay then. Get some sleep. You look exhausted." She kissed me on my forehead and left me alone to dwell in my sorrows.

She'd fought for Kenneth, for their love, and she'd won. I was doing that with Dalton, but I wasn't going to compete for love like my mom had so many times.

* * *

"What are you doing in here?" Dalton asked, stepping into the space of my cubicle.

I'd kept my phone off the remainder of the weekend and hidden out in my room.

"Working," I answered, keeping my attention on the computer screen in front of me. I'd decided not to work in his office this morning. I wanted nothing to do with him. "I figured you needed some alone time to plan your wedding."

"Gabby, please," he begged, rubbing his eyes with his knuckles.

He looked sleep-deprived. Good, I wanted him to lose sleep, not be able to eat, and feel like shit from the way he'd treated me.

I swiveled my chair around to narrow my eyes at him. "Please what? You think begging is going to work?" I huffed. "You want me to put on my scarlet letter and walk around here, being your happy little mistress? Not happening. Find some other schmuck because that girl isn't me."

"Please, just talk to me," he said, reaching for my hand, but I backed up, the wheels on my chair rolling back.

I pointed my finger at him. "Don't touch me. You'll never touch me again."

He circled my chair around and bent down, so our faces were

inches apart. "You have to talk to me sometime. You have to let me explain."

"Explain what? You had a brain lapse and forgot you were engaged while we were having sex?"

"I'm not leaving here until you hear me out," he said, his eyes searing into mine, and I wanted to slap them off his face.

I noticed a few questioning looks coming from people around me. One girl was even leaning up over her cubicle, eavesdropping.

"Fine, I'll talk to you after work," I said. I needed to get him out of there.

He tapped on the armrest of my chair. "I'll be waiting by your car."

I gulped.

He lifted himself up. "And, Gabby?"

I looked up at him.

"I love you."

Those three words burned like fire through my brain.

"No, you don't," I whispered, turning my back to him.

"I'll prove it to you," he added before leaving.

There was no way I could concentrate on work after that conversation, so I pulled out my drawer and finally turned on my cell phone. A notice popped up, letting me know I had forty-five text messages and ten voice mails. I scrolled down the text messages. The majority of them were from Dalton, then Asher, and a few were from Cora, Lane, and Daisy.

I ignored the ones from Dalton and Asher, opening my friends' messages.

CORA: Hey, babe, just wanting to make sure you were okay! I called your casa & your mom said you were sleeping. Call me when you get a chance and keep that head up if you go to work! XOXO

I hit the Reply button.

ME: I'm at work. I'll come over when I'm off and fill you in.

"Can I give you some advice?" a feminine voice asked, and I

jumped in my chair to find Summer standing behind me, one hip bumped out with her hand placed on it.

Her blonde hair was ironed straight, and she was displaying another tight dress.

"Sure," I grumbled. I wasn't in the mood to argue with her.

"Don't do it."

My head flinched back slightly. "I'm sorry, but I have no idea what you're talking about."

She leaned in closer, lowering her voice. "Be a mistress. Don't do it. Dalton's getting married, but from the looks of it, he wants you too."

Great. Even Summer knew Dalton was getting married. I needed to join the office-gossip monthly newsletter.

"It's actually pretty miserable. I've been with Wilson for three years."

I gasped, my eyes bulging at her confession. "You and ... Wilson?" I asked.

She nodded. Now that I thought about it, it made sense. The girl got away with painting her nails on the clock.

"Not once have we ever been able to share a holiday. No Christmases, no Valentine's Days, nothing. Sure, you'll get to exchange presents and stuff, but not until days or weeks later. You can't even go out to dinner or have a date in a public place." She bit out a laugh. "Your relationship will consist of late-night rendezvous in an office or hotel suite."

I stayed silent, still shocked at her revelation. Wilson was such a fucking hypocrite. All of these years, he'd been giving my mom and Kenneth shit when he was doing the same exact thing. Did all the Douglas men have mistresses? Was it a requirement to be accepted into the family?

"So, why not end it?" I asked.

Summer was a gorgeous girl. I doubted she'd have any trouble finding a new man.

She sighed, and I noticed her bottom lip shiver. Shit, I hoped she wasn't about to cry.

"Because I stupidly fell in love with him. It's too late for me, but I wanted to tell you before it's the same for you. Run before you get all sucked up in him and fall in love." She blinked a few times, and I knew from experience, she was fighting back the tears. She blew out a breath. "Anyway, I'm supposed to tell you that you need to go to the boardroom."

I gave her a weak smile. "Thanks, girl."

I appreciated her trying to help me. She had never told Wilson about walking in on Dalton and me. I knew it. As bitchy as she was sometimes, she was a girl's girl at heart.

The only problem with her warning was that it was too late.

I'd already been sucked in and fallen in love with Dalton.

Chapter Twenty-Nine

GABBY

MY STEPS WERE slow on my way to the boardroom. My chest felt weighted as my mind ran through the different reasons of what I was being summoned for. There was nobody in that office I wanted to talk to. My clammy hand wrapped around the door handle, and I shut my eyes, taking in a deep breath before pushing the door open and walking in.

I found only one person sitting in the room. One person I wanted absolutely nothing to do with. My eyes flashed to each corner of the room. I prayed someone else was going to pop out of a corner and come to my rescue but got nothing. I was on my own.

"Hello, Gabrielle," the penetrating voice greeted. He was dressed in a full black suit, sitting in a chair with his legs crossed. An expensive shoe was dangling as he swung his foot back and forth.

I gripped my hands together. "Hi," I mumbled. "Why am I here?"

John's arm shot out, gesturing to the chair across from him. I stayed put while waiting for his answer. I wasn't going to get comfortable because I wasn't planning on conversing with him long. He chuckled at my reluctance to lighten the tense mood. It didn't work.

"I wanted to ask you a few questions," he replied.

"So, start asking," I bit out. I wasn't in the mood to answer any questions that asshole had for me, but I just needed to get it over with, so I could get back to my cubicle.

I jumped at the sound of him clearing his throat. Why was I so jumpy all of a sudden?

"Do you know who your father is?"

I stumbled backward, shocked at his words, and my back landed against the wood door.

"I couldn't care less who he is," I responded, regaining control of myself.

When I was younger, I always asked my mom questions about why I didn't have a dad like all the other kids in school. Eventually, that curiosity morphed into anger, then indifference. I didn't care that I didn't have a dad. I quit wishing on that star a long damn time ago. I hated a man I didn't even know.

"That's unfortunate."

"No, not really."

"Your mother never told you anything about him?"

"Other than the fact he was an asshole who abandoned us when she told him she was pregnant, no, not really," I threw back, my voice getting harsher by the second. I'd had a rough few days, and talking about my bastard father wasn't the hug I needed.

My entire body tensed as he rose up from his chair. I tried to take another step back, but I smacked into the wall.

"I'm your father, Gabby," he said.

My world stopped, my stomach fluttered, and I felt a sudden itch tear at my throat. The next thing I knew, I was bursting out in laughter. "Funny. Did Wilson put you up to this?" I could see Wilson messing with the fatherless girl for his daily excitement.

His hand stuffed into the pocket of his pants. "I'm being serious."

My laughing stopped, and my mind began to race. "You're a liar," I accused.

He had to be lying. There was no way he was telling the truth.

He shook his head, his eyes blazing straight into mine. "I'm not lying."

I shoved my hands against the door to help me balance myself. "You're a goddamn liar."

His words burned into my brain. *"I'm your father."*

The life I always knew was shattered into pieces.

He took a step closer, and my hand shot out, begging him to not come any closer. His feet halted. "Your birthday is November 24," he said. "You were born at 12:58 in the morning ..."

"You could've found that information anywhere. They're public records," I fired back, cutting him off. I glanced down at my hands, noticing they were shaking.

Was this what it felt like when you found out your entire life was a lie? That the one person you trusted had betrayed you? I cringed as my head started to pound against my skull.

"Your grandmother's name was Tilda," he continued to my horror. "Although you've never met her because she was an alcoholic and your mom had to practically raise herself. You were six pounds, four ounces. You were born two weeks early. You were—"

"Please, stop," I whispered, refusing to look at him while I internally screamed *no* a million times repeatedly.

My chest hitched as images of the party flashed through my mind and how my mom had reacted around him. She'd blocked him from seeing me because she was nervous he'd know who I was.

Holy fucking shit.

I was John's daughter.

This was not happening.

"You also have a birthmark on the bottom of your right foot. The same place as your mom's."

Fire swirled into my stomach. "I said stop!" I seethed. "You aren't my father. You are nothing to me! We might share the same blood, but you're not my father. You left me with nothing! You didn't want me. You abandoned me!"

He winced at my jabs. "I understand this is shocking news, and it probably hurts."

"You know nothing about what hurts me," I cried out. "You

know absolutely nothing about me." My knees fell limp, and I stumbled forward to help myself from falling down. I had to get out of there.

"I want to change that," he said, trying to grab my arm and stop me from leaving.

I swatted his hands away from me and stuck my finger in his face. "Stay the hell away from me!"

A sympathetic look crossed his face. "I won't come any closer. I just want us to talk."

"I don't want to talk to you!" My voice rose. "If you come near me again, I swear to God, I'll scream bloody murder."

I jumped as the door burst open. It smacked against the wall when Dalton came barreling into the room with a murderous rage in his eyes.

"What the fuck are you doing to her?" he yelled, his eyes pinned on John.

John walked backward. "This conversation doesn't involve you," he answered him.

"Anything regarding Gabby involves me," Dalton shot back.

I wanted to kill both men in the room, rip their heads off, and never see them again. They'd done nothing but hurt me. Dalton had manipulated me into falling in love with him, only to tear my heart into pieces. John was the reason my heart was so fragile because I'd grown up without a dad to protect and love me.

Dear God, I was now a girl with daddy issues.

Dalton grabbed my head in his hands. "What did he do to you, baby?" he asked, looking over at me. He tried to grab my trembling hands in his, but I crouched from under him as tears began to stream down my face.

"He's my father!" I spat out, signaling to John, and Dalton's eyes practically bulged out of his head. "Congratulations! You both are the biggest fucking assholes on the face of this planet!" My body bumped into Dalton's side as I dashed out of the room.

I hit the hallway and noticed the large crowd staring at me. Their faces let me know they heard me screaming. I wasn't ever showing my face at this place again, so I didn't care. My chin stayed pointed up as I walked down the hallway and snagged my bag roughly to leave. I wiped my clammy fingers against my cheek, swiping away tears violently. Dalton was on my heels the entire time, not saying a word, just walking behind me and following me into the elevator.

"Baby, talk to me," he breathed out, his eyes searching mine.

"Did you know?" That was the only thing I wanted to know.

He ran his hands through his hair. "Fuck no."

I scoffed.

"I wouldn't keep something like that from you."

"Or you could've just forgotten," I replied, letting out a hard laugh. "You know, like how you fucked me, told me you loved me, and forgot to mention the fact that you're getting married." I was still shaking so hard; I could almost feel my teeth begin to chatter.

"Please, let's just go to my place, and we'll talk about this. You need to cool down, and you can't be driving like this."

Dalton attempted to grab me when the elevator doors swung open, but I pushed him away.

"All of you need to stay the hell away from me," I said, walking out and turning to look at him. "Nothing good comes from being around you, any of you."

I turned around and sprinted out of the building, not slowing down until I made it to my Honda. I hit the remote button, unlocking the car, and threw my bag inside before jumping into the driver's seat. It took me a few tries before I managed to shove the key into the ignition.

I swiftly put the car in reverse and sped out of the parking lot. I didn't need Dalton coming after me. I pulled out into the heavy traffic, nearly sideswiping a car and losing control of the steering wheel. Dalton was right. I shouldn't have been driving. The tears began to burn, falling down my face faster, and I wiped them away with my sleeve.

A month ago, I never thought about Dalton. I didn't think about who my dad was. I believed the words that came out of my mom's mouth. Now, all I could think about was Dalton. I knew who my dad was, and it was someone I despised. And I no longer trusted a word that came out of my mother's mouth.

Three people had completely changed my life, and I had no interest in seeing them ever again.

Chapter Thirty

DALTON

I WAS A FUCKING IDIOT.

That was the only reasoning I had for my stupidity. I just fucking stood there and watched the girl I cared about more than anything in the world walk out of my life for the second time. She was hurting, and I didn't go after her. I was the world's biggest piece of shit. I lied, I hurt her, and I still wasn't man enough to go chase after her.

I didn't blink until the silhouette of her body slowly faded away from the lobby and she left the building. The ding of the elevator doors snapped me back into reality as they slid shut, alerting me it was all over. I'd fucked it all up, and there was no going back now. My face burned, and I pounded my fist against the numbered buttons until the one I was aiming for lit up. I shuffled backward to the wall, and my body went limp against it with regret. Regret. It was such a small word, but the meaning was astronomical.

The lift dragged up, and the elevator dinged again when I hit my destination. I sprang forward through the opening doors and darted toward my target. I twisted the doorknob with sweaty hands and swung the door open, causing it to smack into the wall as I barged into the room. The two men stiffened at the sight of me.

I charged toward the man sitting across from my dad. He gasped when I grabbed the collar of his expensive shirt and pulled him up from the chair.

"Why the fuck would you blindside her like that?" I screamed, my throat burning like fire.

He winced at the spit flying out of my mouth, landing on his flushed face.

"Dalton! Let him go right now!" I heard my dad's sharp voice order from behind me.

I tightened my hold on John. I was done taking orders.

John held his hands out. "Let me explain," he choked out, his voice shrill. "Please," he begged, looking apologetic. "I didn't mean to hurt her. I swear."

My hands loosened before letting go of him, and he fell slack back into the chair, breathing heavy and wiping his face with the sleeve of his shirt.

"You need to get the hell out of my office. You're fired," my dad screamed, his voice menacing. He didn't get up from his seat.

Good fucking riddance.

"Thank God," I said bitterly, anger flashing through my insides.

I didn't bother turning around to look at him. He didn't deserve any reaction from me. I was certain he knew what John was going to tell Gabby. He was probably sitting in his office, giggling like a damn schoolgirl, while her whole world was getting ripped away from her. I knew Gabby wouldn't take John being her dad well. She despised the man.

I needed to get the hell out of there before my dad was the next one getting the wrath of my anger. I bent down and grabbed John's face in my palm. He tensed up, and his chest hitched. He was waiting for my next move, but he wasn't fighting back. That surprised me. He gave me a pained stare, and I noticed the muscles in his jaw ticcing.

"You leave her the fuck alone," I demanded. "Stay the hell away from her."

I opened my hand, and his head fell down, his chin hitting his chest.

He sagged into his chair. "I just want her to talk to me. I'm her father."

"A little too late for that. You should've tried that before deserting her," I snarled, walking around his chair and leaving my dad's office.

I hustled through the lobby, ignoring Summer's pleas to talk to her, and kicked open the stairway door before thundering down the stairs. My pace quickened when I heard someone behind me.

"Dalton, please talk to her for me," John yelled, running after me.

I could hear his breathing labor as he tried to keep up with me. He leaned down over the stairway railing to see me, but I turned the corner and whipped around to dodge him. He cried out before falling down a few stairs and landing hard on his side.

Shit! I glanced down at him nervously. I couldn't leave the damn governor lying in an empty stairwell. He held out his hand for my help, and I did a quick sweep of his body to check for any serious injuries. Nothing. He was only having trouble getting up.

"Are you really her dad?" I asked. I was at an advantage, and I wanted all my questions answered. I wanted to be sure my dad didn't set the entire thing up to hurt Gabby for being with me.

He nodded. "I am."

"Did you know when you came to us for help?"

He shook his head. "I had no idea until the party. I saw Shelia and put two and two together. Please talk to her for me. I want to know my daughter."

"Why couldn't you just keep that shit to yourself?" I asked, my voice rising. "You knew she wouldn't want anything to do with you." There was no way Gabby was going to come back after this. I'd kicked her, making her sore, but John's confession broke her.

"I might be a terrible person and a bad husband, but I love my children. I regret walking out of her life every day. It eats me alive to know I neglected one of my own. I was young and dumb. I listened to my parents and allowed them to manipulate me."

His words sounded too familiar, and a hot lump wedged itself into my throat.

"Too late," I croaked. "She doesn't want anything to do with you."

"Talk to her for me. She'll listen to you."

I snorted. "Quick tip: Gabby doesn't listen to anyone. She doesn't let assholes like us control her."

"She will with you. She loves you. I can tell. She looks at you the same way her mother used to look at me. Just don't mess it up like I did."

Thanks for the delayed advice, old man.

My arm shot out to help him up. He gripped my hand in his, and I leaned backward while he moved forward until he got to his feet. I smacked him on the back before running back down the stairs.

* * *

I hit Gabby's name on my phone screen as soon as I made it back to my car. She hit the *fuck you* button each time, ignoring my call. I couldn't blame her, but I needed to find a way to convince her to hear me out.

I scrolled down to another name. I was going to use all my resources.

ME: Do you have Cora's number?

PIPER: Hell no. But I have Lane's.

I dialed the number as soon as she sent it to me.

"Wadddupp?" the voice answered on the other end.

I could hear voices screaming in the background. Was Gabby with him?

"Lane, it's Dalton."

I heard him take a deep breath.

"Dude, why the hell are you calling me?" he asked, his voice lowering to almost a whisper as the screams in the background dissolved. He didn't want anyone to know he was talking to me.

"I need to talk to Gabby," I insisted, my voice almost pleading.

"The fuck you do. You need to stay away from her, you heartless bastard. How could you not tell her you were getting married?"

"It's complicated," I said, starting my car. I needed to get out of this place.

"It's always complicated when you're trying to play two girls at the same time," he fired back.

I admired Lane's loyalty.

"Please, tell her I'm not going to marry Eva," I said, hopeful he would change his mind and talk to her.

He groaned. "Look, I know your parents put you in some messed up position, but that ship has sailed with Gabby. You lied and asked her to practically be your mistress. That's a deal-breaker for her, and you should know that."

"Just please tell her to call me."

"I'll relay the message, but I can't make any promises that she'll do it."

"Thanks, man."

"I'm not doing this shit for you," he screeched, and the line went dead.

"I know," I sighed heavily to myself in the empty air of my car.

* * *

My phone rang when I walked into my house, and I dropped everything in my arms to fish it out of my pocket.

Thank God. She was calling me.

I grabbed my phone, almost dropping it from my sweaty hands, and looked down at the caller ID. Fuck. I wanted to throw it into the damn trash can, but I was too afraid she'd still try to call me.

"What?" I barked into the other line.

"Nice to talk to you too, sunshine. My parents are having a thing tonight. Can you come?" Eva asked, her voice chipper.

"Nope," I answered sharply, picking up my keys and all of the other items I dropped down onto my marble floor.

"Seriously?" she snapped back. "My entire family will be there, and they keep asking about my fiancé, who's never around. Since you didn't go after that girl at the party, I thought our marriage was still on. Everyone thinks I'm dating Casper the Ghost."

I groaned. I still needed to break things off with Eva, but I had more important things to take care of first. "Tell them I got fired and couldn't make it," I said, semi-telling the truth.

"Funny," she said mockingly.

"I'm being serious."

She scoffed. "How do you get fired when your dad's the boss?"

"Long story."

"It always is. I'll let them know you can't make it." Eva was a good person, and she deserved marrying someone who loved her, not someone who was only doing it to get a big bank account and appease his parents.

"I appreciate it."

"And, Dalton?" she said hurriedly before I hung up.

"Yeah?"

"I hope everything works out for you."

"Me too," I muttered, falling down onto my couch and hanging up. I turned my ring volume on high before letting my eyes drift closed.

* * *

With each phone call, my nerves were growing more aggravated. I wanted to forget about them, and seeing his name on my screen every three seconds wasn't helping. I knew the only reason he kept calling was because I skipped out on Eva's parents' event. That didn't make them look good.

Fuck appearances. I was done being their pawn.

The calls began to slow down and then stopped together. Thank you, Jesus.

I fell back onto my bed and inhaled the scent of Gabby still lingering on my sheets. Clutching my phone in my hand, I double-checked I didn't have anything from Gabby before propping my head against my pillow and staring at the ceiling until my eyes began to close.

My phone ringing woke me up, and I immediately grabbed it, praying her name would show up. But nothing. My dad's name had been replaced with Leo's.

"Now's not the damn time," I growled into the phone.

I needed to go back to sleep, or I was going to go fucking crazy. I had to find a way to stop my mind from racing and to stop the urge to go chase down Gabby like a fucking madman.

"You need to get your ass back to the office," my dad's voice snarled on the other end.

Fuck me. Leo set my ass up.

I laid my head back down on the pillow and sighed. "Last time I checked, you fired my ass."

"Ivy's dead, and Gentry is MIA. You were the last person seen with him, Dalton. Quit playing games and get your ass here before it turns uglier."

I jumped up from my bed and stumbled around as I tried to slip on shoes and run out my door at the same time.

This was not good.

Chapter Thirty-One

GABBY

"WERE you ever going to tell me?" I seethed, throwing my bag onto the floor and stomping into the living room.

My mom was sitting on the couch next to Kenneth with a glass of wine in her hand. She was laughing, having the time of her life while her daughter was hurting. It pissed me off. It shouldn't have, but it did. When my mom hurt in the past, I hurt.

Every single damn time.

Every breakup, I was there for her. When she dealt with the aftermath of Kenneth's demon family, I was there for her. But now that she was happy and I was growing up, she'd forgotten to reciprocate.

She looked over at Kenneth, suddenly nervous, and sat her glass down on the table. "He told you," she said. I wasn't sure if it was a question or a statement.

"Oh, so you knew about that asshole blindsiding me at work and telling me he's my dad?" I screamed, my fists clenching tight, my eyes burning.

"He called me last night and wanted me to tell you. I was going to, I promise. I was just trying to figure out the best way to do it," she answered, shakiness in her voice.

I shook my head like I didn't believe her.

"Gabby, sit down," she breathed out. "Let me explain."

I walked around the couch and took the chair across from her. She grabbed the glass of wine and chugged it like she needed alcohol's help to tell me the story of her deception.

"John and I met when we were young. We dated in high school for a while until I told him I was pregnant. He said it ruined his plans. He wanted nothing to do with you or me. His parents despised me and told him to insist I get an abortion. I was trash from the trailer park. But I couldn't do it. I couldn't get rid of my baby."

My head flew up. On every ad I'd seen, John said he was pro-life. Pro-life, my ass. It pissed me off that people had such strong views about something until they were the ones in the predicament.

"Why didn't you ever tell me?" I asked.

A single tear fell from her eye. "I didn't want you to try and contact him."

I scoffed. "I'd never try and contact him. I hate him."

She shook her head. "You don't know that. He's a public figure. All you had to do was tell one person, and that's it; the media would've been on our front doorstep. I didn't want you or myself in the public spotlight like that. I was trying to protect you."

"Protect me by lying?" I gritted my teeth. "And how does he know all these things about me? He knows my birthday. He knows about my damn birthmark!"

"He came by the hospital on the day after you were born. He wanted to meet you and say good-bye. He told me he couldn't have the story leaked and offered me money. I didn't take his hush money."

"How very honorable of both of you."

My mom was too damn stubborn to take money we needed, and John tried to force money down people's throats, so they'd do what he said. What a great pair of procreators I had.

My attention turned to Kenneth, who was sitting silently on the couch. "Did you know too?"

He shook his head, pushing his glasses up his nose. "I didn't," he replied. "I would've never allowed him to walk through our company doors. I know we aren't that close, and I have a feeling you're not my biggest fan, but I do love your mother. And you. I know our relationship hasn't been the easiest with me being married when we met. Now, I understand this information isn't the best news, but you can do one of two things." He held up a single finger. "You can try to establish some type of relationship with him. I'm assuming since he's told you, he doesn't mind it being in the public eye, which is surprising." He held up another finger. "Or two, I can tell him to leave you alone."

I got up from my chair. "I want you to tell him to leave me alone," I said before sending a cold smile my mom's way. "I also want you to tell her"—I pointed a finger straight at her face—"to leave me alone as well."

My mom's mouth fell open, and she whimpered. I was being unfair, but I was so angry. So freaking angry. I grew up hating this imaginary man—someone my mom led me to believe didn't exist. I never expected to face him, and now, I couldn't. The young girl inside of me yearned to know her father, but the wise woman who'd been pained told me to run. Just because he was my dad didn't mean he'd actually become a real father. He'd only hurt me more.

I grabbed my bag and headed upstairs.

"Gabby!" my mom called from behind me.

I glanced over my shoulder. She was still sitting on the couch, not coming after me.

She wasn't trying to console me like I'd done with her. I slammed my door shut when I reached my bedroom and dragged my suitcase out from under my bed. Walking into my closet, I grabbed an armful of clothes and tossed them into the suitcase with the hangers still attached. I opened my underwear drawer, grabbed a handful of panties, and threw them in there too. I leaned across my bed to zip it up, not caring when the zipper snagged some fabric in the process. The suitcase bumped along each stair as I held the handle, walking down.

"Where are you going?" my mom asked, meeting me at the end of the stairs.

"Out," I answered, my voice sounding almost robotic.

She tried to grab the suitcase from my hand, but I pulled away from her. "Gabrielle Nicole! Quit acting childish and talk to me about this!"

I bit back a laugh. "Oh, now, you want to talk about it? You've had eighteen years to talk about it. Ding, ding, your time's up."

I noticed the hurt in her eyes.

"You're not leaving."

Kenneth stepped between the two of us, grabbing my mom and pulling her back away from me. "Honey, she's probably going over to Cora's to cool down. Just give her some time," he said.

My mom sighed, defeat lining her features. My mom and I rarely fought. I wasn't one of those girls who complained about her mother. We used to be each other's backbones.

Without saying another word, I lugged my suitcase out the front door and threw it in the trunk of my car. I glanced back up at the doorway, noticing my mom standing there, watching me. Starting my ignition, I pulled away.

* * *

I shut off my phone and tossed it into my purse sitting in the passenger seat after hitting Ignore for the twenty-second time. The calls were growing more and more painful with each ring. If Dalton's name wasn't lighting up my screen, it was my mom's. I knew my mom would eventually GPS my phone and find out where I was, but I didn't care. The only ones who knew where I was headed were the only people I trusted, and neither of my incessant callers was on that list. They'd both betrayed me.

My hair flapped in the wind coming through my open sunroof as my favorite playlist flowed through my car's speakers. I yawned and turned up the radio. I'd been on the road for hours, but it was nothing a few energy drinks couldn't fix. I'd already downed two and had a few more in my backseat. I wasn't planning on stopping. I was driving straight through, and surprisingly, it was beginning to relax me. In forty years, I could see myself describing this as a soul-searching drive.

Samantha—yes, I named my GPS—was barking orders at me to

merge into the right lane. I did as I was told. Samantha pissed me off sometimes when she led me down one-way streets and sketchy alleyways, but she always had my back when it mattered. I cruised past a sign letting me know I was just a few miles away from my destination.

The streets were dead because it was early. The sun was beginning to rise, and I admired the soft hues from my windshield. I turned down my music to listen to Samantha tell me the last few directions. I made a few turns before swerving into a congested parking lot and pulling into the only open spot I could find near the back.

I blew out a breath, grabbing my energy drinks and tossing them alongside my phone in my bag before hitting the button to open my trunk. I grunted as I dragged my bag out. Pulling out the handle, I grabbed it and strolled toward the front door. Following the directions I'd been given, I walked down the desolate hallway and knocked.

The door swung open, like he was waiting for me. "Welcome to Miami, babe."

Gabby and Dalton's story continues in Worth The Risk, and it's NOW AVAILABLE!
  Click here to read Worth The Risk

Worth The Risk

Risky Duet

RISKY AND WORTH THE RISK

CHARITY FERRELL

Chapter One

DALTON

INTERROGATION ROOMS WERE nothing like in the movies.

They were shitholes.

And speaking of shit, that was how my entire week had been going.

Losing the girl I loved was shit.

Losing control of my first case at my job was shit.

Everything was shit.

I glanced around the room, panic nestling in my bones, and studied the white walls. My nostrils flared at the stench of stale cigarettes, vomit, and desperation. I leaned back in my chair, released a deep groan, and wondered how many people had confessed their transgressions in this room.

How many killers had sat in this same chair?

My patience wavered with each passing minute. This was the last damn thing I needed right now. They had to get in here and explain themselves before I walked out and told them to kiss my ass until they had a warrant.

The longer they left me, the faster my mind sped.

One question haunted me.

What did they know?

They had to know something. The police didn't show up at your front door and bring you into the station for shits and giggles.

I gulped, tasting the bitter aftereffects of my whiskey binge last night, even after three brushes this morning. Kavalan single malt had become my best friend lately. That motherfucker and I were having nightly meetings to erase the fact that the woman I loved had walked away from me, and I had no one to blame but myself. The liquid supplement helped me sleep. That was, until I started dreaming about her. Then, the bottle was back in my hand.

I was hungover, heartbroken, and sitting in the police station.

A shitty situation for an even shittier day.

My muscles tensed up when the door finally swung open. I frowned, feeling my heart kick, while I watched the two men shuffle into the room. I recognized them both. Of course, it had to be *them*. Things were about to go from bad to worse.

Harold Finch and David Whitman.

The Atlantic City Police Department employed both men.

And they despised my family and me.

Everyone stayed quiet as David shut the door behind them. Harold was holding a laptop. The stainless steel table shook when he slammed the laptop down and made a show of opening the screen, so it faced me.

I kept my eyes on the computer screen while the screech of their chairs sliding across the floor echoed through the room. Harold sat down across from me, taking the lead. David took the one beside him.

Harold rested his chubby elbows on the table before clearing his throat. "I'd like to show you something, Dalton," he said. His protruding belly smashed into the edge of the table when he leaned in to hit the play button on the computer.

My stomach twisted in horror.

I saw myself. I saw Gabby.

Nervousness shot through me while fear slapped me in the face.

No. I wouldn't let them drag her into *my* mess.

I straightened up, watching the security footage play out, and tried to mask my anxiety. I remembered the moment like it was yesterday. We were talking to the guy at the front desk to gain access to an apartment. A *now-dead* woman's apartment. The guy reached for the phone, and you could see me, clear as fucking day, stop him. Even more incriminating was me reaching into my pocket, pulling out a Benjamin, and discreetly slipping it to him. Guilt screamed around us like a song, pointing straight at me.

Harold cleared his throat before speaking. "Care to explain why you bribed the man to allow you clearance into a woman named Ivy Hart's apartment?" he asked. His black pornstache rose as an arrogant smile tugged at his lips. The fucker loved this.

I shrugged. Appearing as calm and collected as possible. *Don't let them see your fear.*

"I needed to talk to her," I answered.

"You needed to talk to her?" he repeated. Sarcasm dripped with his question.

My gaze stayed pinned to the screen—*to her.*

A few seconds passed before I looked at them. Harold's uniform was wrinkled, faded, and spotted with coffee stains and who the fuck knew what else. David's, on the other hand, was in pristine condition.

Harold did his best staredown performance, but he didn't look one bit intimidating. The guy used to babysit me and wipe my shitty diapers, for fuck's sake. He and my dad had been best friends once. They were in business together until shit went sour. Now, Harold wanted nothing more than to be the gasoline that brought my family down in flames. I wasn't about to be the hand that supplied the match.

"And what did you need to talk to her about?" he asked.

"What was your relationship with her?" David added, shifting uncomfortably in his chair.

I didn't miss the cold glare Harold gave him for interrupting.

I'd gone to high school with David. He'd been a decent guy but a loner. After graduating from the academy, he made his new position of power known. His new mission was to seek revenge on the guys who had bullied him in high school and the girls who'd turned him down. I'd lost count of the number of speeding tickets the jackass had given me. My friends also racked up a heavy record of DUI arrests.

I was dealing with amateurs, but these amateurs had pure hate in their veins for me.

A deep breath released from my lungs. This wasn't the first time Douglas PR had been in a situation like this, but never for a homicide case. It was usually along the lines of representing someone for committing fraud, corruption, or extortion, not fucking murder.

"That's confidential," I finally answered.

Ivy Hart. The dead woman.

After passing my bar and joining my dad's firm, I'd been assigned her as my first case. I prayed it wouldn't be my last either. So far, I was still employed, but no more work had come my way. My father was punishing me until I fixed the problem.

Which I needed to do fast. Even if I despised my family right now for what they'd done, I had to have their back. Harold wouldn't get a crumb from me. If they found out why we had been there, they'd consider it the perfect motive.

And if they considered that the perfect motive, I wasn't going to be the only one in deep shit. There would be a long list of people joining me in the cell. It was my job to prevent that from happening, to stop what could possibly be one of the biggest scandals of the year.

I was doing a terrible job at it so far.

Harold huffed. "This is a homicide case." He opened a folder sitting in front of him and threw down a photo in front of me. "There isn't shit confidential when it comes to murder."

I slowly looked down at it. Thank fuck I didn't have a weak stomach. It was grotesque and showed every dark detail of Ivy's death. Her naked body was covered in so much blood that it was hard to make out the deep stab wounds. They'd finished her death with a gunshot straight to the temple. Whoever had done this wanted her to suffer before she took her last breath.

My stomach curled. The woman in the picture had fucked me over, but I wouldn't wish that upon anyone. I didn't know who had killed her, but I needed to find out.

I slid the picture back to him without giving it another look. "If you have any additional questions for me, you can take them up with my attorney. Am I free to go?"

Harold held up his finger. "One more question for you, boy. Where's the girl accompanying you in this video?"

I froze at the mention of her, trying to keep a straight face. I had hoped they wouldn't bring her into this. I wouldn't allow that to happen.

My lungs took a lapse of air when he slapped down another picture. It was the first day we'd been on assignment together—when we went to Ivy's place. We were in the elevator. I had her pinned up against the wall with both my mouth and hands on her.

"Gabrielle Taylor. Where is she?" he asked.

I ducked my hands underneath the table and dug my fingernails into my thighs. I wished I knew the answer to his question. Granted, I wouldn't tell him if I did. I wanted to know for self-satisfaction. Gabby had left me with no warning and wasn't answering my calls. It was wrong to be angry with her because it was my fault. But losing her was suffocating, and I needed my air back.

"That's irrelevant. She has nothing to do with this. None of us do," I answered, my voice growing harsher with each word. "You need to quit wasting your time, questioning me, and look for the actual killer. You and I both know my family isn't stupid enough to murder someone, especially someone I'm seen visiting on camera. We're smarter than that."

I settled back in my chair. He could keep me there all day, but I wasn't talking about Gabby. She was the only person who was completely innocent in this mess. My family had already ripped her to pieces. I wouldn't allow Harold to finish her off.

"It is relevant. She snuck into a woman's apartment, harassed her, and then that woman ended up murdered in a back alley. She then skipped town." He laughed mockingly. "If that doesn't scream, *I'm guilty*, then I don't know what does. Oh, and according to the victim's parents, you also showed up at their home, and the dad pulled a gun on you to get you to go away."

My jaw clenched. "We didn't sneak into her apartment," I corrected, knowing damn well I needed to shut my mouth, but I couldn't stop myself when it came to protecting her. "You watched the surveillance video. You can clearly see Ivy letting us into her apartment *willingly*. It wasn't even around the time she was killed. It was over a month ago. Now, as I said, I'm finished with this conversation. You have no warrant to hold me."

Harold chewed on his lower lip. I knew him well enough to know he was brainstorming how to book me.

"Not yet," he replied. "I don't have a warrant *yet*. But don't forget, I'll be here, waiting for you to slip up. And when that happens, I'll get you and your family. I'll stop at nothing until you pay for your part in this woman's death."

I slapped my hand down on the table and pushed myself forward. "Good luck with that. You're going to be walking an empty trail. I played no part in it," I said with a hard sneer. They stayed quiet as I pulled away and got up from my chair. "I'll see myself out."

I kept my head down and ignored the curious stares coming at me from every angle of the station. I smacked open the front doors with extra force and hustled my ass outside. The blazing sun beat down against my black suit as I pulled my phone from my pocket to dial a cab.

"I figured you wouldn't want to ask one of those fuckheads for a ride."

I looked up at the sound of the familiar voice. Murphy was standing a few feet away from me, leaning back against one of the company cars. His hands were stuffed into the pockets of his jeans, and a baseball cap covered his shaved head.

"I'm sure they gave you a good time in there," he went on.

"You know it," I muttered, heading his way. "Door prizes, cupcakes, a celebratory dance." I slapped him on the shoulder when I reached him and ducked into the passenger seat. "Thanks for the ride, man." I turned up the AC and loosened my shirt collar. As soon as he jumped into the driver's side, I asked him what I'd been dying to know. "Did you find what I asked for?"

Murphy was one of the best IT guys at our company. He excelled at finding people and hacking into shit he shouldn't be in. Asher, my cousin, had been on the Ivy case because my dad wanted to keep it in the family, but Murphy jumped on board when he left for football conditioning.

I noticed his hesitation as he slowly nodded.

"Spit it out," I told him.

"Gabby is in Miami," he said, pressing on the gas pedal and heading into traffic.

"Miami?" I asked in confusion. "What the hell is she doing in Miami?" I racked my brain, trying to figure out what would've brought her there out of all places. Then, it hit me. "Fucking Asher," I groaned, throwing my head back against the headrest. "Motherfucker."

My blood went hot, and Murphy's silence gave me the answer I needed. She was there with him. He was my cousin, but that still pissed me off. She was mine, not his. Not anyone else's.

I clenched my fists. Gabby had run straight into Asher's arms the second it got hard in our relationship. She never gave me the chance to explain myself ... to make shit right between us.

"Book me a flight," I said.

"You think that's smart?" He looked at me like I was batshit crazy. "Dude, you were just interrogated for *murder*. If you leave, it'll look suspicious as fuck. You'll have a target on your back."

Everything around me was turning into a shitstorm. Ivy's murder. John missing for days, which made everyone assume he was responsible for her death. My dad and uncle were at each other's throat over his behavior toward Gabby. My dad wasn't smart enough to realize that messing with your brother's stepdaughter was off-limits, whether you liked her or not.

"Book the ticket and keep your mouth shut about it," I answered.

I had to get to Gabby before the police did. They'd go in full force, catching her off guard, and she wouldn't know what to do. She needed to return to Atlanta and clear her name. That was why I was going to get her. At least, that was my story. I was also going for the selfish reason of bringing her home.

Murphy responded with a nod, letting me know he still thought I was making a mistake. The ride stayed quiet until he pulled into the parking garage of our office building.

"I got you, man," he finally said, gearing the car into park. "But if your dad finds out, don't get me in trouble. I can't be losing my job because you always think with your dick."

"It will be my ass, I promise. Trust me, my dad knows you're irreplaceable."

* * *

I stepped out of the elevator and took a deep breath, unsure what side of him I'd be dealing with.

"Your dad wants to see you," Summer said when I walked into the lobby, giving me a hopeful smile.

Since she was my dad's mistress, she was most likely receiving the brunt of his mood swings. I felt bad for her and wondered if she regretted ever getting involved with him.

I lifted my chin in her direction. "Thanks for letting me know."

At first, I'd been shocked he hadn't shown up at the police station, but then I realized he was testing me—seeing if I could handle the problem on my own and then answer to him.

"What did the assholes want?" he asked when I made it into his office and shut the door. He looked at me from behind his massive desk and leaned back in his chair.

I gave him a dumbfounded look. "What do you think they wanted? They questioned me about Ivy's dead body."

"What did you tell them?"

"Nothing, except that if they wanted me to answer shit, I needed my lawyer."

He nodded in approval of my answer. "Good job. Don't talk to them again, you hear me? I've called my lawyer. Everything goes through him."

I sat down across from him. "Got it."

"Did they ask about John?"

"No, but I'm sure they'll be bringing him in soon, considering she was all over the news, admitting to being his mistress."

"We need to make sure his name is cleared."

Ivy had been John's mistress from hell. He came to us when she started threatening him about exposing their affair. We'd attempted to pay her off, but our checkbooks weren't thick enough. John's wife, however, did have enough money, and she paid Ivy to out the affair to the media. She wanted a divorce and needed a way he couldn't touch her money.

Now, Ivy was dead. All fingers pointed to John, and we'd been the one to represent him, which would turn fingers our way too.

"We have another problem," I went on. He raised an eyebrow. "It's Finch."

"Goddamn it. It doesn't surprise me that the motherfucker took the case. I'm sure he was jumping at the opportunity."

"And he's pretty damn adamant on making sure we're the ones to go down for it."

"Did you get any information about her death?"

"They found her in an abandoned alley—naked, stabbed, and shot, execution-style."

"Shit!"

"The DNA was wiped clean, so the cops have nothing. John has big money behind him, so I think they're hesitant to bring him in without having sufficient evidence."

"Did they ask you about the girl?"

"Gabby?"

He nodded, like it would kill him to say her name.

"They have camera footage of us going to see Ivy at her apartment."

"Have they brought her in?"

"They can't find her, but they asked where she is."

"If she talks, her big mouth will ruin everything." He shook his head in anger. "Where the fuck is she anyway? You need to get to her before dimwit Harold does and breaks her down. She could be what gives them the information to ruin us."

"She's in Miami with Asher. Murphy is booking me a flight as we speak."

I hadn't planned to tell him that, but since he'd agreed we needed to get to her before the police, it was a good call.

"The hell you are," he snarled, proving me wrong. "Call the fucking girl and tell her to keep quiet. I know that's a problem for her, but you need to explain what's at stake if she doesn't. Her ass is on the line too."

"She won't answer my calls because she hates me for what *you* did. And I'm sure they're going to have our phones tapped soon." I wasn't sure about the whole phone-tapping thing, but it was another good excuse.

"I'll send someone down there to get her."

"I'm the only one going to her. End of discussion. When she comes back, you're going to play nice. You don't, I'm not stopping her from doing whatever she wants."

"I'm the one who needs to play nice?" he huffed out. "Didn't she leave because of you, not me?"

"She left because of all of us," I corrected.

He whipped his hand through the air. "Doesn't matter. Take care of it."

I brought myself up from the chair and left the room without saying another word. I needed to prepare myself for seeing her again.

It was time to get my girl back.

Chapter Two

GABBY

"MOTHERFUCKER, THAT THING IS ANNOYING," Asher grumbled next to me as the ear-piercing sound blared from the alarm clock sitting on the nightstand.

I was in a room that didn't belong to me. Although I was growing more comfortable there with each passing day. That contentment was because of Asher, and I wasn't sure if that was a good or bad thing.

Bad.

Most definitely bad.

I was setting myself up for disaster. Nothing would result in this but heartbreak and broken friendship. I needed to get up, grab my bags, walk away, and stop being so damn selfish.

I told myself that every day. Then backed out. I'd reconvince myself that I needed just one more day to get my head straight.

Because I couldn't go back *there* yet.

Because I couldn't face *him* yet.

I needed a game plan before facing the man who broke my heart, a moment to pick myself up and get the *I don't care* attitude down even if I was secretly breaking inside. I had to get that down because I was positive Dalton would be at my door the second I returned to Atlanta.

"Sorry for waking you up," Asher muttered, rubbing his knuckles against his eyes.

"It's okay," I whispered.

I tried to stop myself before it happened, but it was unstoppable. I took a deep breath and lowered my gaze to his bare chest that was only halfway covered by the sheets. My mouth watered. Looking at him like that was wrong on so many levels. I didn't have feelings for him like that. No romantic feelings—only friendship. But that still didn't stop my fingers from itching to reach out and touch him.

That was bad.

Real bad.

A loud, exaggerated cough caused me to peel my eyes away from his body and look back to his face. Asher smiled arrogantly, and I sighed as my face warmed, my cheeks blushing in embarrassment. Me checking him out didn't mean I planned to straddle his cock and fuck him.

It wasn't the first time he'd caught me checking him out and probably wouldn't be the last either. Asher was fit from his years of playing football. He had an eight-pack, and his arms were all muscle. He was hot as fuck.

"For someone who loves to check me out all the time, you sure suck at using it to your advantage," he said. "You know you can have your way with me anytime you'd like, right? I'm always at your disposal."

"Yes, you've mentioned that a few times," I said slowly.

I tried to tell myself he was joking every time he said something like that, but I knew better. Asher had confessed his feelings for me, and I walked away from him in fear of ruining the friendship we had. He repeatedly reminded me of our attraction since I showed up at his doorstep. If I wanted a relationship with him, he was all in.

But I was in love with someone else and couldn't throw those feelings away, no matter how hard I wanted to. I didn't want Dalton to mean a damn to me, but I couldn't get rid of our memories together and why I'd fallen for him. Not enough time had passed, and I wasn't sure if it ever would. Having your heart broken for the first time was hard.

Asher gave me a look, expecting more to my response. I hated this part. It was like I was punching him with my words every time.

I rubbed my eyes and let out a deep breath before replying, "Asher, you know how I feel about Dalton. It would be unfair for me to say anything else when my heart isn't in it."

He tried to hide it, but I didn't miss his face fall. "Have you talked to him?"

I shook my head. "I blocked his number."

That had been step one in my Dalton Detox Plan. If he tried to call, I'd never know. I'd also flagged his email address as spam and blocked him on every social media account I had. He had no way of contacting me. I had no way of hearing his excuses.

"He tried calling me last night," Asher said.

I shut my eyes, contemplating whether I wanted him to go any further. "Does he know?"

Asher's long fingers ran over his face. "He sounded wasted, so I didn't understand half of the shit he said. But him calling means he knows something, most likely that you're with me."

"I guess it was pretty obvious if he found out I wasn't staying with Cora or Daisy."

His face softened. "I'm glad you came to me."

Asher was my first phone call when I had to get out of Atlanta fast. The two people I trusted and loved had betrayed me. I wasn't ready to hear their excuses. So, I turned off my phone, turned up the radio, and drove to Miami.

He stretched out his legs under the white sheets. "A bunch of us are going out tonight to watch the fights. You want to come?"

Asher played football for the University of Miami. So far, I'd met a few of his teammates when they stopped by after practice. They were constantly inviting him to go out with them, but he kept declining because he didn't want to leave me. I didn't want him missing out again.

"You go. I'll be fine," I replied.

"I'm not going out and leaving you here by yourself."

"Did you forget I'm only eighteen? I can't even get into bars."

"And I'm only twenty, kitten. But being on the football team has its perks."

"I guess that gives you preferential treatment, huh? You don't have to obey the laws because you can catch a ball and let other men tackle you?"

He shrugged. "Pretty much. That also means your lucky ass gets to come with me. ID or no ID."

He chuckled when I rolled my eyes.

"Oh, yay, I get to be one of your groupies who's allowed in the club because she's with the hot douchebag football player," I said, feigning excitement.

I knew what it was like, getting invited to things because of your profession or who you were related to. Lane and Cora got invited to everything because his family was loaded, and I always tagged along with them.

"Aw, that's sweet, babe," Asher replied, grabbing my side and pulling me into his hard chest. "We'll have to work on the douchebag part, but I'm glad you're finally admitting you're attracted to me. I knew you'd eventually let your honest feelings out that you want to jump my bones."

From the night I'd met him, I always thought he was attractive. I probably would've been all over him if he wasn't my stepbrother. But I only saw him as a friend now. I couldn't lose everything we'd built by getting into a relationship that ended up not working out. There'd be some *very* awkward Christmases.

He kissed the top of my head before sliding out from behind me. "I've got to get to practice. I'll see you in a bit."

He yawned and headed toward the bathroom, wearing only his boxers. I didn't look away until he cut off my view by shutting the door. I twisted around and grabbed my phone at the sound of the shower starting.

I had two missed calls—one from Cora and the other from my mom. I hit Cora's name and listened to ringing come alive on the other end.

"Hey, girl," she answered.

"Hey, what's going on?"

"Nothing too exciting here ..." Her voice trailed off.

Something was up. I knew my best friend well enough to know when she was hiding something from me.

"Okay, what are you not telling me?" I asked impatiently.

"Nothing." Her answer came out too quickly before she faked a yawn. "I just woke up. You know how I am when I'm sleepy. I sound weird and shit."

"Right," I said skeptically. "Are you going to tell me, or do I have to drag it out of you?"

"Good luck doing that when you're thousands of miles away. You're being paranoid. It's nothing. I only wish you had come to me instead of rushing to Asher."

"You know I couldn't because you're too close to everything and ..."

I pulled the phone away when I heard her scream.

"Dalton keeps calling us!" Lane's voice yelled into the phone, and I could hear him fighting Cora off from grabbing it back. "You need to call him. At least hear him out because he won't leave us alone."

"I told him not to tell you that shit," Cora said, taking over the phone at the same time Lane let out a heavy grunt. "It doesn't matter what that asshole wants. He deserves a quick kick in the balls for what he tried to pull. I mean, who doesn't tell someone they're getting married? That's fucked up."

"Tell me about it," I grumbled, pissed off that I still couldn't escape Dalton from coming up.

"Anyway, how's Miami?"

"It's okay," I answered, relieved that the conversation was turning away from him. "All I've done is hang out in Asher's apartment and watch TV."

"Quit sulking like a Debbie Downer and go out. Move on. He's a damn Douglas, for Christ's sake. He can't be that irreplaceable."

She had no idea. Cora hated Dalton's entire family because of their reputation and what Dalton's sister, Piper, had put us through in high school.

"We're supposed to go out tonight," I said.

"That's my girl. Have fun, and if you so happen to get the opportunity to hook up with your sexy stepbrother, do it."

I chuckled and rolled my eyes. Cora was Team Asher right now. She was actually Team Anyone Who Wasn't Engaged.

"That is so not happening."

"You never know. Asher would be good for you. He's a great guy, and he obviously likes you. Quit going for assholes. They're always going to screw you over because that's the only thing they know how to do. Try the nice guy for once. See how much happier you'll be when you don't have to worry about getting hurt every three seconds."

"He's my stepbrother."

"There are no bloodlines shared."

Cora told me the rest of the gossip around the city and then begged me to call my mom. I eventually told her I had to go.

That phone call to my mom was going to have to wait.

I waved good-bye to Asher and waited until the door shut behind him before letting the tears fall. I kept my front around other people, but I couldn't do it alone. No. When I was alone, I had time to think, to remember, and those memories wouldn't stop, no matter how hard I tried to forget them.

Dalton made me believe I was good enough and capable of love—both giving and receiving it.

I shut my eyes, relaxing my head against the pillow, and memories haunted me. My stomach grew nauseated as I remembered the night I found out he was engaged. I was so high but quickly fell. My heart was ripped from my chest and ripped into pieces.

I never wanted to feel that way again.

My heart was off-limits to not only Dalton, but to the entire male population.

* * *

The pub was crowded with drunken college students huddled around tables, focusing on the big-screen TVs plastered to the walls. A group of guys high-fived each other when a boxer hit another boxer. I'd never understood what was so entertaining about watching two guys beat the shit out of each other, but whatever. I was only there to get my mind off Dalton and relax.

"What do you want to drink, kitten?" Asher asked, his hands locking around my waist to lead me toward the bar.

He'd been right. We weren't even carded. The bouncer simply moved aside to let us in, no questions asked.

"Whatever is fine," I answered. "But nothing too strong."

I'd never really been a heavy drinker, so I needed to be cautious. The last time I was drunk around a guy I was attracted to, I gave him my virginity. I obviously couldn't regift that to Asher, but the higher my alcohol content, the higher the chance I'd make a stupid decision.

"I'll take a Coors, and she'll have a vodka with cranberry," he yelled over to the bartender, who promptly started making our drinks. "Here." He handed me the glass. "This shouldn't be too strong, if you take it slow."

"Thanks," I replied with a smile.

He grabbed my hand and guided me to a table in the middle of the room, where a few guys were sitting.

"Asher, my man. What's going on, bro?" one guy asked, his eyes on me when we made it to our seats.

The other guys gave us a head nod and then turned their attention back to the fight.

Asher dragged out a stool for me before taking the one to my right. "Not shit, man," he answered. He grabbed his phone from his pocket when it rang and stared at the screen. "Shit. This is important." He turned toward the guy. "Keep an eye on her. Don't leave her side."

"Got it," the guy said, tilting his beer in response.

Asher got lost in the crowd while his friend gave me a sideways look, making me nervous.

He leaned in, his voice lowering. "I know who you are."

"Okay ..." I answered, not sure exactly how to reply to that.

I didn't recognize him, so I knew he'd never come over while I'd been at Asher's. He looked about the same age as him. He was built, had brown hair, and a short beard.

"And I think you need to take your troubled little ass back to Atlanta and away from my friend. You're not good for him." He kept his eyes on me and took a long draw from his beer.

"You know nothing about me," I snapped, taken aback by his insult.

"You're right. However, I know he came back here, fucking heart-broken because of you, which is something that's never happened. Then, you show up at his doorstep when shit goes wrong with your boyfriend, the guy you chose over him. Asher's my boy. He's been my best friend since he moved here. He's a good guy and not a second option for replaceable bitches. He's not a rebound unless he wants to be. Chicks would kill to sleep with him. So, I repeat, get your ass back to Atlanta unless you plan on being with him and not running back to your ex."

I wanted to slap the shit out of this guy. I raised my chin, not letting his harsh words faze me. "First off, you're an asshole. Secondly, if you call me a bitch again, I'll break that beer bottle over your head."

He shrugged. "If you think someone being honest and protecting their friend is an asshole, that's fine by me."

"For your information—" I was surprised fire wasn't spitting out with my words.

"Sorry about that, guys," Asher said, cutting me off when he came back to the table. He sat back down and slapped the asshole on the back. "You two getting along okay?"

"Getting to know each other," the guy answered. "I forgot to introduce myself. I'm Logan. Asher has told me *so* much about you." He held out his hand, and I shook it, making sure my fingernails dug into his skin. He acted like he didn't feel it and glanced over at Asher. "Guess who I ran into at the bar."

"Who?" Asher asked.

"Morgan." His lips spread into a cocky grin. "She's looking for you."

Logan wanted to get underneath my skin and make me jealous by using a chick as a wedge between Asher and me. Or he wanted Asher to hook up with the girl, so I'd run away. Either way, the dick had an agenda.

Asher shuddered. "Hard pass. She takes shit too serious and tries to suck the life out of you."

"To my recollection, you enjoy it when she sucks. She's hot, and from what you've told me before, she's also a great fuck." Logan's evil smile cut my way.

Asher looked at me, his eyes sending me a silent apology. "She's needy. I don't do needy."

Logan shook his head. "She's not needy. She likes you."

I studied my drink, acting like I wasn't interested in his friend trying to rub my nose in the fact that Asher had screwed other girls. I couldn't be pissed about that. Asher was a free agent and didn't belong to me.

"She likes anyone on the football team," Asher corrected. "She's a jersey chaser. If I don't go pro, I can guarantee you she'll ditch my ass for someone else with a contract."

I looked up when a gorgeous blonde approached us. Her long curls were bleached blonde, hitting just below her ample cleavage, which was more than I was working with.

She wrapped her hand around Asher's arm and sent him a seductive smile. "Asher, baby. I missed your handsome face while you were away," she said, her voice soft and sensual. "But don't worry; I've been waiting for you to come back, hoping we can start back where we left off."

"Hey, Morgan," Asher said, slowly dragging his arm out of her hold. He rubbed the tip of his nose, eyeing the empty seat next to him. He frowned when she hopped on it and made herself comfortable.

"And you're his sister?" she asked, looking over at me eagerly.

"Logan said you were staying with Asher for a few days. Maybe we can get our nails done this week? Get to know each other."

Yeah, that wasn't happening.

"I'm his stepsister," I said, unsure of why I found it necessary to correct her.

"Same difference," Logan chimed in. His eyes burned into mine, flickering with hate.

"Not really. We're not blood-related. We've only known each other a few years." I smiled and took a drink.

Two can play this game, buddy.

Asher and Morgan both looked back and forth between the two of us, noticing the tension.

"Now that we've got the introductions out of the way, let's watch this fucking fight," Logan said. "I've got a shit-ton of money riding on this."

The animosity fizzled, and we spent the next hour watching two men go round after round without having a knockout. People stopped to talk to Asher, and he introduced me to everyone. Morgan stayed by his side, practically sitting on his lap, until he pulled away and said he needed to use the restroom. He came back and sat on the opposite side of me and away from her, giving her the hint that he wasn't interested.

I'd only taken a few sips of my drink but felt dizzy. I pushed the glass in front of me to the middle of the table. Even the sight of it made my stomach turn.

"You okay?" Asher asked, looking at me in concern.

"I'm fine," I said, smiling and patting his arm. "Just feel kind of light-headed."

"You ready to go?"

I nodded.

"Let me pay the tab real quick. I'll grab you a water and be right back." He brought himself up and hustled over to the bar.

"Make your decision," Logan said with a sneer. He hadn't said another word to me since our little disagreement. "It was a pleasure meeting you, Gabby, and I hope never to see you again." He slapped the table and walked away.

I followed Asher to his car, and he held open the door for me to get in.

"I love this car," I told him, making myself comfortable in the leather Mercedes seat. "It's nice."

"Thanks. It was a graduation present from my mom."

During the divorce, Asher took his mom's side, which I didn't blame him for. His dad had an affair with my mom, so it was only right. I would've done the same thing.

That was another thing I admired about Asher. His loyalty. He didn't give a shit about pissing people off. He stayed true to the people he loved—unlike the guy I was trying not to think about.

"Did you have fun tonight?" Asher asked, pulling out of the parking lot. He only had one beer. He wanted to be the designated driver tonight, so I could let loose and forget about my troubles.

"I did. It was exactly what I needed to get my mind off everything."

"You can move here, you know? You can stay at my apartment and maybe take some classes at the university?"

My plan after graduation had been to take a year off, but getting a fresh start sounded appealing. Maybe that was the remedy I needed. A new place. A new plan.

"That doesn't sound like such a bad idea," I answered. "I'll probably have to get a job first though. I didn't even make it long enough to make a lot of money at the firm."

"You do know my dad is planning on paying for your college? You don't have to worry about that shit, Gabby."

"I don't want your dad to pay for it."

That was secretly another reason why I took a year off. I knew my mom's husband would've forked out the bill, and I wasn't ready to hear the rest of his family criticize us for it.

"Put your pride aside. It's free, and he has no problem doing it, considering he married your mom. Even though he's only known you for a few years, he cares about you. Trust me, I know my dad. He wouldn't have offered if he didn't want to." He grabbed my hand. "Spend the rest of the summer here, see what you think, and you can apply for next semester."

I smiled, squeezing his hand. "I'll think about it."

* * *

Asher tossed his keys onto the kitchen table when we made it back to his apartment.

"You want to go to bed, or you up for watching a movie?" he asked, looking over at me. He headed into the kitchen, pulled out two bottles of water from the fridge, and handed me one.

"How about a movie in bed?" I replied.

"Sounds good to me." He stopped, patting his jeans. "Fuck, I left my phone in the car. I'll be right back."

I nodded and headed into his bedroom to change. I grabbed my bag and shoveled through it until I found my pajamas. I pulled out a camisole top and shorts. I stumbled out of my jeans and threw them on the floor next to the bed. I'd worry about them later. My shirt was the next to go.

"Goddamn."

I jumped at his voice and turned around to find Asher standing in the doorway, his eyes hooded. He stared at me, his teeth biting into his lower lip.

"I'll turn around if you want me to, but I'm praying to God you don't."

My breathing hitched when he took a step closer. I needed to cover myself, but I couldn't move.

"I want to see what else is under all of that." He took another step. "Tell me you want me to do that, Gabby."

I opened my mouth, but the words didn't come out. I couldn't do what he was asking. My heart thumped against my chest, constricting my breathing, and I was unable to speak. My mind was spinning. The alcohol was drumming through me, clouding my judgment and telling me to take this step. I knew drinking was a bad idea.

He stopped only a few inches away from me, his breathing labored. "Tell me what you want me to do."

"I want you to kiss me," I replied, taking a step toward him. "I want you to kiss me, Asher."

"Thank God."

His lips hit mine and paralyzed me like a drug. I opened my mouth, allowing his warm tongue entry, and he kissed me hard. Our tongues danced together. I shivered when his hands ran up my sides, leaving goose bumps in their wake. I whimpered, feeling his cold hands sliding down my skin and into the back of my lace panties.

"Tell me this is okay," he whispered into my ear, tugging at my lobe with his teeth. "Tell me you want this as bad as I do."

I do. The words were at the tip of my tongue, but they weren't releasing.

"Tell me you want this, Gabby," he repeated, his voice rough and thick. He needed validation that this was going to lead somewhere.

Reality came rolling through, telling me this wasn't a good idea. I froze. "I ... I can't," I whispered. "It won't be fair to you. I can't."

Asher quickly pulled away from me and shook his head. "Goddamn it, Gabby!" He smacked his hand against the wall. "Get the fuck over him. News flash: he's marrying another woman. He chose her *and money* over you. Don't you think it's time you do the fucking same?" His eyes glossed over as he took in three deep breaths. "What does he have that I don't? Tell me what the hell I need to do to make you realize that I'm the better choice? That I'm the one who will make you happy, not him."

"Give me time," I whispered, wanting to calm him down.

"Yeah, time. Fine. I'll give you a week." He held up a finger. "One week, and then we're having this conversation again. A real conversation. So, be ready."

I dropped my arms to my sides and nodded. I wasn't sure how to explain that I needed longer than a week. How did you explain you hated love and that you'd never take the chance of being hurt again?

"I'll be on the couch if you want to talk," he said, walking out and slamming the door behind him.

Chapter Three

DALTON

THE SUN BEAT down on me as I waved down a taxi, jumped in, and gave the driver Asher's address. My flight had been short but nerve-racking. I had no idea what I would walk into or what Gabby's reaction would be when I showed up, unannounced ... and unwanted.

Murphy had briefed me on Gabby. Her phone was traced to Asher's, which was a smack in the face. I fought away thoughts of her sleeping with my cousin, with someone else, but it was hard.

"Give me ten minutes," I told the cab driver when we pulled up to Asher's complex.

He turned around to look at me and huffed, "I charge for that."

"And I'll pay for it." I stepped out of the car, pulled my phone from my pocket, and checked for Asher's apartment number.

I rubbed my sweaty hands down my jeans before knocking and then held my breath when the door swung open.

"Motherfucker, you've got to be kidding me," Asher grumbled when he answered the door, shirtless.

I ignored his greeting and peeked over his shoulder. "Is she here?" I asked.

Please tell me Murphy was wrong. Maybe he was mistaken.

He took a step back to open the door wider. "Gabby," he called out with a snarl of his upper lip. "You have a visitor."

270

"It's nice to see you too, baby cousin," I commented, walking inside.

Asher and I weren't close, growing up. We ran with different crowds but got along ... until Gabby. Now, it felt like we were in a *whose balls are bigger* competition with Gabby's heart being the prize. And Douglas men weren't keen on giving up easily.

Gabby whipped around the corner and stumbled back when she saw me. "What ... what are you doing here?" Her hair was wet, and her face drained of color as she stomped toward me.

I flared my nostrils at the sight of her wearing only a blue towel and swung my arms out toward the two half-naked people. "I should be asking you the same question."

They stared at me in silence. She wasn't going to answer my question, and neither was Asher. I shook my head and ran my hands through my hair, trying to do my best to fight off my anger. I needed to calm down and convince her to get on a plane with me and go home. We could hash out our problems in private.

"Don't you guys watch the news?" I asked, looking back and forth between them.

"No," they both answered in unison.

I stalked across the living room, snagged the remote from the coffee table, and switched *SportsCenter* to CNN. Standing back, I watched the headlines flash along the screen.

"Holy shit," Gabby whispered, her hand flying to her mouth when Ivy's picture showed up on the screen.

The news of the governor's mistress being viciously murdered had hit the mainstream media. John Gentry, the man Republicans loved and hoped to be their next presidential candidate, not only had an affair, but also killed the woman. At least, that was what it appeared to be.

The anchors shook their heads in disgust while discussing the brutality of her murder and shared their thoughts on who they thought did it.

"While you've been down here, doing *whatever*," I said, staring straight at Gabby when it cut to a commercial break, "this is what I've been dealing with. Ivy is dead. We need to get you back to Atlanta. The police have already brought me in for questioning. You're next on their list, and the fact that you ran off to a different state doesn't look good."

"What?" she choked out. "They can't seriously think that *I* killed her?"

I stumbled back in surprise when Asher's palms collided with my chest. I'd been too focused on Gabby and not seen it coming. As I regained my composure, I looked at my cousin, and our eyes met. I rolled up my sleeves, fully prepared to fight him.

"Fuck you, Dalton," Asher hissed. "I can't fucking believe you dragged her into your dirty bullshit. You're a real piece of work, you know that? You're just like your piece-of-shit father."

Anger surged through me as I tried to ignore his insults, but I couldn't stop myself from pushing him back, harder than I should have. His words hit too close to home. He stumbled back but quickly caught himself.

"Fuck you, Asher," I yelled, looking away from him to Gabby. "We need to talk. We have to fix this before things get worse."

"No, what you need to be focusing on is getting me out of your mess, so I'm not arrested for a crime I didn't commit," Gabby argued, throwing her hands up in the air dramatically. "Do I even look like I could kill someone? I only weigh a hundred and fifteen pounds. I can't even bench-press more than twenty."

"They probably don't think you killed her, but they assume you know something about who did. Pack your shit. We have to get back before they find out I left," I replied.

"You don't have to go anywhere with him," Asher said, jumping back into our conversation, where he didn't belong.

"I don't think you understand the severity of the situation, Asher," I said mockingly. "We're being questioned for murder. Let's worry about Gabby not being in jail rather than you getting your dick wet. We don't have time to do this back-and-forth shit." I looked at Gabby. "The police asked me why you fled the state the same night Ivy was murdered. That means they've looked into you."

Gabby looked too shocked to say anything, but she looked close to tears.

"Get your bags. I've already booked us a flight. You can come back after everything blows over if that's the fucking issue. Right now, we have more problems than our relationship. That's to keep our asses out of prison." I glanced at Asher. "Your bodyguard can come too, if that makes you feel better."

Do I want Asher tagging along? Fuck no. But I was willing to do anything if it meant her coming back.

"I can't miss football, or they'll bench me for the first three games," Asher said, guilt clear on his face.

"It's fine," she replied. "I don't expect you to do that."

Watching them was like a stab to the heart. They looked like a couple. I'd lost before getting the chance to even get back in the ring.

"I'll go get my bag," she said slowly. She didn't look at me once before turning around and walking into another room, what I assumed was the bedroom.

"You'll probably want to put some clothes on too," I yelled after her. "And it seems like you're pissed at me. Good thing we have an entire flight to catch up."

Her head poked out of the doorframe. "Good thing I'll be purchasing noise-canceling headphones," she fired back, giving me a dirty look and disappearing back into the room.

Chapter Four

GABBY

"YOU'RE NOT IGNORING me the entire flight," Dalton said, making himself comfortable in the seat next to me. "It's not going to happen."

"It sure is," I answered.

As difficult as it was, I had to stick to my word. Letting Dalton back in would be a mistake.

He booked our seats right next to each other. I'd asked to be moved, to trade my ticket in for another flight, anything, but it didn't work. It was a full flight, and the attendant was too busy listening to Dalton telling her it wasn't necessary to hear my argument.

I stared over at him and wanted to slap myself for thinking how good he looked. Even after him hurting me, I was still attracted to him. His hair was swept back and messy—my favorite look on him. His blue eyes would glance over at me every few seconds. And his T-shirt showed off the muscles in his arms. Trying not to gawk at him made the flight even harder.

I rummaged through the bag sitting in my lap until I found my Kindle and the headphones I'd bought from one of the terminal shops. They cost me double what I could've bought them for online, but anything was worth avoiding conversation with Dalton.

I jerked forward when the headphones were ripped from my hand.

"You're not getting these back until we talk," he warned, his baby blues shining down on me.

I groaned when he shoved them into his pocket.

Asshole.

The man always liked to take charge and get his way.

I crossed my arms. "Fine, Dalton. What do you want to talk about? Would you like my input on what type of flowers you should have at your wedding? Tulips? Lilies? Oh, and do I get a plus-one?" I raised my voice and threw my hands up. "Hell, am I even invited?"

My ranting worked me up more. The reminder of the way he'd hurt me and the lies he'd told resurfaced.

Did I want an invite to the wedding? Hell no.

I would steer clear of any future events thrown by the Douglas family. Better yet, I was staying away from them, period.

"Or should we talk about how you were the first guy—the *first damn guy*—I ever let in, and you fed me lies?" I added, unable to stop myself.

Dalton opened his mouth, most likely to spit out a bullshit apology, but I continued talking. "*Or* should we talk about how your family messed up my life so much that I might be blamed for murdering a woman?"

I failed to realize how loud I was speaking until I noticed every eye in first class on us. *Well, shit.*

Dalton slammed his hand against the back of the chair in front of us, and they looked away, pretending to be busy with something else.

"What I did was wrong," he said in a low voice. "I hurt you, and I take full accountability for my fuckup. I betrayed our relationship, and that's the biggest mistake of my life. I never told you about my engagement because I was breaking it off."

I stared down at my lap.

"I haven't touched her. I haven't touched anyone but you. You're it for me, Gabby."

I sucked in a breath at his words but tried to keep my face cold, which was difficult.

"You're it for me."

I wanted to believe his words. I really did. But I couldn't. Too much had happened. Too many lies had been told.

"As for any legal trouble regarding Ivy, I give you my word that I'll protect you from any harm or trouble. I will do anything for you. I promise. I love you. I told you I did then, and I wasn't lying. You're the love of my life." He tapped my leg while I stared at him, speechless. "Now that we have that covered, don't act like you're Little Miss Innocent either. Bed-hopper."

"Excuse me?" I shrieked, drawing the attention of the people again.

He'd gone from warming my heart to sending a knife through it. The man knew how to turn me hot and then cold.

"You heard me. We break up, and you run straight to Asher's bed. You were in a damn towel when I got there."

"You have no idea what you're talking about."

I couldn't say it didn't look bad. I wanted to tell him I couldn't give Asher anything because he'd already drained everything from me, but I held back. I wanted him to be tortured, thinking that I no longer belonged to him. Maybe if he felt that, he'd stay away.

I hadn't even had the chance to talk to Asher since last night's incident. He never returned to the bedroom and slept on the couch. I wanted to crawl out of his bed and apologize, but I was too scared. I didn't want to hurt him anymore. It was refreshing to get away from him, to think. I only wished my rescuer were someone else.

"I'm not an idiot, Gabby," he said. "If you hadn't hooked up with him yet, it was coming. You and I both know that."

"I don't fuck people for fun."

"And neither do I. You're the only girl who's been in my bed. In my heart. Can I say the same for you?" He raised a brow.

I leaned over and snagged the headphones from his pocket swiftly before he had the chance to stop me. I plugged them into my phone and turned the volume on high. I didn't have the patience to have that conversation.

* * *

I recognized the guy waiting for us at the airport when we walked out of baggage claim.

Murphy worked in the IT department. I didn't know him and had never had a conversation with him, but he seemed to be the guy in charge there. Asher said he was the best at what they did. He was probably the one who ratted me out to Dalton for being in Florida.

I listened to breakup songs during the flight, a reminder to stay pissed at the man sitting next to me. Not that it stopped him from torturing me. He'd brush his hand along my arm, rest it along my thigh, and send shivers through my body.

"Hey, guys," Murphy greeted, stepping forward and grabbing my bag.

I smiled at him.

He turned, popped the trunk, and dropped my bag inside. Dalton didn't have any bags. He knew he wasn't going to be staying long. I tightened my purse on my shoulder and got into the backseat.

I pointed to the front of the car and groaned when Dalton slid in next to me. "Your name is on the front seat *up there*." I scooted to the edge of my seat, my shoulder smacking into the door.

"The only thing with my name on it is you," he said.

He slammed the door shut and scooted in closer to me. I shivered when his lips brushed against my ear, and his voice lowered to a whisper. "And my favorite is when you're moaning it."

I shoved him away from me. "You're an asshole, you know that? That is never happening again. As soon as I tell the police I have nothing to do with this, I'm staying far away from all of you."

"Where are we headed?" Murphy asked, looking back at us from the rearview mirror. His unsurprised behavior confirmed he was definitely the one who had tracked me down.

"The office," Dalton answered.

"And then if you'll please drop me off at my friend Cora's," I instructed, shooting Dalton a glare. "I'll give you the directions after we drop him off."

I flinched when Dalton stretched his arm out along the backseat. "You can't run away from this, Gabby. We have to go to the office and talk to my dad right now. It's imperative. After that, I'll drop you off wherever you want, but this has to happen, whether you like it or not."

"I'm not stepping foot in that asshole's office," I hissed. "*You* can go talk to him and then relay any important information to me later with a phone call." I'd have to unblock him. Unfortunately. "There's no way in hell I can look at him without wanting to plunge out his eyes with my fingernails."

Torture twisted on his face. He felt bad for making me do this. "Give him five minutes. If he insults you, if he says one wrong thing, we'll leave." He angled himself toward me, his eyes locking with mine. "My biggest priority is to keep you safe. If that means we have to face him for a few minutes, then that's what we have to do. But I can promise you that I wouldn't have you do this if there was an easier way."

I nodded in response, not bothering to say anything else. Even if I attempted to argue, it wouldn't have changed anything. We were almost to the office, and unless I planned on jumping out of the car, I was screwed.

I opened my purse and grabbed my phone to tell Asher I'd landed. My next text went to Cora, asking if I could crash at her place for a few days. She immediately replied with a yes.

Sitting back, I listened to Murphy and Dalton discuss Ivy's death.

"They hacked into her phone and searched her bank and browser history but had nothing. Someone had erased everything," Murphy said.

"What's John saying about her death?" I asked.

Or my father.

I'd never accept who he was to me.

"How does he feel about his mistress getting murdered?" I continued. "Or is he the one who did it?"

Being out of the loop was strange since I'd been so involved in her case. I'd questioned Ivy and helped blackmail and threaten her.

"John is innocent," Dalton said.

"And you know this how?" I asked, looking over at him. "The guy doesn't have the best track record of being honest and forthcoming."

"John might not be a good person, but he's not a murderer. I saw what they'd done to Ivy, and there's no way he could've done something that gruesome."

"He'd never sacrifice everything to kill her," Murphy said, cutting in. "Even when everyone thought he was missing, I tracked his every move. He stayed at his cabin in Chattanooga, and his phone can be traced there as well. There's no way he could've done it."

"So then, who did?" I asked.

Maybe John didn't have blood on his hands, but he could've still been involved. My obsession with *Dateline* taught me that murder for hire was popular for cowards.

"That's what we have to figure out," Dalton answered.

"We?" I asked. "Don't you mean the police? I know you guys are lawyers who fix shit or whatever, but I highly doubt you're qualified enough to solve a freaking murder."

"We're good at doing investigative work," Dalton said.

"The best," Murphy added.

"We're also good at saving our asses."

"You'd better be," I mumbled.

I wouldn't take the blame for Ivy's death, and I didn't care who I had to take down to make sure of it.

* * *

I wanted to make a run for it when Murphy pulled into the parking garage of Douglas PR and remembered how I'd felt my first day there.

"I can do all of the talking," Dalton said, getting out of the car.

"Although you have free rein to tell him how big of an asshole he is. He needs something from you, so he's not going to act out."

My palms grew sweaty as I got out and followed him into the building. "That's exactly what I want to do, but I'm not going to waste my breath. I'll go in there, listen to what he has to say, and then leave."

"I'm heading to the control center," Murphy muttered behind us when the elevator doors opened. He gave us a salute and walked away.

I held my purse tight to my side and followed Dalton toward Wilson's office. Summer's mouth fell open when she noticed us, and I shot her a wave.

"Dalton," she said, scrunching her brows together. "And, Gabby ... this is a surprise."

"A temporary surprise," I told her. "You won't be seeing my face here again."

She frowned. "That's too bad."

Dalton looked between the two of us. We hadn't exactly been the best of friends, but after she told me about her affair with Wilson, we shared a silent bond. I didn't see her as the stuck-up woman or my enemy who'd been trying to sleep with Dalton. We were allies, two women who shared the same experience. We'd both had our hearts broken by men who would never be ours.

"Is he in there?" Dalton asked her.

"He sure is," she replied. "And he's not in the best mood."

"Well, that's not surprising," I muttered.

"Don't piss him off any more if that's possible. I don't want to have to deal with him," she added.

"We'll try, but I can't promise that'll happen," I told her with a smile. I needed to find a nice guy to set her up with, so she'd leave Wilson.

Wilson stood up and walked from behind his desk at our arrival. "Dalton," he greeted before moving his attention to me and smiling. "And, Gabrielle, thank you for coming."

He didn't seem surprised to see me, so Dalton must've given him a heads-up.

Wilson threw out his arm toward the two free chairs. "Have a seat."

I sent him a smug smile before taking my chair and hoped he could see the *fuck you* etched along my lips. He walked back around his desk and plopped down in the large chair.

I looked at Wilson in disgust. I barely knew the man, yet he'd caused me so much pain. He hated me and made it his mission to destroy any happiness that came my way if it involved his family. He'd forced Dalton to lie to me for a business gain and then publicly embarrassed me.

I looked over at Dalton and briefly felt sorry for him. He'd been pimped out by his dad and used as a pawn in a game of hierarchy. Any man who sold out his children for money or personal gain was a coward. I wouldn't be surprised if he was the one responsible for Ivy's murder. The man was ruthless.

Wilson cleared his throat before speaking, "Gabrielle, I'm not sure if you're aware of this or not, but Ivy is dead."

"I know," I answered, proud of myself for how strong my voice sounded.

"The police have ruled it a homicide. They've questioned Dalton, and we don't know if they're going to bring you in. If they do, you tell them nothing, you hear me?"

I'd decided on the way there that I would agree to whatever Wilson wanted. Then, I'd do whatever the hell I wanted. I wasn't taking orders from him anymore.

"Okay, I'll be sure to let them know I had nothing to do with it."

He looked at me skeptically. "That's the thing—I don't want you talking to them at all. Everyone obviously knows about John's affair with Ivy, but they don't know he hired us to cover it up. They don't need to know that either. If they bring you in, tell them you won't say a word without your lawyer."

"But I don't have a lawyer. And I'm definitely not paying for one."

"I'll take care of that. This firm is filled with lawyers, myself included. I'll make sure you have one there the minute you arrive."

"Why are they even questioning us?" I asked before twisting in my chair to peer at Dalton. "Why would they think we did it?"

"They saw the video of you and me leaving Ivy's apartment," Dalton answered, not looking away from me.

"Got it." I turned back to Wilson. "Am I free to go now?"

"You can, but one more thing," Dalton said, getting up from his chair. His face turned serious as he glared at Wilson. "Dad."

Wilson blew out a breath. "I apologize for any harm I might have caused you, Gabrielle. I never meant for you to get hurt. I care about you being my brother's stepdaughter. I never want you to feel disrespected."

His words were sincere, but his tone and his eyes said something different. Wilson Douglas wanted me to become his newest pawn. That wasn't happening.

"Thank you," I replied, turning and leaving the room with Dalton behind me.

The apology wasn't accepted. It never would be, but I needed to move on.

I pulled my phone out of my purse while Dalton pushed the elevator button to the first floor. "Cora is coming to get me, so I need to get my bag from the car."

"I can give you a ride there if you don't want to wait," he said.

I stared at the elevator doors as they closed us in. I looked down at the floor, remembering when we were in the elevator at Ivy's apartment. I'd been trying to push him away then too. But he wasn't having it. I'd lost my breath when he pushed me against the wall and kissed me.

"Yeah, I'm going to decline that ride." I needed to stay strong.

"It's a ride, Gabby. I'm not asking for us to get back together or to fuck you in the backseat."

I shivered, trying to mask the effect his words had on me. "That's never happening again."

I followed him back to the parking garage, and Cora texted me, saying her car was in the shop for an oil change, so it'd be a minute if I needed her to pick me up.

Shit.

"I guess I'll take that ride after all," I muttered.

Dalton didn't even try to hide his grin as he led me to the car Murphy had picked us up in and opened the passenger door for me.

"How long do I have to stay here?" I asked, getting in and buckling up my seat belt.

"Until the smoke clears. I'd estimate a few weeks to a month," he replied after getting in the car.

"A month? I'll be a nervous wreck, waiting around for a month."

He shrugged, starting the car. "Possibly. You never know."

"Let's hope they catch this killer sooner than that."

"That's why we need to figure this out."

"Are you working with the cops?"

"Nope, but we're working *harder* than the cops. We're better at our jobs." He pulled out of the parking lot. "Does your mom know you're home?"

I shook my head.

"She misses you."

"How do you know how my mom feels? You don't even know her."

"I know what it feels like to lose you, Gabby. Uncle Kenneth says she's heartbroken. Answer her phone calls. At least let her know you're okay."

My chest hitched. "She lied to me."

"People make mistakes."

"Of course they do," I muttered.

The rest of the ride to Cora's was quiet, and as soon as he pulled into her driveway, I nearly jumped out of the car. Dalton got out, popped the trunk, and handed me my bag.

I muttered a quick, "Thanks," before walking away from him.

I wanted to say more, but I couldn't. It'd only hurt me more.

Having small talk with someone you used to love, with someone you still loved, was agony. It was worse than ignoring them and acting like they didn't exist because they were in your face, asking questions and waiting on answers when you couldn't even think straight because all you remembered was the heartbreak they caused.

"So, what's the scoop?" Cora asked after answering the door. "I thought you quit that hellhole job."

I followed her into her living room. "There's not any scoop. I quit, but there's an issue with one of the clients we were working with. As soon as it's cleared up, I'm not sure what I'm doing."

"Are you going back to Florida?"

"I don't know. Honestly, I thought I was going to take a year off to find myself, but there's no way I can do that here now."

She pulled her strawberry-blonde hair into a ponytail. "Then, come with me to school."

"It's a little too late to be trying to get into school. It's practically the end of summer. What school will accept me?"

"You could try a community college or something. I'm sure my dad or Lane's could pull some strings and help you out."

"I'll figure it out."

"Okay, I'm here if you need anything, no matter what."

I nodded and smiled. "I know."

"Have you talked to your mom?"

I shook my head. I was already getting tired of hearing that question.

"Gabby, I know it's hard, but you need to talk to her."

"She lied to me *for years*. She always made me believe my father wasn't in the picture, that he'd run off somewhere."

"He technically wasn't in the picture and did run off somewhere. Just because he was close doesn't mean anything would've been different. Plus, are you sure finding out he was your dad would've convinced you to have a relationship with him? He left your mom high and dry when she found out she was pregnant. I wouldn't want to talk about him either."

Chapter Five

DALTON

"REPORTING LIVE from the home of Ivy Hart's parents. Ivy was Atlanta Governor John Gentry's alleged mistress. She was staying here after she went public about their affair to get out of the public eye. We've also received reports that she was hiding from someone else as well. Governor Gentry couldn't be reached for comment, which has convinced people he might be involved ..."

I flipped off the TV.

Damn, I fucking hated the media.

John had to make a statement. The longer he waited, the guiltier he looked. The media, they were hound dogs. They'd dig up every dirty detail about him, the affair, and I was sure they'd find out about us trying to bribe her. That would destroy our business.

I looked up at the sound of my office door swinging open. "Did you forget how to knock?" I asked, leaning back in my chair.

Leo shut the door behind him and chuckled. "I'm your older brother. I do what I want." He walked in and had a seat. "Will this be our last public visit? Do I need to start a commissary fund?"

I flipped him off. "Funny, asshole."

"Dad filled me in. What's your next move, brother? You need to get the police off your back and send them sniffing somewhere else."

Worry filled his eyes. He was trying to make light of the situation, but the concern was there.

He knew the vendetta Harold had against our family. Neither one of us knew why though.

"I have no idea." I raised a brow. "Got any suggestions?"

He ran his hands through his thick hair. "I'm afraid I don't."

"That's a first."

"I'm on the fence. A part of me wants to say fuck it and tell them everything—about John, his secrets, anything to get the heat off you. I mean, fuck, Dalton, I don't want you going down for trying to protect someone who doesn't mean shit to us. It's not worth it."

"And the other part?" I asked curiously.

He always had the best advice. I looked up to him more than my own father.

"The other part is wondering how bad that would tear our family and the business apart. I will stress this though. Like I said, if it gets too bad, throw that asshole politician under the bus, you hear me? Don't lose everything over this deal ... this job. It's not worth it. It's not worth your freedom."

"I will. My patience for this secretive bullshit is wearing thin." I dropped my head back and groaned. "What do you have going on tonight?"

I needed to get my mind off Gabby. As much as I wanted to call her, I had to give her time. She'd had a rough few weeks. I didn't want to stress her out anymore.

"We have Piper's birthday dinner tonight, remember? That's why I showed up here—to make sure you didn't try to bail."

I let out another groan. A night with my family sounded like fucking torture. "Shit, with all of this stuff going on, I completely spaced it."

"I figured. That's why I came to get your ass." He got up from the chair and waved his hand through the air toward the door. "Now, come on."

"I'm not staying long," I muttered, getting up from my chair. "And hey, question."

He raised a brow.

"Will you hire me if I get fired here?"

Leo worked for his father-in-law, who had a plethora of companies. They were all successful and clean, and he'd given Leo a nice position in exchange for putting up with his crazy-ass daughter.

"Kelly hates you. She'd kill her father if he hired you. She doesn't think you're a good influence on me." He laughed and opened the door. "Not to mention, your employment track record sucks. I doubt Dad would give you a good referral."

* * *

We were unfortunately having my sister, Piper's, birthday dinner at my parents' house. Not having dinner in a public place meant private conversations would take place. Leo and I strolled in to find everyone already seated around the long dining room table. Caterers moved in and out of the kitchen.

Kelly, Leo's wife, wasn't there—thank God. She was attending a charity event, and their kids were spending the evening at her parents' house. Leo most likely knew there'd be John talk and didn't want his kids hearing it.

"My big brothers," Piper called out, jumping up from her seat. A bright pink-lipped grin spread across her lips.

My little sister didn't have the best reputation. She'd been called a selfish and manipulative bitch more times than I could count. And to be honest, she could be one. But they didn't know her well enough to understand why she acted that way. She wanted attention because she never got any at home. She wanted someone to love her, and she would hurt anyone that got in her way of getting it.

"Happy birthday," I said, wrapping my arms around her. "The big eighteen."

"I'm officially old enough to make my own rules," she said around a squeal.

"Yeah, that's trouble," I said, and she laughed.

"Leo, Dalton," my dad said, giving us a head jerk without bothering to get up from his chair.

I nodded back while Leo greeted him.

My mom stayed quiet. She was either in a mood or too wasted to think about anything.

As soon as we sat down, Piper laid into me. "What's this I hear about you panting over that homewrecker's daughter?" she asked, a sneer in her voice. She was like the rest of my family. She didn't have a filter and said whatever was on her mind.

I held up my hand, stopping her before she went any further and really pissed me off. "Don't start that shit, Piper. You piss me off, and I walk out of here without giving you your gift. Don't insult Gabby or her mom, and I mean it."

She pouted her lips. "You know you can do better, right? Dad is never going to let you be with her." She let out a snort. "Not to mention, you're engaged."

"I'm not engaged, and I honestly don't give a shit about what Dad says."

I looked directly at my father. His face turned red, but he stayed quiet.

"I'm in love with Gabby. Anyone who doesn't like it can kiss my ass." I looked back at Piper. "You need to quit following in Mom and Dad's judgmental footsteps and form your own opinion of people."

My mom took a long sip of wine before chiming in with her unnecessary input, "Piper, your brother will get over his little crush soon. He's lusting over her, being childish like some love-struck schoolboy. He'll come to his senses, and the engagement will be back on."

I locked eyes with her glossy ones, wanting her to know how serious I was. "Don't hold your breath on that happening. I'm going to be with Gabby, and anyone who doesn't agree with that can get over it or not be in my life. Now, let's stop fucking talking about it."

Everyone's mouth slammed shut, and I noticed Leo grin from across the table.

"At least the girl is acting appropriately, given the situation we're in," my dad said, surprising the shit out of me and everyone else at the table. "I guess I have to give credit when credit is due."

Chapter Six

GABBY

A DEEP BREATH of courage knocked from my lungs before I lifted my hand to knock on the door. I was scared shitless about walking into my own home, practically feeling like an outsider after storming out that day. I shouldn't have acted that way toward my mother, but I'd been so angry.

She didn't get a heads-up that I was coming. No warning. Nothing. I wasn't sure if I was going to chicken out or not. Cora handed me her car keys an hour ago and told me to do the right thing. I drove around the block four times before finally gaining the strength to pull into the driveway.

My mom was my best friend. I had to hear her out, so I could forgive her, and I needed her to forgive me. We had to move on from this. I realized she was only trying to protect me because that was what she'd done my entire life—worked her ass off to provide for me and keep me safe.

I jumped when the door swung open, and she appeared in the doorway.

"Gabby." My name fell from her lips around a gasp.

Guilt crept inside of me as I took a good look at her. She appeared exhausted, and I was to blame for that. No wonder everyone kept insisting I call her. She was a mess.

"Hi, Mom," I greeted, my voice breaking at the end.

There was no stopping the tears from falling down my cheeks. I missed her. She'd been my backbone for so long. There was a special type of bond a child had with their single parent. The two of you were all each other had. She'd taken on the role of both the mother and father and taught me how to be strong.

She opened the door wider and gestured for me to come in. "Come in. I didn't know you came home, but I'm so glad you did."

I followed her into the living room, trying to control my shaking hands, and sat down on the couch while she disappeared into the kitchen.

Why the hell am I so damn nervous?

I already knew the story.

She'd already confirmed that John was my father and that he'd insisted she get an abortion after getting pregnant with me. When she refused, he left her. I wouldn't be here if she had listened to him, if she had chosen his love over me. Accepting that was the hardest part, and I knew there was no way I'd ever let John into my life, no matter how hard he begged.

She wandered into the living room with a cup of tea in each hand. "I know I answered some of your questions when we talked." She handed me a cup. "But I want to get everything out in the open. Ask anything you want to know. *Anything*. I'm an open book."

I took a sip of tea and took my time swallowing it down. "Why didn't you tell me that night? The night of the party when he realized I was his daughter? Or before? Did you know I was working with him?" My mind, along with my mouth, was rambling.

Those were the questions I was dying to find out the answers to. I couldn't understand how we were only miles away from him after moving here and she never said anything.

"I didn't know you were working with him. If I had, I would've told you. I've wanted to tell you for so long, but to be honest, I was afraid for him to be near you. John ... he isn't the most stand-up guy. He destroyed me when he turned his back on us. I was scared to give him the chance to hurt you. He'd reached out before, begging me to see you, but I never called him back. He didn't deserve that, and I couldn't see him cause you any more pain." She sat down, placed her cup on the table, and took my hand in hers before squeezing it.

"Mom, I know what kind of man he is, and I understand why you wanted to keep me away," I said, and her hand didn't leave mine. "At work, we were helping him cover up an affair, and now, the girl involved is dead. She was murdered, but we don't know who did it. The cops brought Dalton in for questioning and then asked about me. He's brought me into his mess."

She let out a heavy sigh and wiped away a few tears. "I know. Kenneth has told me about the situation, but I don't know all of the details. If you think you're in trouble, Gabby, you let me know. As for John, I'm not sure about him murdering a woman. I couldn't see him doing something that terrible, but people do change. I don't want you to let your guard down around him or anyone else around there."

"I won't." I pulled my hand away to wrap my arms around her. "And thank you for telling me everything. I'm sorry for the way that I acted. I know you were only protecting me."

"So, what's your plan?" she asked after we broke away from each other. "Are you staying here?"

I shrugged, taking a sip of tea before answering, "I haven't decided yet."

"And Dalton? Kenneth told me about what was going on between you two and that Wilson found out and embarrassed you in front of everyone." She shook her head. "That asshole. Trust me when I say that you won't be forced to go to any more of their parties."

"What Dalton and I had ... it's over."

"Talk to him, honey. Things in his family, they're complicated. His parents are overbearing and controlling. They use money to take advantage of their children."

"Mom, he was *engaged* to another woman."

"I know, but he didn't want to marry her."

I gave her a look.

"Kenneth was *married* when we met, but he wasn't happy. He didn't love his wife, and quite frankly, I don't think she loved him either. Trust me, I know it feels wrong to get yourself involved with a person who's in a relationship. I wish I'd gone about it differently. I should've waited until Kenneth left his wife, but I didn't. According to Kenneth, Dalton had been trying to cut off his engagement for you, so maybe he's not as bad as you think. In my opinion, he was trying to figure out what to do with the hand he was dealt and hadn't found the solution before his dad decided to dump you with the ugly truth."

I opened my bag and grabbed my phone when it rang, seeing Dalton's name. He'd only been unblocked for a day, and he was already calling. I hit the Ignore button. A message popped up on my screen seconds later.

Dalton: Where are you?

I debated whether to respond. I didn't owe him any answers to my whereabouts. But what if it was Ivy-related?

Me: My house. Why?

Dalton: I'm coming to pick you up. We have a meeting with John.

Me: I think you can do that on your own.

Dalton: No, you said you wanted to know what's going on.

Me: I borrowed Cora's car. I'll meet you at her house.

I gave my mom a hug and kissed her good-bye, promising that I'd be back soon, and got back into Cora's car.

* * *

"How did it go?" Cora asked when I walked into her bedroom.

I sat down next to her on the bed. "It went okay. It's still a lot to take in, you know?"

Cora knew about John being my dad and the whole Dalton situation, and she had a strong dislike for both after what they'd done to me. But I hadn't told her about Ivy's death and our involvement. I didn't want her tangled up in that mess.

"Yeah. You know I'm here if you ever want to talk about it, right?"

I nodded.

"Are you staying here tonight?"

"I think I might stay at home."

She grinned. "As much as I want to spend time with you, I think that's a good idea. Your mom will like that. It'll be good for you two. Do you need a ride?"

"No. I have to do something with Dalton first. He's on his way to pick me up. I'll have him drop me off at home."

Her eyes widened. "Tell me you're seriously not thinking about taking that engaged bastard back."

I shook my head. "I have way more important things on my mind than a relationship right now." I grabbed my phone when it rang. "Hello?"

"I'm outside," Dalton said. "Come out whenever you're ready."

"Okay, I'll be down in a minute."

"Good luck, girl," Cora said after I hung up. "And be smart, okay? I don't want to see you get hurt again."

"Trust me, I've put a barrier on my heart that no one can break through right now."

* * *

"Uh ... where the hell are we going?" I shouted when I noticed we were driving out of the city and in the opposite direction of the office.

Dalton stared straight ahead with his eyes on the road. "To talk to John."

I gestured behind us. "Are you lost? The office is that way."

"We're not going to the office."

"Where the hell are we going then?"

"We're meeting my dad and him at his cabin in Chattanooga, where he's been staying. If someone sees all of us together—all of us *possible suspects*—then that would be a red flag. We need to be as discreet as possible, but we have to see him. I need to convince him to get out of the cabin ... make a statement ... or let someone make a statement on his behalf. The man has to do something."

I looked over at him in confusion. "So, you're saying, we need to lie low yet still try to figure out who killed Ivy at the same time?"

"Exactly."

His answer didn't make much sense, but I wasn't in the mood for an argument. Silence and awkwardness stretched out the long ride. He didn't bring up our relationship. I tried to hide my disappointment of that by staring out the window, watching the city flow into the wooded hills. Deep down, I wanted to hear him tell me how hurt he was, how bad he felt, repeatedly for my own gratification.

I guessed hearing a guy grovel for forgiveness was my thing.

Perfect. I'm that girl.

My stomach twisted at the thought of facing John. The last time I saw him was when he ambushed me and revealed that he was my biological father. He'd begged me for a chance to get to know each other, to have that father-daughter relationship I'd so longed for when I was younger, but I didn't want that anymore. I would've rather stayed in the dark about that part of my life than get hit with the truth.

I preferred him to deny me. It was easier to let go when you knew the other person wanted nothing to do with you. It was easier to not care—to block it out of your mind. It felt like he was a shadow now, haunting me, even when I tried to run away. And to top it all off, I had to accept the fact that he'd be around until we figured out who killed Ivy.

The sun was setting by the time we slowly drifted up the long gravel drive and stopped in front of a modest cabin in Bumfuck, Egypt.

Two matching black Mercedes were parked side by side in front of us, looking out of place. I recognized one of them.

Why is Kenneth here?

He normally didn't work on these cases. He'd practically retired, and he only took on small workloads since marrying my mom.

The interior light shone when Dalton opened his door. I went to do the same but froze up when reality hit me of what was about to happen. I looked over at him in terror.

"I can't go in there," I said. "There's no way I can face him right now." Especially in front of Kenneth and Wilson.

Dalton looked over at me with concern and stretched his arm across my seat to grab my hand. "Babe, yes, you can. Go in there and show him how fucking strong you are. Let him know his absence didn't hurt you." He grinned. "And if the motherfucker tries to talk to you about anything other than figuring out who killed Ivy, we'll leave. I promise if he tries to mess with you, he won't like the results."

I couldn't help but crack a smile. "Look at you, Billy Badass, threatening the future president of the United States."

"I'll always defend you." His response was like a punch in the gut. "As for the whole president thing, there's no way that's happening now. The man had a public scandal. They've already suggested he step down from his position, but he's refusing. People aren't going to vote for him. They can forgive, but they'll never forget. And they don't like cheaters or frauds. They always have more secrets buried."

My cheeks started to burn. "Does that mean you have more secrets?"

His eyes turned hard. "Don't you dare compare me to him, Gabby. I'm not a cheater. I never touched Eva while we were together. Not *once*. Not anyone. I didn't buy her a ring. Hell, I hardly talked to her."

"You kept her hidden from me. Omission is the same as lying, especially about something that serious."

"I know. I was trying to end it with her yet not make my world go up in flames at the same time."

"But you didn't end it with her. You kept riding your family's wagon until *they* said something and completely humiliated me in public."

I'd wanted to die when Eva was introduced as his fiancée. His entire evil family, except for Leo, stared at me as they waited for their entertainment to start her breakdown. There was nothing more fascinating than a public show of ripping a girl's heart out.

"I know, and I'm so fucking sorry." He slammed his eyes shut.

"It's the biggest mistake of my life. I swear to you, if you just give me another chance, I will never do anything to hurt you again."

It was a little too late to be making that promise. I blew out a ragged breath. I was already exhausted, and we hadn't even walked inside yet.

"This is not the time or place to talk about our relationship."

He opened his eyes and nodded in agreement. "But it's going to happen, Gabby. We need to talk."

I didn't reply. He waited until I opened my door before getting out and then stayed by my side as we walked up the porch steps. The door swung open after he knocked, and I came face-to-face with my father.

He didn't look anything like he had when we first met. The smugness, the arrogance, all his confidence were gone. Now, I noticed the wrinkles resting just underneath his hairline, his sunken cheeks, and his tired eyes.

"Gabby." He said my name like it'd been resting on the tip of his tongue for weeks. "You came."

"I didn't come for you," I snapped with fury in my eyes.

He frowned, wrinkles caving into his skin, and shuffled backward to let us in.

"I warned you," Kenneth said, appearing at John's side.

John held up his hands. "I didn't say anything."

I followed the three men into the dining room, where a long table was covered with scattered papers, folders, and open laptops. Wilson was seated at the far end and didn't look up or say one word at our arrival.

"Have a seat," Kenneth told us.

I sat down, and Dalton took the chair to my side.

Wilson cleared his throat. "I want to go over a few things. No one will talk to the police without our lawyer present, period."

Everyone, except for me, nodded their heads in agreement.

"No one will know that we're working on this case behind the scenes," he continued. "Don't ask anyone but our inner circle and people we can trust to help you. The police will ask too many questions about why we're involved."

"Have they questioned John yet?" I asked, interrupting Wilson, resulting in a cold glare from him. The man liked being in charge. I could tell he was containing his smart-ass retort to stay on my good side. "He was all over the news for having an affair with Ivy. Why have they questioned Dalton, but not him?"

Wilson shook his head and narrowed his eyes at me. "They haven't had a chance to question him because he's been hiding out here. I'm sure they're trying to obtain a warrant and sufficient evidence before they bring him in. We want to be ready when that happens."

I glanced over at John. "They're looking for you?"

"I didn't do it," he rushed out in response. "I would never ... I could never ... do that to anyone. I had a special place in my heart for Ivy. I didn't love her, but I cared about her deeply."

I rolled my eyes. She was obviously not tucked away in a too-special spot, considering he told us to destroy her if we had to.

"What about your wife?" Dalton asked. "Have you talked to her? Do you think she might be responsible for Ivy's death?"

John shook his head. "My wife would never do that." He'd said the same thing about her paying Ivy off for outing their relationship. "The sight of blood sickens her. She's a good woman. She's not a murderer."

"Can you think of anyone else who might be responsible?" Wilson asked. "Think back. Think back as far as you can and name *anyone* who might have it out for you."

"Or if you ever heard Ivy mention any rivals she had?" Kenneth chimed in. "Let's not forget that her death might not even be John-related. It could've been an ex-boyfriend or a current one who felt betrayed when she came out as John's mistress. That could've set him off."

He had a good point. The murderer could've been anyone. I only hoped they weren't in the room with me.

John dropped his head down on the table. "I've been trying to think back as far as I can." He snorted. "It's kind of difficult, creating a list of people who'd want to set you up for murder."

"You have a lot of enemies," Dalton said. "Whether you want to believe it or not, you do."

"He needs to be out in the public eye," I blurted.

Every pair of eyes came my way.

"I know you guys said he needs to make a statement or whatever, but he also needs to get himself out there," I said before pointing to John without looking at him. "Go back to work, go on with your daily life, and let people know you're not scared about getting in trouble for this."

"You can't be serious?" Wilson asked. "We're having someone make a statement for him. The media and anyone else will hound him and create a public spectacle. He could say something wrong and fuck himself."

"No, if he's locked up in here, out of sight, it will make him look like he's hiding something. Innocent people don't hide out in a cabin in the middle of the woods. Guilty people do," I argued.

"She does have a point," Kenneth said, giving me a gentle smile. "Get your face out there, and if anyone asks for a statement, you give them one."

"That's a terrible idea," Wilson fired back.

"No, she's right," John said, looking directly at me. "Tomorrow, I'll go back to work. I'll move back in my home. I'll go about my day as normal."

I hoped that wouldn't involve another mistress, but I was too afraid to ask.

Dalton clapped his hands. "Then, it sounds like we have a plan. Let me know as soon as you get back in town tomorrow or if anything comes up before then."

"Got it," John replied.

Everyone got up, and I was the first one to scurry out of the cabin. I jumped into Dalton's car and watched the men congregate on the front porch, immersed in a new conversation that I didn't want to be a part of.

"I'm starving," Dalton said when he got back into the car. "Let's get dinner."

"I'm not hungry," I answered. My lie was then backfired by the grumble of my stomach. *Traitor.*

"One meal. You're hungry, obviously. And by the time we get back to the city, you're going to be starving. Let me feed you."

"Take me to a drive-through and then drop me off at Cora's if you're so concerned about my starvation."

"I don't only want to feed you. I want to talk to you. I want you to hear me out."

I sighed. "I've heard you out. You're not with Eva anymore. You're sorry. That's great and all, but it doesn't change anything between us."

"Why not?"

"Why not?" I screeched. "Where should I start? How about the fact that you lied to me?" My stomach grumbled again. *Damn it.*

"One lie. I told one damn lie. But I never lied about my feelings for you."

I didn't say anything. This was what I'd been afraid of. *This* conversation. The sound of my stomach growling again interrupted the silence.

"I'm feeding you."

"Fine," I grumbled, caving in. I was tired, hungry, and not in the mood to argue. "But as soon as the food is gone, so am I."

Chapter Seven

DALTON

MY FOOT PRESSED down on the gas pedal with too much pressure. The chance that she could change her mind haunted me with every passing mile. I had to get to my condo fast before she decided this was a bad idea.

Talking to her and explaining myself was the only way I knew to convince her to give me another chance. I gripped the steering wheel and silently prayed she'd forgive me. I'd beg. I'd cut off my family. I'd do anything for the woman I loved.

"Dalton, I agreed to eating and going through a *drive-through*. Not coming over to your place," she cried out when I whipped into the parking garage.

"And I said I'd feed you. I never said where. We can eat here. It's nothing different than a restaurant," I said, parking.

"Yes, it is. There are many differences. If we go to a restaurant, we won't be alone. We won't have to sit close enough that you can touch me."

"We're already here." I got out, looking more confident than I felt, and raced over to the passenger door. My pulse sped as I opened the door and stood there, waiting for her next move, which thankfully was stepping out of the car and leading us toward my place.

"What sounds good?" I asked, walking in and flipping on the lights. "Pizza? Chinese? Your wish is my command."

She took a nervous look around. "Pizza is fine."

"Got it. Make yourself comfortable." I followed her to the couch, grabbing my laptop on the way, and sat down next to her. Awkwardness swept over us while I ordered our food. You could've cut the fucking tension with a knife.

"Do you want something to drink while we wait?" I asked.

"Water is fine." Her answer was short, devoid of any emotion, which killed me.

We'd grown so close and comfortable around each other. We'd shared secrets and fears, but now, it felt like we were strangers, struggling for words.

I handed her the remote, snagged two waters from the kitchen, and headed back into the living room, where she was flipping through channels. Everything seemed to be happening in slow motion. I needed to move shit along, get us talking, and take advantage of this situation. I didn't know if I'd get her here again.

"Thank you for coming," I started, trying to get my words in order. *God, why the fuck does this sound so damn formal?* I felt like I was in a business meeting.

She let out a long, ragged breath and threw her hands up. "You win. I'm going to hear you out like you asked, but I'm not making any promises. Me being here doesn't change anything, you hear me?"

I nodded.

"This doesn't mean I forgive you for lying. I'm only here, so there's no awkwardness while we work together."

I tightened my hold on the bottle and bit into my lower lip. *Fuck ... she is definitely still pissed.* Real pissed, and I couldn't blame her. If the roles had been reversed, if I found out she'd been hiding a fiancé from me, I'd have been fuming.

"I'm asking. No, I'm begging for you to give me another chance. Forgive me." My voice cracked in the end from desperation. I was looking at the woman I loved, nervous she'd no longer be mine again and that I'd ruined the best thing to ever happen to me.

It took her a minute to answer. "You have a *fiancée*. You're getting married, for Christ's sake."

I shook my head violently. "I've stressed this so many times. I'm not getting married. I broke it off with Eva."

"That's unfortunate. I'm sure your heart is broken." I didn't miss the nasty sneer in her tone.

"You're right. My heart is broken, but it's not about her. I don't give two fucks about losing Eva. I wasn't in love with her. She was a business deal my parents created when I was in high school. My heart is broken because I lost *you*. I hate myself for the pain I caused you. I hate myself for losing you."

She set her water down on the coffee table before turning and looking me straight in the eyes. "You know what's really sad? It's sad that you'd sell your future and heart away for money and some *business deal*."

I threw my head back before looking at her again. "Love didn't mean shit to me before you. I didn't think love was a real fucking thing. I never was one of those men who thought about who his wife would be or believed in soul mates. I'd been content with the idea of having a wife that was just there. That's how my life was supposed to work. I'd get married to a woman that was okay, we'd have kids, and then I'd take over the family business. No emotion. No love. Only going through life with that plan. There was never anything more to it until you. You changed everything for me. You changed my plans, my train of thought, the way I saw my future. You've made me want the real thing. I finally look forward to my future if it has you in it."

She looked at me, speechless, while struggling to come up with a response. I'd just hit her with a fucking bomb, and I wasn't sure how big the explosion was going to be.

"I honestly don't know what to say to that." She paused, still struggling. "Dalton ... this ... you and I ... we can't do it anymore. It's over."

No. I wasn't giving up that easy. I wasn't going down without a fight.

"Don't turn your back on us." I quickly grabbed her hand in mine. "Have you ever felt this way about anyone else?"

She looked away from me, but I noticed the tremble in her lip.

"You gave your virginity to me. You knew we had a connection before we even got to know each other. Your heart knew we were meant to be before either one of us even realized it."

"I was drunk."

"I told you to quit giving me that bullshit excuse. You weren't *that* drunk. I was pretty wasted too. But I know that isn't why I gave in to you. It was because I felt the connection we had."

"Give me time. Will you please just give me time?"

I squeezed her hand before bringing it to my lips. "I'll give you all the time you need. I'll be here, waiting."

The doorbell rang, and I thanked God he'd given me enough time to talk to her. I jumped up from the couch and had a skip in my step when I went to pay for the pizza. My entire mood had changed now that I knew I still had a chance.

* * *

"Dalton, I really appreciate you coming," John said, answering the door.

The porch light flickered on before he walked out and stood next to me, looking from side to side. He was paranoid as hell, but I couldn't blame him.

I crossed my arms and got straight to the point. "What did you want to talk about?"

It was my second trip to his cabin in one day, and I wasn't happy about it.

I had shit to do.

A murder to solve.

A woman to win back.

But he'd called after I dropped off Gabby, begging me to come over, off the record, and I couldn't say no. Something in his voice told me it was important.

He looked around one more time before waving me over. "Come in. We'll talk."

I looked at him in apprehension but followed him inside.

He slammed the door shut and shoved his hands in his pockets. "I want you working my case."

"I am working your case."

"No, *just you*. Not your father. Not Kenneth. You."

"You signed a contract with them, their company."

Attempting to fire my father was the last problem John needed. My dad was a powerful man. You didn't decide you no longer wanted to work with him. He didn't work like that. He was the one who decided when he was done with you.

"Technically, the contract was for him to get me out of my Ivy predicament, which he failed to do," he said.

"In case you're confused, this is still an *Ivy predicament*. A more serious one than you secretly sticking your dick inside her." I shook my head. "This is really why you made me drive all the way out here? You want to drop my father, you talk to him about that." I turned around to leave, but his voice stopped me.

"I know I'm not your favorite person, but I feel like you're the only one I can trust here." He let out a deep breath. "I can't work with someone if I'm not sure they're incapable of murder."

He thought my dad might've been the one who took care of Ivy.

"I don't trust you though," I told him. "I'm only here because it's my job. Not by choice. Trust me, I can't stand you. The answer is no."

"Please. You know I didn't kill Ivy. I can tell."

"The answer is still no."

He fell on the couch like he'd lost the strength to hold his weight. "You don't think they'll really charge me for this, do you?"

"I don't know. I'm not the police."

His head fell into his hands. "This is going to ruin any chance I had for the Republican bid."

"If there's anything I can guarantee at this moment, it's definitely that."

"Help me. Please help me. I'll do anything you want. I'll pay you anything you want. I won't fire your father, but I want to work exclusively with you."

I looked down at my watch. One a.m. I had to be back at the office in the morning. "I'll give you tonight, but I'm not making any promises."

We took a seat at the table, and I spent the next two hours scouring over emails with him. He told me everything, some stuff I wished he hadn't, but we got our timelines in order. I grabbed the folder that Gabby and I had been working on when we were trying to figure out who paid Ivy. There was a chance one of those men could be the suspect. I took my time examining each one while memories of that night with her lingered through my mind.

All the people in the folder were powerful. Congressmen. Business execs. Millionaires. I couldn't rush into their offices and question them for murder. I had to figure out a more discreet way to find out my information.

"I have a project for you," I told John.

He looked up at me from his notes. "Anything."

"I need you to write down your association with every single one of these men. I want to know if they have dirt on you, if you have dirt on them, or if you've ever had any problems. If any of them stand out, star them, and I'll look into it."

He grabbed the folder and got to work.

It was going to be a long night. Or morning.

"Has she said anything about me?" he asked out of nowhere.

"Who?" I questioned.

"Gabby."

Fuck. I definitely wasn't going there. He was really losing his mind tonight. First, he wanted to fire my dad and hire me, and now, he wanted to talk about Gabby.

"No, she hasn't. Leave her alone. She's not interested in having you in her life. If she changes her mind, she'll be the one to come to you. Stay away from her and focus on keeping your ass out of prison."

He looked at me with sorrow in his eyes. "I understand. I'll stay away, but please tell her if she ever changes her mind, I'll be here. I want to know my daughter."

"You should've thought about that before you decided to turn your back on her and her mother and be a deadbeat dad."

"I deserve that."

"Damn straight you do."

Chapter Eight

GABBY

MY HAND SHOOK as I stared down at the stick I was holding. These skinny, almost-weightless objects had held the fate of millions of women. It warranted so many different reactions.

Mine was fear.

Pure fear.

Running in close second was regret.

Two times.

We'd only done it twice without a condom.

My luck, of course, was that all I needed was two times. I stayed a virgin until I was eighteen. I abstained from sex at homecomings and proms. I'd been the last of my friends to lose my virginity yet the first one to possibly be knocked up.

Karma. Stupid karma.

You slept with a man who was engaged. Bad girl. Your repercussions: missing a period and possibly being pregnant.

I wrapped the cold stick in toilet paper and set it down on the bathroom vanity carefully, like it was made of porcelain. I took a seat on the toilet and opened the Internet browser on my phone. Four minutes was too long to wait. I stupidly Googled unplanned pregnancy. Help hotlines and articles on being pro-life or pro-choice came up. The same shit they preached in sex ed. Only this time, I wasn't only going to be tested on it. I was going to live it.

I waited five minutes, taking an extra minute to prepare myself. The thin blue line told me everything I needed to know.

Adopt. Abortion. Become a parent.

Three calming breaths for each option expelled from my lungs as I shut my eyes.

I was pregnant.

Holy shit. I was only eighteen, newly graduated from high school, and now, I was supposed to figure out how to care for a small, helpless human.

And the cherry on top: it was with a man who'd crushed my heart into a million pieces with a hammer of lies.

I exited out of the browser and clicked on the Messages icon. I wanted to call him, but there was no way my emotions wouldn't bleed through my words.

Me: We need to talk.

My finger hesitated over the Send button. *What if I don't tell him? What if I leave and never talk to him again?* As great of an idea as running away from my problems sounded, I couldn't be that selfish. I knew from personal experience the pain you felt from growing up with the absence of a parent.

I quickly hit the Send button before chickening out. It took him less than a minute to reply.

Dalton: Your place or mine?

Me: Yours.

. . .

The bathroom floor was cold as I moved to my bedroom to get dressed. I slipped on a pair of sweatpants and a T-shirt before slowly walking down the stairs. My outfit of choice probably wasn't the best one, but I'd just found out I was pregnant. That was my excuse.

"Hey, Mom," I called out, my voice squeaky. "I'm going to head out for a while. Can I borrow your car?"

She poked her head out of the kitchen. "Sure, honey. Is everything okay?"

Could she see it on my face? The fear? Was I now a walking billboard for a surprise pregnancy? She'd know.

I forced a smile. "Yeah, just running over to Cora's for a little."

"Okay, have fun, sweetie."

I took the long route to Dalton's place, although I didn't remember much of the ride. My mind was scrambled, my heart jolting with fear. How was I going to tell him? Should I sit him down? Or should I blurt it out when I walked in?

As soon as he opened the front door, I went for the second option. I was never one with great timing—obviously.

"I'm pregnant." I was surprised at how easily the words fell from my lips.

I eyed his unreadable face, feeling numb. I was giving him the chance to be okay with this, to be in our child's life. If he chose not to, if he wanted to turn his back on us, I'd be okay with that. Sure, being a single mother would suck, but my mom did it. I'd survive. I was strong.

His face paled. "I'm ..." He froze. "I'm going to be a father?" His eyes went wide as the realization sank in deeper. "Is that what you're telling me?"

My stomach knotted in fear, and I was unable to spew out an answer. So, I nodded.

I withdrew a step when he fell to his knees in front of me. I waited in fear, nervous of his next move, which turned into a slow smile spreading across his full lips. He stretched out his arm and planted the palm of his hand against my still-flat stomach.

"I'm going to be a father," he repeated. "Wow ... this is ... holy shit."

Is that a bad or good holy shit?

"You're not pissed?" I asked, looking down at him.

He stared up at me, his eyebrows bunching together. "Why would I be pissed?" His hand fell limp to his side before he brought himself back to his feet. "Sure, this was unexpected, but I'm not angry at you. How can I blame you for something we created together? This is both of our doing."

A rush of air I didn't know I was holding in escaped me. He wasn't angry. He was okay with it. He seemed elated. His reaction verified that I wasn't going to face this alone.

Now, I had to break the news to my mom. An ache formed in my stomach as I thought about how I was going to tell her my future was shadowing her past.

But that wasn't my biggest fear.

No.

That was taken by what Dalton's family's reaction would be.

Chapter Nine

DALTON

I WAS GOING to be a father.

Holy fucking shit.

I still couldn't wrap my head around it as I put my car in park. Gabby left my place a few hours ago to break the news to Cora. I asked her to wait until I was with her before telling her mom, Shelia, and my uncle Kenneth. I wanted to be by her side, letting them know I'd be there for her and our baby.

Sure, I hadn't expected to be a dad this young, but I was surprisingly calm about it. Having a family with Gabby felt more refreshing than anything I'd ever imagined my future to be. My once dreams of taking on Douglas PR and being a businessman with a family on the side weren't as enticing as they had been before. I wanted this with her.

I rolled down the windows to get some fresh air and took a minute to go over my words. What was the best way to tell them? There actually wasn't one. I'd asked Gabby if she wanted to come, but she wasn't ready to face them yet. Not that I blamed her. Their reaction wasn't going to be pretty. They were going to flip their shit.

I stepped out of my car and straightened my shirt free of any wrinkles. My steps were hesitant up the walkway and into the house. I walked through the large foyer and straight into the dining room, where my mom and dad were having dinner.

My mom looked up at me in surprise when she noticed my presence. "Dalton, I didn't know you'd be joining us for dinner. I would've had Francesca set you up a place at the table," she said.

"I'm not," I answered, shoving my hands into my pockets. "I stopped by because I have something to tell you."

"What?"

I glanced over at my dad. His face was already burning red. He was a smart man. He knew he wasn't going to like whatever it was.

"I'm going to be a father," I told them, standing tall and strong.

The fork slipped from my mom's hand, falling into her salad. It took her a minute before she said anything. "I'm sorry," she stuttered. "What did you just say? I think I heard you wrong."

"I'm going to be a father," I repeated.

Her face turned ice cold. "The mother had better be Eva."

"I'm afraid to even know who the mother is," my dad huffed. "Although I have an idea."

My mom grabbed her fork and stabbed a piece of lettuce. "I thought we told you to stay away from that girl." She dropped the fork again and covered her face with her hands. "Dear God, please let this be a dream."

"You might've told me to, but that didn't mean I'd follow your commands, Mother. You don't dictate my love life. There might've been some confusion in the past where you thought you did, but I want to make it clear right now. I won't be marrying Eva." I looked over at my dad. "And, yes, the mother is Gabby, and if I have my way about it, she's the one I'm going to be marrying."

My father got up from his chair and came my way. His hand brushed my shoulder while he looked back at my mom. "We'll be right back."

He tipped his head down the hallway, and I followed him to his office.

"How do you want to take care of this, son?" he asked, sitting down behind his desk. "Do you need money for the procedure? Or are you looking toward adoption? It would have to be discreet, and your name can't be anywhere in the documents, but I'll find a good family for it."

I looked at him, baffled. "Procedure? Do you really think we'd abort our child? Your grandchild? I told you I'm going to be a father. Gabby is having this baby—*our* baby—and I'm going to stand by her side, whether you like it or not." I hoped he wouldn't turn his back on his grandchild for his own selfish reasons.

"First, you cut off your engagement with Eva, and now, you got this girl pregnant. You're making a lot of mistakes. Keep making them and you might find yourself out of my will."

"Do what you have to do. You're right; I have made a lot of mistakes, the biggest one being when I let you dictate my life for the sake of being in your will and getting my inheritance. This is the surest I've ever been. This news has made me happier than any dollar, any new car, or job I could ever have, and I won't let you take that away from me."

GABBY

AFTER COUNTLESS TEARS, I'd come to the realization that nothing was stopping me from becoming a mother. It was happening, and now, I had to prepare myself for it.

I slumped down against the pillows on my bed. Accepting that I was pregnant was only step one. Step two was telling everyone. I was so scared of my mom's disappointment. She got pregnant with me at a young age and had shared her struggles.

I went to Cora's after leaving Dalton's. My best friend didn't surprise me when she jumped in the air, squealed in excitement, and told me she was the only option for a godmother. Now, the hard part was telling my mom and making sure I didn't have a panic attack while doing it. Dalton had begged me to let him be there when I did it. He wanted to assure them that he'd be at my side.

I chewed the tips of my nails, trying to figure out the right words to use. My thoughts blurred at the sound of my phone.

"Hey, I'm pulling up right now," Dalton said when I answered. "Are you ready for this?" His smooth voice was gentle and comforting.

I sighed. "I think so. Come up to my bedroom, and then we'll go down and tell them." I had to talk to him first. I had to see where his head was after talking to his parents. Their reaction could've completely changed his mind about being there for me.

"Got it. Coming in now."

I heard the doorbell ring and then my mom greeting him downstairs. I glanced up at the knock on my door. My bedroom door opened, and Dalton slid in, wearing jeans and a black button-up. He shut the door behind him and leaned back against it. He ran his hand over his forehead and blew out a breath.

"How are you feeling, babe?" he asked, locking eyes with me.

"Nervous as hell," I answered. "I don't want my mom to be disappointed in me. I didn't go to college, and now, I'm eighteen and knocked up."

I looked away from him in embarrassment. He was a college graduate with a law degree.

He pushed off the door and came my way. I felt a sense of relief when he sat down next to me and pulled me into his warm hold.

"Your mom would never be disappointed in you. That woman's love for you is so strong; it's unbelievable. I wish my parents felt for me like she does you."

I settled into his chest and looked back at him. "Did you tell them?" I could feel the nausea rolling in my stomach. I didn't want to hear their response, but I had to know what I was going to be dealing with.

"They were bursting at the seams with excitement."

I pulled away from him to shove his shoulder, resulting in a laugh from him. "Very funny," I grumbled.

"Their reaction is what we imagined it to be."

"Angry? Threatening to cut you off and disown you?"

"Something like that, but they'll get over it. Give them time."

"But what if they don't?"

"Then, that's their loss."

"I want to let you know one thing. If they keep insulting me, I'm not letting my child be around them. I won't have my baby around that kind of venom."

He nodded. "I completely agree." His lips hit my forehead before he got up and threw his hand out my way. "You ready?"

"As ready as I'll ever be."

I grabbed his hand, and he carefully brought me up. My hand stayed in his as we walked down the stairs. I grew sweaty with each step as I got closer and closer to revealing the truth. Kenneth and my mom were already at the dining room table, waiting on us. I'd given my mom a heads-up that Dalton would be joining us for dinner.

"Dalton, it's nice to see you," Kenneth said, giving his nephew a head nod.

I tightened my hold on Dalton's hand and froze up, inches from entering the dining room. "I'm pregnant," I blurted out, the same way I'd done with Dalton. Obviously, it was my way of telling people shit I didn't want to say. Get it out and over with.

My eyes were pinned to my mom, waiting to see her first reaction. I flinched when a smile spread across her red lips.

Kenneth cleared his throat while we all waited for her reply.

"Are you being serious?" she asked.

I nodded, still not walking into the room. Dalton stood awkwardly at my side, not sure what to do.

Her hand went to her chest. "Wow. I'm going to be a grandmother." She paused and looked over at Kenneth while taking it all in. "I've always wanted to be a grandma. Sure, it's earlier than I imagined, but I can't wait to meet that special person growing inside of you."

"You're not mad?" I asked. How was she so calm and collected? I was eighteen and knocked up by someone I wasn't even dating.

"I'm shocked but definitely not angry with you." She looked over at Dalton. "I take it, you're the father?"

He nodded in response. My hand jerked and stretched out when he took a step forward.

"I am. I promise to stay by her side and be there for her and our baby," Dalton said. "I'm in love with your daughter, and nothing will change that."

My mouth fell open at his response, and my mom's smile grew.

"I'm happy to hear that," she said. "I expect you to keep your word."

"Have you told your parents?" Kenneth asked. He leaned back in his chair, a glass of red wine in his hand.

"I did. I went there before coming here."

He chuckled. "I'm sure that went well."

Dalton nodded.

"If you don't have their support, I want you to know you have mine one hundred percent. If you two need anything, you let me know. Take care of our girl, you hear me?"

"You have my word," Dalton said.

He looked at me, and I took a step forward for him to lead me into the dining room.

Dinner went by smooth. My mom listed a few things I needed to do immediately. Make a doctor's appointment. Get prenatal vitamins. Then, the pregnancy wasn't brought up again. She was giving me time to take it all in before overwhelming me with questions and plans.

I was headed back to my bedroom with Dalton on my heels when my phone rang.

"It's Asher," I said, nervously looking back at Dalton.

"Do whatever you think you have to do."

Two more rings passed.

We'd texted back and forth a few times since I left his apartment. The night of our almost-drunken hookup was never brought up, and I was sure me leaving answered his question of whether I wanted to go there with him.

"Hey," I finally answered, catching it just before the call went to voice mail.

"Hey, babe. I just got out of practice," he said, sounding almost out of breath. "Coach really kicked our asses today. What are you up to?"

"Just finished having dinner with my mom and your dad."

Dalton raised a brow when I didn't mention his name. I rolled my eyes.

"You're home? That's great. I knew you and your mom would work things out. I'm happy for you."

"Yep." *Tell him. Tell him. Tell him.*

"How's the Ivy killer-hunting going?"

"We're working on it." I paused, fighting for courage. "Asher, I need to tell you something."

"Tell away, kitten."

"I'm pregnant."

Silence. I swore a good minute passed.

"I see. Is this a good or bad thing for you?"

"Well, bad, in the sense of this being the last thing I need right now. Good, in the sense that I think it'll make me happy in the end."

"That's all that matters." Disappointment lingered in his words. "Have you told him?"

"I have." I fell on my bed because my legs were feeling weak.

"And?"

"He seems okay with it." I glanced up at Dalton, who was leaning back against my wall, his eyes blazing toward me. "He told his parents and was with me when I told my mom and your dad."

"At least he's taking responsibility and not running away like a little bitch. You let me know if you need anything, you hear me?"

"You know I will."

"Okay. Get some rest."

We ended the call, and I kept my eyes on Dalton.

"How pissed is he?" he asked.

I shrugged. "He seems okay with it."

He stepped away from the wall to come my way. "Will you come home with me tonight?"

"I don't know. I'm exhausted. I've had a long day." I'd spent the entire day going door to door, telling everyone I was knocked up, and then dealt with their reactions. That shit was rough.

"I understand. What if I get you some dessert? We can watch a movie or something. *True Blood*?"

"I don't know, Dalton."

His hands went together in a pleading motion. "Please. I'm not asking you to sleep with me or get back together. We have shit to talk about. We can do that here, but I'd prefer privacy, and I think you feel the same way."

DALTON

GABBY STIRRED in her sleep while I quietly started to get dressed. I'd wanted to slip out of the bedroom without waking her.

I failed.

"Where are you going?" she asked, startling me as I stuck a leg into my pants.

I frowned, slowly turning around to find her stretching out her arms and yawning.

"I have to go see a man about a dog," I said, zipping up my pants. I stepped to the side to dodge a pillow coming my way, and it smacked the wall.

"Really, Dalton?" she groaned. "It's *way* too early to mess with me."

I blew out a breath, failing to meet her eyes. "Fine. I'm going to talk to some people about Ivy." I slipped my wallet into my jeans, fully prepared to dart out of the bedroom before she had a chance to tag along. I had to do this alone. I didn't want her involved anymore.

Her eyebrows scrunched together as she eyed me warily. "You're going without me?"

"I won't be long. I'm going to talk to them briefly, get what little information I think they'll give, and then I'll be back to take you to lunch."

She whipped the blankets off her and hopped out of bed. "I'm going with you."

She yawned again and brought her arms up. I couldn't help but lick my lips when I noticed her top rise, giving me a glimpse of her smooth stomach. Jesus, even this girl's damn stomach turned me on. I was a goner for her.

"You're pregnant," I argued stupidly, like there was a chance she'd forgotten our baby was growing inside of her.

Her hands clasped on to her hips. "Pregnancy isn't a handicap, Dalton. It's not going to hold me back from getting out of bed, going out in public, or even questioning someone who can get us off the hook and out of this mess. It's not like I'm going to be waving around a gun and shooting people."

I leaned back against the wall, watching her shuffle through her bag and pull clothes out.

"I'm getting in the shower. You'd better still be here when I get back. If you're not, I'm staying at Cora's house tonight."

I shook my head and crossed my arms while holding back a smile. "You evil, manipulative woman."

She knew the best threats to get her way.

"Hurry it up."

I didn't release my smile until I heard the bathroom door shut. My girl was a go-getter. She got shit done, she made sure she knew the details, and I couldn't be upset with that.

Last night, I stopped and grabbed us some ice cream on our way home. We talked for hours on the couch, mostly about our plans for the baby, but we hadn't ventured *there* yet. We didn't bring up our relationship. She was letting me back in, but I was still giving her time. I didn't want to rush in fear of losing her.

I handed her a folder when we got into my Tesla. "These are the best leads I have so far. John wrote some notes on here for us."

She opened it and scanned the first page. "John's wife, Edith, *obviously*." She turned the page. "Malcolm, his brother." Another page flip. "Bill Wheeley?" She looked over at me in question. That name hadn't come up during our brainstorming in my office. Bill Wheeley was a source John had given me at his cabin.

"He's another candidate who was planning on running for the Republican presidential bid," I explained.

I nodded toward the folder for her to read John's notes. We'd composed a short profile and motive for each person, except for Edith. John wouldn't even entertain it possibly being his wife.

"Politicians are sneaky bastards."

"Never put anything past people in power, babe."

I'd spent enough time around my dad and his power-hungry acquaintances to know they'd do anything to stay in their position or move up higher even if it meant sabotaging *or* killing someone else. People were ruthless.

She closed the folder with a groan. "So, where to first?"

"Edith's."

"Oh, yay," she grumbled, rolling her eyes. "I'm putting my money on her. At first, I was rooting for her, but now, not so much. There's something about her that rubs me the wrong way."

I stopped at a red light and nodded in agreement. "She's strange, but do you really think she'd kill Ivy? She doesn't seem like the murdering type."

"Do I think she has Ivy's blood on her hands personally? No. My bet is that she hired someone to do the job for her."

I kept my eyes on her, and my eyes widened in interest.

"Oh, come on. All of her problems would be gone. She'd figure out some way to get her money back in her greedy hands, the mistress who'd been a pawn in her plan of destroying her husband would be quiet, and all would be good in her life. A woman like Edith knows how to get what she wants. I don't put anything past her."

I turned and drove a few more miles until we reached John's gated community. I headed toward their personal entrance leading up to their driveway, and the gate was surprisingly open. It was like she'd been given a heads-up we were coming and was inviting us in.

I told John that we were going to be paying her a visit today. He did what we asked him to do. He left the cabin and went home. He made a statement, sent his respects to Ivy's family, and informed the media where he'd been staying for the past week. He claimed poor cell reception and no cable on his delayed reaction.

Did the people buy it? I wasn't sure.

But he hadn't been arrested yet, so that was a plus.

"This place still gives me the creeps," Gabby said with a shudder. "There's something about it that just makes you feel dirty."

"Tell me about it," I muttered. "You couldn't pay me to live here." I circled around the driveway and parked in front of the massive stone home. I shifted the car into park before shutting it off. "Let's see if she'll even talk to us."

"She'll talk to us," she replied, unbuckling her seat belt. "She'll talk to us and give us some bullshit excuse as to why she had nothing to do with Ivy's murder."

I grabbed her hand when she got out of the car and led her up the stairs. The front door swung open before we made it to the top step. A tall, lanky figure stood in the doorway.

Edith Gentry.

"What a pleasant surprise," she said, coming more into view. Her tone was condescending. Her smile nasty. Just like last time we'd met, a string of expensive pearls were clasped around her neck. She was sporting another pantsuit. She hadn't changed one bit, and she didn't look the part of a distraught woman, worried about her husband being MIA for days.

"Mrs. Gentry," I greeted, forcing myself to smile. "It's nice to see you again. Do you have a minute to talk?"

I was waiting for her to tell us to get fucked and slam the door in our faces.

She didn't. Her face only morphed into a grimace. "Edith," she corrected. "Just Edith. I'm not going to be married to John much longer."

"Okay, *Edith*. Do you have a minute to talk?"

"I guess I can spare a few." She stepped backward with her arm swinging out to the side, directing us to come in. "I take it, this is either about my husband disappearing off to his cabin or his whore's death."

We both stopped at her words. Gabby tensed up next to me. This woman had no heart, only bitter blackness where it was supposed to be. We jumped when the door slammed shut behind us.

"That poor thing," Edith went on, no sign of empathy in her voice. She didn't give two shits about Ivy.

She led us back into the white room. I waited for Gabby to carefully sit down on the couch before I fell next to her.

Edith sat down across from us, adjusting her pearls and crossing her legs. "You want to know if I did it," she said, cutting straight to the chase. "You thought you'd come here and convince me to confess to it." She let out a patronizing laugh.

"Yeah, pretty much," Gabby said, answering before I had the chance to. "It would save us and everyone else a lot of time if you just admitted it now." She shrugged, failing to meet my eyes when I looked at her in question.

Has she lost her damn mind?

This was definitely not the plan we'd talked about earlier.

"What?" she asked, finally looking my way. "We need to get this over with."

Edith didn't look shocked at Gabby's words. She sat there patiently, watching us with her hands folded in her lap, without saying a word.

"Have the police questioned you yet?" I asked her.

"No," she answered.

She'd most likely not been brought in for the same reason John and my father hadn't. They were rich—filthy fucking rich—and affluent. The force didn't want a lawsuit without having enough evidence. They didn't mind fucking with me. I was a nobody in the corporate and political world. I knew as soon as they did though, they'd pounce.

I opened my mouth, ready to ask another question but stopped. She was staring at Gabby, awestruck.

"You ... you look just like him," she told her. "I don't know why I didn't see it before, but I do now. There's no mistaking it."

I looked back and forth between her and Gabby as a heavy feeling settled in my stomach. I wasn't sure how her question was going to affect Gabby.

He told Edith about her?

That surprised me, given John lied as much as the dude pissed.

Edith's eyes still didn't leave her. "You didn't think he'd tell me?" she asked, but I wasn't sure whom she was talking to. "As soon as he found out, he was distraught. He came home that night and told me everything about you and your mom. I had no idea until that night."

I could hear Gabby trying to hide her heavy breathing.

"Lovely," she said, her tone harsh. "But I didn't come here to talk about me. We're here to talk about you and where you were the night of July 6th."

Edith chuckled. "And I see you're just as snarky as before. You probably got that from your mother because your dad ... he follows orders. He follows them to a T as long as he's in public."

"Again, we didn't come here to talk about *me*. I don't talk to strangers about my personal business."

"Personal business?" Edith asked. "It seems it's my business, considering my husband is your father. That would make you my stepdaughter."

Oh fuck. I got myself ready to stop Gabby if she decided to jump up and pull Edith's hair out.

"The husband you're divorcing is my estranged father, which means I'm not shit to you, nor will I ever be. My personal life isn't important. What's important is finding out what happened to Ivy and if you were involved in her murder."

Edith's cheeks flushed. "I was having dinner with my children here that night."

How convenient.

"So, you were here all night?" I asked. "You didn't leave for anything?"

"Yes. My children and housekeeper will verify that, if need be."

"I bet they will," Gabby muttered.

Edith flashed us a fake smile and got up. "Now that you have my alibi and I've assured you I have nothing to do with this, I think our visit is over. I have plans."

"She knows something," Gabby said when we got back to my car.

"She definitely knows something," I replied.

"More confusing pieces that don't fit in this chaotic puzzle."

I turned to look at her before starting the engine. "How are you feeling?" I was more worried about her than any of these other assholes.

She flipped her curls over her shoulder and shrugged. "It is what it is. John is my father. People know that now, and I need to get over it."

"He wants to talk to you." I started the car and took off back toward the gate. We still had a few more people to look into.

"Yeah, that's definitely not going to happen." She leaned her head against the window. "That man is the last person I want to talk to right now."

* * *

My visits to his house were infrequent.

We usually met at a bar, or he came over to my condo because his wife found it necessary to start an argument with me every time I came around. But today was crucial. I was there because I had no one else to talk to about being a father. Lord knows my dad was the last person to take advice from. The guy was a terrible father and human being.

Leo stood up when I walked into his living room and smacked me on the back. "Congratulations," he said, a grin on his face. "I heard the news, big daddy." A gin and tonic was shoved in my hand.

"I take it, Dad told you?" I asked.

"You know it. He called me as soon as your car left the driveway after the big reveal, practically spitting fire through the phone. He's pissed and insisted I try to talk some sense into you."

I sat down, sipping on my drink. Gin always reminded me of eating a Christmas tree. I took another sip and wiped my mouth with the sleeve of my shirt. "Not to be an asshole, but I honestly don't give a fuck about his, yours, or anyone else's opinion. We're keeping the baby. I'm not marrying Eva. If that means I lose my job, my inheritance, my family, then oh well."

Would losing everyone, especially Leo, kill me? Yes. But I had to do what was right. I was finished with being a spineless puppet in my father's game. I had a degree from one of the most prestigious schools in the country. Finding a job wouldn't be that difficult. Sure, I'd have to work my way up, but I didn't mind.

Leo looked at me, baffled. "Brother, I wouldn't expect anything less of you. You really think I'd suggest you neglect or abort my future niece or nephew?"

I rubbed at my tired eyes. "No, there's just so much shit going on right now. I'm scared, Leo. I'm fucking scared. I don't want to be like him. I want to be a good dad like you. I don't want my kid to be scared or disgusted by me. I don't want to be a failure of a father."

"You're not going to fail. Yes, it'll be the most terrifying and hardest experience of your life, but I know you'll be great at it."

"And on top of everything, I have John's bullshit to deal with. That guy, I swear, I wish I had told Dad I wasn't taking on his case. It's been nothing but a disaster."

"I told you what to do. Try to figure it out, but if push comes to shove, get out. Rat his ass out."

"He didn't do it though. He didn't kill Ivy."

Leo raised a brow.

"I'm sure of it."

"Then, who?"

"Fuck if I know. We can't figure that out, but all of the evidence is pointing to him ... to us ... like we killed her." I made myself comfortable on his couch, deciding to change the subject. "So, what's been going on with you? Why do you look so down in the dumps? Smile— you're about to be an uncle."

He lowered his voice, looking at me solemnly. "I asked Kelly for a divorce."

I choked on my drink, sprinkles spewing along the front of my shirt. I waited a few seconds for him to tell me he was fucking with me. He didn't crack a smile.

"Seriously?"

He nodded.

"Thank fuck you finally opened up your eyes. You should've filed those papers years ago."

"I was trying to make it work for my family, but now, I've realized that's never going to happen. She's a miserable person."

"Glad to see how much you love me, Leo," a voice snarled behind us.

We both jumped. More alcohol spilled on my shirt. Shit! Leo told me Kelly was gone. Otherwise, I wouldn't have come over. I wasn't in the mood to hear her squeaky, pestering voice.

"And I don't appreciate you telling him our personal business," she continued.

"He's my *brother*, Kelly. We're divorcing; people are going to find out sooner or later," Leo said, throwing out his arm. "You told your sister. I see no difference in telling him."

"My sister isn't like him," she snarled.

We both jumped when the glass in her hand flew. Leo ducked just in time, and it smacked into the brick fireplace behind him. The aroma of vodka wavered around us. She threw me a dirty look and stomped out of the room.

Leo crumbled back against the couch. "Sorry you had to see that. She told me she was going shopping."

I waved my hand through the air. Kelly needed to hear that. She needed to know how miserable she was making her husband and children.

"Did you meet someone?" I asked out of pure curiosity.

His head flew up. "What?"

"Did you meet someone? Is that why you finally filed?"

"Do you mean another woman?"

"Yes, dumbass. Are you leaving Kelly because of another woman?" I couldn't imagine my brother having an affair, but I could see him having a friendly relationship with someone and ending his marriage before he laid a hand on her.

He drained the rest of his drink. "No. I'm leaving Kelly because she's, well, Kelly."

"What are you going to do about a job?"

"Dad said he'd hire me."

I snorted. "Good luck with that. I wouldn't recommend my job to my worst enemy." I shook my head and smiled. "He's not mad about you filing?"

"You're stealing my shine, little brother. Dad is so pissed about your shit that he's waving mine off. Mom cried though. She just *loves* Kelly."

"Of course she does. She loves Kelly's parents' money."

Chapter Twelve

DALTON

A CHEESY-AS-HELL SMILE was smeared across my face when I pulled into the driveway. I couldn't wait to see Gabby. The excitement was unreal, something I'd never experienced before. She had a way of taking my mind off my problems, making me feel like everything would be okay if she was by my side.

I unbuckled my seat belt when the passenger door flew open, and Gabby jumped in before I had the chance to get out.

"Damn, babe," I said. "I was going to be all proper and come to the front door."

"I think all dating formalities are out the window after you knock the girl up," she said with a laugh.

"That doesn't mean I have to quit trying to romance you. How was hanging out with your mom?"

"It was good." Her eyes brightened, making me smile even more. "We went shopping—*baby* shopping. I tried to tell her I needed to wait until my first doctor's appointment before buying anything, but she insisted. She's so excited. She can't wait to be a grandma."

My chest burned as I fought back a frown.

Why couldn't my mom feel the same way? Why couldn't I have the support of my family?

My mom had left me a voice mail last night, asking if I'd come to my senses and realized Gabby wasn't worth risking everything for. The answer was no. She was worth risking everything for. I didn't call my mom back to tell her that though. I wasn't going to waste my time.

"Speaking of appointments, have you made your first one?" I asked.

"Yep. It's next week. Do you want to come?"

"Yes, I want to come. I want to be at every appointment. I want to be involved in everything, so please keep me updated." I grabbed her hand in mine, feeling the heat of her skin, and massaged it with my thumb. "There's also something else I want to ask you."

My plan had been to wait until we got back to my place before bringing it up, but I couldn't hold it in. The anticipation and fear were killing me.

"Yeah?" Her foot bounced up and down on the floorboard.

Was she as nervous as I was?

"What do you think about staying at my place more ... long-term?" I closed my eyes, waiting for her argument.

"Dalton, look at me."

I opened my eyes, one by one, and flinched when I saw the unexpected smile on her face.

"You want me to move in with you?"

I nodded. "That way, if you need help with anything, I'll be there."

She had her mom, but I wanted to be her main support system.

"Okay, I think we can do that temporarily ... consider it a trial run."

"Really?" I asked, shock overflowing through my voice. I'd been expecting her to shut me down in seconds.

"Yes. I've been doing a lot of thinking. I've talked to my mom and Cora. We're having a baby. We need to work on things for him or her. I don't want my child to have parents who don't get along or didn't give each other a chance to be a real family. You're done with Eva, right? Completely done?"

"I am absolutely done with Eva. The engagement is off, and I haven't seen her since the party."

"That seems too easy."

"She doesn't want to be with someone who's in love with another woman. Shit, anyone can look at me and see how far I've fallen for you. I never thought something like this would happen to me—that I'd be one of those guys who is obsessed with a woman—but I am. You've changed me, made me want to be a better man, and in that, I know letting my parents interfere with us isn't going to happen. I've made it perfectly clear to them that they either have to accept you or I want nothing to do with them."

She finally looked back at me with wide eyes. "Wow."

"We belong together. You, me, and our baby. We're going to be the happiest family in the world. I promise you."

If I could keep us out of jail.

I grabbed her chin in my palm and didn't hesitate before slowly pressing my lips against hers.

Chapter Thirteen

GABBY

OUR KISS ... it took my breath away. Even though I'd kissed this beautiful man before, made love to him before, there was something special about the way his soft lips moved against mine this time. A blanket of security surrounded me, like our connection was a promise that he wasn't going anywhere and I wouldn't be alone.

In that moment, for the very first time, I felt loved by someone other than my mother and friends. I felt intimately and unconditionally loved for who I was.

"Can I say something else?" he asked when we separated.

"Lay it on me," I answered, leaning forward in hopes that he'd kiss me again. *Those lips need to be back on mine.*

"I feel like I need to get everything off my chest."

"What exactly is everything?" Did I even want to know everything?

A deep breath knocked from his lungs.

His hand captured mine. "Before you, I wasn't living. I was only going day by day without caring about anything. I didn't give a shit about anyone but myself. That's how I was brought up—to protect myself, stand up for the family name, and do anything to get what I wanted, no matter the costs. When my parents told me I was marrying Eva, I really didn't give it much thought. I knew I'd eventually get married, but marriage was never *love* to me. I saw it as an agreement, not a commitment, not an experience, not a feeling. I didn't see it as wanting to hold someone's heart in your grasp and never let go. I never thought once about any of those things until *you*."

I stared at him, stunned. He hurt me, he lied, but his eyes bled remorse. I was never one for second chances. You hurt me once? Good-bye. But maybe second chances weren't such a bad thing after all. Maybe it didn't mean you were weak. It meant you understood that everyone, including yourself, could make a mistake and learn from it. I'd been so hurt, so angry, that I never listened to a word he'd said, no matter how bad he pleaded.

"Let me go grab some more bags," I said, squeezing his hand and then opening the door.

"I'm coming with you."

This was insanity. We were both taking a huge step. I was moving in with him, and he was giving me an inside look at the real Dalton Douglas.

* * *

"Take me home," I said after we loaded a few bags in the trunk and got back in the car.

"Home," he replied, grinning from ear to ear. "I like hearing you say that—more than you could ever know. I'll definitely take you to *our home.*"

The smile on his face didn't leave as he sped out of the driveway or even when we made it into the parking garage. It stayed there until I walked into my new home.

"I'll take these to the bedroom," he said, holding up my bags. "I've already made room for you in the closet."

"Feeling confident, Douglas?" I asked.

He turned around, looking at me, and started to walk backward. "A man can always hope."

Without thinking, I followed him. I stood in the doorway, my pulse skyrocketing, and watched him drop my bags onto a chair. He turned around and froze when he saw me.

Maybe it was the pregnancy hormones, maybe it was the idea that we were starting fresh, or maybe it was because I loved him as much as he loved me, but I wanted this man.

I wanted his hands, his mouth, his everything. He hadn't touched me in so long. My body was urging for it.

Without saying a word, I grabbed the hem of my shirt and pulled it over my head. He licked his lips, his riveting eyes turning hungry. He tucked his hands into his pockets, waiting for my next move.

I am the one in control of this show. I carefully unsnapped my shorts and watched them puddle at my feet.

"Keep going," he whispered. "Let me see all of you, baby."

The fingernails of his thumbs hanging outside his pockets dug into his jeans when I unsnapped my bra. I could feel the heat between my legs firing up at the sound of his low moan. His hands shifted from his pockets straight down to his growing arousal. He rubbed himself through his jeans, and it was my turn to moan. There was something so erotic and intriguing about watching a man touch himself.

I slid a finger in between the hem of my panties and skin before suddenly stopping. I raised a brow. "I'm going to leave the rest to you," I said. I put my hands to my hips. "So, Mr. Douglas, what are you going to do with me?"

He erased the distance between us, and I gasped when his hands wrapped around my waist. "I'm going to do plenty with you," he said, his lips nudging my earlobe before replacing them with his tongue. "I'm going to lay you down on that bed, take off those goddamn panties, and finger-fuck you until you can't take it anymore and get off on my fingers. Then, I'm going to do the same thing with my mouth. And if I have it my way, I'll repeat the same process all night long."

Holy. Fucking. Shit.

I thought I was wet then, and now, I was fucking drenched. I could feel my juices almost dripping out of my panties. Another thing to add to the list of things I missed about him. His dirty talk. It never failed to take me over the edge.

"Then, what are you waiting for?" I gasped out.

I yelped when I was snatched off my feet and carefully carried over to the bed. He didn't waste any time sliding my panties down my legs and throwing them on the floor. I shivered at the feel of his cold fingertips tracing the inside of my thigh.

"I've waited to have this back for long enough," he whispered.

And then he did exactly what he said he was going to. Two long, powerful fingers played with my pussy while another one rubbed circles over my clit. It didn't take long for the pressure to build up at my core.

Orgasm number one down.

I wasn't sure how many more were to come, but I felt like I was losing myself at the touch of him. I tensed up, waiting for his second promise, and shivered at the feel of his tongue lightly sliding through my soaked folds.

"Mmm ... still so fucking delicious," he whispered against my skin. "My favorite meal."

His tongue went to work, lapping me up, while I gripped the sheets, my fingernails practically tearing them apart.

Orgasm number two down.

What is coming next?

I knew exactly what I wanted to come next.

Him.

I hitched myself up on my elbows. "Your turn," I said, trying to calm my breathing.

He raised himself up and looked down at me, his eyes penetrating mine. "You have no idea how bad I want you right now." He shook his head, looking tortured. "But I want to make sure you're ready, that you're for real about this, because once my dick is back inside of you, you're mine. You hear me? If we make love and then you leave me tomorrow, I won't be able to take it. It will fucking kill me, Gabby."

"But—"

His words cut me off. "Tonight, I want you to figure out your heart, what you want, and then let me know. When you're sure you want to be in my bed every single night for the rest of your life, I promise I will fuck you senseless."

I threw my arms down and pouted. "Seriously?" I whined. "How the hell do you think it's okay to do all of *that* and then leave a girl hanging when she wants your cock inside of her?"

He shrugged and then leaned down to kiss my lips. I could taste myself on them, which only turned me on more. "Because when I fuck you, I'll make love to you. It's as simple as that."

I gave him the dirtiest look I could manage. "Cut the shit. You know I'm still in love with you."

He kissed my forehead, rolled on his back, and pulled me into him. "Tell me that tomorrow, and I promise it'll be better than tonight."

Chapter Fourteen

GABBY

I SHIVERED at the chill of a strong chest crashing into my back.

Strong arms nestled around my waist. He took a step forward to situate us both underneath the hot water spewing from the showerhead above me. I tipped my head back to look at him, my focus altered by drops of water hitting me in the face. I smiled at the man who held my heart. The man I now lived with. The father of the baby growing inside of me. His lips smashed into the top of my hair, and then he whipped me around to face him, his cold hands resting on my hips.

"Good morning, beautiful," he said, his voice low and raspy. His morning voice was seriously the sexiest thing in the world. "Waking up to *this* is seriously incredible."

Goose bumps sped down my spine when his hands slid from my hips to my breasts. He used his knuckles to lightly massage them, warming me up, and it took me a minute to gain the strength to answer him.

"Morning," I gasped, all my focus on him. I couldn't hold back my moan when he rolled a nipple with the tips of his fingers.

He grinned, loving the effect he had on me. "Did you sleep well?" I could only nod as he continued to play with my nipple, slowly and torturously, reminding me of what he'd done to my body last night. "Me too. I actually slept better than I have in weeks."

I couldn't stop my gaze from roaming down and admiring my insatiable view of him, eyeing the muscles of his hard chest. Beads of water dripped from his muscles and the tip of his cock. I licked my lips when I realized it was already hard. He was ready for me, and the intense beat of my heart confirmed I felt the same way.

His hand stayed on my breast while I slowly reached down and wrapped my hand around his erection. It jerked in my hold.

He tilted up his hips. "Did you think about our talk last night?"

"I did," I answered, slowly starting to glide my hand up and down his dick.

He shut his eyes, his head falling back. "And?"

"I think we can give it another go. No secrets this time."

My breathing hitched when he brought me in closer. His wet lips caressed my neck.

"Absolutely no secrets." He pulled away, just a little, to make eye contact while I continued to slowly stroke him. "You back to being all mine?" He reached down to gently caress me between my legs, his fingers teasing my opening.

I pushed into him, begging for more. "I am. I always have been."

"Fuck yes."

I lost my hold on him and yelped when I was pushed back against the cold tiled wall. I missed the warmth of the water, but I knew he was going to heat me up in a much more satisfying way.

"I love hearing you say that."

His hands went straight to my ass, gripping it tightly, and he hoisted me up in his arms. His mouth went to my tit, sucking greedily on my sensitive nipple while he continued to tease me with his fingers.

I cried out when he plunged a finger deep inside of me. God, this was bliss. Perfect. Something I'd missed so damn much. Deep down, I knew that no one, absolutely no one, could bring out these feelings in me. No one could cause me to tear down my inhibitions and give them my all but this man.

And now, he was mine, *all mine,* and I was all his.

"I need more," I breathed out.

"You want more?" he asked, adding a finger and upping his pace.

"Yes! More than just your fingers. *All* of you."

And he gave me what I wanted. His fingers abruptly slid out of my folds. He tightened his hold on me and replaced them with his cock.

"Damn, I missed you, missed this pussy," he moaned, slowly thrusting in and out of me. His lips met mine, kissing me softly.

He was being gentle, too gentle, and I didn't like it.

"Harder," I pressured. "Give it to me harder."

"No," he grunted out. "I want this to last. I don't want to lose you yet."

"Please," I begged, panting against his lips.

"Are you sure?"

I nodded, and he did as he was told. The sound of our bodies slapping against one another in the water was mesmerizing. Just like I thought, he warmed me up, heat shooting through my entire body, while he pumped in and out of me.

It was building ... my heart pulsating ... until I couldn't hold back any longer. I moaned out and fell slack against the shower wall. He continued to pump in and out of me, not losing his hold, and groaned out his release. We were both panting as he carefully set me back down to my feet.

"Looks like that sealed the deal," he said with a laugh. He tipped his head down to kiss me.

"I think we sealed the deal a while back," I replied, catching my breath. "This is just the icing on the cake."

"No, the icing on the cake will be the day you let me put a ring on you."

I grinned.

Some people thought that I took him back, forgave him too soon, but it was my love life. Not theirs. I was only worried about my happiness now.

The things he did were wrong, but he was apologetic. He was sorry. He was only trying to protect me.

If people didn't understand that, then they didn't understand our love. They didn't understand moving on and realizing what was best for your family.

And I honestly was done caring about what people thought.

Chapter Fifteen

DALTON

"I HAVE to go to the office for a bit. Do you want to come or stay in this warm, comfy bed?" I asked Gabby. I nestled in closer to her warm body and wrapped my arms around her, kissing the back of her neck.

She let out a moan, and her arm reached out to slide around my neck. "As much fun as that sounds, I think I'll stay here," she replied. "My morning is starting off pretty damn well. I'm not going to let that drama kill my mood."

Her hand tightened around me, and I continued to run my lips along her soft skin. The feeling was mutual. Staying there with her sounded more alluring than anything, especially walking into Douglas PR, but I had a job to do. A murder to solve. I had to get this mess figured out. We were having a baby, and protecting my family was the most important thing to me.

"Okay," I whispered against her skin. "I'll be home in a few hours and take you to lunch. Call me if you need anything." I reached down and rubbed her stomach over the sheets. "I can't wait to meet our little one."

* * *

I shut my computer off and was about to get up to leave when I heard the knock on my office door.

"Come in," I yelled, hoping my father wasn't on the other side.

I wasn't in the mood to deal with his bullshit. I held in a nervous breath when the door slowly opened and released it when Summer appeared in the doorway. Thank fuck. Her face was pale, like she'd seen a ghost. Something was wrong.

"What's up?"

"So ... I'm not sure if this is good or bad," she answered, the words falling from her red lips slowly.

"What is it?" I rushed out, waiting for it to be bad. I normally wasn't a rider on the road of pessimism, but shit hadn't been working out in my favor lately.

"Ivy's parents are here to see you."

Fuck. That wasn't what I'd been expecting. "Her parents are here to see me?" I paused, taking in her words like I'd misheard them.

She nodded, and from the look on her face, I knew she was aware of the Ivy situation—most likely from my father. He seemed to always go to her when he either wanted to get laid, have his ego stroked, or rant about work.

I took another breath and released it slowly.

What the hell do I do? Turn them away or contact my lawyer before meeting with them?

"Send them in."

She nodded and turned around to leave.

"And, Summer?"

She stopped to look back at me.

"Please don't say anything to my dad."

A faint smile flashed on her lips. "I won't. You've got my word."

My pulse skyrocketed when she walked away and shut the door.

Is this a good idea? Or am I digging myself an even bigger grave?

I got up from my chair as soon as she brought them in. I'd only met Ivy's father once, and it hadn't exactly been pretty. He'd pulled a gun on me, telling me to stay the hell away from his daughter, after I kept trying to persuade her to retract her affair statement.

Thomas and Becky Hart. I knew more about them than I should have. We'd investigated them—their bank statements, call logs, hacked into their car GPS system to see where they'd been. We didn't find anything substantial. The chance that Ivy's parents had something to do with her murder was slim, but I never said never. They could've found out about the big chunk of money Edith had given their daughter and wanted it for themselves.

I looked for signs of anger, blame, something, but the only look I saw on their faces was devastation. They introduced themselves, and I shook their hands, asking them to have a seat. Summer scurried out of the room, most likely scared to hear anything else my dad would get pissed about her hiding from him.

"I'm sorry for your loss," I said, leaning back against the edge of my desk.

"Thank you," Thomas replied, looking down at the floor.

Becky only nodded.

"This hasn't been easy for us."

I wanted to say some words of wisdom, something to put their minds at ease, but I was drawing a blank. I wasn't the best person to help people grieve.

"What can I help you guys with?" *That was the best thing I could ask them?*

It was forward, but I couldn't keep it to myself any longer. I couldn't put their minds at ease when mine felt like a roller coaster.

Why are they here? Especially since I heard they were the ones who told the cops about Gabby and me.

Thomas folded his hands in his lap and finally looked at me. "We want your help in finding out who did this horrific thing to our baby girl," he answered. "We ..." He stopped, fighting back tears. "We don't have a lot of money, but I hear you guys are the best at finding answers. You were persistent in talking to Ivy. You take your job seriously, and we want that seriousness in finding out the true story. We think you might know what she was up to more than anyone."

It took me a second to digest his words. I pointed to myself. "You want me to help you?"

He nodded.

"After you gave the police my name as a possible suspect, causing them to bring me in and question me like some criminal?"

"We informed them of everyone who'd been in contact with Ivy, to our knowledge. Her friends, ex-boyfriends, coworkers, everyone. We gave them anything we could think of. We're desperate to find her killer."

They could be of some use to me.

"First, I don't care about the money. Consider this pro bono. Do you still have that list you gave them?"

"We do." His hands shook as he pulled out a paper from his pocket and handed it to me.

I frowned when I noticed there were only a few names on there. Apparently, they didn't know who their daughter had been hanging out with.

"Do you mind if I make a copy?"

He nodded. "Does this mean you're going to help us?"

"It does, but if I help you, you have to help me."

"Anything," Becky said. Her first word since she'd stepped in here.

"You find anything else, you come to me first." I needed to be one step ahead of Harold.

They both nodded.

Perfect.

"Do you have anything else for me that might help us?"

"We do. We made copies of everything. They're at the house. You're more than welcome to come over and go through them. She was also ..." He paused. "She was also receiving threatening notes."

"Terrible ones," Becky added. "That's why she was staying with us."

"Do you have them?"

She shook her head.

"We gave them to the police."

Fuck! We needed to get into evidence. I needed to call one of my dad's guys.

I snatched my phone from my pocket and put it to my ear. "Hey,

Murphy. Stop whatever you're doing and meet me in the lobby." I hung up and looked at my visitors. "I'll follow you to your house."

* * *

"Did you tell your dad about this?" Murphy asked when we got in his car and started following Thomas and Becky.

I gave him a look from the passenger seat. I thought it would be a smarter choice to take his car than mine just in case someone was watching their house.

"Of course you didn't. He's going to be pissed."

I shrugged. "And I don't give a flying fuck. This is my best shot at finding out who did this before they start heavily looking into John and us. He'd better thank me for this shit."

"What about the police evidence? Have you got anything from your boy there?"

"I texted him before I left the office and told him to find me something. One hundred bucks for everything reliable."

"You give them dudes a hundred a pop? I'm about to change careers and be a shady cop."

"Shut up. You know damn well you get paid better than that." I shook my head before grabbing my phone and hitting Gabby's name. "Hey, babe. How are you feeling?"

"Good. Starving," she answered.

Shit. I felt bad. I hated canceling on her, but I didn't know if I'd get this opportunity again. "Do you think you can wait a little longer before lunch? Or maybe see if your mom or Cora wants to go with you? I'm so sorry, but Ivy's parents showed up at my office."

"What?" she screeched. "Of course, the day I decide to not come to work, they show up. Go figure. All the good shit happens when I'm not there."

"You can meet us there," I offered.

Do I want her any more tangled up in this? Absolutely not.

But she liked to be updated on everything going on, considering she was also involved.

"No, it's fine. Cora texted me earlier, asking me what I was doing today, so I'll meet up with her. You go, and you'll be telling me every detail when you get home, mister."

"I already planned on it." I knew I'd be getting an interrogation as soon as I walked through the front door. Gabby didn't like to be involved in drama, but that didn't stop her from wanting to hear every single detail about it. "Let me know if you need anything. I love you."

"Love you too."

"Oh, love is in the air," Murphy sang out when I hung up. He chuckled at my dirty look.

Bastard was jealous that I found the girl of my dreams while he was too busy hacking into porn sites for free.

Murphy parked behind them in the driveway of a one-story brick ranch. "I want you to take pictures of everything ... every single fucking thing," I told him before getting out. "Receipts, records, notes. Even if it doesn't look like anything. I don't know if they're going to let us take this shit with us or not, but I know something in there is going to help us."

"Got it," Murphy replied.

We got out of the car and followed them into their home.

"We made copies of everything before giving it to the police," Thomas said, signaling to a cardboard box on the kitchen table.

"Are the threat letters in there?" I asked.

It took Thomas a minute before answering, "Everything but that. We didn't think about it until it was too late, and the cop said they were already in police custody."

"Can we take the box?" I asked.

Thomas hesitated for a moment.

"Or at least make copies of everything? You probably don't want me here all night."

If they said no, that was exactly what I was going to do.

"There's a copy machine in the office down that hallway," he answered, pointing the way.

"And her bedroom?" Murphy asked.

"Directly across from it."

Thomas grabbed the box on the table and followed us. Ivy's bedroom was nothing like the upscale apartment I had visited her at. The furniture was old, scratched, and adolescent. Boy-band posters were still taped on the walls.

I looked over at Thomas, curious whether he'd stay or leave us. He stayed. Murphy pulled his phone from his pocket and started taking pictures of everything.

We stayed in Ivy's room for over an hour but weren't finding anything. She either didn't keep anything there, had gotten rid of it, or was hiding it somewhere else. Broken trails kept coming up, and it was discouraging. I felt like I was running out of time.

"This was a fail," I muttered. "The only thing in this room is stuffed animals, makeup, and shoes. Let's go."

"We'll keep looking elsewhere," Murphy said, noticing my disappointment. "Trust me when I say, we will find something. I'll look at every phone call she made and received and then contact everyone on her parents' list."

We started to head out of her bedroom when something caught my eye.

"Look," I said, snagging the robe from the hook on the back of the door.

I fingered the embroidered logo on the chest. I'd never personally been to the hotel, but I'd know that logo from anywhere. Everyone would.

"The Chancellor," Murphy said, eyeing the robe. "The mistress and hooker capital of Atlanta. Do you think it means something?"

I thought about it for a second and frowned. "Probably not. She was John's mistress, so I'm sure he took her there before getting her the apartment. She probably kept it because these things are nice as hell."

* * *

"Tell me the good news," I said, answering the phone on the way back to the office from Ivy's parents' house. *Please let this be a good phone call.*

"Well ... I got in," Lonnie, my inside source at the station, said.

Lonnie wasn't that high in the rankings yet, so it was more difficult for him to feed us intel, but the man was persistent and liked the extra cash.

"And?"

"To be honest, there wasn't much in there. It looked like they hadn't even started on the investigation yet. Her phone records were gone gone. It's weird as hell, man. Either they're doing a sucky-ass job on the case or someone is trying to hide something."

"What about the notes?" I rushed out. "Were there any threatening notes in there?"

"Yeah. I managed to take pictures of them as well as the evidence inventory."

"Send me a picture of the notes, inventory, everything you managed to get."

"Got it. It's on its way as soon as I hang up."

"Thanks. I'll text you the address where you can pick up the cash." I hung up and looked at Murphy. "He said there was barely shit in there. But he did get snaps of the notes." I relaxed against the seat. "I know this might be out of left field, and I could be completely wrong, but I have a feeling there's a reason why there isn't shit in there. I think someone involved could be on the force."

"And last I heard, Harold is pretty easy to buy off," he replied.

"Yeah, I know. But who the hell is he working with? No one likes the dude, and he's too stupid to be trusted to cover up a damn murder."

"Looks like he's our next person of interest."

* * *

"What the hell do you think you're doing?" my dad asked, storming into my office. He slammed the door shut with extra force and stood in front of me, his arms crossed.

I got back from the office five minutes ago and had been waiting on the Wilson storm to come through.

I leaned back in my chair and kicked my feet up on my desk. "I have no idea what you're talking about," I answered. "And please knock next time you make a trip in here."

He took a step forward, his upper lip snarling. "Meeting with Ivy's parents. I swear to God, if you say one wrong thing, it can come back to bite us in the ass."

I raised my hand to stop him from going on. "They're helping me, helping *us*. They don't think we did it and feel like the police aren't doing enough."

"They're the parents of our enemy right now. They might not think we had anything to do with it, but what are their thoughts on John? They might think he's the guilty one and are trying to get more information on him."

"No one knows anyone's ulterior motives right now, but I'm trying to prove to them that all of us are innocent, and you stomping in here like some madman isn't making it any easier."

"Then, what do you have that's so great? It'd better be something good."

"Ivy was receiving threatening letters," I disclosed.

He raised a brow. One point for me. "Please tell me you got your hands on those letters."

I held the papers up in my hand. Lonnie did as promised and sent me the pictures. I'd just finished printing them out. Every single one had been typed out, and according to the inventory report, there was no trace of DNA on them. They were all short and straight to the point.

I grabbed the first one and read it out loud. "*Keep your mouth shut, slut, or you'll regret it.*"

I grabbed the second one. "*I've already warned you once. You didn't listen. Prepare for the consequences, bitch.*"

The other three were of similar nature.

Who the fuck wrote these?

"Are you thinking what I'm thinking?" I asked.

"Yeah. These sound exactly like they're from John." His face turned red. I swore he was about to pop a blood vessel. "That motherfucker! He'd better not be lying to us. I will not let him ruin my business."

He turned around to leave, most likely to confront John, but I stopped him.

"I think Harold ... or someone else at the station has something to do with it."

He froze but didn't turn around to look at me. "Go on."

"There's hardly anything in the evidence log, and Ivy's parents said they gave them more than what's listed. Lonnie said it looked like someone wasn't even working on the case, which we know is a lie, considering they brought me in. The only things listed are the letters; the statement from her parents, saying Gabby and I showed up at their house; and the video footage of us at her apartment."

He finally turned around to look at me. "Looks like someone is trying to set us and John up, and I bet you Harold is somehow involved."

"What's the beef between you two?" I asked. "Why would he want to do this?"

"Let's just say, Harold wasn't man enough for his wife, and she had to go other places to be satisfied."

His lips formed a confident smirk, causing my stomach to churn. He screwed his best friend's wife and didn't even feel one ounce of remorse. The man continued to make me lose disrespect for him with each passing day.

"Looks like you sticking your dick into places it shouldn't be brought us into this mess."

That smirk collapsed into a frown. "That's what gets all men in trouble: pussy we shouldn't be craving. John with Ivy. Me with Summer. You with Gabby. That's our downfall."

With that, he turned back around and left the room.

* * *

"So, how was work?" Gabby asked on our way to dinner.

"Interesting," I answered. "Definitely interesting."

"I can't believe Ivy's parents came to talk to you." She blew out a breath. "I'm glad they did though. There's no way they'd come to you if they thought you were responsible for her death. That's a big step to prove our innocence."

My girl was looking good in a body-hugging red dress, her hair a wild mess after our quickie session over the bathroom counter. I couldn't help myself when I had walked in, seeing her in only a bra and panties. That was what I wanted to focus on. Her and me.

I knew she wanted more, but that was going to have to wait. I needed a moment without work talk. I grabbed her hand in mine and brought it to my lips. "I know, babe. But no more talk about work, John, Ivy, or my dad. Tonight is about us."

Chapter Sixteen

GABBY

"I WANT to ask you something, but if you don't want to do it, say no. I promise I won't get mad if you do," Dalton said.

We were sitting at the kitchen table after another round of incredible shower sex. The shower had become my new favorite place to get it on.

I was only wearing his T-shirt, sans bra, and panties. That was what I felt the most comfortable in lately. He looked at me from across the table, bare-chested and only wearing a pair of shorts.

"Okay," I drew out. *Please don't be something with your family. Or John.*

"Ivy's parents gave us a list of people she was close with and the contact information of them. I called her old roommate, who was also her best friend, growing up. She agreed to meet with us today. I think it would be to our benefit if another woman is with us, so she won't feel like she's getting ambushed by two men."

He looked nervous, like asking me this was the equivalence of giving him a kidney or something.

"So, that's why you just gave me that mind-blowing orgasm?" I snapped, shoving my plate forward. "You seriously want me to do that?"

He shook his head, his eyes meeting the floor. "Never mind. I was stupid for even asking."

He looked up when I reached across the table and smacked his shoulder, laughing. "Jeez, I'm kidding. This whole situation is seriously killing your sense of humor. Of course I'll go."

He blew out a breath and cracked a smile. "Jesus, why did I have to fall in love with one of the biggest smart-asses in the world?"

I shrugged, biting into my lower lip. "Maybe you should do something about it. Fuck the smart-assness right out of me."

He got up from his chair and stalked the few steps toward me. He turned my chair around, so I faced him. "Mmm ... that might take a while."

My adrenaline spiked when he opened my legs and pulled his shirt over my head.

"But I'm up for the job."

* * *

I frowned when we pulled up to Delaney Melton's apartment. Ivy's building had been ritzy—complete with a doorman, amenities, and all that jazz. Delaney's was quite the contrary. No doorman to be seen. In fact, the entry looked like it needed some TLC. It wasn't the worst. I'd lived in more run-down places with my mom, but it wasn't luxury living. Ivy had moved up and left her bestie in the dirt.

What a great friend.

I stood in the middle of the two men when we made it to her apartment door and glanced over at Dalton. "You made an appointment, right?" I asked.

He nodded and knocked on the door. "Yes, and she seemed pretty cool on the phone. I guess she and Ivy had some kind of falling-out, but she still cares about her and wants to help out in any way she can."

Perfect.

The door swung open before I had the chance to ask any more questions, and just like the exterior of her building, Delaney was nothing like her friend. Thick, red-rimmed glasses rested on the base of her slim nose. Her face was makeup free, her black hair thrown into a ponytail with flyaway strands everywhere. She was sporting a baggy T-shirt and jeans.

How in the hell were these two best friends?

"Hi ... Delaney?" I asked, questioning myself more than her. Maybe we were at the wrong door.

She sighed. "Hi," she said, her voice soft. She looked between the three of us. "I take it, you guys are the ones here to talk to me about Ivy?"

"Yes," Dalton answered. He held out his hand to shake hers. "This is Gabby and Murphy. Thank you for giving us your time. We really appreciate it."

"Sure, no problem." A small yet uncomfortable smile passed over her lips.

Dalton was right. Me tagging along was a good idea. I hoped my presence made her feel more comfortable.

I walked in first, the guys following behind me. The apartment was on the smaller side. The furniture made it seemed even more cramped, but it was extremely clean and organized. A plaid sofa sat in the middle of the room with a TV stand a few feet away. A four-person dining room table was situated on the outside of the kitchen.

"Can we sit at the table?" I asked, pointing at it.

She nodded.

"Thanks." I shot her a friendly smile and took the seat next to her while the guys took the chairs across from us.

Murphy's hand went to his pocket to pull out his phone. "Do you mind if I record this?" he asked, setting it down on the table. "It's easier than trying to write everything down. Plus, we won't miss any details."

"Sure, that's no problem," Delaney answered timidly. "I'm not sure if I'll be of any help. I'm only doing this because Ivy's parents asked me to."

"We understand," Dalton said, and Murphy hit the record button. "We all have one goal—to find out who did this to your friend and get justice for her."

"So, how long did you and Ivy know each other?" I asked, ready to get started.

She played with her hands in front of her and took a deep breath before answering, "Since middle school. We were best friends, practically sisters, throughout high school. We decided to move in together after graduation."

"That's a pretty long time. Is this the same apartment you guys shared?"

She nodded.

"Were you roommates with her when she started seeing John?" I stopped to correct myself just in case Ivy hadn't been on a first-name basis with her boyfriends. "I mean, Governor Gentry?"

"Yes." Her voice shook before she went on. "After she took that job, even though I told her not to, everything changed. She changed. She turned into a completely different person. She lied about it at first, which I didn't blame her for. I mean, who wants to confess to the world that they're banging guys for money? But I knew something was up, so she finally broke down and told me."

"What?" all three of us blurted out at the same time.

Why did shit always seem to get more interesting?

We were always hitting detours, sending us on a completely different path.

"I thought she was an intern for John's campaign?" Murphy drew out.

"An intern?" She snorted. "That's definitely not what I'd call it."

"Then, what would you call it?" I asked.

"She was a hooker before John got her a job."

We still couldn't hide the shock on our faces.

"Not like a *stand on the street corner* kind of hooker."

"Is there a difference?"

"There is. Ivy was a high-end escort. I guess that's a better word for it. It wasn't long-term, probably about a month. She met this girl at the bar she was working at. She told Ivy she knew a way to get fast cash and introduced her to her madam or whatever."

"Jesus," I cried out. "The man was into prostitutes too?" *Why did my mom have to choose the scummiest man to be my father?*

"She did small jobs until one of the girls asked her to tag along on one of hers—a better one with more money. She had no idea that meant a threesome and chickened out. The girl was her ride, so Ivy waited in the lobby until her so-called friend got the job done. That was where she met John. He bought her a drink, and she ended up telling him about the whole situation and her financial problems." She shook her head. "The girl couldn't save money. She blew it faster than her paychecks came. According to her, John offered to make a deal with her. He wanted her to be exclusive with him, no more prostituting, and he'd find her a job and help pay her bills."

Holy fucking shit. The plot keeps thickening.

"So, did that piss off the pimp or madam or whoever was in charge?" I questioned.

"It sure did. Three girls showed up at our doorstep, threatening to kick her ass, but we didn't answer the door."

"Did they ever come back?" Murphy asked.

"Once. Ivy wasn't here, so I ignored them again. They haven't been back since then." She shrugged. "I figured they'd given up."

"Great," Dalton muttered. "So, now, we're not sure if she was killed by her madam and a slew of escorts, her sugar daddy, or an ex-boyfriend."

"Did she have any other boyfriends?" I asked.

She shook her head. "John was pretty much her go-to guy for everything," she answered. "He was really strict about her seeing other men. She stopped seeing them when he gave her the ultimatum of them or the apartment. She obviously took the million-dollar home."

"There was no one else?" Dalton pushed.

Delaney stayed quiet, her gaze moving to the table.

"Delaney, whatever you know will help us find your friend's killer. Anything you tell us will be completely confidential. You have my word."

"And if you don't feel safe, we're more than happy to get you a hotel that you can stay in until we find them," I offered, patting her arm.

Things weren't adding up. The chance that a madam or prostitute waited that long to kill her didn't sound convincing.

"There was another guy," she said timidly. "I never met him, but she told me about him. She said he was manipulative, someone she didn't trust, but loaded. She only slept with him a few times, but that's not what he wanted. He paid her for ... information."

"Information?" Murphy repeated. "Information on what?"

"On John."

The three of us looked at each other.

Bingo.

Now, all we needed to do was find this man.

"Do you know a name?" I asked.

"No."

"What he drives?"

"No. All I know is he used to meet her at some expensive hotel ... The Chancellor or something like that."

"The robe," Murphy said.

"Is there anything else you think we need to know?" Dalton asked. "Anything you think is important?"

"I think that's it. Ivy and I had a falling-out a few months ago when she moved out, so I don't know what she was up to since then."

Dalton grabbed his card and slid it her way. "Thank you. If you think of anything else, give me a call. I don't care what it is—big or small."

I patted her arm again. "Yeah, thanks so much, Delaney."

"Does this mean the cops won't be coming around anymore?" she asked when we started to get up.

"I'm not so sure about that," Dalton answered.

She groaned. "If you talk to them, please ask them not to send that chubby cop here again. The dude seriously gives me the creeps."

"Did you get a name?" Dalton asked, suddenly interested.

"Harold. All he kept asking me about was John and if Ivy feared him. It was weird. He also kept asking me if I'd testify against him."

"If he comes back, give him my card," Dalton said.

"I guess it's time we finally visited The Chancellor," Murphy said from behind us while we walked down the stairs. He tapped my shoulder. "You want to tag along?"

"I think I'll pass on that," I answered, opening the door and heading back to Dalton's car. "I'll leave visiting the hooker hotel to you guys."

"I was thinking," Murphy said from the backseat when we all slammed our doors shut.

"Yeah?" I asked.

He smiled a childish grin. "If you have a boy, I have the perfect name for him."

"Let me guess ... Murphy?"

He pointed my way. "How did you know? That name must've been on the top of your guys' list."

"Oh, hell no," Dalton cut in. "I'm not naming my child after a law that states that anything that can go wrong will go wrong. That's like setting them up for disaster." He looked over at me. "Please tell me you're not a fan of the name?"

"That's rude," Murphy said, faking offense. "You could've just said no."

"Then, no," Dalton and I said in unison, and Murphy cracked up in laughter.

Baby names were the last thing on my priority list.

The only name I wanted to know now was the guy who'd been paying Ivy for info on John.

* * *

"So ... I want to ask you something," Cora said, walking into the living room of the condo. It was my second time hearing that question today, and I hoped hers wasn't as serious as Dalton's. "If you don't like the idea, tell me."

I had Dalton drop me off at home before they went on to their next stop. Going to that hotel was something I didn't want to get into.

"Okay," I drew out. "Shoot."

A grin erupted along her glossy pink lips. "I know it's kind of early and all, but I want to help throw your baby shower. I'm leaving for school at the end of the summer, which means I'll miss out on all of the action if you have it later." Her grin turned into a pout. "This is your first baby shower. I want to decorate it, plan it, do everything on my Pinterest board."

I laughed. "It's definitely early." I was only close to eleven weeks along, according to my doctor that Dalton and I visited yesterday. "I don't even know what the gender is yet." Didn't you need to know these things before throwing a shower? Did I need pink or blue balloons?

"We can make it gender neutral. Daisy is leaving too. You know she doesn't want to miss it either."

She was right. I'd hate to not have my best friends there. I knew they'd both come for the actual occasion, if they could, but I wanted them to be there for the entire process.

I blew out a breath, trying to fight my smile. "Fine, that shouldn't be a problem."

She threw her hands up.

"But I need to check with my mom first. I know she wants to be involved in the planning."

She waved her hand through the air. "Oh, don't worry about that. I've already talked to her. She's game. How's the end of this month sound?"

That was only a little over a week away. I rubbed my forehead and nodded as nervousness trickled down my spine. Everything seemed to be moving in a whirlwind. All my friends were going to be heading off to college. They were going to be focusing on finals, football games, and parties while I was going to be changing diapers and making a feeding schedule.

A part of me felt left behind, like I was losing that component of growing up and finding myself.

"That sounds perfect."

This baby shower was going to be my introduction into a new world and my sayonara to my old one.

Chapter Seventeen

DALTON

"THIS SHOULD BE FUN," Murphy said when I parked across the street from the infamous Chancellor Hotel. "A high-end hooker club. I've never been a fan of hookers, but maybe these ones will have diamond chokers or some shit."

"Maybe you'll find your next girlfriend here," I replied. "And relax. It's not a goddamn harem. You probably won't even see anyone. They're discreet about shit like that here. Why do you think it costs so much?"

"Eh, I guess you're right. Oh well. They're out of my pay grade anyway. My girls get paid with pizza and sex."

"No wonder you're single," I muttered.

"Dude, you were basically single a few months ago, and now, you're acting all high and mighty because you have a girlfriend. What are we in, middle school?"

"Because I am high and mighty now. When you find the right girl, Murphy, you'll feel all high and mighty too. You'll feel pretty damn special that this woman who is so amazing and could have anyone she wanted chose you. You get that, and I promise you, you'll stay on top of the world for as long as she's yours."

Murphy rolled his eyes, obviously not in the mood for my romantic bullshit, and looked over at me in waiting.

I rubbed my hands together before getting out and slamming my door shut. "Let's get this over with."

Murphy stayed on my heels as we headed toward the hotel. He didn't ask any questions when I skipped the front door and walked to the back of the building, straight to the employee entrance.

"You got this?" I asked, looking at him.

He nodded, an arrogant grin coming my way. "Sure do, boss."

He punched in the passcode, like it was an everyday occurrence. Every muscle in my body tightened, waiting to see if we'd get in.

"You got your part?" he asked, holding the door open.

I patted my pocket. "You know it." Only this time, I had to be more careful. I couldn't let a camera catch me paying anyone off.

* * *

I was five hundred dollars poorer with nothing to show for it. Every employee there had been on high alert. Their eyes roamed from one side of the room to the other, barely looking at me or the cash in my hand and most likely on the hunt for hidden cameras. They'd been trained well, which didn't surprise me. The number one reason people came to The Chancellor was for the discretion.

It was like Vegas—whatever happened there stayed there.

And none of the employees were interested in losing their job for a couple hundred dollars. The guests used pseudonyms. They paid in cash. The records were locked tighter than a virgin's pussy.

I got one woman to talk.

One.

A maid.

I followed her into a room, and she gave me what little information she had. She'd seen Ivy there before with a man. He was tall and slim, light-blond hair, and wore an expensive suit. Pretty much most of the men on our list fit that same description. That was all she had for us.

And all that told me was that I still didn't have shit.

I needed to find out who this mystery prick was.

"I need you to find a sketch artist—the best one you can. Give them the details that the maid described, so at least we have something to go off of. Maybe if we show it to John, he'll know who it is."

"Gotcha," Murphy answered.

* * *

I rolled my eyes and hung up the phone. My dad demanded I go to his office. No surprise there. I'd hoped I wouldn't have to talk to him until I figured out who The Chancellor guy was.

I didn't bother knocking before barging in. He wanted to be rude. Two could play that game.

"What's up?" I asked, throwing my arms out. "Why couldn't you talk to me over the phone?"

"Shut the door first, please," he said.

I was surprised at his politeness. I closed it and turned around to see him leaning back comfortably in his chair. Wrinkles shadowed his receding hairline.

"Harold and his little rent-a-cop kid stopped by to talk to me earlier." He shook his head in disgust. "Fucking prick."

"That's surprising," I muttered.

Harold had no problem fucking with me. I was young and easy bait. My dad, however, was a different story. He was more of a force to be reckoned with. Messing with him had severe consequences, and for years, it had seemed like Harold knew that. He always appeared to be afraid of poking the bear too much.

"What did he have to say?"

He snorted before letting out a thick laugh. "He threatened me and told me to watch my back." His cuff links shone as he flung his hand through the air. "Whatever the hell that means. I could smell the motherfucker's bullshit stench from across the room."

"Did you bring up that we think someone at the station might be involved?"

He scoffed. "Do you think I'm an idiot?"

Thank God. No one needed to know that but us.

"I have other news."

"Yes?" He raised a brow and leaned forward in his chair.

"Murphy and I made a visit to The Chancellor earlier."

"And why did you do that?"

"We found a robe from there when we were going through Ivy's room."

"She was a mistress. That's typical."

"That's what I thought. Then, we talked to her old roommate. She mentioned Ivy met a guy there sometimes."

"Was that guy John?"

I shook my head. "No. She said it definitely wasn't John. She told us Ivy had started working as an escort until John insisted she quit. Her friend said she only met with one other guy that wasn't John, and this mystery man was worried more about her giving him information on our dear governor than screwing her."

"Interesting. Very interesting." He rubbed his jaw, and I could tell his brain was working. He was thinking of a twist—something to feed to the media. Now, all we needed was a name or a face, and the chances of the blame game on John would hopefully change. "So, what did you find there?"

"Not shit."

"Typical."

"I'm looking more into it. I'll let you know if I get anything."

"Be careful, son." His sincerity honestly scared the living shit out of me. "Harold is aiming for us, and you're going to be the first hit on his target. He thinks you're vulnerable. Show him Douglas men aren't vulnerable. We're tigers who will rip him apart."

Chapter Eighteen

DALTON

"YOUR MOTHER IS HAVING dinner at the house on Saturday," my dad said, walking into my office. "I know she'd love it if you came. You haven't been coming around, and it's making her sad."

"I have plans."

He raised a brow—a silent *cancel them*.

"It's Gabby's baby shower."

"I don't recall your mother mentioning an invitation."

"That's because there wasn't one sent."

He snorted and shook his head, looking at me like I'd just killed his firstborn. "Well, that's rude."

"And so is my mother. I'm not going to give her the chance to ruin Gabby's big day." I stood up and saluted him before walking out the door.

* * *

"Are you coming to Gabby's baby shower this weekend?" I asked.

Leo scrunched up his eyebrows at my question.

"It's coed."

I stopped by his house before heading home. I'd been so wrapped up in Ivy's case and Gabby, so it had been a while since we talked. I felt like I was getting somewhere with Ivy's murder but still stuck. I needed to know the guy Ivy was meeting. That guy was my missing piece. Murphy was on the hunt to find out everyone Harold had been in contact with.

He shrugged his shoulders. "Sure, I'm in. I haven't really had a chance to get to know Gabby, so it'll be fun."

"Maybe she'll have some single friends you can hook up with." I elbowed him in the side, resulting in a dirty look.

"I'm still married, dumbass. Not happening."

"You're separated and in the proceedings of a divorce."

He obviously wasn't game for my idea, which didn't surprise me. I was only fucking with him. I knew my brother well enough to know he didn't do random hookups.

"Your girlfriend is only eighteen."

"What the hell does that have to do with anything?"

"That means, her friends are most likely eighteen. Eighteen is entirely too young for me."

"Eh, not necessarily," I fired back. "And just because you meet a woman doesn't mean you have to screw her. You could hang out and get to know each other."

"I have children. There aren't many women who are ready to take that on. Your girlfriend's friends are ready for college, parties, all that shit we did when we were their age."

I went quiet and looked down at my shoes when it dawned on me. Guilt swelled up in my belly. Gabby was going to miss all of that. Would she regret not being able to go out and live before having a family? I ran a hand over my face and blew out a long breath.

"Do you think Gabby will feel like that?" I asked him. "Do you think she'll resent me for not being able to have all of that fun before being tied down?"

He shrugged his shoulders and then patted me on the back. "It took two of you to get pregnant, so I don't think she can place all of the blame on you. Should you have been smart enough to wrap it up?

Of course. But what's done is done. As for the resentment, I'm not sure. I think you still need to make sure you guys go out and do fun shit. You have enough money to pay for a babysitter. You both can still have a life and romance outside of your child."

Chapter Nineteen

GABBY

BABY SHOWERS WEREN'T MEANT *to be hell, right?*

They were supposed to be all warm and fuzzy, filled with smiles, balloons, and obnoxious games where you had to be the first one to eat a container of baby food.

Yet, somehow, mine turned out to be.

There were no initial warning signs. The sun was out. It wasn't too hot. Comfortable. No chance of rain.

Cora was hosting it at her house with my mom and Gabby. She had the perfect outdoor entertainment area. I was meeting them there before the guests arrived in case they needed help with anything.

Dalton texted me before I got out of the car, telling me he was on his way. I found the girls working on the finishing touches when I made it to the backyard. I was greeted with squeals, smiles, and hugs.

"What do you think?" Cora asked, excitement pouring through her.

My mom and Daisy stood to each side of her with the same looks on their faces.

I looked around, my mouth hanging open. "Wow," I stuttered out.

Her backyard looked like something out of a movie. It was gender neutral, like she'd promised, and Dr. Seuss–themed. There was food everywhere, some even along the theme of his books—green eggs and ham, clear bowls filled with fish gummies. I even noticed a cotton candy machine. They'd gone all out.

I wrapped them all up in a group hug. "Thank you! I appreciate this so much."

They were too good to me. I had the best mother and friends in the world.

"You deserve it, honey," my mom said after we all pulled away. "You, my darling daughter, deserve this and so much more." She went in for another hug. "You're going to be a terrific mother."

I kept the guest list small. I told them I wanted something small and personal. I had a lot going on with the surprise pregnancy, having an early baby shower, Ivy's case, and working out things with Dalton.

"Keegan and Lane made the diaper cake," Daisy explained. "It was definitely interesting, watching them try to put it together." She laughed. "Keegan swears he's never decorating for a baby shower again."

"Unless you ask him to. The man will do anything you tell him to," I replied.

It was still crazy to me that she'd convinced Keegan, the man-whore who had made it his mission to be an asshole to everyone, to make a diaper cake. Times had really changed, and it only proved that love could really evolve someone into something they never thought they'd be. It was all about finding the right person.

I jumped when a pair of arms wrapped around my waist and moist lips hit my neck.

"Hey, baby," Dalton said in my ear.

My heart fluttered when his hands moved up to my belly, rubbing tiny circles on it. He'd developed an obsession with constantly wanting to touch it.

"This place looks amazing. Remind me to send kick-ass thank-you gifts to all the ladies who did this."

He kissed my cheek before turning me around. My eyes widened when I saw Leo standing a few feet away from us, a smile on his face. A little girl was at his side with her hand tucked into his.

They took a step forward.

"It's my fault we're running late," Leo told me. He brought the girl into his arms. "This little one had to change her clothes three times because she couldn't decide what princess she wanted to be today."

"It's no problem. Thank you for coming." I looked over at the little girl. "Belle. Good choice. She's my favorite too."

She grinned in response, her smile missing a front tooth. "I'm Claire," she said. "Are you my uncle Dalton's girlfriend?"

My cheeks warmed.

Dalton grabbed my shoulder and brought me into his side. "She sure is," he answered.

"Can you take me to get a cupcake, Uncle Dalton?" Claire asked.

Dalton kissed my cheek and then grabbed his niece's hand to escort her to the snack bar.

Leo held up two gift bags. "I didn't want to blindside you in front of everyone," he said. "But my mom and Piper wanted me to give you these. I'll set them to the side somewhere, just in case you don't want to open them in front of everyone."

I nodded. "Thank you."

What the hell would they send me?

Roadkill?

A warning letter?

A check in exchange to leave Dalton?

* * *

"Gabby, we have a problem," Cora said, running into the backyard.

The baby shower was in full swing. All of the women were hanging out and talking to each other. The men were on the other side, playing horseshoes. The kids were running around, playing in the pool.

"A *big* one."

"Already?" I groaned out. "The baby shower just started thirty minutes ago."

"I have a feeling it's about to end." She looked around the yard and screamed Dalton's name. He came running toward us. "You're wanted," she whispered, pointing toward the door leading into the house.

Dalton looked back at Leo and pointed to Claire. "Keep her outside," he said, like he already knew something was wrong.

Leo nodded in response, and I followed Dalton inside, not sure how bad the situation would be.

It was worse than I thought.

Chapter Twenty

DALTON

TWO POLICEMEN STOOD in the doorway.

They took a step forward when they saw me come into view.

"Dalton Douglas, you're under arrest," one said, snagging the handcuffs from his belt.

I heard the gasps around the room. Hands went to mouths, eyes moving straight to Gabby. Fuck, I felt so bad. I was humiliating her on one of the most important events of her life. She'd always remember this day—for all the wrong reasons.

Gabby let out a cry, her face going ashen, and I reached out just in time to stop her from falling. My lower lip trembled.

"Everything is going to be okay," I whispered, tightening my hold on her. "I promise you. I love you, and I'll be home soon." I kissed her cheek and made sure she was balanced back on her feet before approaching the officers. "Under arrest? Under arrest for what exactly?"

Don't say murder. Please don't say murder.

"For the murder of Ivy Hart," an officer answered, disgust on his face.

Fuck!

He said murder.

He really said that word.

I was close to passing out. I looked back at Gabby to find her mom at her side. Daisy and Cora were at the other side.

I slowly mouthed, *I love you.*

She nodded with tears in her eyes.

I gave my attention back to the cops. "You've got to be kidding me. You guys are crazy if you think I killed that woman."

Cop One snorted. "That's what they all say."

Cop Two shook his head. "We'll talk about this at the station. Now, let's go."

I had two choices: cooperate or tell them to fuck off. I turned around, deciding on the first. It would work much better in my favor to work with them.

My hands were pulled behind my back roughly, and I was read my Miranda rights. The handcuffs felt tight around my wrists, which I was sure was intentional.

"I'll call Kenneth," Shelia said, grabbing for her phone.

"We'll fix this," Gabby said, rushing to my side.

I nodded before I was jerked backward and led out to the squad car.

I was being arrested at my girlfriend's baby shower. It was humiliating, and I felt like a total piece of shit. The sadness and disappointment on Gabby's face made me want to rip Harold's heart out of his chest the next time I saw him. Whoever had put them up to this was going down.

* * *

I was back in the same shithole room, waiting for someone to come in and explain to me why I'd been escorted from my girlfriend's baby shower into a cop car. There was no way they actually believed they had sufficient evidence to convict me of a crime I didn't commit.

Harold walked in, a smug look on his face, a pep in his step.

"I'm not speaking without my goddamn lawyer," I said before he even got the chance to sit down. I wanted this over with. Gabby needed me.

He held his hands up in the air. "That's fine," he said, taking a seat. I was relieved to not see David. It was just us two. One-on-one. "I'll sit here and wait until he arrives."

I waited impatiently, not saying another word, and blew out a breath of relief when my lawyer came shuffling into the room. He was dressed in a full suit, and his blond hair was slicked back. He threw his briefcase down on the table and pulled out the chair next to me.

"Why is my client here?" he asked, getting straight to the point.

Billy Herrington was one of the top lawyers in the city. He didn't fuck around. Even though I was a lawyer and so was my dad and uncle, we kept him on retainer. It never looked good, representing yourself.

"We received a tip that he was involved in the murder of a young woman named Ivy Hart," Harold answered matter-of-factly. He was ready to sentence me to life.

"A fucking tip from who?" I blurted out.

I noticed the annoyed look on Billy's face from the corner of my eye. He wanted me to keep my mouth shut and let him do his job. Lawyers hated nothing more than clients who couldn't keep their mouths shut.

"A tip from someone stating they overheard you bragging about killing Ivy Hart, the mistress of John Gentry. Yes, we know you were representing John and trying to hide their affair. We're not idiots. We have the documents your company drew up, trying to pay her to keep her mouth shut. I'm sure you ... your dad ... John, one of you or possibly *all* of you, were unhappy when she didn't go through with the deal you proposed. We found the nondisclosure form as well as the threatening letters. Those letters look like something a man trying to hide an affair might write ... or people trying to help him hide it." He shook his head at me, trying to look disgusted but failing. "Is that why you did it? Because she didn't bow down to you and your family?"

"I didn't do shit," I spat. "You know that." I leaned forward, resting my elbows on the table, and kept going before Billy could stop me. "Why don't you tell me who this reliable source is?"

I ran the possible sources through my mind, trying to come up with anyone else that would be in on their setup, but my mind was drawing a blank. Someone, and I wasn't sure who, had made up me bragging about her death.

Harold folded his hands on the table. "That's confidential."

"Then, I'm not telling you shit."

"The source is Kelly Douglas."

Both Harold and I looked at Billy.

"I know this for a fact. You might not be able to tell him who it was, but I can."

"My sister-in-law?" I yelled. *Or soon-to-be ex-sister-in-law.* "What the fuck?"

"She came into the station, terrified for her own life, after she overheard you confessing the crime to your brother," Harold said.

Damn, he sure wasn't doing a good job with the whole "confidential" thing.

"That conniving bitch," I mumbled. That probably wasn't the best thing to say at the moment, but I was on the verge of snapping. I wanted to run out of the room and confront her ass.

"I see you're a fan of her," Harold said. "Care to tell me why she'd come in here and lie about something this serious? And how she even knows about your involvement with Ivy?"

"The murder is all over the news, and she knows we worked with John about the affair. She attends our family dinners. As for your second question, she most likely did it because she thinks I'm influencing my brother to divorce her."

"That seems a bit extreme."

"That bitch is fucking extreme. She's a basket case." My behavior wasn't yelling innocence, but I didn't give a damn.

"What do we need to do to get him out of here for now?" Billy asked.

"We're not letting him out on bail. He's a flight risk," Harold answered.

I let out a harsh laugh. "I'm a flight risk? Don't you think if I was a flight risk and actually did kill her, I would've run by now?"

Billy looked at me. "Stay here. I'll fix this." He got up and left the room.

"Harold, you know I didn't do this," I said, trying to reason with him. "You know I'm not a killer."

"I honestly don't know what you or your family is capable of anymore," he answered, getting up from the chair and slamming the door shut as he left.

* * *

"I'm going to kill her," I shouted as soon as I walked out of the station and found Leo waiting for me. "I'm going to kill that bitch with my bare hands."

I'd been released, but Harold made sure I knew that this wasn't over. He'd made it clear that he was still looking into my father and me.

After Billy left me in the interrogation room, he went straight to Leo's and convinced him to talk to Kelly. It took Leo a few hours, but he finally managed to break her down. She told him she made it all up to get back at me.

"I advise you to shut your mouth, Dalton," Billy said, walking alongside me.

"Sorry," I grumbled.

He turned my way and shook my hand. "Let me know if anything else comes up. Have a good night."

"Brother, calm down," Leo said, coming my way. He was my ride home ... well, my ride back to my uncle Kenneth's, so I could get Gabby. "She's still my wife and the mother of my children. Watch what you say, especially in public, dumbass."

I walked to Leo's car and threw open the door. "She tried to destroy our family," I said, getting in. "Her ass is the one that needs arrested. False informing is a crime."

Leo looked down at his lap, shaking his head. "She was mad at me, at you. She felt like you were the one who pushed me to file for divorce. She overheard you talking about finding me a girl at Gabby's baby shower. That apparently made her angry enough to get back at you."

"I've got to find the killer before this gets worse. I can't have this hanging over my head when Gabby has our baby."

Chapter Twenty-One

GABBY

"HE'S ON HIS WAY," Kenneth informed everyone in the room, but his attention zeroed in on me, waiting for my reaction.

My hand flew to my mouth, and more tears fell down my cheeks —these ones of relief. "Oh, thank God," I cried out.

I'd been pacing back and forth in his living room for the past five hours. So many emotions had hammered through me with each step. Shock. Sadness. Anger. Fear. I couldn't go back to the condo. I couldn't be there alone. The thought of Dalton not coming back and my staying there without him was terrifying.

Dalton's arrest was the bitter sign of my baby shower coming to an end. There was no fun to be had after the daddy-to-be was carted off in a cop car. It pretty much put a damper on the occasion. The guests had given me strained congratulations and patted my shoulder, looks of pity crossing their faces.

"Gabby, I think it's time you tell us what the hell is going on," Cora said, her tone stern. She along with Daisy, Keegan, and Lane were all there with me, waiting on any updates.

"I agree with Cora," Daisy said while the guys nodded in agreement.

I looked at each one of them and shook my head. "I can't. I don't want you to be involved. There's too much at risk." I didn't want the police or anyone else getting to them.

"What's at risk?" Cora asked. "Girl, you're seriously scaring me."

"We have wealthy parents," Lane said and grunted when Cora's elbow rammed into his side. "What? All I'm saying is that if you think we're going to get in trouble for knowing too much, I doubt it. Our parents can most likely get us out of it. None of us actually thinks Dalton offed some chick. Tell us the truth, so we can understand and try to help you."

I blew out a breath, growing light-headed, and sat down. They all listened closely, absorbing every detail, while I told them everything—about John hiring us to cover up his affair, about us trying to bribe Ivy, her death, and then about John being my father. They all joined my side, forming a circle of support.

"Holy shit," Daisy whispered. "It's like a movie."

"I can't believe all of that happened and you didn't tell me anything," Cora said. "How the hell could you keep that to yourself? That's serious." She'd been the only one who knew about John being my father, but I'd kept the rest a secret.

I only shrugged, not wanting to tell her I didn't keep it to myself. Dalton had become my new confidant. He knew everything.

"I can't believe that douchebag is your father," Lane said. "I swear, the old dude is always coming to my dad for campaign money."

"Is Dalton on his way here?" Daisy asked.

I nodded.

"Then, we'd better go," Cora said. "Let me know if you need anything. We're here for you."

* * *

"Baby, I'm so fucking sorry," Dalton said, rushing over to me as soon as he made it into the living room. He picked me up and lifted me into his arms. I shivered when his cold lips hit my ear. "I'm going to fix this. I swear to God on everything, I'll fix this." His voice cracked at the end.

"Is it true?" I stuttered when I finally pulled away. "Was it really Leo's wife who lied and set this entire thing up?"

I'd only met Kelly a few times. She wasn't the most cordial woman, but she'd never been nasty toward me. She mainly just ignored my existence. But you could sense her distaste for Dalton from anywhere. Even after not knowing her well, the thought of bitch-slapping her in the face definitely seemed appealing.

He nodded, his shoulders slumping. "Can we please go home? I don't want to talk about John, Kelly, my parents, or anyone. What I want to do right now is go home with the woman I love, wrap her in my arms, and sleep."

My heart ached, and I took his hand in mine. "Then, let's go."

* * *

Our steps were slow to the bedroom. Dalton trailed behind me, his hands on my waist, guiding me. He flipped on the lights and turned me around to face him. The torture and guilt were clear on his face.

"I will make this up to you," he said. He'd repeated those words nonstop on the car ride home even though he said he wanted to quit talking about it.

He rushed over to the bed, pulled down the sheets, and came back to my side. His hands pressed into my shoulders as he carefully sat me down on the bed. He dropped down to his knees and started to drag my flats off my feet.

"Dalton, look at me," I demanded.

It took him a few seconds to do what I asked, and I gulped when I noticed his glossy eyes. I leaned down and wiped them dry the best that I could.

"You don't need to make anything up to me, okay?"

"But—"

I cut him off with my words. "You spent your entire night in an interrogation room and you're apologizing to me?" I shook my head, running my hands over his cheeks. "Nuh-uh. This isn't your fault. I won't let you take the blame for it."

He pulled my hand away from his face and kissed my palm. "I said no more talk of this, remember? Tonight is about you and me."

He went quiet and started to undress me. My arms instinctively flew up, so he could pull my dress over my head. I sat there, wearing only a bra and panties, and watched him undress.

My breathing labored when he came my way. He stopped directly in front of me, his hands at his sides.

"Lie back, baby," he whispered.

I did as I was told. I felt his weight against mine as he followed me, our bodies practically becoming one as we made ourselves comfortable.

"Do you want me to shut off the lights?" I asked.

"No," was all he said before his lips brushed against mine. "I want to see all of you tonight. I want to keep reminding myself that this is real."

We then made slow, passionate love in the comfort of our bed. His touch seemed to erase the day's events and put me at ease.

Chapter Twenty-Two

DALTON

THE LIGHTS and coffeemaker were off when I walked into the office. I'd left before the sun came up, before Gabby woke, before the city came alive. Sleep didn't come to me. Too much was on my mind.

My phone rang at the same time I sat down in my chair. I fished it from my pocket.

Leo.

I guessed I wasn't the only one who couldn't sleep.

"Good morning," I grumbled into the speaker. I shouldn't have been taking my anger out on him, but it was too hard to hold back. He was the one who brought Kelly into our lives.

Scratch that.

Our parents did.

"Morning, brother," he replied. "I want to apologize again for yesterday's events." The sadness was evident in his voice. "Please give my apologies to Gabby as well. I feel like this is all my fault."

"It's not your fault, but you'd better keep that woman the fuck out of my sight." Anger hammered through my veins. "You know she'll get a big piece of my mind if I see her. I got arrested at my girlfriend's baby shower. She embarrassed Gabby and completely ruined that moment for her." It was like my family couldn't leave her the hell alone. "I'll never forgive Kelly for that—*ever*. So, thank God you're divorcing her crazy ass."

He let out a long sigh. "I understand. If there's anything I can do to make up for it, let me know. Kelly has issues, I'm well aware. I knew she could be vengeful, but I never thought she'd go that far."

I held in my sarcastic reply. I didn't want to make him feel even shittier for her doing. "How did you get her to confess?" I knew that wasn't an easy task for him. Kelly was stubborn and never admitted to her faults.

"I had to rip up the divorce papers."

"You can't be serious."

"I'm serious."

"So, you have to stay with her for me? Now, I feel bad about that."

That was probably Kelly's whole plan. The scheming woman knew Leo would sacrifice his own happiness for the sake of his family.

He let out a chuckle. "She's under the assumption that ripping them up means the divorce proceedings are over. It's not hard for me to have them drawn back up."

"My man. She's going to be pissed she's getting played at her own game."

* * *

"Please say you have something for me," I told Murphy as soon as he stepped into my office. "*Anything.*"

He held up his hand. "Man, first, I want to say I heard about what happened," he said, shaking his head and taking a seat. "That's probably one of the most fucked up things I've heard lately, and that's saying a lot, considering I work here."

I nodded. I was already getting sick of talking about Kelly. I didn't give a shit about her anymore. I only had two things on my mind—Ivy and her mystery dude.

"But that happening only gave me more motivation to work harder and smarter," he went on. He held up a folder. "I got the sketch you wanted. I spent all night going through scenario after scenario, possible suspect after possible suspect. I drew a blank, so I decided to look more into Harold, going off the idea that this might be an inside job. There wasn't much in his recent records, but I went back farther."

Murphy was having trouble hacking into the police system, but Lonnie had been sending him anything he could get. Nothing else had been added to the evidence log. All fingerprints had been wiped clean. Her fingernails had been torn off, most likely because she fought back and they didn't want to risk their DNA being found underneath them. Whoever did this was a smart killer—a professional. There were no eyewitnesses. They had nothing, and I still wasn't sure if that was done purposely.

"And?" I pushed.

"Take a wild guess who Mr. Cop has been talking to."

I gave him a stern look. "Not really in the mood to be playing guessing games at the moment."

"Oh ... yeah ... right." He leaned forward in excitement. "Malcolm Gentry."

I snatched up the folder as soon as he slapped it down onto my desk.

"They were in constant contact two days after Ivy went public about her affair with John. I mean, eight calls in one day. Then, after that, nothing. I'm not sure if it's anything big, but it screamed out for me to look into it."

"Why the hell would those two be talking?"

"Something smells fishy," he drew out. "And the stench is coming from that shady cop."

"Any texts between them?"

"None that I could find. If they were talking about anything illegal, I'm guessing they got burners."

Of course. They weren't *complete* idiots.

I pulled out the sketch and studied it. Shit! Even though it was exactly what the maid had described, it was generic as fuck. It was impossible to put a name to. It looked like every friend of my father's. The sketch wasn't going to do shit for us.

But what reason would they have to kill Ivy?

Then, it hit me.

It was the perfect setup. Rumor had it that Malcolm was mad because John ran for governor. Malcolm wanted that position. Their parents supposedly got involved and told Malcolm he needed to step aside for his older brother. As for Harold, he hated my father.

Kill two birds ... or mistress with one stone.

But why did they use Ivy?

"Accusing them of murder is a serious accusation," I said.

He nodded in agreement. "I know."

"We need more information. A lot more. We have to have all of our ducks in a row before even bringing it up to them or anyone else. Do you think you can find this burner phone?"

He scrubbed his hands over his face. "Burner phones are complicated. They don't have an account attached to them and aren't easy to trace."

"Find a way."

"And how do you expect me to do that? I can't exactly strut into the police station and ask him to give it to me."

I snapped my fingers before pointing at him. "Then, we'll sneak into Harold's house and find it."

What the fuck? How did finding a burner phone lead to breaking and entering?

"If there's anything that man has to hide, it'll be in there. I guarantee it."

Murphy let out a sinister laugh. "You're a crazy son of a bitch." He clapped his hands together and jumped up from his chair. "And I'm in."

"Hack into his schedule. See when his house will be empty."

* * *

I didn't tell Gabby about our plan to break into a police officer's house. She would've either objected or demanded I let her come.

Harold had downsized since his divorce, now living in a small one-story home that needed a serious mow and landscaping work. We were parked across the street, a few houses down from his, in Murphy's car —both of us wearing ball caps that hung low. I ducked down when Harold pulled out of the driveway in his cruiser.

Perfect timing.

Murphy unbuckled his seat belt when Harold's taillights were out of view. "You ready to do this, boss?" he asked.

I wrapped my hand around the door handle. "It's now or never," I replied. I was desperate for answers, and if breaking and entering a police officer's house was what I had to do to get them, I was taking my chances.

We got out of the car and sprinted into Harold's backyard. Murphy managed to open the door with an old gym membership card. I assumed a police officer would've been more careful about the security and locks on his house. I followed him inside and froze at the sound of the alarm going off.

Oh fuck. Alarms were more difficult than cheap-ass door locks.

"Don't worry. I got this," Murphy said calmly.

He punched in a code, and my shoulders relaxed when it silenced.

"Dude, I need you to teach me some tricks," I muttered, shutting the door behind us. "Now, let's find something before he gets back."

He gestured down the hallway. "I'll take the kitchen and living room. The bathroom and bedroom are all yours."

I nodded, turning down the hallway. The place was only a two-bedroom. I went to Harold's first. The bed was unmade. Clothes covered the floor. Soda cans took over the nightstand. This man was going downhill from when I'd known him, growing up.

I went straight to the nightstand. That was where the good shit always was. I examined every piece of paper. Receipts. Junk mail. Nothing.

Fuck!

His dresser was next. I rifled through the drawers, moving away wads of unmatched socks, when I felt it. I knew the feel of money from anywhere.

"Jackpot!" I hissed. I grabbed it, dashed down the hall, and found Murphy in the living room. "You got anything?"

"This." He held up some cash. "Found it stuffed in a cereal box." He pointed to a laptop sitting on the table. "Also spotted this underneath the couch. I'm transferring all of the data onto my thumb drive as we speak, just in case there's anything on there. What about you?"

I showed him the wad of cash. "Found this in his sock drawer."

He snapped his fingers. "I think we're getting somewhere."

Chapter Twenty-Three

GABBY

I GLANCED up at the sound of the doorbell with concern. Dalton said he wouldn't be home for a few hours, and no one else would come by without calling first.

I looked through the peephole to see two people I didn't recognize. A girl and a guy were arguing back and forth. The girl threw her hands up in the air while the guy scolded her in harsh whispers.

What the hell?

Do they have the wrong door? Are they here about Ivy?

Hopefully, the last one was negative.

This whole situation had me way too paranoid.

I clutched my phone in my hand, took a deep breath, and slowly opened up the door. They froze up, their hands and whispers stopping.

They looked like teenagers who were sent to boarding school by their wealthy and strict parents. They somewhat reminded me of Dalton and his siblings. The guy was probably around my age. His dark hair was neatly slicked back, and boyish dimples popped from his cheeks. The girl looked barely old enough to have her driver's license. Her hair was lighter, more of a chestnut blonde, and pulled back with a Burberry headband.

The guy straightened up his back and cleared his throat. "Are you Gabby?" he asked.

"Yes?" I drew out. *Who are these people? Why are they at my door?*

"I'm Patrick," he replied and then pointed to the girl. "And this is Marissa." He looked at her for a few seconds before giving me his attention again. "We're your brother and sister."

My jaw dropped, and I stared at them, speechless. I didn't need any more surprises at the moment.

"John ... he's our dad," Marissa went on. "He told us about you." Her voice was smooth and sweet, almost childlike.

"Your father is a pig," I said before I could stop myself. I looked down at the ground, feeling bad, but I was so pissed. *How dare he use his kids as pawns to get closer to me!*

They didn't look surprised at my response.

"We know he has some bad qualities," Patrick replied. "But nevertheless, he is a good father."

"We wanted to come in ... talk ... get to know each other ... if that's okay with you?" Marissa asked, clasping her hands in front of her. "Our other siblings couldn't be here, but they want to meet you too."

I briefly wondered how rude it would be to tell them no and slam the door in their faces. But I couldn't. They weren't John. They didn't deserve my aggression. They'd come out of their way to talk to me, and I needed to have the courtesy to return the favor.

I took a step back and waved my hand in front of me. "Sure, come in." I shut the door behind them and pointed to the couch. "You can have a seat over there. Can I get you anything?"

They both shook their heads.

"No, we're okay," Marissa answered while Patrick followed her to the couch.

I sat down across from them in a chair, my nervousness holding me back from getting too close. We all looked at each other for a few seconds, taking one another in. I could see the resemblance between us. We shared the same nose, the same small cleft in our chins.

I had a brother and sister.

Wow.

"We wanted to meet you," Marissa said softly. "I've always wanted a big sister, and when our parents told us about you, that's the only thing I could think about."

Patrick nodded. "We don't know the whole story about what happened between your mom, you, and our dad. He said you're not really interested in having a relationship with him, but would you consider one with us?"

Marissa's deep brown eyes stared into me, waiting for my answer. Saying yes would change everything in my life. I'd be opening a door I wasn't sure I wanted open yet. I hesitated, unsure of what my answer would be, but hoped my lips could form the right word.

I gulped. "Okay," I said slowly. "I'd like that as well."

Two childlike smiles spread across their lips.

"Then, let's get to know each other, shall we?" Patrick asked.

Chapter Twenty-Four

DALTON

"WHAT'S WRONG?" I asked, rushing through the door. I threw down my briefcase on the floor and headed straight to her. I'd sped home as soon as I got her text message, telling me she needed me.

I found her sitting on the couch, nursing a cup of tea, and looking straight ahead at nothing. She blew out a breath before looking at me.

"I had visitors today," she answered.

Visitors? Don't be the cops.

"Good visitors? Bad visitors?" I said.

"I really don't know." She paused. "They were John's kids. My, uh ... brother and sister."

Well, shit. I still wasn't sure if that was good or bad.

I sat down next to her and ran my hand over my forehead. My girl didn't need any more stress right now.

"Did you slam the door in their faces? Invite them in?" I asked.

I didn't want to give a reaction until I found out what hers was. If she was happy, I wanted to share that excitement. If she was upset, I wanted to console her.

"I ... I don't know. I'm still trying to process it. I grew up, wishing for a father, but finally realized that was never going to happen. I came to terms with it. Then, bam! Enter father. Enter pregnancy. Enter siblings. It seems like everything is smacking me in the face all at once," she replied.

I nodded in understanding. It seemed like her world had gone crazy since she got involved with me, and I was terrified she'd end up leaving when she realized it.

I grabbed her hand, gently swiping my thumb across her soft skin. "You know I'm here for you, right? If you need anything or there's something you don't feel like doing and want me to do, I'm game. Anything, you hear me?"

She squeezed my hand before laughing. "I think you, my mom, Cora, and Daisy are the only reasons I'm seriously not going off the deep end right now. For some reason, you ground me."

It felt damn satisfying, hearing her say that. *I ground her.* Little did she know, she was the one holding me together.

"Did they just want to meet you? Or really get to know you ... like relationship status?"

"They want to get to know me."

"Tell me everything."

I leaned back, allowing her to situate herself in my arms, and gave her my undivided attention. She told me about them showing up at the door and asking to come in. She told me she agreed but wanted to take things slow.

"And there's something else," she said, drawing out the words as soon as she was finished with her story.

"Yeah?" Again, why did new information seem to always worry me?

"Leo brought gifts to the baby shower from your mom and Piper. With everything that's happened, I completely spaced it, but I finished unpacking all of the gifts today and found them."

I gulped, hoping my mom didn't send her something threatening or weird. I wouldn't be surprised if it was a check to stay the hell away from me, a bribe to run away with our baby. I lost her when she pulled away and headed into the room that was going to be the nursery. She came back with a gift bag and sat down.

"These are from your mom," she said, pulling objects from the bag.

I recognized the baby blanket and silver spoon that had belonged to me. She then pulled out Rufus, my first stuffed monkey. My mom had kept those?

She opened another bag. "And these outfits and a mini Louis Vuitton bag are from Piper."

Wow. The fact that they did this for Gabby put some happiness in my terrible day.

"Do you think this is them coming around?" she asked.

"I think it is," I replied even though I wasn't completely sure.

My family were experts at the manipulation game, and I hoped they weren't trying to play us.

* * *

I sent my mom and Piper a text message, asking them to meet me for a coffee.

"Hey, guys," I said, joining them at the table. I gave Piper a kiss on the cheek when she got out of her chair. "There's my favorite sister." I waited until we received our drinks before bringing up the gifts. "Gabby told me what you guys sent to the baby shower. We both really appreciate it."

My mom played with the handle of her coffee cup and cleared her throat. "It was the right thing to do," she said. "Your father and I have been talking. As bad as we dislike the young lady, we feel—"

"But why do you dislike her?" I asked, interrupting her. "What has she done to you?" I looked over at Piper. "To any of you?"

Piper looked down, failing to make eye contact.

My mom only stared at me, trying to come up with anything she could use against Gabby.

"Exactly. Nothing," I said.

She stared at me for a few more seconds before saying anything. "I suppose you're right."

Piper nodded. "Yeah, I guess I'm graduated now. I need to get over the high school drama. Tell her I'm sorry."

"Thank you," I said. "You have no idea how much this means to me." I winked. "And for that, I'll buy your coffees."

Chapter Twenty-Five

DALTON

"THERE HAS to be something I'm missing," I muttered to myself. I'd been staring at my computer screen for the past hour, going through Harold's hard drive. I was on the hunt for something that I wasn't even sure existed.

Murphy made me a copy. Two brains were better than one, and we needed to start working harder. Murphy did a great job, getting all of Harold's information. It was like I was inside his computer.

My hand froze on the mouse when I spotted one of the biggest things I'd been looking for.

Fucking bingo.

I clicked on the folder named *Police Reports* and scrolled down until I found Ivy's name and case number. I was surprised he'd even kept this information on his personal computer.

Homicide Report 65671
  Name of Victim: Ivy Hart
  Age of Victim: 28
  Sex of Victim: F
  Race of Victim: White/Caucasian
  Date of Death: July 6, 2013 or July 7, 2013

Time of Death: Estimated between 10:30 p.m. to 1:30 a.m.

Last Seen Alive: July 6, 2013

Weapons Used: Firearm (make and model TBD), knife/cutting instrument

Rigor: Present.

Cause of Death: Blunt force to the head, 15 stab wounds (listed in detail on page 6), and 1 gunshot to the front temple

Offender: Unknown

I scrolled through the rest of the details until I found the Evidence Page.

Physical Evidence:

No DNA present on body or at the crime scene.

Circumstantial Evidence:

Item 654: Security footage from victim's home showed two individuals bribing a worker for access into victim's apartment. ID'd as Dalton Douglas and Gabrielle Taylor.

Item 655: Reports of an affair with Atlanta Governor John Gentry.

Item 656: A nondisclosure form found from Douglas PR, attempting to pay off victim before exposing affair. Parents say Douglas and Taylor had been stalking her.

Possible Persons of Interest:

John Gentry

Douglas PR employees, including Dalton Douglas, Wilson Douglas, and Gabrielle Taylor.

. . .

I moved on from there and went to his other documents until I found the one labeled *Passwords*.

Jackpot.

I went on from there to his browser history. My jaw dropped, and it took me a minute to gain my composure. I picked up my phone and hit John's name.

"I'll see you first thing in the morning."

* * *

I was meeting John by myself. Just the two of us. He'd asked me to help him, and now, it was time he did the same for me. John hadn't been doing much to help us, except for making his statement. He'd been brought into the station once for questioning but was released two hours later after Billy came in to represent him. Harold was grasping for straws, but I knew he was close to planting evidence if he didn't find enough.

The sun was barely up when I parked in the empty alley. I unlocked my door when I noticed his black Escalade pull up. He hurried over to my car, his head hung low, and slipped into the passenger seat.

"What's going on?" he said, looking over at me in concern. "Why was this so urgent?"

"Did your wife know Harold Finch?" I asked.

"Who?" He paused to think for a few seconds. "The detective investigating Ivy's murder?"

I nodded.

"No ... not that I'm aware of, but Edith seems to know everyone around Atlanta. She's a popular socialite and philanthropist. She's also donated her fair share to the police department."

"Ah, she must be a pretty generous woman."

"Yes, she is. She loves charity work."

"Generous enough to give one officer in particular six hundred thousand dollars?"

His eyes widened.

"Can you guess who that officer is?"

I had almost lost it when I got into Harold's browser. The idiot had all of his usernames and passwords saved in his records, so it took me only three seconds to log in.

That was when I noticed the transfer from a familiar offshore account.

Celine Dion.

Is Edith a fucking idiot? She knew we'd caught her giving money to Ivy. *Why would she use the same account to pay Harold?*

"My wife wouldn't give anyone that much money." He faked a chuckle, but I noticed the uncertainty on his face. "There's no way."

I pulled out my evidence. "Yes way. I made copies. This account is the same one that paid Ivy, which your wife admitted to. She paid Harold to do something. I'm not sure what it was yet. But there's a reason he got put on this case, and there's a reason why we're the only suspects."

"You're ... you're mistaken."

"I'm not. Now, buckle up."

"Why?"

"We're going to talk to your wife."

I locked the doors before he had the chance to try and make a run for it. Holding a state official captive in your car? I was sure there was a charge for that, and I honestly didn't give a flying fuck.

* * *

I followed John through his front door and down the long hallway of his house.

"Edith?" he called out.

We found her in the bedroom. Two suitcases were sprawled out on the bed, both almost full.

"What the hell is going on here?"

She slowly turned around to look at him. I didn't miss the look of disgust she sent his way.

"I think it's a good idea if the kids and I left for a while. This is too much for them," she answered, pointing a finger at him. I noticed the absence of her wedding ring. "You caused this. You're hurting our children. I can't even stand to look at you."

Damn, this woman deserved an Oscar.

She maneuvered around John's still body, heading toward the dresser, but froze when she noticed me standing in the doorway.

"I don't care why you're here, but you need to leave this house before I call the police," she told me.

I sent her a sinister smile. "Go ahead, call them. Are you going to ask for Officer Finch? You know, I'm sure he'll do whatever you want for a couple more thousand dollars."

She stumbled back a step, her hand going to her chest. "What in the world are you talking about?"

I opened my mouth to call her out on her bullshit, but John beat me to it.

"He's talking about the six hundred grand you sent him!" he yelled. "For some reason, you keep sending money to people that are trying to ruin my life."

She scoffed and gave me a dirty look. "You might want to reconsider your sources. I haven't paid anyone anything." She threw some more shit in her suitcase, her shaking fingers trying their best to zip it up. "If this is some sort of setup to void our prenup, just stop. Desperation never suited you, dear husband."

Fuck, the woman was brutal, and in that moment, I realized Edith Gentry thought she was untouchable. She thought she was indestructible because of her family name and the money they had.

I studied John, and for the first time ever, I felt sorry for the man. His face was blank, void of any expression, and his hands fell slack at his sides. I could hear his breathing from across the room.

I leaned against the wall and briefly wondered if that was what my life would've been like if I'd married someone I wasn't in love with to make other people happy. Thank God I'd gotten my head out of my ass.

"What happened to you?" he whispered to her.

"Love. Love happened to me," she answered, unable to meet his eyes.

"*Love?* If you love me, why are you leaving? Why are you lying to me? Why are you involved in something that's trying to get me pinned for Ivy's murder?"

She shook her head and snorted. "John, the love isn't for you. I haven't loved you in years, and I honestly don't blame you for cheating. I'm actually glad you did. It definitely worked out in my favor."

And with that, she whipped around and scurried to the bathroom. The door slammed shut, the lock clicking in the silence.

Is Edith in love with Harold?

I couldn't help but laugh.

There was no way.

"Whatever you do, make sure she doesn't leave the country," I told John, pointing to the bathroom door.

* * *

"You got any scoop for me?" Gabby asked. Her voice was chipper, but I could see the worry in her eyes. What happened at the baby shower had scared her.

I leaned forward in the patio chair outside her favorite frozen yogurt place. "You ready for this?"

She blew out a breath. "On a scale from whiskey to beer, how bad?"

"Whiskey. The whole damn bottle and add a few shots of vodka."

She let out a whistle and ran her hand over her hair, controlling the flyaways. "Jesus, I'm not sure if I even want to know."

"We managed to get our hands on Harold's computer hard drive, and let's say, he was hiding some good stuff in there."

"And how did you manage to get your hands on it?" she drew out.

My lips spread into a cocky smile. "Now, babe, I can't tell you all of my secrets."

She let out a grunt and rolled her eyes. "Whatever. I probably don't even want to know. So, what did you find?"

"He had all of his passwords and account information saved. I logged in to one bank account and noticed he had a substantial amount of money in there. Way more than what a city cop could even dream about saving."

"So, someone sent him money?"

I nodded.

"How much?"

"Six hundred thousand."

She dropped her spoon in her bowl. "I'm going to take a wild guess that Celine Dion is who sent the money?"

"Winner, winner, chicken dinner."

"That woman ... I knew she had something to do with it." Her face fell before turning serious. "I want you to make her pay, you hear me? If she had Ivy killed, she needs to go down for it."

"Don't worry, babe. We're on it and getting closer and closer to the finish line."

"Do you think she acted alone? Like paid Harold to do it and then cover it up?"

"I'm not sure. Murphy got into Harold's phone records. Unless he talked to Edith on a burner phone, we have no record of them talking to one another. But we do have record of him talking to Malcolm Gentry."

"And let's add another vodka shot. So, what are you going to do? I mean, the only evidence you have is something I'm sure you illegally got your hands on."

I nodded in agreement.

"You need to figure out why Harold is protecting Edith. You find that out, and I think stuff might come together."

"She paid him six hundred thousand dollars. That's why he's protecting her."

"Do you think he's the one who killed Ivy?" She snorted. "How damn perfect is that? You can't find the killer when the dude investigating the crime is the one who committed it—or at least was involved. There's no way he is going to release anything that he doesn't want exposed. It's messed up, but I've learned to expect the unexpected."

* * *

I grabbed my phone as soon as I dropped Gabby off to meet up with Cora at the movies. Cora was getting ready to leave for college, so Gabby wanted to spend time with her.

"You busy?" I asked Murphy.

"Perfect timing. I was about to call you," he answered. "I have some good but probably bad news for you. Edith booked her father's private jet to leave tonight, and my guess is that she's headed off to a different country, which makes the woman look guiltier than a motherfucker."

"I knew she had something more to do with this. Anything else?"

"No. I've been looking everywhere. We obviously know they all had *something* to do with her death, but I'm not sure who had what role. And I don't think we'll ever find out unless someone spills, which I doubt will happen."

"I have an idea."

* * *

I walked straight into the apartment, Murphy strolling behind me, and headed down the hallway.

"Oh, David, David, David," Murphy called out.

I swung the door open and waited for the surprise.

"What the hell?" David yelled, looking up at us from his bed.

The dude was still in bed at two in the afternoon? His eyes were sleepy, and he blinked a few times, like maybe he was imagining us.

I guessed we made breaking into cops' homes our new hobby.

"We only want to talk," I said, walking into the room. I looked at Murphy and tilted my head toward the nightstand.

He nodded in understanding.

All the blood rushed from David's face. "You broke into my apartment!" he yelled.

"The door was unlocked," I lied and shrugged. "You should probably have someone look at that. Maybe it's broken."

"You can't just walk into my apartment." He reached for his phone on the nightstand, but I beat him to it and snatched it up. "Are you an idiot?" He scoffed. "I'm the police. They'll have your ass for this."

"Eh ... I have a feeling you might not be the police for much longer," Murphy chimed in. He pointed to the nightstand. "Cocaine. Are cops allowed to do that now?" He pulled out his phone, turned on the camera, and directed it toward David. "Say hi to the camera!" He moved the phone to the nightstand. "Oh, say, hello, blow!" The camera moved to the police uniform folded on the dresser. "Oh, hello, cop uniform."

"You're going to answer our questions," I told him. "And *maybe* we won't tell the world what a scumbag liar and addict you are."

"I don't know what you're talking about," David stuttered out. "Those drugs, they're not mine. I don't know how they got there."

"Don't insult my intelligence. I know the drugs are yours." I honestly didn't care about the drugs. That wasn't why I was there. "Now, what I want to know is, why would they put a rookie like you on a homicide case?" I was bluffing. I honestly had no idea what his ranking or responsibilities were. "We know you're working with Harold to cover up the evidence of Ivy's murder. Now, spill, or Murphy will post that video on YouTube."

"I'm not telling you shit."

His eyes widened when I pulled out the Taser from my pocket. Did I plan on actually using it? Possibly. I'd already broken one law, so might as well go on a full streak.

"Seriously? You're going to threaten me with a Taser?"

I raised a brow. "Would you prefer waterboarding?"

He stared at me, speechless.

"Now, get up. The faster we get this over with, the faster we leave here." I turned around to leave the room but stopped. "And I can promise you that you'll want to talk because we already have enough evidence against you to make your life a living hell."

He flipped the covers off him. "Fucking asshole."

"I think this is going to be the longest day of my life," I muttered, sitting down in his living room.

* * *

"Your wife has chartered daddy's jet and is planning on fleeing the country," I told John when he got into my car. "I've got Murphy working on a way to delay that."

He shook his head before resting it in his hands. "I think you know by now that I can't control anything that woman does." He let out a deep breath before removing his hands and looking at me. "Shit, you knew about her leaving before I did."

I had a list of things to get done. I had to get sufficient evidence to take to Lonnie that all four of them were involved. I then needed to make sure Edith didn't get on that plane and a story was sent to the media, exposing them.

I didn't want to break the news about what David told us yet. I was waiting until the perfect moment.

"You still own the place that Ivy was staying in, right?" I asked him. *Why the hell hadn't I thought of that earlier?* Probably because Harold had gotten that surveillance video of Gabby and me, and I figured they'd already had their hands on everything.

"Yeah."

"Good."

"Why? Is that where we're going?"

"We sure are. You're going to march in there, tell them you are the owner of a unit, and demand to see the security footage."

His dark eyes widened. "The police already have the footage. That's why you and I were brought in."

I parked in front of the apartment building and looked over at him. "That doesn't mean shit, John. Right now, we can't trust the cops, so don't say a damn word to them, you hear me?"

"You're really starting to make demands, Douglas."

I threw my arm out. "If you don't like it, I can walk away from this, and you can figure it out yourself."

He pushed open the door without answering me, and I followed him into the lobby. He demanded to talk to someone in security immediately. As soon as he showed his ID, we were escorted to a small room, where a young guy, Heath, was waiting for us.

"What do you need?" he asked, sitting behind a row of computer screens with his legs crossed while security footage played out in front of him.

I looked over at John. "When did you get her the place?" I asked.

He looked over at me in confusion.

I snapped my fingers in front of his face. "John. Think!"

"Uh ... about a year ago, I think."

I dug into my pocket and pulled out a hundred-dollar bill. "I want all of the footage in the past year."

Heath hesitated for a moment, contemplating whether to risk his job for the extra cash. "I can give you everything up to the end of March. The detective took all of the footage from April to July."

I grinned. Harold's stupidity kept working in my favor. He'd been too lazy to get all the footage.

We stayed in that stuffy room for five hours, watching footage until we found exactly what I was looking for.

"I need a copy of this," I told Heath.

He shook his head. "I can't do that, man. It'll be my ass."

I pulled out two more hundreds. He snatched them from my hand.

"Just don't say you got anything from me. I need this job."

* * *

"I'm telling you that we're wasting our time doing this," John said. "Sure, we don't get along at times, but there's no way he's involved in Ivy's murder. He didn't even know her."

Oh, yes, he did.

We were back in my car and on to our next destination. I felt like I was playing a game of cat and mouse.

"You saw the evidence with your own two eyes. You asked me to trust you," I said. "Now, it's time you do the same with me. You told me you wanted me on this job, to figure out who was trying to set us up, and I'm getting closer and closer. Your problem is that you trust people too much. I don't think you realize that people you love, people that are close to you, can hurt you."

Ivy had turned on him. His wife had turned on him. His own political party had turned on him. And now, his own blood was. Sometimes, the only people you could trust were the people you barely knew at all.

I wouldn't disclose what David had told me until I had the proper evidence. Something like that could destroy a family, but after seeing the video footage, I knew for sure.

"You need to wake up, John," I went on. "Your brother and Harold were involved in Ivy's murder along with Edith, and for some reason, they were trying to make you take the fall for it."

John shook his head violently and refused to look at me. "You're wrong."

"I'm not wrong," I argued. "You were with me in that room, watching him go into Ivy's apartment. Why would he be there? To visit you? To ask for sugar?"

I couldn't hold back my excitement when I saw that Malcolm had visited Ivy on multiple occasions. He fitted the maid's description, and he somewhat had a motive. Everything was coming together.

"Uh ... it could've been ..." John stuttered, obviously having nothing to argue.

"Exactly. You have no idea. That's why we're going to him for answers."

John didn't say another word during the short drive to Malcolm's house.

Murphy tracked Malcolm's cell location and confirmed he was home, so I walked straight into his house, John on my trail, without even bothering to knock. All I cared about was getting this done, and I was edging closer and closer to the finish line.

I found Malcolm in his office with a drink in one hand and his phone in the other. He was bitching at someone on the other line, calling them a mindless whore, before he noticed me walk into the room.

"I'll fucking call you back," he shouted and then ended the call. He looked past my shoulder, straight at John, and grinned wildly. "My older brother. What a surprise." His attention went back to me. "And the Douglas boy. Are you two a team now or something?"

"You should really think more about the people you plan a murder with. David told us everything, Malcolm," I said, cutting straight to the chase. "So, cut the shit."

He lifted his chin and rolled up his sleeves. The man was probably twenty pounds lighter than I was, lanky and lean, but he thought he made up for his size with confidence. He reminded me of my father.

He took a sip of his drink, not letting one emotion show, before replying, "I don't know anyone named David." He shrugged. "You have the wrong person. Sorry."

I pulled my phone from my pocket and played the recording of David telling us the details of their deal. His fingers flexed around his drink while he listened.

David had developed a drug addiction, which Harold decided to use to his advantage. He offered David the opportunity to work on a big case that would further his career as well as extra cash to maintain his addiction. He wanted him to bullshit the Ivy case and pin everything on us. David was also positive that Malcolm paid Harold to kill Ivy, which didn't exactly coincide with our story of Edith paying him.

"I told Harold we couldn't trust that junkie," Malcolm muttered, downing the rest of his drink. He saluted us with it, placed it on his desk, and then clapped his hands. "But good luck, trying to prove it. The little evidence the so-called police have points straight to you. Harold and David aren't going to even let that little recording get used as evidence." He pointed to John. "You need to start being smarter."

"Why?" John asked, stepping forward. "Why would you want to do this to me? We're brothers. We're family."

Malcolm let out a menacing laugh. "You're a blind fool. You always have been. You thought you were sneaky, but you weren't. I found out about your little mistress, fucked her a few times, bribed her with some cash, and she gave me every little detail about you. It was a nice little arrangement until she started getting money hungry and threatened me like she did you. But unlike you, I took care of the problem. I took matters into my own hands and started screwing your wife. I convinced your sweet Edith that we were in love, so she'd pay off Ivy. Then, I kept screwing her to convince her to pay Harold to off that dumbass girl. There was no way I was letting my name come out of her mouth. I threw in a little cash bonus to Harold to make sure all fingers pointed straight to you." He let out a sarcastic snort. "And there's nothing you can do about it." He shrugged. "I win. Mom and Dad can't get you out of this one."

"Eh ... not so much, baby brother," John said.

I turned around to look at him and grinned.

In John's hand was his phone, and on the screen was a person on video chat. "Say hello to CNN."

The media loved a good scandal, and they were going to have a field day with this one.

Chapter Twenty-Six

GABBY

MY JAW HUNG OPEN the entire time Dalton told me about Edith and their setup. I was stretched out on the couch, my feet resting comfortably on his lap, while he told me the whole story.

"Wow," I finally drew out when he finished. "I can't believe all of them got together and planned something like that. *Murder.* That took some serious thought and balls. With that many people involved, someone was bound to let something slip." My stomach twisted in disgust. "Was it really worth it? To take a woman's life?"

He wrapped his hand around my ankle and slowly began to massage my foot. "Love, money, and jealousy can do that to people, babe."

I shuddered. "Not to everyone."

I noticed the burden lifted from his shoulders the minute he strolled through the front door an hour ago. I could tell something had changed, and that something was good—but I hadn't been expecting all of that.

"Now that this shitshow is over, I don't even know what to do with our time," I said with a chuckle. "So much of our relationship has been wrapped up around John's scandal and then Ivy's death. It's going to be weird not to think about it constantly."

409

His hand elevated over my ankle and up my thigh. "Oh, my love. I'm sure we can find plenty of other things to do with our time."

I raised a brow and slightly opened my legs. "Oh, really? What do you have in mind?"

My eyes stayed glued to his hand as it slid between my thighs and then underneath the hem of my shorts. He looked over at me, a boyish grin on his face. "If you want me to have fun with you, babe, you'd better give me more than that."

I grinned and obliged, opening wider to give him better access. I was already throbbing between my legs, aching for his touch. I gasped when he slipped a finger inside of me. I let him get a few thrusts in, feeling the pressure build up, and then grabbed his wrist.

He looked at me in confusion. I pulled away, stepped off the couch, and stood in front of him.

"You've had a hard day," I said. "Let me make you feel good."

He grunted when I pushed him back against the couch and fell to my knees.

His mouth parted. "I think this will make even the shittiest day better." His eyes were glued to me, watching as I slowly slid his zipper down and pulled down his pants along with his boxer briefs.

His cock was already hard, a bit of pre-cum resting on the tip. I licked my lips before tightly wrapping them around him. I looked up at him to see his eyes drinking me in, watching me as I moved his rock-hard cock in and out of my mouth. He shuddered when I circled my tongue around the tip.

"Yes," he groaned. "This is amazing." He bit into his lip. "But now, it's time to stop. I want to finish inside of you."

I gave him one last lick and then slowly released it. It took him a minute to catch his breath. I gasped when he jumped to his feet, grabbed my waist, and bent me over the couch.

This was my second favorite place for him to give it to me.

I arched my back when he patiently slid inside of me.

"Is this much better than work?" I asked, looking back at him.

"So much damn better," he replied with a grunt.

"Then, fuck me as hard as you work."

I lost my breath with the first thrust. It was amazing with him every single time. He wrapped his arm around my waist and pounded in and out of me, telling me how much he loved me with every pump, until we were both a hot, panting mess.

Chapter Twenty-Seven

DALTON

"I COULDN'T SLEEP LAST NIGHT," I said, swerving into a parking spot. "I've been waiting for this day for what seems like forever." I was trying to hide my anticipation, but my heart was racing like a jackhammer. I was going to remember this day for the rest of my life.

Gabby let out a deep sigh before looking over at me with a smile. "I know, right? If someone had told me a year ago that this was what I'd be doing, I would've laughed in their face." She gestured out the window. "But here we are."

It was the same with me. I'd been freshly graduated from law school with building my career being my only priority.

She laughed and looked down at her phone when it chimed. "Cora wants me to FaceTime her," she told me.

"Right now?"

"No, when we go in."

I chuckled. "Babe, we are not FaceTiming your best friend during the ultrasound."

Her fingers typed away on the screen. "I know. That's what I'm trying to tell the pain in my ass, but the girl doesn't listen."

All of Gabby's friends had left for college, and I was thankful I had more time to spend with her after quitting my dad's firm. I'd been afraid she'd get lonely, but getting ready for the baby seemed to take up all our time—which I was completely okay with.

My dad said I was an idiot for quitting and throwing away my chance of someday taking over the business and I'd never get an opportunity as good as that. I didn't care. Nowadays, my happiness reigned over my career and money. If I was making enough to provide for my family, I was content.

Plus, Leo and I had a plan. We were in the process of starting our own law firm. We'd already been approved for the lease and had people interested in being clients. Before signing any documents, we agreed on one thing: we weren't taking on the same clientele that our dad did.

Gabby tossed the phone in her bag. "She'll have to get over it. We'll record the reveal for her."

She looked over at me, her beautiful eyes meeting mine. My excitement intensified.

"You ready?"

I leaned forward and kissed her. "Sure am."

All of Gabby's checkups had been positive. She was healthy. Our baby was healthy. But that didn't stop me from being a nervous wreck. In the back of my mind, I knew there was always a possibility that something could go wrong. Too much shit had happened in the past year for me to *not* think about that stuff.

I got out, hurried around the car to open her door, and helped her out. She was starting to show, and I loved it. The more she grew, the more our baby grew.

I looked down when we got into the room and realized my foot was bouncing. Was this how all expecting dads were? Jesus. I wasn't even sure what shape I'd be in when she had our baby. I'd heard the horror stories, and I prayed to God I wouldn't be one of those dudes who passed out.

Gabby shivered when Maura, the technician, rubbed the gel over her stomach. I sucked in a breath when she ran the transducer over it. I took Gabby's hand while I stared at the screen and squeezed it at the sound of our baby's heartbeat, which had become my favorite sound in the world.

The room was silent while we listened, taking it all in.

"Everything looks great," Maura said. "You have a healthy baby in there." She gave us a sincere smile. "Are you waiting to find out the gender?"

Gabby nodded. "We are."

"But we can change our minds," I rushed out. Gabby's eyes narrowed my way when I looked at her. "Can't we say screw the reveal because I kind of want to know right now? The anticipation is killing me."

"No," she replied sternly.

Maura laughed. "Trust me, you're not the first expecting parent to say that. Patience is a virtue. You'll be happy you waited to share the moment with your loved ones."

* * *

Four hours later, our condo was packed with friends and family, all of them as excited as we were. My hand was clasped around Gabby's while we made our way around the room to greet everyone and thank them for coming.

We chose to have a small party, something intimate, and I'd gone all out, sparing no expense, in hopes of making up for the disastrous baby shower.

My gaze zeroed in on the white frosted cake centered on the long table set up in the dining room. I had to keep stopping myself from rushing over to that damn thing and grabbing the knife to cut into it early.

Gabby leaned into me when I squeezed her side and brought my lips to her ear.

"Is it time yet?" I asked.

She smacked my stomach and laughed. "Jesus, I think it's killing you more than it is me."

I stumbled forward when she pulled me toward the table. The crowd parted and got the hint that it was finally time.

We circled around the table, and everyone came our way.

"Dalton can't wait another minute," Gabby announced.

"She's right," I added. "So, how about we get this party started?"

The crowd responded with claps and smiles. Cameras and phones came out, fully prepared to capture the moment.

I put my hand around Gabby's when she grabbed the knife.

"You ready?" she whispered.

"I'm more than ready," I replied.

Time stood still as we cut the cake.

Cheers erupted.

All I saw was pink.

GABBY

Two Years Later

"OH MY GOD," Cora screeched, jumping up and down. "I can't believe this is happening."

"You?" I said, blowing out a breath. "*I* can't believe this is happening. My nerves are on fire. I'm pretty sure I'm about to hyperventilate."

She came up from behind me in the chair I was sitting in and wrapped her arms around my shoulders. "Relax. It's your big day."

"I'm only hoping it doesn't end up the same way my last big day did."

"Are you talking about the baby shower?" Daisy asked, sitting across from me while the hairdresser finished up her hair.

I nodded.

"Girl, that is history. You've had plenty of big days since then. You and your man have been drama-free for years. You have the perfect family, and the firm seems to really be taking off."

Daisy was right. After the news broke about who'd been in on Ivy's murder and their attempt to frame us, everything seemed to calm down. Harold had received a life sentence for his part in the murder. Malcolm and Edith both ended up with thirty years each with the help of their big-shot attorneys. David got off easier with only three years of prison time and the loss of his badge for helping Harold with the cover-up. Even after two years, what they'd done still baffled me.

Our baby girl was born on the day of Edith's sentencing. Karlee Nicole Douglas came into the world, weighing seven pounds and eight ounces. I was in labor for six hours, and it was as excruciating as everyone said it was going to be—but completely worth it.

"You look so perfect," Cora said, helping me out of my chair. "He's seriously going to die when he sees you."

I grabbed my dress from the hanger and my bridesmaids helped me into it.

I turned around to look at myself in the mirror. I'd spent hours searching for the perfect gown, and I knew in that moment that I'd chosen the right one. Beautiful lace and silk made up the sleeveless A-line dress, and the veil hit just below my waist.

"The most beautiful bride I've ever seen."

I looked back to see my mom coming into the room, tears already falling down her cheeks.

"Mom," I yelled. "You're not supposed to be crying yet!"

More tears fell. "I can't help it!"

I sucked in a breath, hoping it would help me hold back my own tears. "You crying will cause me to cry, which will mess up my fresh makeup."

She laughed. "Of course that's what you're worried about."

"It's time for us to go out there," Cora said. "I'll see you out there when you become *Mrs. Douglas.*"

She and Daisy gave me hugs before walking out the door.

"You ready?" my mom asked.

I sucked in a deep breath. "I'm ready."

She took my hand and led me out the door. It was warm out, but the weather was perfect. Kenneth was waiting for me outside the door. He took my arm, and my mom scurried to her seat.

"I'm honored to do this," Kenneth said.

"Thank you. I'm so glad you're the one doing it," I answered.

The music started, and our steps were slow as he led me down the aisle. Everyone's eyes were on me, but I only looked straight ahead at *him*. I could feel the moisture building up in my eyes as I got closer to Dalton. His face was red and blotchy, and I could tell he was holding back tears as much as I was.

Kenneth released me, and Dalton took my hand when I reached him.

"Wow," Dalton whispered. "This is my life, and it's perfect. Thank you for making my life a hundred times happier."

"No, *thank you* for showing me I can be loved," I whispered back.

"You're amazing. You saved me and changed me into a better person. There are a million reasons why I'm marrying you. There are a million things I love about you." He took my shaking hands and cupped them in his. "You're beautiful and the strongest woman I've ever had the pleasure of meeting. You're an incredible mother. I can't wait to find out a million other reasons why I love you as my wife."

I took a deep breath, feeling the sweat between our fingers, when the priest stepped up to start the ceremony.

We didn't make it until the end before the tears started.

Shoot, half of the audience was crying when we headed back down the aisle, this time as Mr. and Mrs. Douglas. Dalton scooped up Karlee, our flower girl, in his arms.

We were one.

* * *

"Thank you for coming, everyone," Dalton yelled, standing up from our table at the head of the room.

I looked through the crowd at the reception and smiled. People I'd expected to be at my wedding were there.

My mom was at my side, the brightest smile on her face. Kenneth was there along with my bridesmaids—Daisy, Cora, and Piper. Yes, Piper, who had tried to make my life a living hell in high school. But she'd apologized. We moved on and were actually getting along really well.

She wasn't the only one coming around. Sitting next to Dalton was his mom, who'd finally divorced Wilson and become a much happier person. And next to her was Leo, Dalton's best man.

I waved at Asher, who was sitting across from us with his new girl-friend, Liza. He hadn't graduated from college yet and already had NFL teams scouting him out. He called me last week and told me he was planning on popping the question to Liza.

I looked to the next table, where Patrick and Marissa were sitting. We'd really gotten to know each other, and I was there for them after the news broke about their mom being involved in Ivy's murder. I'd contemplated inviting John, but I decided against it. Even though two years had passed, I still didn't feel there with him yet.

"Oh, and by the way," Dalton went on. He took my hand and helped me up. "I'm going to be a daddy again!" He threw our arms up. "Woo!" He grabbed my face and kissed me.

Jaws dropped. Cheers erupted. A smile broke out along everyone's lips, mine being the biggest. I looked over at my husband. Damn, it felt good saying that, and my stomach fluttered at the excitement on his face.

We'd been trying to hold off on getting pregnant until after the wedding, but we couldn't keep our hands off of each other lately. Just the thought of us being something bigger—husband and wife— seemed to jack up our hormones.

It might have started out too early. Our ride might've been rocky. Unplanned situations happened. But no matter what, I wouldn't trade it for the world.

My heart and life were complete.

Also by Charity Ferrell

Thank you so much for reading *Worth The Risk!*

Want to read more of my books?

TWISTED FOX SERIES

(each book can be read as a standalone)

Stirred

Shaken

Straight Up

Chaser

Last Round

BLUE BEECH SERIES

(each book can be read as a standalone)

Just A Fling

Just One Night

Just Exes

Just Neighbors

Just Roommates

Just Friends

STANDALONES

Bad For You

Beneath Our Faults

Pop Rock

Pretty and Reckless

Revive Me

Wild Thoughts

RISKY DUET

Risky

Worth The Risk

BOOKS UP FOR PREORDER:

Only Rivals

Only Coworkers

About The Author

Charity Ferrell is a USA Today and Wall Street Journal best-selling author of the Twisted Fox and Blue Beech series. She resides in Indianapolis, Indiana with her fiancé and two fur babies. She loves writing about broken people finding love while adding humor and heartbreak along with it. Angst is her happy place.

When she's not writing, she's making a Starbucks run, shopping online, or spending time with her family.

Made in the USA
Monee, IL
27 June 2022